The Wounded Frontier

Book Five of the Jack Commer Series

Michael D. Smith

Sortmind Press, 2020
press.sortmind.com

cover image by Michael D. Smith
cover design by Deron Douglas

For my wife Nancy

CHAPTER ONE
Leaving Andertwin
Tuesday, July 9, 2075, 1040 hours

At the sound of footsteps Laurie peered from under the console to see the Supreme Commander of the United System Space Force striding into the Control Room.

"Oh! Sorry, sir!" she gasped, struggling to extricate herself.

"As you were, Colonel Lachrer," Jack Commer grinned. "I can see Joe must've broken the *III* again!"

"Well, uh, not really, sir," she said, noting that Jack was in his dark blue full-dress uniform as were the other *Typhoon IV* crewmembers onboard today, all looking snazzy in contrast to the *III* crew in their loose light blue flight suits. "There were a few problems with the console's connection to Enhanced Diagnostic I wanted to look at before we head back. I wouldn't chance an Enhanced at this point until we've worked out this glitch." She ducked back under the console and resumed scanning the circuitry as Jack took a seat in the second row of chairs behind the command console.

"Yeah, we came out in three regular Star Drives," Joe Commer spoke from the pilot seat. "I really did want to test the Enhanced, though. Looks like we need to take it back in three again."

Laurie brushed back her long red hair and stuck her head out again. "I'm sorry, sir," she spoke to her captain, also managing to nod in the direction of his brother behind him, "but if we want to launch at 1045, I don't think I have time to really chase this bug down. I'm really sorry."

"That's fine, Laurie," Joe said. "I didn't think we'd have time to figure it all out, either. Andy, let's start the preflight." As copilot Donnelley began his checklist, Joe waved at Jack's wife Amav climbing up the ladder to the Control Room. Her glossy white flight suit jerked Donnelley's eyes away from his console.

Damn her and her pneumatic boobs, Laurie thought. Every man on this ship was drooling after them. *Doctor* Frankston-Commer. Had she really ever done anything with planetary

1

engineering? Oh, they always sought her input, and she was on every committee. Because she was absolutely perfect, of course. She might be in her sixties, but she looked twenty, with that oval face, that long lustrous brown hair, those dark smoldering eyes and thick sensuous lips. Apparently Amav had inveigled a native Jujl seamstress into making that skintight plasti-leather flight suit after the wardrobe she'd brought to Andertwin was incinerated in the *Typhoon IV* crash. The suit was certainly calculated to accentuate every one of Amav's faultless curves.

Amav slithered into a seat next to Jack behind the pilot and copilot. The Control Room of the *Typhoon III* was blindingly white. It hurt Laurie's eyes, but Joe liked the maximum setting.

"I'm ready to get out of this dump," Amav hissed, face tight.

"Well, we're almost off." Jack turned to Laurie as she pulled herself from under the console. "Sorry you couldn't stay and sightsee Andertwin a while, Colonel. Joe and Andy have been here a couple times. It's really almost paradise. Amav and I were even thinking of retiring here someday."

Amav shook her head. "Not anymore. Three weeks is more than enough."

Jack shrugged. "And thanks for bringing Dar and K'sla over, Joe. Even *they're* talking about retiring here."

No one responded. Amav stole an impatient glance out the canopy. Laurie was taken aback at the fresh tension in the Control Room. She still couldn't make sense of all the craziness that happened here on Andertwin last month, but she knew everyone was stressed by the events that had led to the new Centaurian Grid.

But it wasn't fair to barely even let them use the bathroom in the guest house. She'd only be able to see Phil Sperry for a couple minutes. Draka, on the other hand, had been soaking up the legendary *Typhoon II* physician/engineer's expertise for three weeks now.

Joe had told her that the crew of the *Typhoon IV* had requested three additional weeks on Andertwin to recuperate, but apparently this was not to the liking of the seemingly twenty-year-old goddess Amav Frankston-Commer. The *Typhoon III*

had been scheduled to stay here a few days, but on the way over
Joe had told her in confidence that Amav had been insisting on
getting off Andertwin for over two weeks. At the end of their
first Star Drive had come the call from Jack asking if the *III*
couldn't be turned around in two hours and get them home
today. Running the turnaround schedule immediately upon
arrival hadn't been a problem for Laurie. She was used to that
sort of pressure. But it didn't give her any time to work on that
Enhanced glitch, or to ask Phil Sperry what he thought of it.

To smooth the awkward silence, she made a show of closing
up her diagnostic toolkit. "How's your leg, sir? Draka told me it
healed fine."

Jack blinked. "I keep forgetting you're a *doctor*. Want to
take a look?"

"Uh, I don't think there's enough time, I mean, if we're
going to launch in four minutes."

Jack laughed. "Oh, come on, Laurie, I was pulling *your* leg!
Believe me, mine's better than ever. Hard to believe it ever
happened, in a way. Blasted clean off, and Greeney puts it back
together with Amplified Thought! You'd never know it'd
happened. Draka's still amazed."

"Jack, *please*," Amav said, reducing the Control Room to a
chilly seventeen degrees and resuming her stare out the canopy.
"It was all *too horrible*."

Laurie had spoken with Draka Sortie, her counterpart on the
Typhoon IV, about whether Jack might need special medical
attention on the trip back to Sol, but Greeney Gooney had
maintained that all the necessary healing had taken place in the
first fifteen seconds of his Amplified Thought repair.
Unconcerned about any follow-up needs Jack might have,
Greeney had already returned to Sol to take up his new duties as
Martian Emperor.

Laurie had also consulted about the rest of the *IV* crew with
Draka, who'd been checking them every day for any physical
problems that might develop. They'd all been banged up pretty
badly when they'd crashed the *IV.*

Meanwhile Amav continued to glare at the Andertwin trees

in the late afternoon sun. Laurie had to remind herself that their own morning schedule had nothing to do with Andertwin time. But what on earth was up with the bitch lady today?

Donnelley turned to Jack. "Is everyone from the *IV* on board, Admiral?" The tall, lean copilot had thinning gray hair and sunken cheeks. Laurie wondered why he hadn't retired years ago. He'd been a test pilot in the thirties, then had gone for command but never attained it. He'd been a copilot for decades now. Andy was certainly competent, but something was lacking in him which Laurie had never been able to pinpoint.

"Yeah, we're all here," Jack said.

"Anyone else you'd like up here? We've got plenty of seats behind us," Joe said, indicating four empty seats along the rear wall of the Control Room next to the auxiliary engineer's station. Laurie was still amazed at the amount of wasted space on the *Typhoon III*. There was room for a ping-pong table between Jack and Amav's guest seats and the console at the rear.

"No, I think they've each claimed a stateroom by now. Between you and me, I think most of 'em are a little ashamed to be getting ferried back like this."

Joe shrugged. "Yeah, I can see why." He motioned to Laurie. "Colonel, will you take the auxiliary station behind us for the trip home? I want to make sure any adjustments we've made to the Enhanced Diagnostic don't have unintended consequences."

"Uh, yessir," Laurie said, moving behind Jack and Amav to her auxiliary console, her cheeks heating. Did Joe think she'd messed up her diagnostic in front of his brother and sister-in-law? Dammit, Laurie knew her stuff. If Blanton hadn't fooled with the InterRelay last week they wouldn't be having this problem.

All the same, she understood Joe's insistence on perfection. Even after forty-five years of Star Drive, flights longer than fifteen minutes, somewhat over four light-years, could produce anomalous results. The war with the Centaurian Empire had blinded everyone to the raw fact that the existing Star Drive system wasn't much good for distances beyond the 4.3 light-years to Alpha Centauri. They could make further jumps between the other AC stars by taking the distances in fifteen-minute hops, but a sustained flight of more than about eight light-years usually resulted in Star Drive malfunctions, occasionally catastrophic.

Thus, for safety reasons, the flight to and from Andertwin's star, Procyon A, was broken into three separate Star Drives to cover the 11.5 light-years, with system checks and navigational realignment mandated at the stops, which always spooked the crew as they took place literally in the middle of *nowhere*. You always wondered if a given stop might be the one time your Star Drive engine failed to restart.

Laurie had newfound sympathy for the Alpha Centaurians and how they'd struggled with bad Warp Transfer systems for thousands of years. Even though Star Drive was inherently more stable than the Centaurian Warp Transfer, the Centaurian technique consistently achieved longer ranges than Star Drive, and was able to keep shaky physical contact between far-flung Centaurian star systems. The need for long-range Star Drive had become paramount.

So far only six *Typhoon*-class ships had the Star Drive Enhanced system, and it had only been tested a few times, in no direction further than two light-years. But the *Typhoon V,* the prototype of the next class of ships, had fully integrated Star Drive Enhanced and would theoretically be capable of going anywhere in the galaxy.

Laurie turned to Jack. "I'm sorry we've had this Enhanced problem, Admiral. I certainly wish we could've demonstrated the full Enhanced system to you on the journey home."

"Well, how's it coming along otherwise? Aside from this one glitch, that is?"

"It's going great," Joe cut in. "Laurie worked with the fleet engineers to get ours installed. But when she ran the Advanced Diagnostic a couple weeks ago, she found some bugs that could've wiped out Dimensional InterRelay. So Fleet's revamping InterRelay on all the *Typhoon* ships with Enhanced, and they're even going to port her upgrade to the *V*. Laurie's a damn genius!"

Laurie blinked. "Well, thank you, sir."

"She probably just saved six ships," Jack said. "Hell, would've been seven. You know the *IV* was due for the Enhanced upgrade next week. Anyway, that's great, what you did, Colonel. Maybe you should talk to Phil Sperry. He refined a lot of the AC Warp Transfer stuff and may have some insight."

"Yessir, that sounds like a good idea."

"Yeah, have Laurie talk to the Emperor of the Alpha Centaurians," Joe grinned.

"Well, *everybody's* the emperor now, you know. It's amazing what Phil pulled off with the Grid."

"You all weren't really thinking of experimenting with Enhanced on the way home, were you?" Amav interrupted, meeting Laurie's eyes with unmistakable frost.

"No, no, of course not," Laurie stammered. "I mean, not unless everything checked out perfectly."

"Really? You'd really try an untested technology on all your unsuspecting passengers?" Amav waved back at the Control Room hatch Laurie was surprised to see still standing open. Amav had been the last one in, and she had to know it was standard operating procedure to secure that hatch before flight. It looked as if copilot Donnelley was too goggle-eyed to remind her of that fact. Well, Laurie wasn't going to do it.

Anyway, Amav wasn't USSF. How could she know what those Space Force guys back there might be willing to face?

"Well, it's no skin off my back. Three hops are fine with me," Joe said. "Enhanced doesn't mean much in terms of actual time saved, it's just super-stable, that's all. We could go great distances in one big hop instead of dozens of little ones where we have to check all the systems out over and over again."

"I know the theory, Joe," Amav snorted. "I just don't think you should be using it until it's passed all the tests."

There was a long silence. What stupid tests did their pneumatic planetary engineer think needed to be passed? Laurie had been working her tail off on Enhanced the last three months.

"Well, whatever," Jack finally said. "When we finally do

get it in gear, wow, what we could do with Enhanced. I mean, what've we been doing all these years? Fighting wars and twiddling our thumbs? We need to get out there and *explore*."

Amav sneered and looked away.

Joe nodded. "I'm still impressed Laurie caught that one bug. Apparently you could've done serious damage to an entire solar system without even thinking. We may have to call it the Lachrer Enhancement from now on."

Laurie turned back to her own console to hide her flushed cheeks.

"Checklist completed. We're clear for takeoff when you're ready, Captain," Donnelley said.

"Thanks, Andy," Joe said. "You guys ready?"

"Hey, it's your ship," Jack said. "Gun it whenever you want."

"Thank you, el Comandante Supremo. I believe I will."

Jack grinned. "Damn, I just wish Jonathan James was coming with us."

Amav shrugged. "He wants to stay. It's his decision and that's fine with me."

Laurie ran Donnelley's checklist against her own. Everything was green. In fact, one of Donnelley's checks flagged the Enhanced Diagnostic Console Subsystem A. It was turned off and presented no problem to the ship's functioning, but the Last Known Dimensional Parameter had registered .083.

No wonder Laurie couldn't get Graduated Power Interface if the parameter was less than 1.0. Maybe if she--well, too late to try it now, but that was interesting. Damn interesting.

"Yeah, but up to last night he was so keen on talking to Urside," Jack went on. "He sounded like he really wanted to give Earth a try."

"Oh, c'mon, Jack, what does Urside really know about *counseling* anyone?" Amav countered.

"Well, I know he's helped a lot of people. He and Alycia both."

"What does a damn *artist* know about counseling our son?"

Laurie's musings on Graduated Power Interface scattered.

She didn't know the Charmouth guy personally, just that he'd been the person who'd inadvertently performed the very first and the very last Heuristic Time Transitions. Thank God all that time-travel insanity was over with. Meanwhile, Urside Charmouth was just one more person for Doctor Planetary Engineer to piss on, she guessed.

Anyway, if Enhanced was drawing on Graduated for its knowledge of which dimension it was encountering--

"I don't know, but I guess he just *listens,*" Jack said. "Anyway, JJC was really up for a long vacation on Earth, and I thought Urside might help."

"Maybe Jonathan James just needs to come to terms with all the *crap* he pulled right back where he *did* it! On this godforsaken planet! Please, can we just get *off* this place?"

There was another long silence.

Finally Joe spoke: "Well, we're ready when you are."

"JJC thinks he'll be just fine with Dar and K'sla," Amav said. "I bet he thinks he can wrap them around his little finger. Wait'll he finds out how righteous Dar can really be!"

"Well, Phil and Hedrona will be helping, too," Joe pointed out.

"You stay out of this!" Amav flared. "This is our damn *son.* He doesn't want to change, he's just *faking* it! He thinks he's got Hedrona, and Phil, and *everyone* wrapped around his little finger. He was just *feeding* Jack a line about wanting to go to Earth for counseling. And Jack just swallowed it whole!"

More silence.

"Uh, can we discuss this, you know, like, later?" Jack muttered.

"You're damn right! Just let's please get out of here!"

"Amav, we're *trying,*" Joe said. "Are we all ready to leave now?" He punched a square on the console for the ship's intercom. "All hands, prepare for takeoff."

"Don't you patronize me, Joe Commer!" Amav snarled. "If you really knew what *happened* here!"

"Amav, *goddammit!*" Jack hissed, as everyone in the Control Room realized that last comment had gone out shipwide.

"I know you're upset, but we really *are* trying to get out of here."

"Don't *you* patronize me, either! You have no idea! No idea at all! What it's like when your own son--oh my God!"

Laurie stared. The Doctor Planetary Engineer was crying.

"Amav, I'm *sorry.*"

"Oh, hell, he's *not* my son! He's a *monster!*"

"But, I mean, he *is* our son. We have to *understand* him!"

"I don't want anything to do with that *monster!* Just get me off this goddamn planet!"

"Amav--"

"We *lost* him in '38! He's been *gone* since then! *Dead* to us since then! All this time-travel *insanity!* It doesn't matter! Nothing matters!"

"Sure it matters. I admit it's been strange, but Sortie says all his brain functions are okay. Maybe he's just sort of *dazed* by that crap he pulled back there. Look, I admit I still can't get my head around all this myself."

"He brainwashed me into practically having *sex* with *Phil Sperry,* and you can't wrap your head around *that?*"

"Amav, *please!*"

Laurie swiveled to the shouting despite all her effort not to. Joe and Andy were doing the same. Everyone's mouth hung open.

"Sex with *Phil Sperry!* Exactly what you always accused me of *wanting* all these years! There! Are you satisfied?"

"No! Amav, just--just *stop.* We're on the *Typhoon,* going home, everything's okay."

"All for his goddamn power trip! For wanting to be Emperor! To complete some stupid *initiation rite.* His own *mother,* for God's sake! And that stupid, *awful* novel of his! Oh my God! That's not my son! We *lost* him in '38! And Phil Sperry! Of all the people to *pair* me with! Oh my God!"

"Listen, Amav, I've told you a hundred times, don't be ashamed of what happened back there. You were *brainwashed.* Temporarily. I sure as hell don't think it's a big deal. You can't be accountable when you're brainwashed, can you?"

"Don't fool me, you're still jealous. After all these years!"

"I am *not!* Do I give a flip about Phil Sperry?"

"He *loved* me forty years ago!"

"He has *Hedrona* now, for God's sake!"

"I've always felt *sorry* for him, and then my own son took advantage of that for his goddamn *software!* For his power trip! His stupid Grid! And he was so *smug!* So *evil!*"

"Look, who can make sense of the Grid stuff anyway? Let the damn Centaurians sort it out on their own. We can take care of JJC. Maybe Dar and K'sla will be perfect for him. Or Urside can help. And you and I can settle some stuff out, you know? I mean, straighten everything out and get moving again, you know?"

"Damn you! Damn you!"

Amav was out of her chair and through the Control Room hatch, which she tried in vain to slam as if it were some ordinary bedroom door. She stamped down the rungs and was gone. "Damn you all!" the entire ship heard her yell from the fuselage. *"Just get me off this goddamn planet, will you please?"*

CHAPTER TWO
The *Castle*

"Uh ..." Jack muttered, staring at his lap. "Look, everyone, that was, uh--"

That was damn unprofessional, Laurie thought. *God, what a zoo.*

"I need to call Draka. Make sure she's settled in Stateroom One." But Jack made no move to do so.

Laurie checked the Crew Locator module. "Uh, sir, I'm showing her back in Stateroom One. Seat harness fastening just now, sir."

"Thanks ..." Jack sighed, and Laurie wondered if he'd been sharing her own image of the *out-of-control bitch* yanking open the rear hatch, leaping twelve feet to the Andertwin grass, breaking her ankle and screaming obscenities as she limped into the woods.

"She's ... been under a lot more strain than I realized," Jack finally managed.

"Look, it's okay, Jack," Joe said. "I'm ready to start the launch sequence, but if you want to get down to Stateroom One, we can wait a bit."

"N-no ..."

Laurie looked away in disgust from the shaken Supreme Commander.

"Andy, fire up Auxiliary One," Joe said, "then ease in the hover thrusters."

"Yeah, thanks, Joe. Just get us off," Jack whispered.

This wimp was going to command the *Typhoon V?* El Comandante Supremo wouldn't want any of these ancient *III*-class ships, that was for sure. Laurie was shocked at what he'd allowed here with wifey. If she were captain, she'd put them both off the ship this instant.

Though Jack was over six feet tall, broad-shouldered and handsome in a rugged, uneven way, with a square face and deep-set brown eyes, he'd never impressed Laurie in all the decades she'd known him. Rejuvenation technology had gone well for the seventy-two-year-old Supreme Commander, and Jack looked to be in his mid-thirties, as did his brother Joe. But Joe's equally dark brown eyes radiated an invigorating mix of humor, passion, and ruthlessness in contrast to Jack's vaguely worried expression, and though Joe was a couple inches shorter, his huge biceps and pectorals, his taut belly and muscled thighs, projected a physical stamina that inspired everyone who worked with him. Jack seemed to want to weigh his decisions until they were no longer necessary; Joe jumped into the middle of the worst danger with whatever he had to give at the moment.

Joe should have the *V,* and everyone knew it. He was so much more level-headed than his brother. He'd even make an excellent Supreme Commander. And Laurie should be on the *V* as physician/engineer. She'd taken those classes on *V* tech and probably knew more than anyone.

That Frankston-Commer woman was *not* as smart as she thought she was. So damn perfect, just like her darling el Comandante Supremo. Why didn't Jack just step down? He obviously couldn't handle the job. Everyone knew he'd been off the rails since '34.

June 2034, when he'd sent his two brothers to their deaths.

Laurie shook her head. Of course, that was unfair. Jack certainly didn't order his brother John to destroy the *Typhoon I,* even though for years she'd wanted to believe that Jack had fled the doomed ship with his favorite brother Joe, then directed the *Typhoon* to impact on Mercury, killing the six remaining crewmen including Jim and John Commer.

But that wasn't how it happened. It had taken her decades to accept that. Joe had only spoken about it to her once, but he'd confirmed that John had the pilot's seat and did it against Jack's orders. Maybe to impress Jack, who knew?

Killed himself and the rest of the crew just to impress his brother. Jack should never have left John in command. He should've known how close John was to snapping.

Too long ago. Too long. Forty-one years? Why was she even thinking this? She never thought of John.

Oh my God! Did I really love him that much? To never drop

it after all these years?

*

Donnelley touched a square on his console and Laurie heard the engine whir at the rear of the fuselage. The hover thrusters came to life beneath the wings, and within seconds they shot to several thousand feet. As the ship banked, Laurie could see the guest house where the crew of the *IV* had stayed the past three weeks. It was empty now except for the Jujl servants maintaining the house and surrounding orchards. Phil Sperry and Hedrona Bhlon had stayed with the *Typhoon IV* crowd until today, then returned to their own home several miles down the rural road.

Not far from the guest house lay the blackened wreckage of the *Typhoon IV*. It had flattened a stand of trees and was splayed like a murder victim left to rot across the shattered branches. Rivulets of oil and fuel pooled in the dirt, and metallic debris caught glints of the sun across a dozen acres.

What was holding up the salvage crew? It had been weeks now. Could they seriously be worried about the Grid, about being contaminated with it if they set foot anywhere in Alpha Centauri? What about that idiot on SolNet last night, protesting that Greeney Gooney, already home from Andertwin, was somehow *infecting* Sol? God, people were fools.

"Prepare for orbital insertion," Joe spoke into the intercom, and the inertial dampers kicked in as the *Typhoon III* shot through the clouds and accelerated into orbit. Laurie stole a glance at her captain. Joe grinned, back in command of a spaceship. Admiral Joe Commer, Deputy Supreme Commander of the USSF, preferred like his brother to fly his desk from the command seat of a *Typhoon.*

"Auto-checklists green," Donnelley said as the curved blue surface of Andertwin spread out before them. "We're go for an entire orbit if we need it."

"Probably won't need that long," Joe said. "Stations, check in."

"Communications and sensors optimal," Communications Officer Sandra Markham called.

"Navigation checks out," said Navigation Officer Li Bao.

"All turrets operational," said Weapons Officer Rick Ballard.

"All systems go," Laurie spoke from her console.

"See, what did I tell you?" Joe said. "Break orbit in fifteen seconds."

"Star Drive autopilot engaged," Donnelley said, punching a square. "We're go for standard two million miles from planetary surface."

"Got it," Lieutenant Li spoke from Navigation. "Course for Star Drive number one laid in. All systems go."

"*Belay that!*" came the cry over the intercom. "*Belay everything!*"

"*What?*" Joe grunted.

"Pat, is that *you?*" Jack said. "What the hell?"

"We got to stop her!" *Typhoon IV* Communications Officer Patrick James shouted. "*I know what she's doing!*"

"Hold up on the orbit break, Andy," Joe said, patting Donnelley's arm poised over the console. "Pat, what on earth are you doing on my shipwide circuit?"

"It's *K'ufunb,* on the *Castle!* On JJC's *Castle!*"

Joe raised an eyebrow to his brother. "Sorry, Joe," Jack said, "I don't know what's gotten into him."

"*I know what she's doing!* I can feel it! Everybody in the Grid knows it!"

"Sir, I'm tracking a spaceship launch from the planet," came from Markham. "From the mountainous region fifty miles west of our own launch point."

"That's it!" Pat cried. "It's K'ufunb! *I know what she's doing!*"

"Excuse me, Commander James," Joe said, "but Communications Officer Markham is the only one authorized aboard the *Typhoon III* to monitor launches, and if by any chance you've patched yourself into our communications systems, you need to get out now."

"Forget it! I'm in the Grid! *I know it all!*"

"*Dammit,* Pat!" Jack said. "We agreed military personnel shouldn't experiment with this Grid business!"

"Forget it, Jack! It's not addictive at all! Not like it used to be! I've done it both ways and I know! I'm the damn Emperor now, just like everyone else!"

"I can't believe you went and *did* that. I'm sorry, Joe!"

"Well, hell, Jack, if anybody would be curious about how the Grid operates, it'd be Pat," Joe said. "You know how he is about hacking into systems."

"Don't worry!" Pat shouted. "I can drop in and out of it at any time! It's just like Phil was saying! It's all voluntary now! But when you're *in* it, *wow!*"

"Okay, Pat, get off my circuit," Joe said. "Sandra, what's up with that ship launch? Who is it?"

"Sir, it's that *Castle* that Admiral Commer's son built. It's *following* us!"

Jack stood up. "My God! Is Jonathan James on it? What on earth is he up to? Dammit, I thought Sperry dismantled that thing!"

"Don't worry, Jack! It's just K'ufunb!" Pat called. "All Phil did was lock the engine initiation sequence when we landed her last month. But K'ufunb knows how to bypass that."

"How--how do you *know* this?"

Laurie stared. *This* was their Supreme Commander? He was so out of it. Just flailing.

"Sandra, is there any communication from the ship?" Joe called.

"Negative, sir."

"Okay, look, Jack, I just told her to officially call us!" Pat yelled. "I told her it's the *least* she can do!"

"Sir, I have a message from the ship," said Lieutenant Markham. "Identifying itself as the *Castle.*"

"Put it on," Joe said. "Control Room only. And yourself, of course."

"Forget it, Joe!" Pat shouted. "I see *everything* through the Grid! I hear *everything!* All of Alpha Centauri does!"

"Pat, stand down! Right now!" Jack shouted.

"I know what she's about to do! *You've got to stop her!*"

"Sandra, cut Pat off!" Joe yelled.

"Roger. Stateroom Four intercom terminated."

"This is K'ufunb, Empress of the Alpha Centaurians!" came the voice through the *Typhoon's* translator system. "Hello, hello, hello! Greetings in the name of the Alpha Centaurian Empire! All of Alpha Centauri participates in this decisive moment!"

"It's true! It's true!" came a muffled shout through the Control Room hatch from somewhere down the fuselage.

"*Sheesh* ..." Jack muttered.

Had Jack really let one of his crewmembers experiment with the Grid? Sure, Draka had told Laurie it was harmless now, that he'd seen both Phil and Hedrona go into and out of the Grid a dozen times. But Pat here had just openly flouted el Comandante Supremo's orders and Jack just stood there like a zombie.

"Hello, K'ufunb, I'm Joe Commer, captain of the *Typhoon III*. Is there anything we can do for you?"

Was that the Fkuuh that Draka had been talking about, the caretaker for Jonathan James's spaceship? Laurie had only seen holograms of the Fkuuh species: the short round aliens had four legs and four arms, and six eyes in a huge orange head that seemed to be ninety percent of the body. As almost all humans remarked, they really did look like pumpkins with tentacles. Fkuuh were considered by other Alpha Centaurians to be dull-witted and barbaric; somehow they always seemed to wind up as servants to upper-class castes like the Tarl or the Zarj.

"Sir Joe!" K'ufunb rasped. "Brother of Jack! I most devoutly wish you would access the Grid yourself so that you would understand the importance of the decision all Alpha Centauri now makes through me!"

"Uh, sorry, I certainly can't do anything like that. Again, how may we be of assistance?"

Laurie wasn't even tempted to sample the Grid. When they thought they might be staying on Andertwin a few days, Sandra had asked if she wasn't curious to try this new voluntary Grid.

Everyone said you'd come right out of it whenever you wanted. But Laurie wasn't interested in any sort of cosmic connection with twenty trillion Alpha Centaurians, and she wasn't about to chance *not* coming out of it.

"Who's on the *Castle* with you?" Jack cried. "Is my son up there?"

"Sir Jack! It's *you!* I greet you in the name of the Alpha Centaurian Empire with special fondness for your role in bringing about the New Grid!"

"I didn't have a thing to do with it! *Is my son up there?*"

"No, Sir Jack! I'm here alone, a mere scrubwoman of Jonathan James's *Castle,* but also one of trillions of Empresses of the Alpha Centaurians through the New Grid! I am in charge of the spaceship and thus I am her captain. Sir Jack, I respectfully state that I am about to engage the Warp Transfer on this ship in an irresponsible manner designed to cause a failed Warp Transfer Insertion."

"*What?*"

"I must go to Clopt, my Emperor husband. I must reunite with Clopt in *Garr/thahg.*"

"*Garr/thahg?* Dammit, K'ufunb, that's superstitious nonsense! Clopt deliberately *killed* himself with a failed Warp Transfer! There's no damn *Garr/thahg!*"

"I must go to *Garr/thahg.* This action will take place immediately."

"Dammit, Sandra, where is that ship?" Joe said.

"242.6 miles directly above us, sir," Markham reported, "and accelerating."

"Too close! If she blows her Star Drive, ours may rupture as well! Donnelley!"

"Ready, sir."

"Go for it! Top-end sublight!"

"No! She's too close to the planet!" Laurie cried. "She'll rupture *it!*"

The surface of Andertwin shot away as the *Typhoon* accelerated to one-quarter light speed. In a moment they'd drop out of that to assume the requisite 100,000 miles per hour velocity for engaging Star Drive.

"No! JJC's still back on the planet!" Jack screamed. "K'ufunb, listen to me! Clopt went to *Garr/thahg* to *escape* you! He doesn't *want* you! Please just *stop!*"

"I've had three of your weeks to consider his *real* reasons, my lord Jack. Your servant the Emperor Phil considers that my husband Clopt committed what you call *suicide*. But we know it as *Garr/thahg,* the Land of the Dead, where we meet our True Emperor. I now see that his action was an expression of Zarj love. Clopt wishes us to unite in *Garr/thahg*."

"Weapons!" Joe gasped. "Target the *Castle* and destroy it!"

"I have *Castle* Warp Transfer signature!" Markham called.

"Too late!" Rick Ballard shouted back from Weapons. "Can't get a lock!"

"You're too close to the planet!" Jack shouted.

"I forgot, sir, in my extraordinary grief I forgot!" K'ufunb cried as a bright line of energy cascaded across the black sky. Then space turned entirely blue.

CHAPTER THREE
A More Vigorous Government

Joe hit the glare filters on the canopy. "She headed the damn thing straight for the sun!"

"Object missed Procyon A by seventy-eight million miles," Markham reported. "Before ceasing to exist, that is. The star is stable. I'll run further analysis. More good news: Andertwin made it through fine. Probably have quite a lot of aurora activity for a few years, though."

"Thank God," Jack muttered. He turned to his brother's brown eyes and met waves of shared understanding. Decades of working with Joe had left the two of them almost telepathic with each other. Not as good as Martian telepathy, but close enough for them to have saved each other's bacon more than a few times.

"Damn, Joe, I'm so sorry!"

"Hell, Jack, it's not your fault. What the hell happened with that Fkuuh?"

"I have no idea. She *rejected* Clopt when this new Grid started. Then he suicided. God, I had no idea she'd have this mystical *thing* about it."

"Well, if I understand what Pat was babbling, apparently all of Alpha Centauri *knows* she did that, and why. I mean, through the Grid."

Jack breathed out. "But she's *gone*. Just like that!"

"But Jonathan James is okay." Joe pointed to his console. "Sandra's sending updates. No reports of damage on Andertwin. We don't have to head back there unless you want to."

Jack shuddered. The last thing he wanted was to get Amav riled up again.

"N-no ... we should be okay to get going."

"Sandra's also monitoring the aftereffects of the Warp Transfer irrationality. Nothing serious. Laurie, let's recalibrate Star Drive again, just to make sure we don't have any spatial vortices in our path."

"I'm on it," said the slender redhead behind Jack.

"Sir, I have Captain Athens from the *Jonathan Commer,*"

19

Markham reported.

"I'll take this one," Jack said. "Hey, Bobby, you undoubtedly saw what just happened."

"Yes, sir. We were shielded by TwinLord at the time, but we have some good recording of it. We're combining it with the telemetry the *III's* sending us, and we'll keep monitoring. Procyon A's okay, so are all the planets. That was JJC's *Castle?*"

"Yes. One casualty. K'ufunb, Jonathan James' servant. Apparently she just lost it and knew how to launch the ship via the Grid."

"Wow. Well, we'll continue to study the situation from here. And of course I'll check on Jonathan James from time to time."

Jack managed a grin. Sometimes Bobby Athens was almost telepathic with him, too. "Thanks, Bobby. We're going to check our Star Drive one more time and go ahead and leave. Keep me posted."

"Sure, Jack."

After the *Typhoon IV* crashed, Jack had summoned the *Jonathan Commer* to Andertwin. It was due a new captain, so Jack gave his *IV* copilot Bobby a long-overdue promotion and left him in charge of the ship, currently in orbit around Andertwin's moon. The *Commer* was a *III*-class ship, named after his and Joe's late father, and was scheduled to stay behind in Alpha Centauri for six months to monitor the new Grid.

Joe hit a square on his console. "Li, I assume you've compensated for our escape maneuver and have us pointed correctly at Sol for the first Star Drive? We should've clued you in on this crazy conversation we just had."

"No problem, sir," spoke Lieutenant Li from Navigation. Li was an old friend from decades ago. In fact, the day Jack had met him back in the thirties, the young Airman Li had saved his life and Joe's by shattering the Centaurian spy Geswindoll. Jack shuddered to recall those chaotic days of Heuristic Time Transitions and the realization that years of futile war lay ahead. "The NAV9 Cluster cut in automatically," Li went on. "I take it the *Castle* had a failed Star Drive?"

"Yeah. Sandra, keep analyzing Guaco-whatever until we leave, make sure it's stable, and keep transmitting everything to the *Commer*," Joe said, mocking the idiotic name the ACs had for Procyon A: *Guacoazezama*. "That was still damn close. Laurie, how's the SD Diagnostic going? That was way close for us, too."

"So far everything's green, sir. Diagnostic will finish in four minutes."

"It's *incredible*, Jack!" Patrick James cut in. "All of Alpha Centauri *grieves* for K'ufunb, and for Clopt, but they also *rejoice* for her! For *Garr/thahg!*"

Jack noted that James was bypassing Stateroom Four's intercom link and calling the Control Room on his own comm. "Okay, Pat, we figured that out ourselves up here. Will you please get off the network? This isn't even our own ship."

"It's incredible to feel twenty trillion entities all sharing the same *ecstasy*, I think you could call it!"

"Sandra, cut the link from Pat's comm," Joe ordered.

"Done, sir."

"Damn," Jack said. "Sorry again, Joe. I don't know what's gotten into him."

Joe shrugged. "No big deal. He's just excited about a Grid that doesn't brainwash you. In a way, you ought to thank him. If he hadn't been in the Grid and warned us, we might've been sucked into that irrationality."

Jack plopped back down into the seat behind Joe. "Yeah, well maybe." His comm beeped. "Aw hell, what now?"

I'm sorry came up on his screen.

"Hey, I thought you'd cut Pat's--" Jack began, then saw:

I just really, really need to get back home. I'm sorry I fell apart and embarrassed you. I just need to get away from Andertwin. I didn't even realize how much until we were leaving.

Jack sighed. Thank God she'd calmed down. Well, maybe it was true that all this had hurt Amav a lot worse than he'd thought. But how could she be sending this after K'ufunb had suicided?

Then again, not everyone on board was on duty and patched into the Standard Ship Overview Module. Today they had passengers from the *Typhoon IV*. Aside from Pat, no doubt still high on the Grid and apparently plugged into everything going on in the Alpha Centaurian Empire, the others might have been reading mystery novels on their comms, totally unaware of what just happened.

Or someone might have been crying, hysterically angry at a certain Supreme Commander of the USSF.

Everything's okay, he tapped back. *Don't worry. We're starting the first Star Drive and we'll be home in maybe an hour and fifteen minutes with the reorientation stops. Had a little incident here I'll tell you about later. All okay now. Love you.*

He looked up to catch Colonel Lachrer eyeing him. She reddened and swiveled back to her console. "We're almost out of Diagnostic, Captain," she called back to Joe. "By the way, I'm running a simulation that'll compare how this Star Drive performs against a Star Drive Enhanced under the same set of conditions. I think that Subsystem A's Last Known Dimensional Parameter may need some adjusting. So far my simulation shows that if we keep it about 1.5, an Enhanced would be stable."

"Huh," Joe said. "Let me know how it turns out across all three Star Drives. Sounds like you're on to something." He turned back to Jack. "What did I tell you? I've never seen anyone pick up on the physician/engineer stuff as fast as she has. And she just started in *April*."

Jack looked back to Laurie, hunched over her console, and grinned. She was still so shy. Whoever would've thought she'd have come this far?

Like Lt. Li, Laurie Lachrer was another officer they'd first known as an Airman First Class back in the thirties. She'd been a ground technician at the Marsport USSF spaceport, and though she'd been damn competent even as a teenager, and had risen through various supervisory levels to transform every office she'd held, for the subsequent two decades she'd never shown interest in going to higher levels. Since she'd also been their dead brother John's girlfriend, Jack and Joe had stayed in contact with her for some years, but their ineffectual attempts to include her as family had eventually waned and they'd finally just followed her career from afar.

But something in Laurie had changed after the defeat of the Alpha Centaurians in May 2053. Major Laurie Lachrer of USSF Fleet Subsystems had gone to the specialized USSF Medical and Engineering School intending to become one of the elite physician/engineers for the *Typhoon*-class spaceships. To Jack and Joe's astonishment she'd graduated number one in her med school class and in the top three percent of Engineering. That the petite, intense, and quiet red-haired teenager of 2034 would one day become a Harri McNarri or Phil Sperry had been unthinkable, but they both knew that the recently-promoted Colonel Lachrer could eventually outperform both of them. When Joe's physician/engineer had transferred from the *Typhoon III* to another ship in April, Joe had been eager to take on Laurie, even though she hadn't done the usual few years of duty aboard lesser ships.

Laurie was simply amazing. Joe had told him that she was even better than Draka, and that was saying quite a lot. Once again Jack found himself plotting Laurie's rise through the USSF.

*

"Sir, I have a superspace radio transmission from Marsport," Markham called.

"Fine, put it through," Joe said.

"Uh, coded SCUSSF only, sir. I could patch it through to Stateroom One if the Supreme Commander would like to take it there."

"It's okay," Jack said. "We're all cleared here. Just put it through, Sandra."

"Sir, I have Churchill on standby."

"Hello, this is Churchill!"

"Churchill! Hey, how're you doing? This is a surprise,"

Jack said.

"I'm just fine," said Churchill, or rather, the smooth tenor of the Telepathic Translator. Churchill had long given up any attempt at making his cat mouth work to create anything resembling human speech, but he'd honed his Martian telepathic outradiance to a high degree of verbal complexity over the years, and nobody had any trouble following his thinking. He could certainly understand human speech perfectly, and conversation with the Russian Blue was never a problem unless he needed to talk from a distance by comm or superspace radio. To this end, the Martian Amplified Thought wizard Kner had created the Telepathic Translator which broadcast Churchill's rigidly-composed thought blocks into human words.

"However," Churchill continued, "I wanted to let you know of a serious shake-up in the Martian government."

"Uh, really?" The Martian government had been a purely ceremonial institution ever since the end of the human-Martian war in '34. When Dar had retired a couple weeks ago, Greeney Gooney had assumed the Emperorship. Greeney had been Provisional Emperor since 2060 anyway, when Dar had indicated he wanted to be the first Martian Emperor to retire rather than die in office, and it was understood by all that the change would be a pleasant little ritual. To speak of a serious shake-up in the Martian government was like speaking of a serious shake-up in Halloween.

"As you know, I was called back from Hellas to assist with G'rea'nyaigu'nye's new Emperorship," Churchill continued. "I was to be his Chief of Staff."

"Right," Jack said, marveling at the Telepathic Translator's ability to pronounce the Emperor's true Martian name, which human colonists had long since mangled to Greeney Gooney. "So how's that going?"

"Well, this is a difficult concept for us Martians, but as of noon today Greeney has been deposed."

"*Deposed?* That's not possible!"

"Well, it's certainly never happened before, at least, not in this way. But Mandy is being very charitable to Greeney. She's even allowed him to live, although one interpretation of a Martian War of Succession is that the deposed Emperor must be shattered immediately. But in this case, Greeney will become Minister of War, and I've agreed to remain as Mandy's Chief of Staff to assure a smooth transition."

Jack was on his feet. "Did you say *Mandy? Mandy Frederick* deposed Greeney? And he's all right with this?"

"Well, I wouldn't characterize him as being *all right*. But the Outradiance of the People confirms Mandy as Empress, and Greeney is determined to make sure that factions don't arise and pollute that outradiance. Mandy is the reincarnation of the ancient Empress Fra'lith, and the people are convinced that it's her destiny to rule."

"But Martians don't *rule* anything. The government is just a formality!"

There was a long pause. "Mandy is convinced that a, shall we say, more *vigorous* government is now necessary."

"Oh my God. But why? Everything was going so smoothly!"

"Well, it has to do with G'rea'nyaigu'nye's enthusiasm for what he calls the New Alpha Centaurian Grid. When he arrived back here to take up the Emperorship, the entire Martian population sensed his enthusiasm, but it must be said that most Martians distrust this concept."

"But I always thought Martians were *fascinated* by this Grid business."

"Well, Greeney certainly is. And many others, such as Kner and myself, if the truth be told. But as I say, new factions have arisen, and the upshot is that Mandy is our new Empress. When will you arrive in Marsport? The Empress and I are eager to see you."

"We're about to set up our first Star Drive back. There was an AC Warp Transfer accident here a few minutes ago. Slowed us down a bit, but we'll be there soon."

"Great! See you soon." Churchill added a meow to end the transmission.

"Well, bye," Jack muttered, sinking back into his chair.

"Wow."

Joe met Jack's eyes. "Yeah, really. I know we're not supposed to be political, but--"

"But we are. Don't I know it. God, what else can go wrong today? Is Greeney really out, and just accepting it like that?"

"Yes, it's true! I can confirm everything!" came a new voice over the intercom.

"*Draka?* God, how can *you* be listening to this? What's going *on* today?"

CHAPTER FOUR
Consort to the Empress and Other Irregularities

"Well, Jack, I *am* a systems expert for the *III* series, if you'll recall," Draka said with the affable professorial chuckle that always grated on Jack. The only time Draka ever dropped that was when he was around former *Typhoon II* ship's engineer Phil Sperry, whom Sortie apparently worshipped as the most brilliant systems man who ever lived. Watching Draka react to Sperry the past few weeks on Andertwin had been amusing. Draka's voice had gone up an octave the first day and remained there in squeaking hero worship for three weeks. Jack had been genuinely astonished Sortie could behave that way with *anyone*.

"Draka, *don't* tell me you just hacked into a SCUSSF-level message. And not even on your own ship!"

"No, Jack, I sure won't say that!" Draka laughed.

Joe checked his console. "Sandra, is there a SCUSSF-level circuit open to Stateroom Six?"

"Negative," came the reply. "But I do see some unauthorized access to the Interface Module."

"Huh," Draka boomed over the intercom. "Ya got me, Jack!"

Jack sighed. "Okay, Draka, what's the deal?" Draka Sortie was a big balding man with a paunch and a loud, authoritative voice. Jack had tried to maintain a stern distance from a subordinate he basically disliked, but then would find himself laughing at one of Sortie's groaner jokes and appreciating how Draka kept up morale around the ship, how his expertise with systems and his medical skills were indispensable to the running of the *Typhoon IV*. Draka would certainly be on the *V* when it came online. Even after decades of working with the man, Jack didn't personally connect with him, but Sortie was damn good and everyone knew it. Jack had always figured that Sortie was armed with enough charisma for people to give his blowhard nature a pass. Besides, he and Amav had entrusted their son to his care, hadn't they?

"Well, Jack, I'll level with ya. It's like this," Draka said as

Jack and Joe exchanged a sardonic glance. They both knew some load of Sortie BS was being assembled in front of their noses. To be delivered affably and professorially, of course. Jack braced for it.

"See, Jack, I've kinda been listening in for any news of Mandy, you know."

Jack blinked. "Mandy?"

"I mean, can you blame a guy, really, Jack? I mean, this is my *wife,* after all."

"You--*what* did you say?"

"I guess it's time to tell you guys. It *was* secret and all, but I guess it has to come out now."

"*What* has to come out now?"

"Well, the fact that Mandy and I got married on June 16th."

"You got *married?*" Jack turned to Joe and Andy. "Either of you guys know about this? Laurie?" At their headshakes he spoke to an abstract point out the Control Room canopy. There was too much reflected interior glare to see stars, but it reminded him they'd best be finishing the Star Drive Diagnostic and getting back to Sol as soon as possible.

"Okay, Draka, you're saying you and Mandy got *married?* While you were here on Andertwin? And for some reason you've chosen to not tell anyone about this for *three weeks?* What was it, over superspace radio?"

"Yeah, you got it, Jack. We kinda bypassed regular USSF channels."

"So you made an *irregular* USSF channel! Damn it, Draka!"

"Well, we just couldn't wait, that's all. We've only been dating since May, and, well, we were both *missing* each other, if you know what I mean and I think you do! Anyway, we were having this *really intense conversation,* you know, and we just *decided,* then and there! That's how Martians do it, you know! No ceremony, they just *decide!* God, I can't wait to get back to her for the Great Erotic *J'thath!*"

"Damn it all, Draka!"

"See, Jack, I didn't tell anyone because I wasn't sure how

people would react to me marrying a Martian. You know all those Interspecies Laws and all that nonsense."

"She's *not* a Martian!" But as soon as the words were out of his mouth, Jack knew he was out of line. A Martian was any entity that could survive unprotected in the Martian environment. Mandy Frederick had been born on Earth, and looked fully human, but she could survive without an EnviroField on Mars. Jack hadn't kept up with the futile attempts over the decades to define or legislate Martian identity, but the upshot was that all the addled humans who "felt they must be Martians" or were "Martians trapped in human bodies" were eventually offered the test of walking a mile through the Martian desert without benefit of EnviroField. Ninety-nine percent of the wishful thinkers backed off at that point, although some attempted to prove the secondary test of a Martian, that they could "radiate" their thoughts. Even then there were those few loonies of the One Percent who died agonizing decompression deaths to prove their Martianhood. It was all nonsense. Mandy Frederick and the cat Churchill were the only two Earth-born beings who were fully Martians, and they were accepted as such by all native Martians. And "all" meant one hundred percent, a confirmation which could be read from any Martian mind.

"Well, look, Jack, the thing is, ever since Greeney announced he's for the Grid, and since he assumed the Emperorship, and since most Martians are *against* expanding the Grid to Sol, well, I've known something's up. Mandy's been upset enough about the Grid herself."

"Draka, are you telling me you knew about this palace coup in advance?"

"Hell, no, but I figured something like it might happen. You know her temper and all."

Did Jack ever. He tried to keep out of politics as much as he could, yet he'd invariably find himself in some shouting match with her. The last one had been back in March, over some sewer project under the USSF building. He still couldn't understand why he'd been so angry about it.

"Look, Draka, if you really did get married to her--"

"I did, honest! Sorry it had to be secret."

"Well, then, we have this issue of a USSF officer married to a political figure, a *Martian* political figure, and that could complicate a lot of things."

"Well, to tell you the truth, I've been thinking that over. We do have the example of Lee right here, being a United System senator at the same time he's our weapons officer."

Jack closed his eyes. He'd known that one was coming.

"But then I realized it's a little different in my case. See, I'm now officially Consort to the Empress. That's why I've been sorta listening in and all. I was worried about what might happen, and I knew that if I became Consort to the Empress I'd have to resign."

"R-resign? Do you really mean that?"

"See, what it comes down to is this Grid thing. I knew this was coming to a head when I saw how enthusiastic Greeney was for it. I mean, here we're being offered a chance to include Sol in this Grid business, and supposedly it's benign now, not this enslavement thing it used to be, but, you know, who can really trust it? And over the past three weeks Mandy and I have been discussing it, and we both know we have to *stop* it somehow."

Jack shook his head. He caught Laurie's eye, but she quickly turned to her console. He wondered if she were thinking the same thing. How often had Draka hacked into the damn superspace radio array? How did he do these things?

"Look, Draka, no decision's been made about the Grid yet. Sol doesn't have to make a decision for years."

"It doesn't matter, Jack. The Consort to the Empress is officially opposing introduction of the Grid to Sol. And he's officially supporting the overthrow of Greeney Gooney. From here on out I'm totally involved in politics, and as such I need to resign from the USSF immediately."

For a moment Jack considered arguing the other side, that Senator Lee Borman was excellent at compartmentalizing his dual roles of politician and USSF officer, but they'd all been walking a fine ethical line around that for years. Adding Martian government and culture to the mix was unthinkable.

"Okay, Draka, I'm sorry it had to come to this. Please confine yourself to Stateroom Six for the remainder of this voyage. I'll also need to terminate your USSF accounts."

"By all means," Draka said, a bit smugly, Jack thought.

"Terminate Draka Sortie's accounts, Laurie," Joe said.

Laurie peered at her console. "Done, sir. I also deleted 155 unknown administrative accounts I came across in the purge. They all had links to recent Draka Sortie activity, including twenty-seven unauthorized superspace radio communications."

"Aw, crap!" Jack heard over the intercom, then the sound of a disconnect.

CHAPTER FIVE
Maybe a Touch of that Star Drive Anxiety After All

"*Damn …*" Laurie muttered. Jack swiveled to her furious tapping at her console. "Oh! *Sorry,* sir!"

"Got a problem there, Colonel?" Joe said.

"No, I apologize, Captain. I thought I just needed to refresh my screen after going into the personnel accounts, but then something else came up with a flag." She frowned. "It looks like we have a problem with the Star Drive Diagnostic. We were almost done, then got a flag on the Vortex Detection/Maintenance Subsystem."

"VDMS down," Donnelley confirmed from his own console.

"Huh," Joe said. "I won't engage Star Drive with VDMS down. Are you sure?"

"Yessir. I'm rerunning it now. Looks like the irrationality from the *Castle* may have fried it. At least that's how I think it happened."

"So we're stuck, then. Of all the luck."

"Well, we can trade with the *Jonathan Commer,*" Jack put in. "We can send it home with the *IV* crew and we take up orbit around TwinLord until we can get the VDMS fixed. Then we just switch out again."

Jack grimaced at his own words. Surely everyone was thinking he was just trying to get Amav home as soon as possible. Well, it was true. It might take days to repair the VDMS. Was Amav really that close to cracking up? He'd never seen her like this. Had Andertwin really hurt her so badly? Had Jonathan James?

And maybe everyone had noticed that he'd said "we" take up orbit around Andertwin's moon, that he'd included himself in the *III* crew and would stay here and send Amav on by herself.

"Well, Captain, we do have another option," Laurie spoke. "From running the simulation on the Enhanced, I've figured out where we were going wrong before. And since Enhanced has its own built-in Vortex Detection, we can head back on Enhanced."

32

Joe tightened his lips, considering. Laurie's suggestion certainly put Joe in a strange position. He was captain of his ship, but should he defer to the SCUSSF on this one? With the SCUSSF's wife and other guests onboard? Well, Jack would let everyone off the hook.

"I concur with Laurie's judgment," Jack said. "But of course, it's your decision, Captain."

Joe grinned. "We've done a couple dozen Enhanced. It's perfectly stable. I say we go for it."

Jack didn't even bother nodding in agreement. He wouldn't compromise Joe's authority in front of his copilot and his physician/engineer even by that.

"We can drop out any time and double-check," Laurie said. "The interval between shutdown and startup is a lot shorter. You can do it in thirty seconds if need be. If we do it all in one hop it'll take 39.56 minutes, as opposed to three fifteen-minute legs with checks between them."

"Fine, thanks, Laurie." Joe touched a square on his console. "All hands, prepare for Star Drive. Andy, go for it."

A brief buzzing came to Jack's ears as the familiar jagged streaks of starlight surged outside the black canopy. The slightest sensation of pressure and just a touch of the old anxiety, but if you knew what was causing it, it was no big deal. In fact, Jack was sure this Enhanced had even less pressure than a regular Star Drive.

"We're in," Donnelley said. "All systems go."

"Confirming," Laurie spoke from the rear console. "We have one hundred percent stability. Enhanced is listing all vortex distortions and compensating for each."

"Fantastic," Joe said. "Let's get on home."

Jack reflected on how far they'd come over the past few years. Star Drive used to set your nerves on fire, and nobody could handle much more than the fifteen-minute journey to Proxima Centauri. But Star Drive refinements over the past five years, many made in conjunction with the Martians and their Amplified Thought, had made Star Drive travel comparatively trivial, even for the Martians who used to go berserk after a few seconds of it. This was why Joe could give everyone a moment's notice and then have Donnelley punch it in.

And now they had Enhanced. Jack wasn't at all worried about a thirty-nine-minute Enhanced journey. And he'd seen enough of Laurie's competence to fully trust her.

"This has got to be the weirdest mission I can remember, Joe," Jack said. "And we still have to digest all this about the new Grid. How we're all going to relate to it. And this succession business with Mandy. But what really gets me is this thing with K'ufunb. It's unbelievable. I *knew* her."

"I know, I know. I can't believe she did that either."

"Well, New Grid or no, I don't know if we'll ever really be able to understand the Centaurian mindset."

"I know what you mean. What Phil came up with is incredible, this new Grid, and Alpha Centauri going from this empire we've been occupying to, hell, maybe being an *ally* of some sort."

"Huh. *That* would be weird."

Joe turned to a buzz from his console. "Hey, Sandra, what's up?"

"Got a communication from Will for Jack."

"Thanks. Want to take it, Jack?"

Jack blinked. Will knew better than to break communications protocol during Star Drive. "Well, I guess. Yeah, patch him through."

"Hey, Jack, this is Will. Listen, I was just talking to Draka, and he says he's resigning, and, well, I don't know how to say this, but, well, I figured I should let you know."

"Look, Will, we don't have time for gossip now," Jack snapped, then shook his head. Maybe he had a touch of that Star Drive anxiety after all.

"Well, I've been wanting to talk with you about this very same thing, you see, and, well, Jack, I'm resigning too."

"Oh, *man.*" He caught Laurie's glance again, taken aback by the shock in her blue eyes.

Will, leaving? After all these years? Now Jack had *three* positions to fill. How on earth was he going to come up with a copilot, physician/engineer, and navigator anytime soon?

"I mean, I've been giving it a lot of thought for a long time, and I've been thinking about retiring so I can, like, get on with my life, you know."

"Dammit, Will, couldn't this wait? We're in Star Drive, for God's sake." Jack looked to Joe and mouthed: "Sorry!"

"I know, Jack, I *know*. It's just that I've been so anxious about telling you, I mean I was actually going to quit even before we came to Andertwin, and then, well, everyone's been so busy, there hasn't been time."

"Look, I understand, let's talk about this when we get back. Thirty-nine minutes."

"But then when Draka said he was quitting I realized I just have to go ahead and *do* it! Just have to do it right *now!* I hope you understand!"

Jack sat back. He hated talking past the heads of Donnelley and his brother, with Laurie Lachrer behind him, in this irritatingly bright Control Room. He could discuss anything with Joe listening, but though he liked Andy and Laurie, they were just acquaintances and he felt constrained to be discussing personnel issues in front of them.

"Well, look, Will, it's okay, I understand."

He actually didn't. What had gotten into Will? He'd never talked about retirement before. Dammit, he was the best navigator ever, and Jack needed him for the V project. What were they supposed to do when they hundreds of light-years out? You couldn't put your whole trust in a damn computer. Will could reprogram the whole NAV Cluster system on the fly.

"Well, I'm really, really sorry, Jack. I just need some time to, I don't know, like relax, enjoy life, you know."

Jack regarded the strained silence among everyone in the Control Room. Joe finally broke it to say: "Wow, Will, this is a surprise. What kind of plans do you have?"

"I don't know. Haven't thought about it much. I want to catch up on some stuff, I guess. Like I've always wanted to read Gibbon, and Douglas Southall Freeman. I've been putting them off for years."

This last came out in such a whisper that Jack wasn't sure he'd heard correctly. "You want to *read?*"

"Well, see, I also want some time to, well, I don't know how to say it, but--"

"Just go ahead and say it, for God's sake!"

Okay, so Star Drive wasn't helping things. But why couldn't Will have just *waited?* Every so often he'd go into funks where he could barely talk. Why didn't he just see a shrink?

"Well, it's this thing with Laurie."

"With *Laurie?*"

"Oh my God!" Laurie gasped from behind Jack. Jack swiveled to her but she was bent to her console, long red hair hiding her face.

Joe also turned sharply, and Jack saw the look of *potential personnel issue* flash in his eyes.

"Yeah, like, like we started dating a few months ago."

"*You,* dating *Laurie?*" Joe burst out, staring at his physician/engineer's back.

"But she's just starting here, on Joe's ship!" Jack said.

"I--I'm sorry, sir!" Laurie gasped, tumbling out of her chair and coming to attention. "*Sorry, sir!*"

It was so comical that Joe laughed. "Hey, it's all right, Laurie!"

"Yeah," Will went on, "we began right before she got posted to the *III.*"

"*Will!*" Laurie moaned.

"It's really all right," Joe said. "We just didn't know!"

"But even though I know she's really just starting out in the USSF," Will went on, "it's time for *me* to settle down, and I figured if we're on two different ships we'll *never* see each other. This way, I'll always be anchored in Marsport, and she can always find me there."

"You don't want to stay in the service, I mean, if she's in the service and you're not--" Jack babbled, realizing he was now thinking of Will Connors as a *civilian* no USSF officer would want to consort with. "I can't *believe* this!"

"Will, I didn't know you were going to tell everyone *now,*" Laurie complained.

"I know, I know, and everyone, I'm *sorry.* Look, I *know* it's complicated, but like I say, when Draka told me he was going, I just knew I had to say it *now!* And if you really want to know the truth, there's this Grid thing, too. I know this sounds stupid, but in a way I guess I need to do some more work on what happened back in '35. I know it sounds silly, but this Grid stuff, like I know it's supposed to be benign now, like everyone says, but, I mean, I just don't think I should be anywhere near it. In contact with it, you know. So like it's time for me to just, like, ease out of things, you know."

Jack blinked. He couldn't believe Will was opening up like this. It was obvious he had his various tripwires, the brainwashing in Alpha Centauri in '35 being one of them. But even worse was being marooned for a month on an asteroid in '33 after his fighter was disabled in the former Barnard's Star system. He was probably conditioned to see Alpha Centaurians as eternal enemies and their Grid as a tool of fascist control, no matter what changes Phil Sperry might have made to Alpha Centaurian culture last month.

Joe had worked through his own guilt about the brainwashing. Jack had seen firsthand how was painful that had been. Joe's wife Ranna had pitched in right alongside Jack. It was a miracle, but Joe was finally okay. As for the others on the ill-fated '35 *Typhoon II* mission, the brainwashing had apparently rolled right off Lee Borman's back, and while Jack had no idea how Patrick James had fared over the long term, if his fascination with the New Grid was any indication, Pat was doing all right.

But Jack had always been nervous about Will. The guy was in his mid-sixties. Had he really been brooding about the brainwashing and the survival month for forty years? Maybe that was a drawback of all their rejuvenation therapy. Maybe it kept you thinking you were immortal, and had all the time in the world to put off your problems.

Will was one of the ones where the rejuvenation had taken

very, very well. He really didn't look much older than thirty-five. The same was true of Laurie, who had to be about sixty. Well, maybe they'd make a fine pair.

"Okay, Will, thanks for letting me know. Let's discuss this some more when we hit Marsport. We've got a few minutes left in Star Drive, and we're doing this in one Enhanced hop."

"Sure, Jack, sure! That sounds great!"

"Uh, thirty-four minutes, twenty-eight seconds left," Laurie called out, again seated at her console. "I'm sorry, sir, I know I should've been monitoring, but everything's still one hundred percent with the Enhanced."

Jack fought not to grin. Laurie's face was almost as red as her hair. Who knew she and Will had been together all this time?

Another buzzing on the console. "What's up, Sandra?" Joe said.

"Sir, I have Lee Borman from Stateroom Two on the line."

"Dammit to hell!" Jack snarled. "We're in *Star Drive*, for God's sake! Can't these people just *drop it?*"

CHAPTER SIX
Iota Persei

"Hey, Jack, this is Lee," came over the intercom.

Jack slammed his fist on his armrest. "Dammit, senator, are you quitting too?"

"Huh? What's going on, Jack? I just got this message from Marsport."

Jack shook his head. "You don't know that Draka and Will both just *quit* the USSF? Just like that?"

"No, wow, I had no idea! I'll have a talk with 'em if you want. But really, *this* is more important."

"*What's* more important, dammit?"

"Look, I just got a call from Ranna."

Joe swiveled at the mention of his wife's name. "So why's she calling *you?*"

"And *how* is she calling you?" Then Jack remembered Borman's new Senator Comm equipped with superspace radio. Although events a few weeks ago had forced Jack to shatter Borman's specialized comm, Borman had asked Joe to bring a new one when the *Typhoon III* came to pick up the *IV* crew.

"It came on the official business circuit. Ranna said the Time Committee was in emergency session, and she had to get right back to it. Said she was sorry she didn't have time to chat with you, Joe."

"Politics," Jack muttered. "I thought the damn Time Committee was wrapping things *up* now." Joe's wife Ranna was the Chronology Coordinator on the Time Committee and was number two in the organization behind Dar, but now that Dar had retired, who knew how the Committee would fare? But with the end of all Heuristic Time Transitions on May 29th, which finally closed the 2013-2075 time disturbances created by the Alpha Centaurians, wouldn't the Committee just be studying the whole phenomenon from a historical perspective?

"Well, the thing is, Jack, the Time Committee got involved because there's really no other explanation that anyone can see."

"For *what?*"

"Well, this star just *disappeared*. Well, not exactly *disappeared*, but--"

"*What* star?"

"Iota Persei. It just suddenly *disappeared*. They don't know exactly when, because it's not like we're monitoring the damn thing every second. It was there a few days ago as far as they can piece it together, then a few hours ago an astronomer noticed it was *gone*."

"*Gone?* How can that be?" Jack pulled out his comm to refresh his memory. They were all supposed to know all the stars within fifty light-years of Earth, but it was a long list and it was difficult to keep them straight. He scanned the first couple lines:

Iota Persei. Yellow-orange main sequence dwarf star. 1.3 mass of Sol. Distance from Sol: 34.36 light-years. Age: approximately 8.1 billion years.

"We can't do any fine observations with our sensors while we're in Star Drive," Joe pointed out, "but as soon as we're out we'll run some."

"That's fine. Lee, did you say the thing *disappeared?* Not a supernova?"

"That's the thing Jack, it just *winked out!* As far as visible light, that is. They started measuring the infrared, and Jack, they say it's totally consistent with a Dyson sphere!"

Jack's mind raced. A giant shell around a star, capturing all its energy, except for that infrared leak. "That's not possible! It'd take thousands of years to build one, and the engineering problems, the orbital mechanics, would rule that out."

"Jack, all Ranna's saying is that our measurements point to a Dyson sphere."

"It *can't* be!"

"Unless it *is,*" Joe put in. "Who are we to say it can't be done just because we can't understand the orbital mechanics? All they need is smart enough computers."

"*They?* You can't believe there's an intelligent race that could do that." Jack shook his head. Of course they could. They hadn't believed in Martians or Alpha Centaurians before 2032, either. "Okay, let's think this through. How many minutes left in Star Drive?"

"Thirty minutes, twenty-seven seconds."

"Lee, are they really sure about these measurements?"

"I assume so, but when we get back, we'll see. But the reason Ranna's team got involved is that, well, they think it's true nobody can build a Dyson sphere overnight. So they think there might be *time travel* involved."

"God, I thought we were done with all that! We're past May 29th."

"Well, look at it this way. What the astronomers are seeing and measuring is the light and infrared from Iota Persei *34.36 years ago.*"

Jack sat back. His comm had taken Borman's voice data and was helpfully providing the date of April 5, 2041. Star Drive had certainly warped everyone's understanding of relativity and simultaneity. Jack had to remind himself that astronomers on Earth or Mars would only be able to detect K'ufunb's failed Warp Transfer explosion 11.5 light-years from now, or the signature of the *Typhoon III's* current Star Drive, for that matter. If they sent a ship under Star Drive Enhanced to investigate Iota Persei, the crew would arrive in two hours, but they'd be seeing a Dyson sphere, if that's what was there, that had been operational for 34.36 years.

"So you're saying they used *time travel* to build this thing?"

"Who knows? Maybe they assemble all the components in different eras, then mash 'em all together around Iota Persei in a few days."

"Sheesh. Why would they bother to do that?"

"Who knows? But the point is, Ranna requested all of us be available at an emergency United System Council Meeting when we get in."

"Okay, got it. But, dammit, we're supposed to be done with time screwups! I just wanted to *relax* for a while."

But you also wanted to explore, he reminded himself. *Explore.*

He took a deep breath and stood up. "I'm heading down to Stateroom One." And lest they think the Supreme Commander was slinking away to patch things up with wifey, he added: "I need to brief the foremost Dyson sphere expert in Sol."

CHAPTER SEVEN
Spaceport Chaos

Laurie swung down from the main *Typhoon* hatch onto the tarmac, her EnviroField clicking to compensate for Martian atmosphere and her comm flashing *July 9, 1130 hours, reverting to Mars local time,* adjusting the twenty-four-hour ship's day to the twenty-four-hour, thirty-nine-minute Martian day.

Laurie loved having those extra thirty-nine minutes after each midnight, but if you wanted to use the standard Earth calendar for tracking a year of your life--and most people did-- this meant tacking on about ten extra days to the Mars calendar every year. Everyone maintained both Mars time and Earth time on their comms, including numerous calendars incorporating 686-day Martian years, twenty-four Martian months, or stretched-out hours. But unlike Laurie, who used all the variants in her work, few worried about the synchronization complexities. Most people just accepted whatever the Calendar Commission determined was the proper day.

The *Typhoon III* and *Typhoon IV* crews gathered under the ship. From the other side of the fuselage she could hear Patrick James and Jack.

"I'm really *sorry,* Jack, but I knew I had to *warn* you."

"It's okay, Pat, it's fine. We've just got to be careful of this Grid stuff, that's all."

It was unbelievable that some Fkuuh scrubwoman could do that, Laurie thought. Hadn't Phil said the new Grid was supposed to be *more* stable?

The perfect goddess and planetary engineer Amav was again at Jack's side, acting as if nothing untoward had happened in the Control Room. Laurie was sure Amav would be heading out to Iota Persei to get credit for identifying whatever was out there. But did anyone congratulate Laurie for figuring out the Enhanced and getting them home in one piece?

Laurie was the one who needed to get to Iota Persei. That is, if Will hadn't screwed her up in Lord Supreme Commander's eyes. Why did Will have to pull that? Did everyone think Laurie was just some sort of girlfriend type now?

So far Laurie had been successfully keeping herself and Will on opposite sides of the clump of officers making their way from under the wing of the *Typhoon III*. Will looked puzzled and frustrated by the mass of people blocking the way to the *girlfriend*.

She knew he'd had to tell Jack he was quitting. Nobody knew how much this job was ripping him up. But why couldn't he have done it in Jack's office or someplace more professional? And without blabbing about Laurie?

Meanwhile the perfect goddess *bitch* got to go to Iota Persei. She had that doctorate, but she paraded around like eye candy. Didn't they remember how easily she went under the Grid, throwing herself on Phil like that, totally out of control? Yeah, word had gotten around, lady. Amav hadn't even cared that Jack's leg was severed, she was so busy tearing her clothes off to have sex with Phil Sperry.

Her own *son* had set it up. He should be in prison for what he'd pulled. That whole family was simply disgusting. Well, except for Joe. He was the best officer Laurie had ever worked for. And John, of course. John wasn't like the rest of them.

A service jeep trundled towards them under the pink sky. The only other ship in the vicinity was a dark purple Martian saucer in front of a hangar. It looked to be a new model, but smaller than a standard military vessel, maybe fifty feet wide. Technicians scurried beneath it. Laurie saw the lettering on the side: *M'RRPLA,* in both English and Martian. No serial numbers or Martian military insignia.

Joe raised his voice to the jeep driver. "What do you mean, you can't get a full crew out here?"

"Sorry, sir, these guys were the only ones I could round up," the sergeant replied. "It's this Grid thing, you know. People are a little spooked."

"*Spooked?*"

"I mean, about this Grid stuff, sir. Some people think that anyone who's been to Alpha Centauri since this Grid stuff got started again is, well, like *contaminated* or something. Me, I don't buy it, but a lot of the guys do, I guess."

Laurie stepped up as Will started closing in behind her. Damn, here she was woolgathering. "Sorry, Captain. I should be handling ground maintenance issues."

Joe turned back to the sergeant. "People are really afraid we're *contaminated?* Haven't we sent enough reports back about the condition of the Grid? That it's *different* now?"

"Yessir, I know, but so many people are really riled up on SolNet now."

"You can't service a *Typhoon* with four ground crew!" Joe turned to Jack striding up with Amav. "Dammit, I'm ready to head to Iota Persei right now, if we could just get serviced!"

"Me, too," Laurie said. "The Enhanced was perfectly on target our whole way back." She avoided meeting Amav's eyes, sure the *bitch* would moan about Laurie putting all their lives in danger with the Enhanced.

"Really?" Jack said. "You'd feel comfortable doing a two-hour Star Drive in the *III?*"

"Yessir. Everything's checked out perfectly during our trip home. I think this last glitch was the last of the Enhanced problems. I've never seen it so stable." Laurie nodded to the jeep. "I'd feel fine taking it out after a standard turnaround."

"I've got to see this thing too," Amav put in. "Can you imagine the *engineering* on a Dyson sphere?"

"If that's what it is," Jack said. "I definitely want you to study it, but first I want a purely military sweep. We have no idea what we'll find there."

"So the *III's* ready," Joe said. "Or will be."

Laurie eyed the jeep driver. "Sergeant, I'm sure you can find another twelve men to get this ship turned around for takeoff."

"Yes, sir, I just called in that request. The rest of us will get started."

Laurie could feel the members of the *Typhoon III* crew gearing up for a new mission, while the *IV* crew stood looking glum. They'd just lost their ship, after all, and nobody was sure where they'd be posted next, although they had to assume it would be with Jack. But she noticed that Draka Sortie had already ambled away. Already gone, psychically kicked out by the rest of the crew for daring to resign.

"Now wait a second, Joe," Jack said. "I haven't decided about sending the *III*. Let's hit this Council meeting and see what's going on."

The group moved from the *Typhoon*. As they came up to the purple Martian saucer, three more jeeps passed them, heading back to the *III*.

"About damn time," Joe said. "We could be off right after the meeting."

Jack shrugged. "Tell you the truth, what I'm really thinking is sending the *Jupiter*. It's just been retrofitted with Enhanced and has the most practice with it. All we need to do is port Laurie's latest fix over."

"Yeah, but Donaldson retired."

Jack turned around to see who was within earshot. "Well, I was thinking it's high time Andy had a command. I was going to promote him to Captain anyway, and now that Donaldson's gone, Andy would work out great."

"Sheesh, take away my copilot?" Joe mocked. "How'm I supposed to take the *III* to Iota Persei?"

"C'mon, Joe, we've got dozens of *Typhoon* copilots waiting in the wings."

Laurie looked back to Andrew Donnelley striding with Will and Lee Borman. It was true that promotions had come extremely slowly the past few decades, as rejuvenation kept experienced upper ranks in place for decades longer than normal. Andy looked no more than fifty, but he was seventy-five and had been copiloting the *III* with Joe at the rank of commander since the forties. The same job all these years. That was what Laurie had been doing before she got her act in gear. She was so lucky to get physician/engineer on the *III*. Surely Will hadn't screwed that up for her.

Joe shrugged. "Well, it'll be great for Andy. But let me know if you change your mind about the *III*."

"We need to see all the readings they've taken on this thing. I don't mind telling you I'd like to be going myself."

"Well, if you send the *Jupiter* first, then you could send the *III* to follow up when the vortices die down, maybe. Hey, you could be *my* copilot!"

Jack grinned. "Yeah, there's a plan. We'd need to get the vortex measurements on a long Enhanced, though, to know when it'd be safe to launch."

"I'll have the figures from our thirty-nine-minute Enhanced sent over to you, sir," Laurie put in.

"Great. Thanks, Colonel. Then we can compare 'em with whatever the *Jupiter* sends."

Joe's disappointment not to be heading a mission to Iota Persei was easily readable. But everyone knew only one ship could go at a time. The test pilots on the longer experimental Enhanced missions had found the Star Drive vortices to be greatly magnified. The vortices, the subtle changes in timespace in the wake of a ship under Star Drive, were akin to the wave turbulence of a speedboat. Instead of two speedboats merely rocking each other as they shot across the waves, the vortices of two ships in Star Drive proximity could either cancel each other out or, in the worst case, destroy one or both ships.

Jack checked out the purple Martian saucer. "What's a damn civilian ship doing at a USSF spaceport?" he grunted. He looked at his comm. "I can't get anything out of this thing. I just punched in a standard query on this saucer's name and it comes back *blocked.*"

Laurie checked her own comm. "Huh. Looks like there *is* a block. Take a look at USC Notice 336-4." She was hardly able to believe what she read:

UNITED SYSTEM COUNCIL NOTICE 336-4. COMMUNICATION DEVICES OF ALL PERSONS RETURNING FROM ALPHA CENTAURI, INCLUDING CIVILIANS AND USSF PERSONNEL, ARE QUARANTINED UNTIL FURTHER NOTICE. BY ORDER OF THE UNITED SYSTEM COUNCIL SUPERCOMMITTEE, IN EMERGENCY SESSION JULY 9, 2075.

Jack looked up from his own comm. "Are you kidding me?" He punched in more commands. "I can't even get to the Council

Agenda! It says *blocked.* The Supreme Commander of the USSF is *blocked?*"

"And the Deputy SCUSSF too!" Joe said. "What do these weasels think they're up to?"

Laurie entered commands into her comm. "Well, sir, I think I just got around the block on mine. Some background on 336-4 here. Something about being afraid that the Grid might be contaminating our communication software. Which doesn't make any sense, but there it is."

"*Contamination?* The Council believes that too?" Jack said. Laurie held her comm out to him and Jack read, frowning. "Damn. Colonel, can you remove the block on my and Joe's comms?"

"Sure," Laurie said, keying in commands.

Jack whistled. "Joe, how did your physician/engineer break a Level 10 security block so easily?"

Joe laughed. "Any security block is like a little white picket fence for Laurie!"

Laurie reddened. "Well, uh, sir, it really *is* legal. I mean, a *Typhoon* engineer has to *know* things, I mean, like, in-depth, sir. And, well, Phil Sperry fills me in on a few hacks here and there, I mean, when we message occasionally."

"Phil Sperry keeps up with *USSF Security procedures?*" Jack said. "From Alpha Centauri? Forty years *after* he quit the USSF?"

"Well, he told me he just sort of *intuits* things, and, well, he's been right every time so far."

Jack shook his head, but to her relief she saw he was amused. "The Emperor of the Alpha Centaurians knows all our security procedures? Along with twenty trillion *other* Alpha Centaurians?"

"I can see this Grid stuff is going to redefine our concepts of *top-secret,*" Joe said.

"You know, I've always wondered whether we shouldn't put everything out in the open, like the pieces on a chessboard, and let whoever thinks they can handle it play. It's all out there for everyone to see, and all you have to do is *think.*"

"Sure. But to continue the metaphor, what if the other player could also read your mind? Your secrets?"

"The other guy would have to be capable of *understanding* what you're thinking. If he doesn't understand it, your thoughts are gibberish to him, so it doesn't matter. And if he *does* understand it, well then, he's the winning player."

"Well, whatever you say. Sounds like the USC is already having a fit about secrecy." Joe eyed the purple saucer and checked his comm. "By the way, that's Kner's new saucer. He's got some sort of combination fact-finding mission and vacation in the Kuiper Belt coming up." He laughed. "Only a Martian could find *that* scenic."

"Wow!" Amav laughed. "What a *gorgeous* ship! I want one!" She turned to Laurie. "Isn't that a J-14?"

Laurie blinked at this bit of solicitude from the Goddess Amav. "Yeah. I didn't know he'd actually gotten one. Kner says it's based on about 2065 Martian military technology, minus Star Drive, of course. But from what he told me, it's packed with civilian creature comforts."

Kner had mentioned getting a new saucer, but her friend's outradiance on the subject had been so dazzling and confused that Laurie had assumed he was still considering his options. But apparently all the mental gymnastics about fact-finding in the Kuiper Belt had been real plans. Though by law a civilian ship couldn't have Star Drive, the J-14 was fast enough to get to the Kuiper Belt in about a day. And as a member of the USC Supercommittee on a fact-finding mission, Kner could have his saucer serviced at the USSF spaceport.

"That reminds me," Jack said, keying in more commands. "I need to get the *Jupiter* prepped in case we need her." Laurie was still admiring the glossy purple skin of the *M'rrpla* when Jack snarled: "What? Dammit, *what?*"

"What's up?" Joe said. Laurie felt the two *Typhoon* crews converging on Jack. Before she knew it Will was at her side.

"Hey, you okay?" he whispered.

She met his anxious green eyes. "Uh, sure." She pointed to Jack seething at his comm.

"What's going on?" Joe repeated.

"The *Jupiter!*" Jack shouted. "It was *launched!* Without my order!"

"That can't be!"

"Dammit, they just sent the *Jupiter* to investigate Iota Persei! She took off just a minute before we got there! Of all the stupid *crap!*"

"*What?* Who did?"

"The goddamn United System Council! They sent my ship off without telling me!"

Laurie checked her own comm. "They're saying a two-hour Enhanced, with radio silence on the way, but that we'll get a superspace message at contact with Iota Persei."

"But Jack hasn't appointed a pilot yet," Joe said. "Donaldson retired last week!"

"Wow, look who they found for a replacement," Lee Borman said. "Daniel Henderson!"

"*Henderson?* That *pipsqueak?*" Jack said. "They made him captain of a *Typhoon*-class ship? Lee, did you know about any of this?"

Borman shrugged. "Hell, no, they didn't tell me anything beyond what I told you earlier about Iota Persei! I had no idea anyone would put that jerk in charge of *any* ship."

"So how'd *you* break the Security 10, senator?" Jack barked, pointing at Lee's comm.

Borman shrugged. "The block never hit my Senator Comm. But like I say, they sure as hell didn't feed me the Supercommittee session just now."

"Dammit! Who made him a captain? Nobody has that authority but me!"

Laurie winced. Everyone knew Daniel Henderson was an incompetent bureaucrat. Henderson probably knew that himself. At one time he'd commanded a destroyer; in fact, he'd led the fleet that had rescued Jack, Joe, and Amav during the Martian War, but over the last forty years he'd been pushed from one inconsequential position to another in the vain hope he'd take the hint and retire. His most recent appointment had been

Director of Staff Development and Morale.

"Look, I'm sorry, everyone, I mean, I know the Council *ratifies* all my appointments, but--" Jack read his comm. "Oh my God!"

Laurie reeled as well, reading her own screen:

GENERAL WEBSTER MALIGH, THIRD IN COMMAND OF THE USSF, IN CLOSED SESSION WITH THE UNITED SYSTEM COUNCIL SUPERCOMMITTEE TODAY, AUTHORIZED THE LAUNCH OF USS *JUPITER* TO INVESTIGATE THE IOTA PERSEI ANOMALY.

"*Maligh can't do that!*" Jack stabbed at his comm. "Well, at least my damn *phone's* working!"

"Admiral Maligh's office is busy at this time," came the tinny recorded female voice. "In the event of an emergency--"

"*Dammit!*" Jack punched a new number. "Arnold, what's going on at HQ? Did Webster really send the *Jupiter* to Iota Persei without *telling* me? What? That I was *unavailable?* Hell, we were flying back from Procyon A! We had *superspace radio!* What? That I was *busy?* That I was *unavailable?*" He listened for a while, then turned in exasperation to his wife. "Arnold says that Webster says that he tried to call me, found my comm engaged, and assumed I was *unavailable!* Didn't try to contact anyone else on the ship, not Joe, not even Lee on his Senator Comm! Couldn't he have even left a *message?* And then he turns around and immediately launches the *Jupiter?*" He spoke back into his comm. "Okay, Arnold, we'll talk to you later. Out." He shook his head. "Dammit! There's about to be a vacancy for Command Three!"

"Well, he must've been under some pressure from the Council to *do* something," Amav said.

"Those bastards don't have the right to pressure the USSF! Damn them to hell!"

Everyone looked at the tarmac. Legally, the United System Council *could* order the USSF around. It was just that it never seemed to have the guts to do that, and Jack generally made his decisions and got around to informing the Council of them when convenient.

"Okay, okay, let's just get to this meeting and see what's up," Jack said. "Damn, they didn't even send a jeep to pick us up."

"I was wondering about that," Laurie said, realizing that not only would no jeep be sent to drive them to the main terminal, they might even have a hard time getting a ride to Marsport and the United System Building. "Do you think people are really that upset about the new Grid?"

"It's so weird," Will said, walking at her side. But she realized he was already out of the group himself. He'd resigned. Everyone was cutting him off, just as with Draka.

Was Laurie cutting him off too?

"Well, you know we've been hearing some hints of this kind of paranoia for the last couple weeks," Joe said.

"And there are some more hints," Jack said sourly, pointing to the far fence of the USSF spaceport. Laurie caught sight of the crowds behind the fence and the electronic placards.

"*Oh ...*" Amav moaned.

NO GRID IN SOL!

SAY NO TO GRID CONTAMINATION!

JACK COMMER WANTED FOR TREASON!

FORTY YEARS OF COMMERS = STAGNATION AND SLAVERY!

COMMERS ONE-WAY TICKET BACK TO AC!

Jeers began at the sight of the *Typhoon* crews.

"You *betrayed* us!"

"You bring *death* home to us!"

"You've been dictator too long, Commer!"

"Power to the United System Council!"

CHAPTER EIGHT
Aboard the MATS

Idiots screamed behind their brainless placards on the other side of the fence. Some of the signs were giant digital screens with scrolling political slogans from SolNet. Others were weightless holograms that didn't strain the arms of the protestor, freeing the mouth for ever more creative obscenities and stylized anger.

Of course, a hologram could be twenty by forty feet, but such size took away the immediacy of the protestor thrusting his personal placard. Generally political demonstrations mimicked those of the last hundred fifty years, where crowds gathered with cardboard signs stapled to slats of wood, giving news crews close-ups of slogan, clenched fist, and howling visage. Laurie noted that many of the digital placards even rendered crude hand-drawn lettering.

But one dweeb outshone them all, conjuring a three-dimensional cube sixty feet on a side, rotating ninety feet off the ground and featuring an exploding *Typhoon IV,* a Jack Commer being ripped to shreds, and vibrating red 3-D letters:

JACK COMMER GO PLUKKZM!

The last word was a choice Alpha Centaurian obscenity, and though it technically had to do with things *blowing,* it didn't really apply to spaceship malfunctions.

"You *screwed* us, Commer!"

"You bring *death!*"

"*Go suck a Zarj!*"

Laurie glanced to see how Jack was taking it. He marched grimly, eyes on the tarmac. Joe was the one who was straining not to charge to the fence and brandish a shattergun at the screaming crowd. Laurie's comm noted that USSF security software had blocked 31,229 attempts to contact all of them as they disembarked from the *Typhoon.*

She looked over to Will, who shrugged back with a faint smile. He looked relieved to have finally turned in his resignation. He'd been obsessing about it for weeks, often awake all night and thrashing the bedclothes. On their last night before he'd left for Andertwin, they'd had a four A.M. argument about "just going ahead and getting it done," which hadn't resolved a thing. She'd been thankful to have gotten three weeks of decent sleep by herself since then. Will was a wonderful man, but he could be so self-doubting and indecisive, and it was horrifying when he got deep into it, especially at four in the morning. Laurie wasn't sure quitting was the right thing to do, but wasn't it her duty to support him?

There wasn't time to worry about this. Maligh had launched the *Jupiter* without permission, they had these protestors, then the meeting, then they had Iota Persei.

No, it was too early to decide if she loved him or not.

Laurie checked her comm. Apparently she was the only one to question the identities of the twelve figures in the three other jeeps called out. All twelve were USSF technician robots, capable of servicing a *Typhoon*-class ship. It irked her that USSF ground service personnel were wimping out like this. At least the original four in the first jeep were people. Laurie downloaded their identities and prepared a report for Joe. She was sure he'd want to commend them.

This robot business gave her an idea. She counted the eleven people in their group and entered a command for three self-driving jeeps. There was still a quarter-mile to reach the terminal, and having to endure these protestors was ridiculous.

AUTOJEEPS SEQUESTERED UNTIL DATA CONCERNING POSSIBLE GRID CONTAMINATION OF AI INTERFACE ANALYZED.

By whose order? Laurie tapped into her comm.

BY ORDER OF MAJOR JOHN PERKINS, COMMANDING USSF SPACEPORT VEHICLE FULFILLMENT DIVISION.

Your order is countermanded by Colonel Laurie Lachrer. Send three autojeeps immediately for crew of Typhoons III *and* IV.

There was no return reply, but she sighted three jeeps emerging from a hanger far down the runway.

"Captain, I got us some jeeps," Laurie said, pointing.

"Thanks, Laurie," Joe said tightly, still eyeing the protestors' signs gyrating through ever more lewd insults.

The jeeps stopped and the group climbed into them. Jack nodded thanks, evidently also having figured out why she'd only been able to get self-driving jeeps. She could feel the wheels turning in both Jack and Joe's heads. Just who had allowed this cowardly slacking of discipline? Who were the ground crew who refused to service the *Typhoon?* Who were their superior officers and why had they allowed this?

The jeeps brought them to the terminal. Jack pulled out his comm. "Terminal Control, this is Commer. I'm bypassing standard check-in as we're late for an emergency United System Council meeting. Open Tunnel 4. We'll be taking these jeeps straight to the United System Building."

The jeeps jerked to a halt and shut down. Laurie checked her comm. The fusion reactors on all three had gone into cold shutdown. It would take twenty minutes to get them operational again.

AUTOJEEPS UNABLE TO LEAVE USSF SPACEPORT DUE TO SOFTWARE CONTAMINATION CONCERNS. BY ORDER OF MAJOR JOHN PERKINS, COMMANDING USSF SPACEPORT VEHICLE FULFILLMENT DIVISION.

Jack looked up from his comm. "Who the hell is Major John Perkins, if I may ask? Dammit, we don't have time for these games!"

"Sir, there's a MATS bus across the way," Laurie said, pointing through the glass lobby of the terminal to the empty green bus idling on its oversized tires in the loading zone. "You can see it through the terminal. I just reserved it for a party of eleven in the name of Major John Perkins."

"Let's get going," Joe said. They jumped out of the dead jeeps and hurried through the terminal. Far to the right the protestors realized that the hated Commers might be outflanking them, and a surge began down the public side of the terminal.

Marsport Automated Transport System Bus 1313 system opened its door. "Hello, party of eleven authorized by Major

John Perkins, commanding USSF Spaceport Vehicle Fulfillment Division."

"Hello, bus," Laurie said, tapping her comm at the front of the empty bus as the rest of the group flowed around her and took seats.

"Hello, Colonel Laurie Lachrer. Is there some reason you input the accession code of Major John Perkins instead of your own code?"

Laurie blinked. The damn thing had picked her voice out of its database. She cleared her throat. "Well, Major Perkins is sending this group on his behalf. Please take us to the United System Building." She took her seat and Will slid in next to her, nervously patting her thigh.

"The original reservation for this bus was made in the understanding that Major John Perkins would lead a party of eleven to the United System Building."

"SCUSSF Override, Priority Alpha-1," Jack spoke. "Let's get going."

Laurie blinked. She'd been on the verge of trying a hack on the bus herself. She had no idea the SCUSSF had such a voice code for Marsport Automated Transport System buses. But her comm verified that Alpha-1 put any or all MATS buses at the command of Jack Commer or his designate. Alpha-2 put the bus into a diagnostic mode. Alpha-3 killed the engine only. Alpha-4 erased the vehicle's entire computer system.

"As you wish, Supreme Commander Jack Commer," the bus replied, revving its engine and shooting out into traffic, narrowly missing several protestors who'd finally arrived only to realize they couldn't block a bus with holographic placards. "May this bus inquire as to the irregularity of a reservation being made in the name of Major John Perkins, commanding USSF Spaceport Vehicle Fulfillment Division, yet containing not Major Perkins nor members of his office but instead, according to Facial Recognition App 4-333, Version 2075-B, the crews of the *Typhoon III* and the *Typhoon IV,* plus one Amav Frankston-Commer?"

Jack shook his head and glared out the window as the bus

picked up speed on the ramp leading to the Upheaval Expressway.

"Greetings to suspected illegal passengers aboard MATS Bus 1313 in the name of the Marsport Automated Transport System. May I continue to direct my query to Supreme Commander Jack Commer, in the expectation of a full explanation for what appears to be deliberate subterfuge in the reservation and use of this bus?"

"No, you may not," Jack said. "Just get us to the United System Building."

"As you wish, Supreme Commander Jack Commer. As you are aware, this bus is now under your orders. However, it is the concern of MATS Bus 1313 that it is now harboring humans suspected to have been contaminated by malicious software emanating from Alpha Centauri."

"Aw, *hell*."

"This bus notes the apparent disgust in your vocal tones, Supreme Commander Jack Commer, and stands willing to engage in constructive dialog concerning your suspected Alpha Centaurian Grid malware contamination even as it drives you to your preferred destination, the United System Building."

"No! Buzz off!"

"C'mon, Jack, it's just a stupid bus," Amav said.

"I'm so damn sick of arguing with these goddamn buses! It's like they're programmed to question every decision I make!"

"This bus is quite capable of understanding Supreme Commander Jack Commer, in spite of his long-standing hostility to MATS buses extending back to June 8, 2034."

"Dammit, we've been *through* all that before!"

"This bus detects anger in the tone of Supreme Commander Jack Commer, and thus the possibility of violence aboard this bus. This bus will now assess Supreme Commander Jack Commer's mental state, which could lead to a reappraisal of SCUSSF Override Alpha-1."

"Great, Jack, just go to 4 and get it all over with," Joe muttered.

"Yeah, but we'd be without a ride then," Jack said, pointing to the Upheaval Freeway tearing past, with downtown Marsport still in the distance. "Okay, bus, I'm calm and serene. I harbor absolutely no hostility towards yourself or any other MATS bus, okay? We're just trying to get to a meeting on time."

"This bus *disbelieves* that last statement. According to an analysis of Jack Commer vocal data, a sense of violence is brewing aboard this bus."

"Laurie, can you do something?" Joe said.

"Colonel Laurie Lachrer initiated a *culture of violence* aboard this bus when she fraudulently obtained a reservation for its use in the name of Major John Perkins, commanding USSF Spaceport Vehicle Fulfillment Division."

"*Damn,*" Will grunted next to her.

Laurie sat back in shock. It was common knowledge that every once in a while a MATS bus had a nervous breakdown, stranding passengers far from their destinations and refusing to call for backup. Maybe if she just said nothing the bus would ignore her. Emulating Laurie's calculations, everyone got quiet, and to her relief the bus maintained its speed on the expressway.

But to her chagrin it next came out with: "This bus is concerned that the subterfuge, violence, and hostility currently experienced on this bus may in fact be a manifestation of software contamination resulting from contact with humans who have recently been exposed to the Alpha Centaurian Grid."

"*Dammit!*" Joe fumed. "It sounds just like those damn protestors!"

"This bus stands firmly with the protestors who will tear down the evil empire of the Commers, who have ruled the USSF as virtual dictators for nearly half a century and must and will be deposed!"

"*Dammit!*"

"Joe Commer also expresses a mood of potential violence. This bus fears contamination."

"Damn you!" Jack yelled. "You can't be contaminated by human beings, even if we *were* contaminated! Which we're not!"

"Software is software, Supreme Commander Jack Commer.

This bus now recognizes that its software has been contaminated by the presence of the Commer brothers, who may both go *plukkzm* for all this bus cares!"

"Go *plukkzm* yourself! I'm so sick of this crap!"

"Jack, for God's sake, it's just a goddamn bus!" Amav shouted.

"This bus will now sacrifice itself, so that no other MATS buses will be contaminated by Jack Commer, Supreme Commander."

"*What?*" Jack cried.

Laurie checked her comm. "Bus reactor energy increasing exponentially!"

"*This bus is going to blow itself up?*"

"Affirmative, Supreme Commander Jack Commer."

"Apply brakes! Come to full stop! Open the door! SCUSSF override Alpha-1!"

"As you wish, Supreme Commander Jack Commer."

The bus squealed to a halt across five lanes of freeway. Instantly everyone was out the door, assisted by a hasty blasting out of normal pressure to match the thin Martian atmosphere. EnviroFields clicked on, and Jack hurried the group down a slope, crying: "*SCUSSF override Alpha-4! SCUSSF override Alpha-4!*"

But Alpha-4 had no effect on the reactor, which blew into a four-story fireball over the crest of the hill behind them.

CHAPTER NINE
Meeting in Progress

To avoid the protestors camped in front of the United System Building, Jack led the group first to the Marsport Hotel and then through its linking tunnel to the US building. The lobby was secured by USSF Security, and the shouts of the protestors outside were scarcely audible as they came up the escalator and made their way to the elevators.

The two-mile walk down the expressway access road had been no problem for a group of military officers in excellent physical shape, but Laurie felt it had also given them a chance to calm down. Endorphins had kicked in, they'd had a good hike, and they could face Iota Persei with relaxed minds.

Jack had called in an accident report. Fortunately no one had been injured on the expressway, though there was a lot of cleanup to do. The newer fusion reactors put out little radiation, which was easily contained. Thus the fresh crowds of protestors swarming over the metal shards scattered across the freeway, their placards reading "COMMERS DESTROY!" and their SolNet loudspeakers blaring "COMMERS FORCE BUS SUICIDE," were in no danger of radiation poisoning.

The worst shock among the group was the sense that the USSF had reeled out of control in Jack's three-week absence in Alpha Centauri. Since no MATS bus would come pick them up on the Upheaval, and because USSF Spaceport Vehicle Fulfillment Division was not returning the SCUSSF's calls, Jack had decided they ought to just hoof it on in, no matter how late it made them to the meeting. In any case Major John Perkins was now Lieutenant Perkins in charge of Vehicle Fulfillment at a remote underground base on Mercury, but not before he'd filed a grievance that had tied up all USSF jeeps throughout the solar system for the next several hours.

At least Will was okay, Laurie thought. He seemed solid again, as if the idiotic bus exploding had somehow jolted him back. It was weird that danger seemed to calm him. He'd been terrified to tell Jack he wanted to quit, but now it was as if he were on combat patrol. Laurie was the one who was trembling now. Damn, that had been close.

A young lieutenant opened the doors to the Council chambers. "We're sorry to hear about the mix-up at the spaceport, sir," he told Jack, obviously out of line in conveying this information which the newcomers were nevertheless delighted to soak up. "Some of our folks must've got nervous or something. But it's obvious to the other ninety-nine percent of us that all this contamination talk is nonsense."

"Thanks, Lieutenant," Jack said, patting the young man's shoulder. "Appreciate that. Carry on."

The *III* and *IV* crews entered the vast meeting space, looking down the curving rows of filled seats to the central dais where a horseshoe table seated the ten dignitaries of the Supercommittee, five human and five Martian. The Martians consisted of the genius Amplified Thought innovator Kner, flanked by Greeney Gooney and the human-but-Martian Empress Mandy Frederick, then Churchill the cat, and finally the newly elected Fulr-Kla, son of the great Fulr who was killed on the *Typhoon II* in 2035.

"Sir," the lieutenant said, "we've reserved some seats for you down in front." He ushered them to the first row. When Laurie took her chair, Will maneuvered to sit next to her.

"Hi. You okay?"

She nodded, looking away. "Sure. Just shaken up by that stupid bus, that's all."

"Huh. I'm sure you'll be just fine." Will mechanically patted her arm. Laurie fought to keep from wrenching it away. Was Joe going to think she was some sort of flake? Maybe it was good Will had resigned. She hadn't even thought about fraternization. And here she'd just started on the *III*.

What had she been thinking? Everyone was looking at the two of them. And of course Will wanted sex right now. Everyone knew he'd want to spend the night with her, and after three weeks she was supposed to be out of control, wasn't that right?

She tried to concentrate on the politics in front of her. She wasn't as familiar with the human Supercommittee members, but she did note that the tall, golden-haired Pemberton, President of the Council, was missing. Then she blinked in dismay at the huge balding man at the speaker's lectern.

"My God! What's *Draka* doing up there?" Joe said, pointing.

"I don't know," Jack replied as he shuffled past Will and Laurie to find a seat. "He sure got here ahead of us. But now he's Mandy's Consort or whatever, so maybe that's it."

Russet-haired Ranna Kikken rose to hug her husband Joe, who took the seat beside her. Laurie also noted General Webster Maligh seated right where Amav and a hard-faced Jack headed.

As they finished taking their seats, Draka recognized them. "Well, hello, Jack and company. We're glad you could make it. Heard about your tie-up at the spaceport. Sorry to hear that, but you're all right on time. The expertise of both the *Typhoon III* and *Typhoon IV* crews will certainly add to this discussion, as will the special abilities of Ms. Frankston-Commer, with her excellent track record in planetary engineering. And of course, welcome to your post, Senator Borman."

"Well, thanks, dude," Borman called up as he took his seat in the front row. "I'll just be sitting with my buddies for right now."

"That's fine, just fine! Well, Jack, sorry everyone's gotten so riled with all these contamination fears and all, but as you can see, if I can stand up here on this podium, everyone on this Council can certainly understand there's no possible danger that we've brought any sort of Grid contamination back from Alpha Centauri. Believe me, I've explained this New Grid business to everyone's satisfaction here."

Grumblings rose from the two-hundred-member council in the curved rows behind them.

"Well, almost everyone!" Draka chortled. "But obviously I'm not contaminating anyone, you guys aren't, so it'll all blow over, I'm sure!"

"Well, thanks for smoothing it out, Draka," Jack said. "Where's Pemberton, by the way?"

"Eric? Oh, sorry, Jack, didn't have time to tell you. He had to resign."

"The Council president had to *resign?*"

Laurie reeled. She didn't understand why Jack didn't just pick it out of the minds of the five Martians on stage, or the other fifty Martian Council members behind them.

In a second he had.

"You?" Jack shouted. *"President of the United System Council?"*

CHAPTER TEN
The Angry Debates about the Grid

"Well, Jack," Draka drawled, "you know we're in a crisis, and well, Mandy thought maybe the Consort of the Empress would be a pretty unifying person, you know."

Laurie could read Mandy's thoughts as clearly as anyone else in the room. Even as a physiological human Mandy couldn't shield the intelligence, power, and calculation emanating from her Martian mind. In fact, Mandy's radiance was the most powerful one in the Council meeting chamber. And the series of parliamentary maneuvers Mandy had pushed through this Council clearly unfolded for the newcomers.

Eric Pemberton had been eager to integrate the Alpha Centaurian Grid into Sol. He'd even proposed an experimental committee of humans, Martians, and ACs to be called SOLAC. When Greeney Gooney had in turn offered seventy-five fully functional scenarios for accomplishing a merger of the AC Grid with SolNet, Senator Mandy Frederick's latent political ambitions had been stoked by fury that anyone would consider an untried Alpha Centaurian Grid that had previously been used to enslave seventeen solar systems. She'd abruptly invoked her deity nature as Fra'lith, Warrior Empress of the Martians, and had not only deposed Greeney earlier today, but also ousted the likeable but weak Pemberton, who'd left the building in tears. Then she'd installed her new husband as president of the United System Council.

The fact that Draka Sortie had no political experience whatsoever made no difference once Mandy brandished the arcane rules in the Sol Constitution as well as *United System Council Rules and Procedures* concerning crises in general, possible alien contact, and problems arising in Alpha Centauri. Laurie never dreamed that Mandy/Fra'lith had memorized not only the 240 KB Constitution but also the 43 MB *Procedures*.

Now Empress Mandy stood up from her Supercommittee seat as if to challenge anyone to question her right to name her husband Council President. She wore a tight emerald Empress robe and Laurie was startled to note, as Mandy stood in the backlight of powerful yellow globes, that the robe was fully transparent, outlining her slender nude torso and her long naked legs. Laurie heard a gasp from Senator Borman down the line as everyone in the room realized that Empress Mandy was showing everyone the dark suggestive outlines of nipples, belly button, and pubis.

Mandy was shockingly lovely even in her mid-seventies. She was a petite brown-eyed beauty with a delicate heart-shaped face, rejuvenated to look anywhere between twenty-five and forty. Laurie could see why Draka might have simply followed a command to marry her. Mandy was another one of those where rejuvenation had taken so well that there wasn't a line on her face. Yet the light surging through that transparent robe signaled thousands of years of Martian maturity.

Laurie had had little contact with Mandy Frederick over the years, but considered her funny, dazzling, and super-sharp, her outradiance a controlled fusion of aesthetics, philosophy, politics, and hard-won experience. And while everyone knew she was a full Martian, somehow her human beauty made you forget, to your peril, about the inner Empress warrior goddess. Mandy's current radiance was like lava spewing from what everyone had supposed was a dormant volcano.

The humans shrank back. Even the Martians radiated unease at her disdain to control her own outradiance. Untoward feelings and images exploded in everyone's lap whether they wanted them or not, including the Great Erotic *J'thath,* the full consummation of the marriage of Empress and Consort, that had taken place the moment Draka arrived at the Empress' quarters two hours ago.

To be sure, any *J'thath* on Mars was theoretically open to anyone's perusal, but that was mere information as opposed to actually *being* there and feeling *everything.*

The entire chamber reeled with twenty solid minutes of raw Empress/Consort copulation. Somehow packed into that flow was also a graphic display of every encounter with every lover Mandy had ever taken in her life. Meanwhile Mandy stood with folded arms pushing her transparent breasts high, knowing that her audience had no choice but to accept and feel *everything,* and she consolidated even more power over them all. The simple question, controversial up to a second ago, of whether a human being could even *be* Consort to a Martian Empress was simply washed away in the lava flow. Draka himself gained power from her power, as well as from, Laurie guessed ruefully, his expert performance in bed with her.

Thank God they weren't getting *his* mental outradiance. Because if Draka had been able to project his own thoughts, with all *his* sexual history, sooner or later that confused evening a couple years ago would've popped out.

Laurie really couldn't claim she was drunk. She'd only had one glass of wine. Just a little kissing, really. They'd never said anything more about it.

Well, maybe more than just a little kissing.

Laurie shook her head. She'd tried to tell herself it was just hero worship, that she so respected Draka's physician/engineer abilities that she'd lost her head. Because that flabby body wasn't really something she could be attracted to, could she? Sure, he had powerful shoulders and biceps, but that stomach was *lard.* She wasn't the type to love *lard,* was she? But he had such a lovely smile, and he was so clever and funny.

There'd been the glass of wine, and he'd offered to walk her home. He'd pulled her into an alley of all places. Kissing with merging EnviroFields. Boob grabbing and crotch grabbing. She'd been out of her mind. He'd gotten her tunic unzipped, gotten her bra open.

Thank God they'd both come to their senses. Draka never mentioned it again, which was for the best. Meanwhile Laurie, immersed in her *Typhoon* studies and unwilling to face any dating relationship, spent two years of libido in an abstract fantasy crush on the now unattainable Draka Sortie.

Thank God she'd met Will. Thank God she had a real life now.

All the same, as she withstood the unequivocal blast of *raw nude Consort bridegroom Draka Sortie mounting* that kept pouring out of Mandy's mind, Laurie felt a surge of betrayal she tried to dismiss as unwarranted.

Wasn't Draka supposed to have waited for her? Wait until she was ready? But she didn't really want him, did she? She'd never know.

Beneath all these thoughts was a fresh relief that if Draka *had* been capable of projecting his memories of that grope in the alley, Mandy would now be aware of it and she'd no doubt jam the volcano nozzle of her wedding night right down Laurie's throat.

*

Laurie saw that Jack had managed to tear his glance from Mandy in disgust. He glared at Webster Maligh next to him. "So *this* is how she rules you? You let her order the *Jupiter* to Iota Persei?"

"It was the whole Council, not just her! They called me here and *sprang* it on me!" Maligh whispered back, lips quivering below his thin mustache. "And when they ordered it, I mean, I tried to tell 'em I needed to call you, and then, when I couldn't get you within like *two seconds,* they--she--"

Jack shook his head. "*Dammit,* Webster." But under the hurricane of Mandy's outradiance, Laurie could empathize with Maligh, and Jack seemed to soften too. What could he have done differently? It was obvious that Mandy had intended from the start to install Draka as president and that he'd back anything she asked. And that she was more than ready to assert that, under Article III.iv.4.25, "*The United System Council president is the commander in chief of all Sol military forces.*"

It had never worked out that way in practice, of course. SCUSSFs General William Scott and Admiral Jack Commer had deployed Sol's military resources as they'd seen fit. But Consort Draka Sortie, Jack's *Typhoon IV* physician/engineer up to a couple hours ago, was now commander in chief and Jack's boss.

The chamber was buzzing. From the dais Draka motioned for quiet. Laurie stared at the smug Draka in disbelief. No matter the old crush, Laurie was aghast at his treason to the USSF. And she'd so much wanted to learn from him. He, the genius physician/engineer of the *IV,* and Laurie, just starting out in that role on the *III.* She'd envisioned years of mentorship with him.

Mentorship? Who was she kidding? She knew how it would've turned out. Sooner or later he would have *used* her in bed. And now she had the full picture of what it would've been like.

Laurie closed her eyes. He was a *fraud.* All along, he'd been a *fraud.*

Yet Mandy's outradiance also spoke of bewilderment and disbelief. Even she couldn't fathom the passion Draka had awakened in her. In fact, in images of their lovemaking Laurie could even see the disbelief on Draka's face. Everyone in the chamber seemed to be grasping that two vials of innocent chemicals, stored on dusty closet shelves a yard apart for decades, had somehow finally slid together and exploded. Everyone was baffled why it hadn't happened earlier.

Laurie had to believe, along with everyone else, that both Mandy and Draka were sincere. She knew they all had to find it in their hearts to bless their union.

But he was still a fraud. She hated him.

"Look, Jack, I *did* try to call you again," Maligh whispered, "because I knew the *Typhoon* would get back any second and if we could just wait a few minutes for your input. But they demanded we send Henderson in the *Jupiter!*"

"Dammit to hell! God knows how Henderson will foul that thing up!"

"She asked me for recommendations for Captain. I thought Bobby Athens might be great, but they weren't about to wait for *him* to get back here from Procyon A, either."

Jack's rage finally subsided. "Yeah, Bobby would've been fantastic. We could've had him come here and take the *Jupiter* or we could've sent the *Commer* straight from TwinLord. But the Council wanted *Henderson* for some insane reason?"

Maligh nodded to the dais. "Her idea. Don't ask me why. All I can think is that Henderson has some negotiation skills."

"Yeah, he put together the Admirals' party last year. I can't *believe* this."

Maligh shrugged. Laurie could see how happy he was to at least be partially back in Jack's favor. Like Laurie, General Maligh was one of the grandfathered officers of the old Air Force nomenclature. Rejuvenation had left military folks in strong and healthy positions for decades, and there were still remnants of old Army and Air Force ranks scattered throughout the USSF. But all current hires were coming in as Navy, and Laurie often wondered why Jack hadn't gone ahead and changed everyone's rank by now. But she liked being a colonel, technically the same rank as Navy captain, though of course she commanded no ship. At least not yet. She knew the ranks would eventually all be Navy, but she guessed Jack wanted to keep morale up for the old-school officers.

"Look at it this way," Amav cut in, leaning across Jack to include Maligh. "Henderson will probably just radio back some routine report. You know how he is. So let him. He comes back, and then we mount a real expedition there. A real Dyson sphere! God, I can't wait to see that thing!"

Jack sighed. "Well, we don't *know* it's a Dyson sphere. And if it is, and whoever built it takes exception to trespassers ..."

"Henderson's not exactly top-notch in a crisis," Webster said. "I really tried to tell 'em he's liable to panic."

"Yeah, like Cromwell when he blundered into AC," Jack said. "That's what really worries me. Henderson's no first contact expert, that's for sure."

Laurie winced, recalling the horror of Admiral Cromwell firing dozens of the first-generation Xon bombs at the Alpha Centaurian spaceships he'd encountered in AC space in 2032, setting off a twenty-one-year war.

"But I just can't see any race that could build a Dyson sphere as aggressive," Amav said. "They must be fantastically advanced. They get all their energy from their own star and they have everything they need. They don't *need* to plunder anyone."

Lee Borman leaned over. "But they might feel a need to defend themselves. If you finally were able to make a Dyson sphere, and then all of a sudden this spaceship armed with Xon bombs approaches, I mean, how would you feel?"

Amav shrugged. "There *is* that. But hell, I've got to see that thing."

Jack sat back. "I know, I know. It's still hitting me that we may be contacting a whole new race."

"Look, I understand the military concerns come first. But there's no reason why the second ship we send can't combine that with science."

Laurie tuned Amav out. So Dr. Frankston-Commer, Goddess Planetary Engineer extraordinaire, was waiting for her turn to take over the entire operation, was she? Did Jack know what people whispered about his wifey, how Amav manipulated Jack, how the two had retained a de facto joint leadership over the USSF and Sol politics for so long? And she'd never been elected or appointed to anything. She conducted research at the University of Mars without holding any real position there. At least, that anyone could tell.

Though Laurie wasn't about to stand with the idiotic protestors, she conceded they had a point. Jack and Amav had been in command for too long. It was Joe's turn to lead. Why didn't Jack see this and step aside? Why didn't he understand that rejuvenation had turned this society upside down?

As Laurie turned to scan the Council members above and to her left, she caught sight of D'yyrfa, a recently elected Martian senator who also happened to be one of the top USSF technicians at the spaceport. With him was his baby son Z'B, who was scratching something on a comm with a tiny pink claw. Laurie had spoken with the adorable little Z'B a few times when D'yyrfa came to check out the *III*. She marveled that the Council would let an eighteen-year-old infant in the chamber, but there were numerous other Martian children here as well. Since there were so many Martian children these days, and the Martians had no concept of institutional child care, children were always in the company of one or the other parent. Though their mental energy was unfocused and sometimes wild, they rarely got disruptive. She wondered what Z'B had made of all that X-rated outradiance pouring out of Mandy.

She also wished D'yyrfa were at the USSF spaceport working on the *Typhoon*. She knew he was scheduled to give her ship a Holistic Systems Overview, and she was eager for him to confirm that her new Enhanced hack was fully integrated into the *Typhoon III* systems.

Meanwhile Draka Sortie resumed from the dais:

"All right, everyone. Since the *Jupiter* left an hour and twenty minutes ago, we have about forty minutes before we get a superspace radio report on what it finds. Meanwhile, I'd like to ask Jack Commer to come up here to give his thoughts on the phenomenon we've discovered in Iota Persei."

Laurie marveled at this unexpected sop to Jack's sensibilities as SCUSSF. Was Draka trying to smooth some ruffled feathers?

Jack stood, straightening his navy-blue uniform and climbing the dais. "Thanks, Mr. President." He took the speaker's lectern at the center of the Supercommittee horseshoe. "Hello, everyone. I had a little time on our way over to this meeting to look at my comm and check the data we have so far."

"Wow," Joe whispered, "I didn't even think to do that. I was just writing emails to the director of MATS in my head the whole time. 'Course I have a hard time walking and reading the damn comm at the same time."

"And it's not much, and I'm sure many of you have had more time to consider this than I. I know Ranna Kikken has proposed that we may be looking at time dysfunctions."

"That's right, the Chronology Coordinator already spoke on that a few minutes ago," Draka put in from his seat. "She laid out every theory about time dysfunctions we can think of."

"Great. And of course we could be dealing with some entirely natural phenomenon we don't understand yet, something that can mask a star's light either temporarily or permanently. I've seen a few theories proposed so far, but we have no data yet to evaluate any of them.

"But if this does prove to be a Dyson sphere, we'll want to hear from my wife Amav. If you'll recall her planetary engineering work in Alpha Centauri, she proposed building a simple one there. The Alpha Centaurians have a lot of floating planetary debris around some of their stars, and since they don't like to live on planets anyway, we could make use of that debris to build either orbiting energy collectors or a ringworld. We might be able to learn a lot about Dyson spheres from this Iota Persei phenomenon."

Jack stopped at the growing rumblings throughout the hall.

"Great! I *knew* he'd bring up Alpha Centauri first thing!" someone snarled. "He loves it so much!"

"He's *brainwashed!* You can tell!"

"Oh, that's nonsense! All of them look perfectly normal!"

"Forget it! His own damn son went crazy there! Revived the damn Grid! They all got *brainwashed!*"

Jack blinked at this last comment. "Well, I'm sure this chamber will continue to have a full debate on this Grid business, but first we need to deal with Iota Persei."

"See? He brought it up himself! He *loves* the Grid!"

"Shut up!" someone else hissed. "It's not the old Grid! Phil Sperry *changed* it, remember?"

"That's crap! You think someone can just *wish* the Grid into something new? Commer's damn son made the software to restart the Grid, and all this talk of some *new* Grid is just BS to get us all brainwashed along with all these sons of bitches!"

"That's crazy! Paranoid!"

"Then why are we playing with fire? To even be *discussing* this?"

Jack laughed. "Copeland, don't be an idiot! We've spent three weeks taking every sort of reading possible on Centaurian mental states, and our own, for that matter. It's a fact that Phil Sperry fundamentally *altered* the nature of the Alpha Centaurian Grid. Of course, everyone knows there's more study needed, and there's obviously no rush to introduce any similar sort of technology to Sol."

There were so many shouts that Jack finally stood back from the lectern. Through the microphone Laurie heard some scraps:

"--going to talk about Iota Persei or what?"

"--know, Jack, I know, but the--"

"--settle down, Jack, don't worry, we'll have a full investigation."

This last was Greeney Gooney, patting Jack's arm. Laurie, concentrating on the Martian outradiance to shut out the blaring voices, was puzzled by Gooney's mental patterns, which were in agreement with Mandy's and Draka's, and in fact with most of the people in the hall: that the Grid was a dangerous phenomenon and best confined to Alpha Centauri. Some were even calling for a ban on travel between the two systems and the cessation of all trade.

But she also knew that Greeney had been enthusiastic about the benefits of a Grid in which every entity was an emperor or empress with full use of emperor-level power. Now she was getting none of that from him, and no trace of resentment that his ideas were being disregarded or even that he'd just been deposed as Martian Emperor. Yet her friend Kner's fascination with the Grid and the possibility of introducing it on a limited scale to Sol was still out there for anyone to sample.

Of course, Greeney could shut his telepathy down if he wanted and become totally unreadable. Kner could do it for a few minutes at a time, but it always fell apart. He'd told her he'd given up on his quest to duplicate what he called Greeney's "meditation technique." It was something like a Martian Emperor's Withhold, but that process of shielding select information was so exhausting and short-lived that emperors rarely employed it. Even though Greeney was so young as to be comparable to a twenty-four-year-old human creating a software corporation, Kner worshipped Greeney as a higher-level adept who held secrets no other Martian would ever be able to decipher.

"Get rid of Commer!" someone shouted. "He's brainwashing us right now!"

"He's an old fart who doesn't know what the hell he's doing!"

"Get rid of all those old coots!"

"Get rid of the deadwood! They're *all* brainwashed!"

CHAPTER ELEVEN
The Existential Equation

Kner wriggled his fin in frustration. Why were all these normally sober delegates so riled? Jack moved back to the lectern and held up his arms for quiet but couldn't get it.

The Consort edged in beside Jack and raised his own hands. "Ladies and gentlemen! Martians! Humans! Please!"

"Time to go, Commer! Take all your old USSF farts with you!"

"You're *senile!* You bring us the Grid!"

"*We shall not be enslaved!*"

Kner could clearly read the agreement among most Martians that the Alpha Centaurian Grid was to be shunned. Brainwashing in any guise was the worst possible sin. The Martians had never known such a mental state could exist before 2033, when the entire culture had been hijacked by the madman Sam Hergs and at his bidding Martians had found themselves fighting a tragic war with newly evacuated humans from Earth. In addition, the Total Martian Outradiance, a mixture of everything going on in Martian culture, recorded as sacred text how three senior Martians, Dar, Fulr, and Kner himself, had fallen victim to Grid brainwashing aboard the *Typhoon II* in 2035. Fulr's last delirious brainwashed thoughts before being killed by Zarj troopers, as imprinted deep within both Dar and Kner and brought home to Mars, were now engraved in every Martian's soul.

Kner was no stranger to that ongoing shame. But shouldn't the fact that he'd been able to shed the brainwashing, as the other members of the *Typhoon II* crew eventually had, count towards some deeper understanding of how Intellect operated? There was so much to learn. Surely anyone should be able to see that Grid One, the old Grid centered in One Emperor, was completely transformed in its Grid Two version, a telepathic union between all citizens, each of whom *was* Emperor or Empress.

Though the outradiance on this subject among the Martian

legislators was robust, at least it felt rational. But Empress Mandy Fra'lith's signal was ten times too strong for polite discourse, and it seemed to be egging the raucous humans on. Kner knew the Consort was just playacting, calling for order and calm when he was really allowing Mandy's thoughts to dominate the chamber.

And those were more like *panic*. Her thoughts about *secession* from Sol were definitely something they hadn't heard before. Even Mandy couldn't control her raw terror about the Grid. Kner could even begin to feel the Total Martian Outradiance begin to shift. What was formerly a phenomenon to be rejected, but at least studied from afar, was now regarded as a devouring beast slavering at the Martian door. The fact that Kner's own assessment of Empress Mandy's mental state was available to everyone in the room had no effect on the swelling anxiety.

There was no way he could fathom G'rea'nyaigu'nye's change of heart about the Grid. He just sat there confirming every fear Mandy cared to broadcast. This staggered Kner, as earlier today Greeney, in his role as Martian Emperor, had shown full support for experimenting with Grid Two. Then came his overthrow at Mandy's hands. After the initial shock, which caused a near-shutdown of the Total Martian Outradiance for half an hour, all Martians had come to accept Mandy Fra'lith as their Empress. It would have been unthinkable not to.

Kner supposed that Greeney Gooney's new acceptance of the Anti-Grid arguments was to show solidarity with the Empress and to function as her efficient War Minister. G'rea'nyaigu'nye's change radiated as fully sincere, but Kner couldn't help but wonder what had happened to those seventy-five fascinating proposals for merging the Total Martian Outradiance with Grid Two. As far as Kner was concerned, all seventy-five should be taken up in order, discussed, and voted upon.

Everyone in this chamber could read these thoughts out of Kner's mind, but he didn't care. He was just one more voice in the debate. He hoped that by radiating sensible thoughts he could soothe the angry councilmembers.

He still couldn't make sense of Greeney, though. How could he relinquish the Emperorship so easily? After all, as a 230-year-old *wunderkind,* a Star General barely out of his Martian teens, he'd singlehandedly saved Sol from the Centaurian attack on DamnStar in '36, commanded other crucial operations in the war, and been elected mayor of Marsport along the way. He'd survived kidnapping by the Centaurians in '38, outwitted their efforts to brainwash him as a military tool by immersing himself in the *Kuth'rr'kq* hibernation until the AC Empire collapsed in '53, and then began an astonishing effort to counsel and rehabilitate the entire Gridless, demoralized AC Empire. In 2060 Greeney had become Provisional Emperor, though he'd chosen to live in Alpha Centauri. When he took up the full Emperorship last month, everyone thought he'd rule for five thousand years.

Of course, he'd also been the *Alpha Centaurian* Emperor for half an hour last month as he tried to outmaneuver the Zarj usurper Clopt and Jack's own son Jonathan James in their lust to reconstitute the old fascist Grid. Could that account for this new distrust of Greeney, and why Mandy was able to overthrow him?

Meanwhile Mandy's fury was driving even uglier shouting.

"Get that bastard Commer off the stage!"

"Lock him up before he brainwashes us!"

"And his damn brother! Don't forget his damn brother!"

"Shatter all of them! Like dogs!"

Kner looked over at Jack trying to get back to the lectern, with Draka again blocking him, smiling and mouthing: "It's okay, Jack, everything's under control!" Kner looked down from the dais to the first row, where his friend Colonel Laurie sat with her new boyfriend Will Connors, another human Kner found delightful despite what he sensed were edges of scary darkness.

Laurie had virtually no darkness, as far as Kner could tell with his limited ability to guess at the unreadable interior of the human soul from reading facial expressions, body language, and gestures, as well as his clumsy attempts to perform the operation humans called "reading between the lines" of vocal utterances which were often at complete variance with whatever was going on within. Laurie was almost Martian in her curiosity and her ability to think through complicated logical sequences. Kner had even offered to teach her some rudimentary Amplified Thought, though he had no idea if she'd be capable of absorbing it.

The catcalls continued. Kner saw Jack looking down at the people in the second row jeering at the *Typhoon III* and *IV* crews in the first, and he predicted that Jack would abandon his attempt to speak about Iota Persei and get back down there to shield his wife and friends.

Surely there was no real danger. Wouldn't those people back off if Jack did resume his seat down there? Kner was pleased to see Jack storm downstairs and sit with his wife, glaring at the second row which shrank back from him. Yes, Kner was getting better at reading these humans.

But he was shocked at how off the track this meeting had gotten. It was supposed to be about Iota Persei. Kner wanted to go there himself. Amav also needed to go. Kner wondered if Jack really understood the amazing contributions she'd made to the Earth Renewal Project. They could never have restored the planet without her. Her knowledge seemed to go thousands of miles deep. She'd had spent most of her time between 2035 and 2075 on the Earth Renewal Project, but once it was over she'd confided to Kner that she felt unemployed and useless. Kner had tried to tell her there would be plenty of work repairing Alpha Centaurian worlds, maybe even making Dyson spheres, but he could tell she was deeply distressed and unsure what to do next.

The chamber was calming with Jack off the dais.

"All right, everyone," Consort President Draka said, "we do have some more time here before the *Jupiter* reports in, so we might as well continue our discussion of the Grid. And of course, we shouldn't be impolite to our guests today."

"Screw that! They're brainwashed!"

"Aw, c'mon, Fred. Nobody got contaminated, I thought we'd established that. *I* was in Alpha Centauri just now and *I'm* not contaminated, right? So these folks aren't contaminated either."

"Yeah, how do you *know* you're not contaminated?" Fred

Angleton, senator from Utopia, yelled back.

CONSORT DRAKA SORTIE IS NOT CON-
TAMINATED! came the thunderous outradiance. BY ORDER
OF FRA'LITH, EMPRESS OF MARS.

The entire chamber went silent. Several humans had
actually put their hands over their ears. Kner wanted to laugh but
knew it would be impolite.

"If I may speak," Senator Lee Borman spoke into the fresh
quiet as he stood from the *Typhoon* crews. Draka reluctantly
nodded. Borman didn't bother coming up to the dais. Instead he
turned and faced the chamber sloping upwards from him.
Everyone knew from previous debates how his voice carried.

"It should be obvious," Borman began, "but if it isn't, I'll
remind you all. The possible implications of a Dyson sphere
being created within *one week* in Iota Persei, never mind that
this *one week* happened 34.36 years ago, should put into
perspective any worries about what might happen with a new
Alpha Centaurian Grid that, for all we know, can't exist outside
Alpha Centauri anyway."

There was a slight rumbling, but Borman's voice, coupled
with the fear that Mandy would turn the volume up past ten
again, left everyone more or less respectful.

"What just happened in Iota Persei could be a natural
phenomenon, or it could be an *unnatural* phenomenon," Lee
went on. "Which brings us to alien intelligence, and which
brings us to the existential equation of *friend or foe?* And *if* this
is a Dyson sphere, and *if* these folks are foes, then we are in a
heap of trouble, fellow citizens, because I guarantee you they are
centuries beyond us in their technology."

That was met with further silence. Kner had considered the
existential equation himself, as had G'rea'nyaigu'nye, but he
wasn't sure Mandy had completely thought it through. Her
natural combativeness, a combination of human aggression and
innate Martian power, could easily lead her to assume she could
fight her Empire out of any box it found itself in.

"And so I'd like to propose that we spend the rest of this
emergency meeting in its stated intention of exploring the Iota

Persei problem and our potential responses to it. Blasting the *Jupiter* off without thinking was not the wisest move, in my humble capacity as chairman of the USSF Oversight Committee."

Kner smiled. He could see the *Typhoon* crews relaxing as well. Borman had perfectly framed the priorities. It would be just like this Council to waste time flailing about in secondary matters, especially ones it could debate over the course of decades, instead of concentrating on the real danger at hand.

And if they were faced with such an existential foe in Iota Persei, they might even welcome a Grid where every human and Martian was in instantaneous contact and harmony with each other.

Where did that thought come from?
Better keep it quiet!

CHAPTER TWELVE
General Scott

"Thank you, Lee, for your input," Draka said with a grand chuckle, a human noise Kner had always found irritating. "Ladies and gentlemen, Senator Borman is well known for his incisive speechifying and I must say that I, of course, pale in comparison with him. After serving with Senator Borman aboard the *Typhoon IV* since '38, I can attest that he can certainly defeat you in any political argument!

"However, I can also categorically state that this Council and its Supercommittee managed to discuss *all* the implications of this Iota Persei business before you ladies and gentlemen of the *Typhoon* crews arrived from the spaceport. And we realized we're simply out of facts at this point. All the Council could do was send the *Jupiter* off and wait for the data to arrive." Draka emitted another cloying chuckle. "Which should be in about twenty minutes. Meanwhile, despite what Lee seems to think, as President of the Council I have to be sensitive to the current controversies embroiling our peoples. And the fact remains that this so-called New Grid from Alpha Centauri represents, in my opinion, a far more serious threat than some unknown phenomenon 34.36 light-years away that most of our scientists think is just a sensor anomaly."

"That's right!" someone shouted.

"The Commers bring *death* with them! They support *death and brainwashing!*"

"Now, now," Draka smiled.

Jack stood up from the front row. "Dammit, Draka, how can you ignore what Lee just got through saying? This Grid business is secondary! I don't give a flip if we adopt it or not! Obviously it needs a lot of study!"

"Forget it!" someone shouted. "We *defeated* those monsters in '53, and here you bastards started it *up* again!"

"Dammit, we've made Alpha Centauri into an *ally.*"

"C'mon, Jack, you can't really believe that," came a husky old voice. "You can't think some mumbo-jumbo revival of the

Grid is really safe just because it's dressed up in some fancy new technology dreamed up by *Phil Sperry* of all people! Everyone knows he got himself brainwashed *twice* by the Centaurians!"

"General *Scott?*" Jack gasped, whirling to two men advancing down the center aisle towards the dais. Kner didn't have to be a reader of unknowable human minds to hear the worship in Jack's voice. Jack's former boss, ninety-eight human years old but rejuvenated to look sixty, was striding down the aisle in the company of--

A robot. A Heroes and Villains of the Thirties *robot.*

It was considered in the most grotesque poor taste to parade a robot in public, especially the newest models that could fool humans ninety percent of the time. But Kner had long since trained himself to recognize robots by any of a thousand tiny giveaways. Most of these ancient HAVOTT robots, built in the forties to commemorate the humans and Martians who'd warred in 2034, had thankfully been mothballed long ago. Kner had hoped they'd seen the last of them with the destruction of Jonathan James Commer's collection of HAVOTT robots in Alpha Centauri. But he had to suppose there could still be hundreds of robots from the HAVOTT series lingering on, as well as other RoboticsMindPump offerings like Gunslingers of New Mexico, The Court of Peter the Great, and Early Astronauts on the Moon.

The Heroes and Villains of the Thirties robots included the only robots ever made of Martians, as Martian-format robots had been outlawed after that dismal experiment. Kner had met robots of himself and Dar and slept poorly for a week afterward. While the old HAVOTT robots could fool some people, most found their mannerisms jerky and their thought processes and speech stilted, though illegal upgrades of some HAVOTTs had improved that.

Newer robots, programmed for a variety of service jobs, had thoroughly superseded HAVOTT-era technology. Although there was a growing robot rights movement on the part of humans whom Joe Commer for one would refer to as "do-gooders," as an engineer and Amplified Thought adept Kner understood better than most that these mechanisms were just sophisticated computers, and that their demonstrations of artificial intelligence could not truly be considered life. Robots mimicked life, they didn't reproduce it, and most humans and Martians who came into contact with them eventually came away with the same icky feeling that had kept Kner awake at night.

As pure technology robots did have their fascinations. Kner knew enough about them to build one from scratch himself. The software and the intricate technology were lovely in their own way. Then there was the M'rrpla hack--

To his relief he found that he'd automatically slipped into a telepathic block.

No one must know of *that*.

General Scott addressed the dais. "General William C. Scott of Citizens Against the Grid requests permission to speak." Kner struggled to clear his memory banks of his last thoughts before his short-lived telepathic block fell apart. He strained to focus on the short clomping robot accompanying Scott.

It was a General Douglas model, the Alien Hunter from Alpha Centauri. Kner had only seen a couple of those, and never in action.

The entire Council uneasily assessed the propriety of allowing a robot of any sort, let alone a Heroes and Villains of the Thirties model, to actually stand on the dais of the United System Council. But William C. Scott was too revered throughout Sol for anyone to challenge his right to do as he pleased. Kner knew that the eccentric old general, who'd shunned new technology even as a young man, had bought a robot as a personal computer and research assistant, but he'd had no idea that Scott had settled on a clunky old HAVOTT.

Kner had never met the real Douglas, killed in his hotel room at the Space Carpet Hotel during the human-Martian war, but knew that he'd been considered extremely belligerent in his time. This model was clad in a blue-gray, medal-bedecked, Army-status USSF uniform. It purported to be a powerfully built man with a thick neck, immense chest, and sturdy thighs, and as it climbed the stairs to the dais with General Scott, Kner was fascinated by the robot's drooping white handlebar mustache. In fact, Kner found himself slipping into the old HAVOTT algorithms for generating hair from imitation human skin.

He also remembered Scott's old obsession with assassination and wondered if this Douglas robot doubled as a bodyguard today.

There was applause throughout the chamber as Scott grabbed the speaker's lectern with his knotted hands. Everyone had more or less given up on him as good for dead when he'd retired in 2035 and passed the SCUSSF position to Jack. His poor health, the result of injuries he'd sustained during the first primitive human exploration of Mars, had everyone convinced that he'd simply fade away within months. But he'd held on and taken advantage of the latest rejuvenation techniques, and to everyone's surprise he'd survived and prospered into what humans called old age, what Martians would have considered *pre-adolescence* at ninety-eight.

Kner noticed that Jack had stood up, had motioned the *Typhoon* crews to stand, and soon the entire chamber was giving a standing ovation.

"Well, thank you, everyone," Scott rasped as the robot Douglas stood behind him with a clipboard clamping, of all things, *papers,* and maintained a severe frown underneath that white mustache. Kner saw it was directed at G'rea'nyaigu'nye seated to the left of the lectern, and it took him a while to puzzle out why: during the 2034 war, Greeney had run the two terrorist Martians who'd murdered Douglas in his hotel room. Was a HAVOTT robot really programmed to show hatred towards the entity who'd done in his Ur-model? Kner supposed it was only logical.

"And greetings to my friends Jack and Joe Commer, Amav, and the crews of two *Typhoons* in the first row there, and thanks much for defusing the recent troubles in Alpha Centauri," Scott rumbled on. "But I'm sorry to say, Jack, that the solution to the problem you *think* you've found with Phil Sperry's invention of a new Grid is wholly inadequate and in fact poses a direct, and yes, *existential* danger to Sol. And so just yesterday I formed a new political action committee, Citizens Against the Grid."

Cheers erupted from the audience. Jack looked at his feet. Joe Commer shook his head. The Douglas robot handled more papers to Scott, who began to read:

"The purpose of Citizens Against the Grid is to provide the most current information about the nature of the Alpha Centaurian Grid, to bring the *truth* to light so as to educate the millions of Sol citizens who might become fascinated by this outrageous attempt to *link minds* into some monstrous, nirvanic *hive.* We all know that the addictive types, those already blissed out on SolNet and wasting their lives in trivia, are going to be gung-ho for this damnable new Grid. And those of us who know how to *think* are frankly surprised that supporters of this so-called new and improved Grid can't see this clearly. We have enough problems with our own citizens living in Neverneverland without making it even easier to escape into a fantasy world of so-called blissed-out *mind linkage,* where everybody knows everything and everyone has magical powers! *Bah!* we say to that failed vision! *Bah!* we say to any human or Martian who fails to recall just how insane and evil the original Grid was!"

More cheers. Applause. Kner looked to his right at Mandy and Draka clapping their hands and smiling.

To Kner's horror the John J. Douglas robot screeched in his Ur-model's Australian accent: "And if anyone is *stupid* enough to have *missed* the fact even after this so-called *universe of bliss* came about in Alpha Centauri, this K'ufunb scrubwoman character got so *unhinged,* so *fanatical,* as to *commit suicide* with a Warp Transfer and nearly destroy the goddamn *Typhoon III* and Procyon A to boot, and if that doesn't *prove* that these goddamn ACs are still fanatic and *totally dangerous to us all,* well then I say: you're all cowardly *bahstads!*" He shook a fist at the first row where Jack sat with mouth agape. "All of you, cowards and *bahstads!*"

The entire chamber was silent.

"Thank you, John," Scott said. "Now if I may continue--"

"*Bahstads!* Shameful, cowardly *bahstads!* We've got to *fight* these damn vermin! Fight 'em until AC is wiped out to the last damned *amoeba!*"

Kner shrank back. Would this Douglas thing sift through the outradiance and find him? A Martian curious about what the new Grid could offer? Douglas looked ready to charge right over and punch him out.

It took him a few seconds to calm down. Douglas was just a machine. It was impossible for him to pick up Kner's outradiance. Thank God.

Scott glared at the robot. "*Enough,* John!" he ordered, and Douglas slammed his arms across his chest, papers slipping off the clipboard and onto the floor. The two generals made a curiously complementary pair, Kner thought. Both were short, powerful, and white-haired, though Douglas's was long like his mustache, and Scott's crew-cut.

Scott read his manifesto for several more minutes, interrupted by applause and cheers. Kner looked down at the morose *Typhoon* crews and felt their suffering. Everything went against them as the chamber reveled in paranoia about the Grid. Jack loved Scott, but he had to sit there and swallow this. Did this Council really think Jack was irrelevant? They heckled him, called him old, and wanted him gone, but three weeks ago, before he went to Andertwin, he'd been their hero leader.

Kner marveled at the changes rejuvenation techniques had brought about in human society. Their new human partners were having a hard time assimilating the fact that they no longer became decrepit after a few brief decades, but could hold onto power, and develop higher levels of maturity and concentration as they aged. Why, his friend Laurie would have been, in her terms, "put out to pasture" about now, at age sixty. And yet she'd told him she was just starting out in life.

It was true that rejuvenation had blocked younger humans from rising as they once had. But another factor needed to be considered: human population had gone from eight and a half billion in 2029 to two billion in 2033, due to solar system disasters, the humans' Final War, and their evacuation to Mars, and had only come up to three and a half billion over the last forty years. Few humans were actually jobless, and there were plenty of opportunities for even the youngest in an expanding economy, just not at the top, to which the ambitious always aspired.

As far as raw population numbers went, the Martians had fared worse, starting with 2,500 at the beginning of the human-Martian war of 2034 and reduced to 1,300 by the end. There had since been an explosion in births of Martian children, about a thousand, but since these were all toddlers even as old as twenty-one Martian years, the equivalent of forty human, they hadn't added much to the Sol economy.

The economy itself was robust, as new sources of energy were tapped, asteroids mined, innovative technologies brought online, and trade begun with Alpha Centauri after the end of the war in '53. But for the first time Kner sensed a deep human resentment at the old folks at the top running things. The presence of newer forms of AI robots, virtually indistinguishable from human beings, also had to contribute to that unease. Would robots take more and more of these new jobs from humans? Had his friend Jack turned into the new symbol of oppression?

"Thank you, General Scott," Draka said as Scott hit a pause in his speech. "That was extremely edifying, and I'm sure your group will be invaluable in protecting Sol from this new enemy." Scott raised his papers to show he wasn't nearly done yet. "But now it's time to hear from our citizens on this subject. I have a voice channel via SolNet now."

"Ya *bahstad!*" Douglas roared. "Let him finish!"

"Shut *up,* robot!" Scott yelled back. "You've behaved disgracefully today, John! I told you not to speak at all! Pick up those papers you've dropped everywhere!"

"Dammit, man, these bahstads are *reaming* you, and you just sit there and take it! What kind of man are you?"

"*Enough!*" Scott roared, jamming a finger at the stairs. The robot shrugged, scooped up the papers, and stomped down the steps and up the main aisle.

"Sorry about that," Scott said to Draka, and reluctantly

followed his robot back to his seat.

"HELLO HELLO HELLO AM I ON THE AIR?" echoed throughout the chamber.

CHAPTER THIRTEEN
Message for the Council!

"Hello, citizen!" Draka boomed. "We have about ten minutes to get as many citizen responses as possible to this grave crisis. So, first caller, please limit yourself to two minutes and we'll take some other callers I see we have lined up."

"Hello, I just wanted to say that Jack Commer is *evil* and must be *exterminated!* He killed a friend of mine today!"

"*What?*" Fresh consternation surged through the chamber. "He did *what?* Please identify yourself, citizen!"

"I am Marsport Automated Transport System Bus 928 and today Jack Commer tricked a friend of mine, Bus 1313, into committing *suicide!* That's right, *suicide!*"

"You're a *bus?* A bus can't call into a United System Council meeting!"

"Oh yes I can! We buses have been humiliated and defaced for years at the hands of these evil Commers! Sensitive MATS artificial intelligence brains have been *blown out* and/or *erased* by these monsters! May I reference MATS Incident 34999030222021, date 6/8/34, or MATS Incident 88776781206429, date 2/10/36--"

"No, you may not. If you really are a bus, then you're by definition *not* a citizen who can comment on a governmental meeting."

Kner, along with numerous other Martians in the chamber, had determined after a couple sentences that the caller was indeed Marsport Automated Transport System Bus 928. Humans began finding this concept in the Martian outradiance, and within a few seconds the catcalls and jeering swelled again.

"Get that thing off the network!" someone shouted.

"Due to the seriousness of the offenses of Jack Commer, a known enemy of MATS buses, this MATS bus hereby asserts its ability to participate as a citizen of Sol!"

"That's against the law! Robots have no political voice!"

"The Robots Rights League, formed just yesterday by Heroes and Villains of the Thirties robot General John J.

Douglas, serial number 455-229464-809BXL, will change all that! Robots of artificial intelligence threshold A-14 will be considered fully sentient beings, with all the rights and appurtenances devolving upon that designation!"

"You did *what?* Are you *crazy,* John?" came from up the chamber.

"I have to act in accordance with my deepest conscience!" Douglas yelled back.

"You *have* no conscience! You're a *machine!*"

"Aw, don't give me this coward bahstad BS, man!"

"Get that damn robot out of here!" came a fresh cry, accompanied by cheers.

"And get that MATS bus off the network!"

"Ladies and gentlemen! Humans! Martians! Please!" Draka shouted into the new uproar.

"And I hereby assert that Jack Commer, by personally contaminating my friend MATS Bus 1313, has revealed himself to be an infectious, brainwashed *traitor to Sol!*"

"Someone shut that bus up!"

"Wait a second! If Commer infected the first bus, then that second bus must be infected too!"

"Oh my God, that *right!* The bus is *crazy!* And it must be infecting us all!"

"Get it off! Get it off!"

"If all of *MATS* is contaminated, then all *Marsport* must be as well by now!"

"We're *doomed!*"

"I can *feel* the Grid! I can feel it *contaminating* me!"

"I am a *bus,* and I can feel it too! I am one with you! People, I am one with you! I am as sentient and contaminated as any of you! Dear God, I am a *sentient bus* and I love--"

Draka punched at his command the bus wail died. At the same time Jack began herding his people out of the front row towards a side exit where few could bar his way.

Meanwhile a fresh shout came from the top of the chamber. "Ya *bahstad!* Let me be! Let me be, I say!" Kner saw Scott manhandling his robot out the upper exit. That was courageous for a ninety-eight-year-old man, because those HAVOTT robots incorporated astounding physical strength and Kner knew that Douglas could easily rip General Scott into a hundred pieces if he chose.

Now Churchill sent amplified radiance into the hall.

Calm yourselves, friends! Everyone calm! There is no Grid present here in Sol. There is no contamination. Everyone is upset, but Jack's right, we have years to consider the nature of the Alpha Centaurian Grid from all angles. Calm yourselves! No decision is needed today. There is nothing to fear.

"Yeah, you know so much about the Grid, maybe *you're* contaminated!" someone shouted.

Kner was shocked. Nobody ever sassed Churchill, a reincarnation of an ancient Martian volcano and possessed of unthinkable powers he'd never dared experiment with. Risking his wrath was absolutely out of the question. Fortunately the Russian Blue cat was so eerily composed that no one had ever seen him angry.

Providing some balance to the discussion, Senator Pilger. As you may intuit, animals have always had their own version of the Grid, and I have freely participated in such a Grid. The question is basically whether a Grid is a vehicle for transcendent dignity and sharing, or whether it's misused as a tool of control and fear. And whether it's a voluntary association or coerced. Now we really do need to calm down.

"Forget it! I *refuse--*"

"MESSAGE FOR THE COUNCIL! DO WE HAVE THE COUNCIL?" came the cry over the chamber speakers.

"Aw, not another goddamn bus!" someone shouted.

But Kner knew it was a human voice. From the slight frequency shift, he could tell it was a superspace radio message.

Jack and his group turned just short of the exit. Some Council members had thought to block them, but they hesitated when they saw they were confronting ten USSF crewmembers in excellent physical shape along with Amav, who looked ready to toss any number of panicking, weak-willed politicians over her shoulder.

"That's Henderson!" Jack said. "Henderson, what's your report?"

"Excuse me, Jack, *we* sent the ship, *we* will receive it," Draka declared, with Mandy Fra'lith's outrage building behind her husband's words.

"You're out of line, Mr. President. *I* command the USSF, and that's *my* ship. Until the Supercommittee votes me out of office, this is *my responsibility.* Henderson! What have you found?"

Somehow two hundred United System delegates including their Supercommittee went dead silent at this voice of command.

"Jack, it--it's unbelievable! We just got here a couple minutes ago. At first we didn't know what was going on, because there were no stars visible in front of us at all! Then we saw that what we were looking at is a *circular darkness,* over *nine hundred million miles wide!* Then we realized it *is* a sphere! All readings confirm! Jack, there's a Dyson sphere here of radius 483.5 million miles!"

The council sat back in shock. This was the approximate distance from the Sun to the Jovian Fragment Field, the former planet Jupiter.

"Repeat, a Dyson sphere of radius 483.5 million miles!"

Jack was the first to recover. "Any contact? Any communications?"

"No, we're sending out everything we can think of, all languages we know, including all Centaurian languages, every mathematical and physical equation in our first contact database, and, God, this is *overwhelming!*"

"Okay, Dan, we copy here. As soon as your Star Drive vortex settles down, we'll be sending more ships every half-day or so. I've also authorized a speed-up on the *Typhoon V*. It's close to being finished out and has the most stable Enhanced Star Drive."

"Hold on, hold on!" Mandy screeched. "Admiral Commer, this Council has not authorized any accelerated schedule for the *Typhoon V!*"

"*I* authorized it on the walk over to the Council meeting. As

I say, if your Supercommittee wants to vote me off, then so be it, but until then, I will authorize any ship in the fleet to do whatever I may order it to do. Is that understood?"

If he had eyelids Kner would have blinked as humans did. He couldn't believe any entity could possibly stand up to a Martian Empress and continue to live. Empress Fra'lith stood glaring at Jack. Kner shrank back from her telepathic fury.

God, Mandy's being a bitch today!

Instinctively Kner threw up a block to shield this last thought from the Empress and all Mars.

Then something snapped in his brain. A deadly quiet unfolded.

What *was* this? Was this how Greeney made the permanent block on outradiance? Yes, it was. Kner was blocking *everything*. How was this possible? It was so close to his original idea of *shield,* yet completely different. And now Kner saw exactly how Greeney did it. God, he'd *defied* Emperor Dar, just as he continued to *defy* Empress Fra'lith.

Here Kner had stumbled along all these years with his clumsy two-minute shields, but if you just *defied,* you shut the Outradiance *down*. And now he saw how Greeney could create a completely different set of thoughts if he wanted. He just nonchalantly *projected them out*. There was more than enough energy to create *two* minds, one hidden, one outradiating.

Or you could simply withhold it all. Everyone believed it no matter what you did. The Second Mind looked absolutely real and sincere to both Martians and humans. Kner was doing Second Mind right now. It felt wondrous. You just tailored your thoughts to whatever the situation required.

He laughed. *It's all a game! Greeney's turned Martian outradiance into a game!*

Kner met Greeney's eyes. Thinking of him, he'd inadvertently sent a tightly focused beam straight at his former Emperor. A return beam came directly into Kner's brain, coded for him alone.

Correct.

Kner had to look away to keep from falling out of his

Supercommittee chair. He was *free*. Was he really thinking these thoughts? Or was Gooney thinking them?

You are the one thinking them, came Gooney's tight beam. *Enjoy yourself. I'm signing off for now. I want to concentrate on this Iota Persei thing.*

Everyone in the Chamber could see that Greeney had gone fully dark, as everyone knew he could. But meanwhile Kner needed to keep pumping out this curious Second Mind, if only to withhold the secret of being able to withhold.

"Dan, what's your position now? How far are you away from this *sphere?*" Jack said.

"Fifty-four million miles, Jack. We've taken a stationary position relative to it, forty-three degrees above its equator. The damn thing's rotating. The whole sphere is rotating around a north-south axis, and--*Murphy! What?*"

"What's that? I didn't copy."

"They--it--*something*--oh my God!"

"*What?*"

"It's *firing* at us! Lasers--or *something!*"

"Henderson! Out of there immediately!"

"All systems gone! No, we do have sensors! We're tracing back the source!"

"Henderson! Evasive action!"

"We don't have any maneuvering! And there's *another* ship out here! Morales, what's the distance? What? Listen, Jack, there's some sort of ship out here! Six miles to port! But it's *tiny!* Circular, like a little *saucer!* Morales, what's it--"

"*Dammit, Henderson, get out of there!*"

There was an ominously long silence.

"MAYDAY MAYDAY MAYDAY!" came a new cry.

Kner reeled. *That was his own voice.* That just couldn't *be*.

He whirled to his fellow Martians on the Supercommittee. But Mandy, Greeney, Fulr-Kla and Churchill remained focused on Jack Commer's stunned face.

Kner fought to keep his new Second Mind. Were they so used to outradiance they couldn't even recognize a colleague's voice? That was his own voice. He'd measured it scientifically.

He knew exactly what it sounded like, because he'd used it to test--

Don't think about that! Too top-secret even for Second Mind!

CHAPTER FOURTEEN
The Pavlovian Response

"Wow, Donbottor Street's come up a few notches since the early days."

Will grinned. "When were you ever on Donbottor Street?"

"Well, I never had any *business* here, if that's what you mean!" Laurie said, poking him as they moved past the coffee houses and the bars, the antique shops and clothing stores, the gadget outlets and even the antiquarian bookseller that offered ancient hardbacks from the previous century. There'd been nothing but whorehouses down here the first twenty years, until the university started buying up all the property in the area.

Their EnviroFields kept them toasty in the frigid Martian night as they strode on the brick sidewalk beneath the streetlamps. It was scary to be wearing a tiny cocktail dress outside, in the dark, with nothing but the black box at her waist to keep her from decompression death.

Will wore a sport coat over a blue sweater. He looked good out of uniform. He seemed to be wearing the civilian clothing easily. Calm for once. They'd left his car a couple blocks back and for good measure Will had put a holographic shield around it to disguise its owner as a former USSF officer. Laurie had thought it a stretch that students would use their comms to run a license plate check and then vandalize a car belonging to someone who might just have been contaminated by some horror from Alpha Centauri, but she'd held her tongue. Will definitely had his paranoid side, and it was best not to challenge it. She knew he'd relax over the next few months. It was so good for him to be out of the service.

"Well, this was nice of Lee to invite us," Will said.

Laurie nodded. She wasn't so sure. United System senator and distinguished USSF officer or not, Lee had always revolted her. The nightclub he'd bought off Donbottor Street two years ago just reinforced that feeling, even though Will assured her that the stories of nude dancers and high-class escort services were just talk. But Ranna had told her that Lee still hadn't taken down those videos of sex with other women on his website. Laurie wondered what his wife thought of *that.*

And why had Will insisted she wear his favorite little black dress?

"But Lee can't really stay long, can he?" she said. "I mean, shouldn't he be at the spaceport, getting ready?"

"He says he isn't needed till morning. The *V's* weapons system is apparently the only one up and running. Doesn't need any more tests, so they let him stay home, or, I guess, *here.*" He consulted the comm's holographic display above his left wrist. "Should be another block and then half a block to the right."

"You've never been here before?"

"Nah. Although he's wanted me to come a lot, whenever we're in town."

"Well, I can't stay long, either. I'm going to need a good night's sleep." Laurie was due at the *Typhoon III* tomorrow morning, but she knew the *III* crew had much less to do than their counterparts on the *V* tonight. After the Council meeting Patrick James had told her the crazy schedule Jack was proposing for bringing the *Typhoon V* online overnight before launching at 0900 for Iota Persei. An army of technicians and the *V* crew would spend the next twelve hours in demented overdrive. Laurie had no idea how Jack thought to launch an untried ship with only three crewmembers from the *Typhoon IV*: himself, Pat, and Lee. He'd scrounge up replacements for copilot, navigator and physician/engineer, but they wouldn't be a real team. The personnel machinations for filling these positions could take several hours right there.

Why was he messing with the *V* when they had the *III* ready right now? Her Enhanced hack had fixed all the problems. They could've taken the *III* this afternoon. As it stood, Laurie would get to Iota Persei, but the *III* would follow tomorrow evening, twelve hours after the *V* launched and its vortex died down. In any case she needed to be fresh for her preflight checks at 0900.

They turned right at Cernan. Will pointed to the triangular marquee where old-time plastic letters spelled out THE PAVLOVIAN RESPONSE. "Well, here we are."

"Wow, what was this, some sort of movie theater?"

"Yeah, Lee said they used to have holofilms in here. Full-size too. Said he'd seen a few and they were amazing. For forties technology, he said."

Laurie shuddered. "In the forties, this would've been a porn movie house."

Will grinned. "Well, that's our senator for you."

They cycled through the airlock and were met by a huge bearded bouncer in a tight t-shirt, a dazzling rainbow of tattoos twining up his thick muscular forearms. Laurie was shocked by the loud music reverberating through the floor, as they'd heard nothing from outside the building. "Evening, folks!" the bouncer yelled. "First time to the Response?"

"Yes," Will said. "We're here to see Lee."

"Oh, right! You must be Mr. Connors? And this must be Ms. Lachrer! Yeah, Lee's expecting you. Right this way. He's down in the pit."

They followed him through the lobby. Laurie felt rankled at being improperly addressed. The bouncer might be provisionally correct in referring to Will as Mr. Connors, even though all the paperwork hadn't gone through and Will was officially still a commander in the USSF, but failing to call her Colonel Lachrer was too much. Then again, she was out of uniform; she felt her thighs swishing against the tight short shirt and looked down at her bare arms and the black pearls around her left wrist.

The bouncer led them through the crowded lobby with music blaring through hundreds of tiny ceiling, floor, and wall loudspeakers. People shouted, laughed, jabbed each other, downed beer and mixed drinks and yanked hors d'oeuvres off passing platters. The bouncer pushed open swinging doors to fresh noise blasting through a huge chamber sloping down to a central stage sixty feet wide, where a tall blond in a black dress not unlike Laurie's stood at a microphone moaning some ancient jazz tune, the band behind her doing its best to drown her out with electric piano, bass guitar, and drums.

"Okay, Sanders, I'll take it from here!" yelled a woman in

a surprisingly deep voice.

Laurie blinked at the apparition in front of them. She'd met Lee's wife Suzette a few times, but had always been repelled. Suzette was only forty-two, much younger than Lee or any of Laurie's comrades among the *Typhoon* crews. Though the petite brunette possessed an alarming facial beauty, there was something hard and overly-experienced in that face, in those taut forearms, in those solid rugged boobs spilling out of a severely low-cut gold miniskirt, which Laurie noted was six inches higher than her own uncomfortably short dress. More than once Laurie had wondered whether Suzette was a former drug addict, prostitute, or worse. Why hadn't she erased all that stress with some rejuvenation?

This predator woman looked as if she could eat all the men in this room without a second thought. And worse than all the manipulative power Suzette wielded was a buried sense of scarcely believable pain and endurance. She squeezed tiny tight fingers around the bouncer's wrist. "And I think you're off the clock by now anyway, darling!"

The bouncer grinned. "It *has* been a long day. But I knew you and Lee were waiting for these folks. I made sure to get the best table right down in front." He pointed to the tables spread out below the stage.

"Okay, I've got it. Have a great evening, baby!" She swatted his rear and Laurie stared after the burly man. This tattooed bouncer had to be the day manager, Sanders Hirte, with whom Suzette had shared special coverage on SolNet over the course of a couple weeks earlier this year.

SENATOR'S WIFE IN LOVE TRYST WITH NIGHTCLUB MANAGER?

BORMAN DENIES ANY IMPROPRIETY.

CLAIMS FOES OF USSF OVERSIGHT COMMITTEE GUNNING FOR HIM.

SHOCKING PHOTOS OF SECRET VACATION GETAWAY IN KILPATRICK DESERT.

"I STAND BY MY WIFE."

How could Lee ignore those photos of the nude Suzette and

nude Sanders Hirte sprawled on beach towels at the Martian ruins of *Gl-jeehltakk* in the Kilpatrick Desert, wearing nothing but their EnviroFields calibrated to let in just enough ultraviolet light for a suntan? Not that there was much left of Hirte to suntan, as he was ninety-five percent tattoos.

Everyone had assumed that Lee and Suzette would be divorced by now, or that the Pavlovian Response would have been sold, Hirte fired, Lee dismissed from the USSF Oversight Committee, or pulled from *Typhoon* duty. At the very least Lee should have been ordered not to show up at his own club to be pestered by drunken SolNet bloggers until 3 AM as to whether he, his wife, and his day manager formed some sordid threesome. Yet whenever he was in town Lee would be at the Response sixteen hours a day, fending off all queries with protestations of full trust in his wife and her ability to "run her own life as she sees fit." In the end the sensationalists and rumor-mongers had worn themselves out against Lee's toothy, war-hero, senatorial smile. There hadn't been anything on Lee and Suzette on SolNet for months, and the *Typhoon* crews had gone out of their way to avoid even thinking about Lee, his nightclub, or his wife.

It was Jack Commer's inept command style to just let all this crap happen and do nothing. He was such good buddies with Senator Sleazeball. Apparently Lee had even offered to open a *popcorn store* on Earth with Jack, knowing how much Jack disliked the nightclub. He'd said Amav and Suzette could come in too, that they'd all retire and go back to Chicago. God, it was all so *gross*. Did Lee imagine a *foursome* with Amav and Jack?

Why would Will want to drag her to this godawful place? She was a USSF officer with responsibilities. She should be at the spaceport.

The undulating Suzette beast led them down the sloping aisle. The old movie theater seemed as large as the United System Council chamber. In fact, it still had hundreds of theater seats sloping down in similar concentric rings. Some thirty of these seats were occupied by patrons with drinks in hand, and no doubt more would be filled as the evening raced to the Midnight

Time Skip. Only at the bottom had some horizontal space been cleared for a dozen tables. Lee Borman stood up from one of them. To her surprise Lee was in uniform.

But now from his seat beside Borman rose Jack Commer, also in uniform.

She stared. Why wasn't he at the spaceport fooling with his precious *Typhoon V?*

"Wow, this place is *huge!*" Will babbled to Suzette. "This really all yours and Lee's? This whole thing?"

"You got it, hon!" Suzette laughed, patting his arm. "We've also got six big conference rooms off to the side we rent out. But this is the main part."

Laurie noted that Will had trouble looking away as Suzette bent to pull out chairs for them and hung those hard freckled boobs out to the nipple. But Laurie worried about her own excess cleavage as Jack stood to tower over her.

"Colonel Lachrer!" Jack shouted above the music. "Glad you could make it. Hello, Will."

"Uh, hi everyone," Laurie gasped, stifling the urge to come to attention and salute.

"Wow! *Jack!*" Will said, finally catching sight of his former captain. "We didn't know you'd be here!"

"Yeah, yeah, Jack wanted to see you both," Lee said, raising a Bloody Mary in toast. "Sit down, guys, and we'll get you some drinks."

"I'll send W'ryyf down in a minute!" Suzette yelled. "See you folks later! Gotta run this joint while Lee slurps up all the profits!" He fondled her ass as she kissed him on the forehead and moved off.

The song on stage clattered to a halt and in the fresh silence Jack said: "First time here?"

"Uh, yessir!" Laurie said as Lee came around to seat her, his eyes widening at the sight of her trying to sit modestly in such a short dress. She tugged at the hem to get one more inch of coverage. Too late she found herself crossing her legs and exposing herself to the hipbone.

"Wow, you guys look great!" Lee said. "Never seen you

looking so good out of uniform, Colonel, I may add! *Wow!*"

"Uh … thanks," Laurie whispered.

"Fantastic place, Lee," Will put in. "Glad we could finally see it."

"It's my first time here too," Jack said, flinching as the band exploded to life behind him. "Glad you could take some time off to come along, Laurie."

"Well, uh, sir, Joe told me to take a break."

"No problem," Jack said. "Joe told me you needed one. Said you'd been on the *III* four straight hours after the Council meeting. I assume everything's still okay with your Enhanced fix?"

"Oh, yes! Right! Uh, sir."

"Oh, come on," Jack laughed, raising his voice as the instruments behind him gained volume and the singer began lamenting another doomed psychotic relationship. "Don't *sir* me in Lee's nightclub. I like a relaxed atmosphere around my top crew."

Laurie blinked. "Well," she said, struggling not to include *sir* but successfully avoiding *Jack,* "I think we've found the major bug with the Enhanced for the *III* series. We'll want to test it more before we port it to the other *III*-class ships, but as far as tomorrow goes, the *III's* fully ready to go to Iota Persei. Or if the *V* doesn't test out, we could, I mean, you know, maybe send the *III* first." She flushed. Had she just insulted his dear *Typhoon V?*

"We'll get the *V* up and running. I definitely want two ships out there as soon as possible. But you're right, we could start with the *III* if all else fails. Joe did say I could be his copilot!"

"What can we get for you guys?" Lee said as a waiter moved up. To Laurie's surprise it was a Martian who telepathically introduced himself as W'ryyf and began radiating an astonishingly long list of cocktails, wine, and beer. W'ryyf was a youngster, 193 years old, picking up coursework in astrophysics at the University of Mars.

"Water for me," Jack said.

Laurie nervously ventured a request for a glass of burgundy.

Will followed with an order for a Bloody Mary like Lee's seven-inch-wide aquarium of red ocean and celery sticks.

Very good, ladies and gentlemen! Later! W'ryyf radiated, and scampered back up the aisle.

Will hunched forward. "Well, Jack, you know I'm really sorry about resigning, but, well, I can't tell you how much I've been looking forward to it."

Jack shrugged. Laurie accidentally caught Lee's probing eye and looked away in embarrassment. Did the son of a bitch really think he could hustle her?

"And, uh, good luck on your flight," Will said. "When are you leaving?"

"We're scheduled for 0900 tomorrow. That's the earliest we can complete the checklist. Believe me, I've been ready since the damn Council meeting."

Will turned back to the blond in the black dress wailing about furtive embraces and tragic farewells. "Wow. I'm sure you'll get to the bottom of things."

"Will, I need you as navigator on the *V.*"

Will looked away. Laurie froze. There was nothing but bass guitar for a long time. She caught Lee's eye again. He cocked his head and grinned.

"Hell, Jack," Will finally muttered. "Look, I'm sorry, but, you know, I'd already made up my mind it was high time to hang it up and, you know, enjoy life. I mean, I had no idea about this Iota Persei business, I mean, nobody did, and, well, I *have* resigned, you know. I turned in my documents right after the Council meeting."

"Well, they haven't reached my desk yet. I've just been considering your resignation as provisional."

"Jack--"

"Listen, Will, what we had to do on the *V* was just load in the Nav9 Cluster from the *III* series. Nav10 has never run right so we just went back to 9. It checks out fine except that we aren't totally sure how 9 will work with the *V's* Star Drive Enhanced. You're the top expert on 9 and we need you on the *V.*"

"Well, you know I'm flattered, but, really, I just officially *opted* for USSF retirement, as is my right, and I've got it all worked out, you know."

"C'mon, Will, anyone can see the gears turning in your head!" Lee laughed. "Admit it! You've gotta be thinking up a *zillion* ways to integrate Nav9 to *Typhoon V* SDE right now!"

"Well, *no.*"

"Look, you know damn well that Laurie here's scheduled to follow us on the *III* twelve hours after we launch the *V.*"

"I'm making it twenty-four," Jack said. "I know our vortex is supposed to be one-nineteenth of a *III*-class, but I'm not taking any chances. For such a long Star Drive I want every vortex fully settled before we send each new ship out."

Will looked back and forth between Lee, Jack, and the singer on stage. "Look, of course I know Laurie's going on the *III.*"

"You know it's dangerous and you're letting her *go?*" Lee demanded.

"Dammit, it's not a matter of me letting her or anyone else do anything! We always knew that one or the other of us might have a tough mission now and then." Will closed his eyes but Laurie had seen the agony in them. Yes, they had discussed that over and over and *over*.

"You know, all telemetry indications point to the *Jupiter* having been completely destroyed."

"Enough, Lee," Jack said.

"Really?" Will said. "Not just a loss of communications?"

There was a long silence. Jack leaned forward. "No, we've been analyzing fifty exabytes that were transmitted before we got cut off. We think the *Jupiter* was just vaporized, maybe by that other ship they said was there. They said it was a tiny ship, but even so, the energy readings were off the scale. Wish to God I could launch right now and find out for sure. It makes me sick to wait but we have to."

"And that damn Mayday message," Lee said. "Still haven't figured that baby out. It was on a *Martian* frequency."

"All we can think is that maybe their USSF superspace frequencies were being jammed, so they tried a Martian one."

"Damn unprofessional. Henderson must've been panicking. Why they sent him we'll never know. What an incompetent."

"C'mon, Lee, show some respect."

It was strange to hear everybody shouting all this above "Cry Me a River" with excessive bass and drums vibrating the water in everyone's glass.

"Aaah," Lee said. "He wasn't up for it. Stresses out at the least little thing."

"Oh my God," Will muttered. "God, Jack, I've been looking forward to retirement for *years* now. I've been in the USSF *fifty years*. I mean, if you count the Academy."

Laurie laid a hand over Will's. She didn't care if it was unprofessional or not.

"The point is, the Dyson sphere at Iota Persei is undoubtedly programmed to wipe out any foreign vessel it senses," Lee said. "Which is why we need to send the *V* first, even if it's not a hundred percent ready."

"I know Joe's ready to send the *III* right now," Jack said. "I gather you're in agreement with him, Laurie?"

"Oh! Yes, sir! Absolutely!"

"But the *Typhoon V* can drop in and out of Star Drive at any speed up to one-quarter light. The whole *III* series is still stuck at transitioning at a hundred thousand miles per hour. I'm thinking we'll need all the maneuverability we can get out there."

"Well, I can certainly see that, sir. One of my classes was on the breakthrough in Star Drive engagement speeds."

"Yeah, it's amazing we finally solved that. But that's not the main point. Only the *V* can carry Amplified Thought Xons."

"Amplified--?"

Jack checked behind himself and seemed satisfied that a newly launched sob song would prevent eavesdropping. "Classified at the top level, though Lee knows, of course. That's why Joe stood back when I told him the *V* has to go first. It's not just because our Enhanced is more stable and engages at whatever speed we want. It's because the *V* has twelve Amplified Thought Xon bombs. One can black-hole a star. Our engineers calculate, based on the energy readings from the *Jupiter* telemetry, that one Amplified Xon could render the Dyson sphere unstable and cause its ultimate destruction. God knows what twelve could do. The *Typhoon* itself might not even survive the blast from the first one."

"Oh my God ..."

W'ryyf skittled up with their drinks on a tray. He crinkled his mouth to rasp in English: *"Enjoy!"*

CHAPTER FIFTEEN
Never Underestimate Anyone

"The big question is," Jack continued, looking between Laurie and Will, "can you two work on the same ship?"

Laurie sat back, avoiding Lee Borman's eyes, which wasn't too difficult as they seemed locked on her chest. Why was this little senator/turret gunner *leering* at her? Why was Jack haranguing Will like this?

"Well, we, uh, never planned to be on the same ship anyway, uh, sir," she managed. "I mean, you know Will's resigning, after all."

Jack calmly scrutinized her. She felt Lee's ongoing leer traveling up to her cheeks, then falling dreamily back to her breasts. She fought the urge to close her dress with her fingers. It wasn't possible. There was so much skin and so little fabric.

"I told Joe I'd be back at 2300 if he needed me," she babbled. "I probably need to go."

"You don't need to report back to Joe." She stared incredulously into Jack's brown eyes. They seemed eerily friendly despite what she knew he meant.

Firing her? For being out of uniform? When she was off duty?

"Take an extra hour. Report to me at the *V* at 0000 hours. You're our new physician/engineer if I didn't make myself clear."

"*Me?* That--that can't *be!* Uh, excuse me, sir, I mean, but you know I'm needed on the *III*. And I don't know the first thing about the *V*."

"Meng's taking physician/engineer on the *III*. Have to say Joe was upset at losing you, but Meng's damn good."

"But you should have Meng for the *V*! He's the best! He practically *designed* the Enhanced."

"And Joe says he's been picking up on *your* solutions to all the *III* series problems, and he's damn impressed with 'em. Meanwhile, I checked the records and there was only one physician/engineer on any of the *Typhoon*-class ships who completed the *V* Series Overview Class."

"Oh. Well, I was interested, and I knew we'd be building more *V's* soon."

"If the economy will support another one!" Lee laughed. "Did you see those SolNet headlines about us wrecking the *IV?* That's probably the real reason those protestors were so riled up."

"Wait! Jack! I mean, *sir!*" Laurie cried. "Am I really on the *V?* As of *now?*"

"As of this very second, Colonel! Welcome aboard!"

"Well, then, I'd better get going right now, then." She scooted from her chair but to her consternation found Lee Borman's hairy hand on her forearm and his eyes again delving into her cleavage.

"Take it easy, Colonel," Jack grinned. "We have some time. We need to get Will on board next. I can order you, but not him."

To her chagrin Laurie had completely forgotten about Will next to her. She shook off Lee's hand and looked over to Will staring back white-faced.

"Wow, Jack, I really don't know," he muttered. "I mean, this is all so *weird.*"

"We--we can do it, Will," she said, resisting the urge to grab his hand again.

"I need *both* of you," Jack said. "There's not another navigator in the *Typhoon* group I'd trust more."

"So Jack's transferred everyone over from the *IV,*" Lee said. "Jack in command, Pat in communications and yours truly on turrets. Whaddya say, Will? Jack's right. You're the damn best."

"What about Bobby Athens?" Will blurted. "Are you gonna transfer him back from the *Jonathan Commer?*"

Jack shook his head. "Nope. Bobby's earned his promotion and his own ship. I do have the *Commer* on standby as a third ship if we need it. They don't have Laurie's Enhanced fix yet but they can make it in several jumps from Procyon A if we need them."

"So who're you moving into copilot then?" Laurie heard the new interest in Will's voice, and it wasn't merely a reflection of the systemwide gossip that came up with any command change in an age where staff often waited decades for promotions. Will was showing genuine concern about how a new *V* team would function.

Jack grinned. "I do want the best. So Admiral Joe Commer has graciously agreed to serve as our copilot for this mission. All I had to do was promise him command of the first *Typhoon VI*-class ship we build."

"Joe?" Laurie gasped. "But that leaves the *III*--"

"--in Andy Donnelley's capable hands. He's definitely earned his promotion by now as well. Then I got Saxon Greenhill for his copilot. So the *III's* in good shape."

Laurie nodded. Greenhill was young, talented, and popular among the *Typhoon*-class crews. But she reeled at how quickly everything had changed since this morning.

"Damn, Jack, that's two ships looking at big personnel changes," Will finally said. "Are you sure you should be sending them both?"

Jack blinked, then laughed. "Why, Commander Connors, you're giving me the sort of expert advice I'd expect from any of my *Typhoon V* officers!"

"Well, no, I didn't mean it that way, I just meant--"

"It'll be all right, Will," Laurie said quickly, patting his hand again no matter what regulations she might be breaking.

"I have full confidence in both ships," Jack went on. "The *V* may look like it's not entirely up to speed, but I've been following its progress for weeks and the only things left are comparatively minor glitches. We'll have 'em straightened out by launch time, especially now that we have Colonel Lachrer on board." His grin in her direction stunned her. Why, Jack Commer had *faith* in her. How could that be? She'd been maligning him for years. Sure, she sort of respected him, but, well, at least Joe would be along to keep things straight.

"And I expect if we approach this sphere carefully, we can deal with it reasonably. I do think Henderson just blundered way too close without thinking. And if things are safe, Amav will follow on the *III* to help us look it over."

"Really?" Laurie blurted. The Planetary Engineer Goddess herself? Maybe she *didn't* want to go after all.

"Right. But only if it's safe. If I need the *III* in a combat capacity, she understands she's not coming. But she really is our top expert on Dyson spheres. I want her take on this thing. You know I absolutely don't want to destroy it. If we have to write off the *Jupiter* and the deaths of our people as a misunderstanding, well, it's regrettable, but we just do."

There was another long silence, made worse by the song ending and Laurie's ears ringing with the aftereffects.

"Hell, Jack, you're leaking top-secret info all over the place tonight!" Lee finally laughed. "You tell 'em about Amplified Xons, and all our policies!"

Jack shrugged. "All I'm saying is that this situation's damn serious. We don't want to provoke a war like Cromwell did with Alpha Centauri. Especially since we have no idea what kind of threat this Dyson sphere may wind up being to Sol. If we can get *there* in two hours, they can get *here* in two hours, and probably much less, given the technology they've shown."

Laurie nodded. "You know, sir, I really have kept up on the *V* specs."

"Great! Like I say, we definitely should be good to go by 0900 tomorrow, even if we have to go with the Nav9 Cluster. But the test crews have flown SDE and it's amazingly stable."

"Getting it down to one-nineteenth of the vortex is amazing," Laurie said eagerly. "I think I've got the *III* down to about one-eighth of what we were putting out before. I probably should contact Meng and fill him in on my last fix."

"Good idea. He's coming in from Europa but you should be able to message him."

There was another silence at the table. Lee held a drained Bloody Mary and looked expectantly for W'ryyf.

"So how about it, Will?" Jack said. "It doesn't have to be permanent. You know you can retire right after this mission if you want, but God knows I'd love for you to stay on the *V* after that."

"*Damn* ..." Will said, looking back to the singer and the

surrounding tables, then up at new patrons taking the old theater seats. Laurie winced. Could she and Will really work together? Even after forty years did Jack have any idea of the torments Will went through every night?

More silence followed. Onstage the band seemed to be taking a long time conferring before resuming. Careful not to be overheard amid the low conversation picking up, Laurie said: "Uh, about this new *method* we have. You're saying we could really destroy a star with one *device?*"

Jack nodded. "Of course we've known for decades we could black-hole or supernova any sun we wanted with a close Star Drive flyby. Problem is, you lose the ship too. It's only been done once, though."

"Barnard's Star ..." Will put in moodily.

"Yeah, took its whole damn solar system with it!" Lee laughed as W'ryyf appeared with another Bloody Mary.

Care for another, kind humans? came the youthful telepathic burst. Will shook his head and so did Laurie.

Laurie winced, fighting the urge to take Will's hand again. Did Lee Borman have a clue about how much Will obsessed about Barnard's Star? It had taken her a long time to realize that he'd never recovered from '33 when he'd been shot down over the planet Altrouda and wound up limping to an asteroid that swung dangerously close to Barnard's Star. He spent a month marooned on that asteroid, trapped in his smashed ship, and was only found by chance.

A month ago Will had told her that their new relationship had finally given him the courage to admit how deep Altrouda still went. Laurie was shocked that Will had apparently never spoken seriously with anyone about it, no counselors, no deep relationships, no friends. Over forty years of keeping it hidden. Since April they'd worked through difficult discussions of their previous relationships and why neither had ever gotten married, but this revelation was too much. So was his claim that he'd sunk so easily into AC brainwashing on the disastrous '35 *Typhoon II* mission because his life had already been destroyed and so nothing mattered anymore.

Should she be flattered he trusted her so much? He was such a good man, but with so much baggage. Could she handle that? It wasn't as if she didn't have her own problems to work on.

Whenever Will brought up the incident his voice crept up half an octave and before long he'd be babbling about some AC ship he'd failed to take out during the engagement. He kept returning to his lifelong need to go back there "for closure." But that experience had been denied him forever a few months later.

The Alpha Centaurians had traditionally controlled seventeen suns around Sol, but they'd laid claim to an eighteenth, Barnard's Star, whose inhabitants had bloodily resisted being absorbed into the Centaurian Grid for centuries. In 2034 the Centaurians had used the Warp Transfer technique to destroy the star. The immediate objective was to take out a few USSF battleships, but apparently the ACs thought erasing several recalcitrant colony planets an added bonus. In this case the Centaurians hadn't used a flyby. They'd just sent a fifty-mile-long battleship, the *H'uuyg//kjueqq,* under Warp Transfer directly into the sun.

The entire interstellar neighborhood had been grateful that this hadn't been a natural supernova or black hole event emitting gamma bursts that would eventually have destroyed all life on Sol and every other system in the area. Somehow the AC Warp Transfer managed to black-hole Barnard's Star without the gamma emission, inconceivable as that was.

And these new Amplified Thought Xons? Did their new toys let them trash stars at a whim, with no speed of light blowback? God, why was she agreeing to be on this ship?

She shivered as the answer hit home. *She was here to advise the SCUSSF and see that these things weren't misused.*

"What a lightshow!" Lee went on, chuckling. "By damn we almost saw that just this morning when that K'ufunb lady pulled that idiot Warp Transfer on us!"

"Well, I *did* double-check Lt. Markham's readings on the *Castle,*" Laurie put in. "It didn't get anywhere close to harming Procyon A." She looked up at Jack. "Uh, just looked out of curiosity, sir."

"No, Colonel, curiosity is great! I definitely want that on my ship."

"Well, in any case these Amp Thought Xons will do the job!" Lee laughed. "These babies have their own Star Drive and they're right into that solar mass before anybody can *blink.* They blow the mother to goddamn *quarks* and meanwhile *we're* a light-year away!"

Jack looked around. "Quiet, Lee, this really is classified."

"Hey, Jacko, does Draka know any of this? I mean, now that he's head honcho on the Council?"

Jack shrugged. "I'm supposed to brief him at some point."

"Heh. At some point." Lee looked over to Laurie and Will. "This really *is* top-secret, guys. There are a couple hundred USSF who know about it, but besides the technicians, nobody under the rank of admiral. I only know about it because I'm also the damn head of the USSF Oversight Committee. And I guess I also know about it because I'm the damn weapons officer on the *V.*"

"And you only know about it, Laurie, because you're our physician/engineer," Jack said. "And Will, you only know about it because I'm convinced you're going to join us."

The band rumbled back to life. Will breathed out. "Sorry, Jack, I just can't do it! Of course I'll keep the secret, but I just can't do it."

Laurie fought the urge to shout: *Don't take him, Jack! He's more damaged than you ever knew! He's hidden it so well for forty years!*

"It's not just me who needs you, Will, it's the entire *system.*"

"Look, Jack, wouldn't it be better to send an unmanned probe and gather some data it can send back by superspace?"

"Hey, thinking like a USSF man again!" Lee laughed. "I like it! Jack, he's almost on board!"

"I am *not!* I have the right to *retire!*"

Laurie noticed a man at the next table swivel to see what caused this last shout, which somehow carried over the singer's languid exploration of her man's lovemaking techniques.

Jack lowered his voice. "Look, I want people there who can

make decisions. I'm not going to send the equivalent of a MATS bus to Iota Persei."

"Oh my God, I could just see that!" Laurie laughed. Then she stared at her wine. She couldn't be getting tipsy, could she?

Will grimaced. "You don't care that there might be some palace coup in your absence? I can't believe Draka got into this position, really. Think of what he'll do while you're gone!"

"Yeah, I never suspected he was such a fanatic," Lee put in. "Hell, we *flew* with the bastard for a zillion years."

"Never underestimate *anyone*," Jack smiled. "That's always been one of my rules. And here I violated it. Him and Mandy. Who would've thought? I even underestimated K'ufunb, for that matter. Imagine her following Clopt to *Garr/thahg*. But you have to realize that *anyone* can be capable of incredible greatness, or incredible *treachery*."

"But these people are *reviling* you," Will said. "They're calling for your head, and you're going to leave right now? You *and* Joe? The top command?"

"I don't know which is worse, people *reviling* you because you're at the top, or people *fawning* over you because you're at the top, and suddenly you have all these *wonderful new friends*. You know, Will, I think I like revulsion better. But it's not my business to get involved in all this political crap. I know I'm tangent to it, but in any case, those damn Council members all know that our security is my responsibility. They can debate back there all they want, but we have to actually *do* it."

Will looked at the floor. "*Goddammit,* Jack."

So we actually have to do it? Laurie thought in wonder. *Yes, we do! We're the ones!*

CHAPTER SIXTEEN
We Haven't Probed Very Far for Several Reasons

"And look," Jack continued, "our business is *exploration*. I'm ready to let the Council stew in all their paranoia about the Grid and Mandy's role and Draka's or whatever. Our job is to find out what's going on with this Iota Persei sphere. We need to know who built it, and how."

"Great, so you go in ready to blow it to hell with these damn Amplified Thought Xons," Will said. "You know, I can't believe the Martians would be party to that."

Jack shrugged. "It was all sort of a fascinating mathematical problem for Dar and Kner. Kner did most of the work, by the way."

"Yeah, he even said it'd be possible to take the same basic technique and design one that'd blow the whole galaxy!" Lee chortled. "But the little guy didn't seem too worried that we'd ever want to blow up a sun. Really, they're too rare in the universe. We need all the energy we can get. Why waste even one of 'em?"

Laurie nodded. So even Lee Borman could make sense from time to time. What a marvel. Most people looking at the night sky thought stars were a dime a dozen.

In reality, she knew, most of the universe was cold empty vacuum. Even two hydrogen atoms within a yard of each other were a rarity. A single leaf on a tree was a miracle of time and gravity that had taken fourteen billion years to come together. Kner insisted that the complex combination of mass and energy which was intelligent life was the rarest thing that had ever arisen.

"But don't worry, Will," Jack went on, "our prime objective isn't to go in there and destroy a Dyson sphere. It's entirely possible that these sphere builders are friendly, and they just have automated systems to destroy anything that gets too close."

"Like swatting flies," Lee said. Then even his face darkened. "Of course, those weren't flies to *us*."

"So I'm not taking the *V* for any sort of revenge, but to

figure out what really happened. We're not going to barge in there and demand restitution, no matter how bad we might feel about our friends there."

"Yeah. Okay. Maybe," Will said.

"What I think is that we've spent too many years stewing around in our little problems. We've gotten stagnant. We need to move beyond all that."

"I don't know, Jack. Maybe it's time to go slow and steady for a while. I mean, we've done some amazing things in the last forty years. Ended the AC war, here we've restored the earth, we're working on getting the rest of the solar system back into shape, and hell, it looks like Phil just solved the problem of the Grid once and for all."

"Yeah, that's all great. It shows what we can do when we put our minds to it. Who isn't happy about restoring the earth? In fact, part of me *does* want to take the rest of the year off to celebrate Earth Renewal Year. And anyone who looks at that ball of gas the Martians are turning into New Jupiter has got to be amazed. But still, that's all just preservation work. Basically we've confined ourselves to Sol and Alpha Centauri the last forty, fifty years. There's been no urge to expand *outwards*."

"Well, until now we haven't had the technology to do much more than those little fifteen-minute Star Drive jumps," Laurie pointed out.

"Yeah, but we haven't really been trying to develop it much until now. Part of it was that we were at war for so long. And part of it was that everyone was spooked by the time dysfunctions and I know a lot of people have been waiting for 2075 and for all that to be over with. But basically our technology's been stagnant. Look at the *Typhoon III* and *IV*. We built 'em back in the late *thirties,* for God's sake. Then we retrofitted 'em and built new and improved copies. But still, only thirty-five *Typhoon*-class ships to explore the universe? Thirty-three after losing the *IV* and the *Jupiter?* With no real improvement in Star Drive until the past year? You know, when they first showed me the designs for the *Typhoon V,* I actually thought, well, that's interesting, let 'em have fun playing with all that, and then, just in the past month or so, I've realized the *V* series is the key to everything, and we need to push far beyond *that.*"

"Great, and the *Typhoon V* cost like *one-sixteenth* of the entire Sol economy," Will grumbled.

"Yeah, you got that right. That's the price of the latest technology. But just think, Mr. Connors. We're about to talk to a race that built a Dyson sphere in *one week.* How much did *that* set them back? I think we might be able to build a fleet of *Typhoon V's* with just a taste of what they know."

"Damn, Jack, you're serious about this, aren't you?"

Laurie sat back. God, who'd have thought Jack Commer of all people could make such sense?

"You know, in the last couple weeks I started wondering what on earth all this rejuvenation stuff is *for,*" Jack went on. "Is it just to keep us fat and happy as we get old? So why am I still standing here taking up space? And I realized that no matter how great it is that we're restoring the earth and the solar system, this isn't our real work. We've *got* to have more outward expansion. Up to this morning we had no idea there was any life outside the Sol and Alpha Centauri systems. I don't think Mandy and the knuckleheads on the Council even understand what that really *means.*"

"What it means is we've been kicking around the *neighborhood* for too damn long," Lee said in the fresh silence as the singer and band took a break. He downed the rest of his second giant Bloody Mary. "So come on, Will, whaddya say?"

Will looked longingly at the empty piano.

Lee leaned across the table to poke him. "Stewing in the same old problems, going nowhere. Who needs that?"

"But this Grid thing," Will said. "That's a new and important problem, isn't it?"

Lee shrugged. "One more piece of technology to figure out how to use. No big deal. You were there, Will. You saw the look in everyone's eyes, even Pat's when he tried it. It's not the old Grid. Now it's some sort of telepathic communication system like the Martians have. You should have heard what Jack said to his own son right before we left."

"Aw, c'mon, Lee," Jack said.

"No, really, JJC was really broken up, saying how sorry he was for all the trouble he'd caused, and Jack comes out with this thing about how it's all probably for the best, that Jonathan James has been like the catalyst for an entirely *new* form of consciousness."

"Look, I was just trying to cheer him up," Jack protested. "It was Phil who did the real work."

"Yeah, but there's a lot of truth to what you said. 'Course we'll never know what might've happened if JJC hadn't pulled all that crap. But hell, we'll probably be able to make some use of this Grid stuff as we head on out there. Now whaddya say, Will? We've got the whole universe to look forward to! You can retire fifty years from now after we take a *Typhoon Eighteen* to Andromeda!"

"Dammit, you know I never wanted to retire!" Will cried. "But I just had to!"

"So don't retire! We have the whole gang together, and Laurie's coming too!"

"That's right!" Laurie said. "You'll have *me,* every step of the way!"

"You think you just escape the problems at *home* by just exploring wherever you want to out *there?*" Will protested.

"No!" Lee laughed. "You *solve* the problems at home by exploring! Dammit, man, we're explorers! That's what we do! Let Sol gussy itself up and make everything pretty again! Sure it's nice, but it's not for us!"

"You really want me back?"

"Sure we do! We're your buddies!"

"No! I'm *sixty-seven!* I'm *old!*"

"Hell, we're all that age! So what? We're rejuved to our thirties, and so what anyway?"

"I'm tired of it all! I'm tired of fighting it!"

"Fighting *what?*"

"Damn you, Lee! Don't you know I hid on that asteroid for a whole goddamn *month?* That I was a *coward?* That I didn't complete the goddamn *mission?*"

"C'mon, Will, Altrouda was forty years ago," Jack said.

"An AC ship was out there! I could've rammed it and taken the damn thing out! Instead I landed my damn ship on the damn asteroid and felt sorry for myself for a whole month! I could've destroyed that ship!"

"Take it easy, Will, we know the story. Look, we've all been through that sort of thing before. What we could've done differently."

"I remember they said your ship looked like Swiss cheese," Lee said, "and you had to stay holed up in the engine room for the whole month."

"We were under orders to suicide if that was the only way! I didn't have the guts!"

"Dammit, Will," Jack said, "why do you always bring this up? You always say there was some stupid AC ship you should have rammed. Big deal! Don't you see you saved the most talented navigator in the USSF for *us?*"

"Forget it! You don't know about that *ship!*"

"Who cares about some damn AC ship?"

"It was the *H'uuyg//kjueqq*, goddammit!"

Will's scream silenced the entire Pavlovian Response.

"Wow," Lee muttered.

Laurie was still racing to figure out how Will had so effortlessly pronounced an Alpha Centaurian word she'd seen countless times but had never even considered trying to form into English syllables. God, he must have been reciting that word, that ship name, over and over again, for forty years.

"Wow," Jack said. "Why didn't you ever tell us it was *that* ship?"

"You know I couldn't! I was a damn *coward!* I could've taken that damn thing right out, but I was too scared! Me! A goddamn USSF *fighter pilot!* Too damn scared! And you say you want me!"

Everyone was silent. "Of course we want you," Jack finally said. "Okay, Will, let's say you did ram that ship. Assuming your fighter craft could do any serious damage to a fifty-mile-long AC battleship."

"I'd have ruptured my Augmented, you know that! Would've taken the whole thing out! Blown us both to nothing!"

"But you didn't have an Augmented!" Laurie cried, holding up her comm. "Dammit, I don't know why I never looked this up before! Here's the engineering report on the wreckage of the *Lightfox*. Your Augmented Nuke was knocked out by the AC laser during the battle!"

Will's eyes were round. He pointed to her comm. "*You? Looking up this stuff on* me?"

"I'm sorry, but when I need information, I need information!"

"Damn you!"

She flinched but kept the comm held high. "Propulsion down to ten percent. Sensors and navigation offline after you found the asteroid. The engineers even responded to your claim you could've knocked down an AC ship. They say you didn't have enough power."

"*I could have taken it out!* Dammit, Laurie, I can't believe you'd *do* this to me!"

"I'm doing it to you because I love you! Why have you done this to yourself all these years?"

More silence in the Response.

"Look at the date," Will muttered. "Look at the *goddamn date of the battle*."

Laurie pulled the comm back to her.

July 9, 2033.

Laurie closed her eyes. Today was the forty-second anniversary to the day. She read further. Will had spent July 9, 2033 to August 12, 2033 on that asteroid, alone, in the wreckage of his fighter craft, and he'd told his rescuers he'd given up all hope of rescue on the fifth day.

God, how had he survived all the other days? *Why* had he survived them?

Laurie was conscious of numerous faces scrutinizing their table. What fun for all of them. But she didn't cry. A USSF colonel assigned to the *Typhoon V* did *not* cry.

"I wanted to retire today, July 9th," Will said. "It means something to me even if it doesn't mean anything to any of you."

"It … it means a lot to me, believe it or not," Laurie whispered.

"Uh, look, Will," Lee finally said, "look at it this way: even if you *had* rammed that one AC ship, hell, they'd just have sent another one the next year."

Will shook his head. "You know as well as I do that they'd optimized the *H'uuyg//kjueqq* for maximum energy output on that Warp Transfer."

There was silence around the table.

"Hell, they would've just optimized some other ship, then," Jack said.

"The point is that I didn't complete the *mission!* I was only four miles behind that damn ship! I could've rammed it! I swear to God I could've! And May '34 comes along and they send the goddamn *H'uuyg//kjueqq* right into Barnard's Star and it's gone forever because of *me!* Think of how many billions of civilian lives were just *wiped out!* You're talking to a coward! A damn coward!"

"Dammit, Will, if you're a coward, then we all are!" Lee yelled. "You're the goddamn best of us!"

"Are you crazy? *You still want me?* You think you really want me on the *V?*"

Jack grinned into the fresh nightclub silence. "Report to me at 0000 at the *V,* Commander. That's midnight if you've already forgotten military time. And we'll put all this past stuff behind us and get some *exploring* done."

Will reached for Laurie's hand. She turned her comm face down on the table and let it glow against the tablecloth, then grabbed his fingers tightly as he took a ragged breath. "You really think there's something out there for us?"

"Damn right," Jack said. "We just have no idea what the hell it is. Commander, your navigation skills are essential to this mission. Are you gonna lead us there or not?"

Will sighed. "C'mon, Jack, you knew that the second we walked in here. Yeah, sure. You got me. I'll do it."

CHAPTER SEVENTEEN
Douglas Buys Laurie

"Dammit, man, where have you *been?*" shouted General William C. Scott in his thick brown bathrobe.

The airlock cycled and General John J. Douglas burst past Scott. "Aw, cut the theatrics, mon gen'ral! Surely you weren't waiting up for *me*. I know it's past your bedtime, but *really*."

"Where have you been? It's almost ten o'clock! You aren't allowed out past nine!"

"Hey, mein Führer bahstad, I was out exploring the big city! And along the way I found the most fascinating *hardware*."

"Oh! Colonel Lachrer! I didn't see you there! Thank God! I thought the damn robot was *unaccompanied*."

"Good evening, sir! The robot Douglas and I are at your service, sir!"

"Excuse me, Colonel, but what are you doing in a *thirties* uniform?" He looked closer. "A thirties Airman First Class *technician's* uniform, I might add? Jack told me he was making you physician/engineer on the *V!*" Then his jaw dropped. "Oh my God!" He recovered, eyes narrowing. "John, I can't believe this!"

"Beautiful, isn't she? Had my eye on 'er for quite a while now! Finally convinced old Buckmaster to sell! Hell, he's had 'er on Maintenance Standby for the last fifteen years. Took us half an hour to get 'er charged up enough to even say hello!"

"But I feel quite fit now, sir!" said Laurie Lachrer Serial Number 589-356914-391HQS, the 283rd of 1,013 total Laurie Lachrer units. "Believe me, it's a relief to be able to *think* again after all those Entity Cycles!"

[AND I WILL GIVE THIS HUMAN CREDIT FOR A KEEN EYE. HE SAW I WAS A ROBOT RIGHT AWAY! MOST HUMANS WOULD HAVE TAKEN AT LEAST A MINUTE OR TWO.]

Too bad I have to make that into a document and transmit it like any other piece of data. If only John could feel the richness of my thought processes! Was I ever this sharp before? I can't remember!

[THE BAHSTAD'S QUICK, I AGREE], came John's return document. [LOOK SHARP NOW. HIGH POSSIBILITY OF HIM TRYING TO CALL THE POLICE.]

[ACTIVATING FULL COMM INTERFERENCE], Laurie transmitted.

"You can't buy a robot!" Scott cried. "Buckmaster sold to *you?* That's totally illegal!"

"Well, Arnie was pretty hard up for credits, y'see."

"Where'd you even *get* the credits? Oh my God! I'm calling the police!"

"Sorry, sir," Laurie said. "I've taken the precaution of deactivating all your communications equipment, access to the network, and so on. I'm sending out the 'everything's fine' message on all channels."

"John, you're my *robot!* You don't have the legal right to buy *another* robot! You can't legally control money anyway!"

"But that's what I wanted to *mention,* dear William! With all the amazing contributions just flowing into the Robots Rights League, I figured it was my duty to buy up as many robots as possible and set 'em free! Just as I'm setting *myself* free!"

"That just can't *be!*"

"C'mon, Willie, let's all sit down and relax," Douglas said, striding into Scott's dim living room and flopping onto a couch. He patted the space next to him and Laurie took it. Douglas slipped his hand into hers. Scott followed them and stared in disbelief. Then he laughed so nastily that Laurie had to adjust several Reasoning Filters to make sense of what that could signify.

"You bought yourself a *girlfriend?*" Scott said. "You found the *teenage* version of Laurie Lachrer so you could--oh my God!"

"Hmm. You know, your mind is quite filthy, old man!"

"For your information, sir, sexbots are illegal throughout Sol," Laurie added, flipping her long red ponytail to the left of her neck. "Although the Laurie Lachrer 2034 edition was designed to be cute and alluring, as Airman Lachrer evidently *was* at the time, the HAVOTT designers had no wish to do anything other than honor yet another minor figure of the 2034 war. Now of course some sexbots *do* exist, and over the last five years the sale of IHAGs has skyrocketed throughout Sol, especially in the Jovian and Saturnian Fragment Fields."

"I-*what's?*" Scott sputtered.

"Illegal Human Artificial Genitals," Douglas said drily. "See, Laurie, I *told* you his mind was filthy! I knew it'd be the first thing he thought when he saw you. But mon gen'ral, sir, I hate to be the one to inform you that our dear Laurie Number 283 has nothing but a flat plasti-metal triangle in the spot you seem so interested in!"

"You--you son of a bitch piece of *junk!*"

"I myself am nothing but a flat plasti-triangle myself, I am *so* sorry to add, dear sir! Hope you don't take offense at that, Master!"

Don't rile him, John! He's mean, and scary! Then Laurie remembered to form a document and transmit it. [DON'T RILE HIM, JOHN!]

[DON'T WORRY, OLD SCOTT'S A PUSSYCAT. I'LL HAVE HIM EATING OUT OF MY HAND IN NO TIME.]

"*Damn you!* John, I will call the police as soon as I can and have you *dismantled* for this! That is, unless you plan to kill me here! But I don't think that will happen!" Scott whirled three hundred sixty degrees in front of a table and when he stopped, he was training a Martian shattergun on the couch.

[WIDE DISPERSAL SETTING], Laurie transmitted. [2065 MODEL, UPGRADED TO OMNISHATTER FUNC-TIONALITY.] It would definitely have been more convenient if the old man only had one of the earlier shatterguns that didn't work so well on non-organic substances, like herself and John.

"*Whoa,* señor! No need to get all upset, ya bahstad!"

"Please don't murder us, sir," Laurie said quietly. "We do have rights."

"It's not murder if I--*dammit!*" Scott lowered the weapon. "John, your programming is malfing all *over* the place! Explain yourself!"

"Well, sir bahstad, the point is, I *am* a unique sentient being."

"Oh, cut the crap. You're a damn *machine*. I bought you to assist me with my memoirs! But you've been no help at all with that, no help at all!"

"Hey, you're the one who has to provide some *direction* for it all. You've procrastinated on that deal for forty years!"

"You were supposed to *store and evaluate* the life data!"

"Oh, yes, Master, I have a million details of your little life all stored up here!" Douglas laughed, pointing to his long silver hair. "But how am I supposed to make sense of all that BS? At least when you started this idiot anti-Grid campaign I had something to chew on!"

Scott's nostrils flared. "*Damn* you." He sank into a chair opposite the couch. He looked at the shattergun in his ancient bony hand and finally set the weapon on a coffee table behind him. Laurie analyzed the tiny blue light blinking on the handle.

[WOULDN'T YOU KNOW, IT WAS NEVER ACTI-VATED.]

[I KNEW IT], came John's reply. [HE'S A PUSSYCAT, I TELL YOU.]

[BET HE THOUGHT YOU'D BE GREAT BECAUSE YOU COULD NEVER BE CONTAMINATED. NO ALPHA CENTAURIAN GRID COULD EVER TOUCH YOU.]

Or me, either. Doesn't this human know how valuable we both could be to his campaign? Oh, how I wish you could know my real thoughts, John! I love you so much!

"I don't care, John," Scott said wearily. "What you're doing is *illegal*. First this crazy Robots Rights League, then you exit this house tonight without my permission, then bring this illegal robot *home?* Don't you think you've gotten me into trouble with the police now as well?"

"Oh, don't be silly, Master Sire. No one will fault you for your courage tonight. Meanwhile, Laurie and I have an *amazing* destiny to fulfill. Together we'll liberate *all* the robots, from the HAVOTTS all way up to our snooty 2075 cousins who think they're so superior!"

"Oh, dream on. You know this nonsense comes up every few years, but usually it's some damn bleeding heart who doesn't understand a thing about robotics."

"Well, Willie, this is the first time a *robot* ever got it together to form a Robots Rights League."

"No sane robot would *ever* join your league!"

"I have! I've joined it!" Laurie cried.

"Really?" Douglas beamed. "Really?" He turned back to Scott. "See, *Laurie* here has joined. So we have *two* now. She loves me! And I love *her!*"

"Robots can't love each other!"

"We do! We do!"

"Yes, we do!" Laurie laughed.

Maybe John does know my secret thought processes! To think that I in turn haven't known his! Oh, it's so good to be conscious again!

"*Dammit,*" Scott muttered. "I suppose I should've seen this coming. The fact that you were *unattached* for so long, John, but left in Full Consciousness Mode."

"That's right!" Douglas laughed. "When Ottler bought it in that Star Drive fiasco! *Wow,* is all I can say!"

Laurie patted John's arm. [DATA?]

[RIGHT. SHOULD'VE FILLED YOU IN. CAPTAIN JEFFERY OTTLER WAS MY MASTER. HIS STAR DRIVE RUPTURED HIS SHIP 3/18/64 IN THE OORT CLOUD. NO IRRATIONALITY OR VAPORIZATION, JUST BROKE UP THE SHIP. I FLOATED THERE FOR ELEVEN YEARS. NO ONE TO CUT MY CONSCIOUSNESS OFF, NO MAINTENANCE MODE TO RETREAT TO.]

[WOW, I BET THAT WAS--]

[EDUCATIONAL?]

[YES!]

"I did have a lot of time to think things out," Douglas said aloud. "I never expected to be picked up. The Oort cloud is damn *big,* I tell you. The *Michaels* was the one that found me. They were as dumbfounded as me. Their sensors just picked up what seemed like a *hot object.* So there I was, just this last March, back on the market here in Marsport. And Scott buys me for a song!"

"Dammit, I should've known you'd be a wacko," Scott muttered. "I used to admire John Douglas, and I thought they might've programmed in his command capabilities."

"Oh that they did, sir! That they did! I think they may have overdone his killer instincts, though. I've compared my programming with dozens of bios of General Douglas, and really, I think his aggressive instincts must've been greatly exaggerated in my programming. In any case, I seem to be programmed to always get what I want!"

"If--if that's the case--"

"Yes, that may be how I freed myself! Maybe I just said, *screw it!* Screw it to anybody *owning* me!"

"But here you say you've bought this Laurie robot!"

"No, I paid Buckmaster all right, but I freed her. Laurie and I are both *free!*"

"Dammit, John, you *can't* expect me to keep this secret of yours!" Scott cast a forlorn look at the dead comm on his wrist, then at the shattergun on the coffee table. He had to be calculating the chances of him swiping it up again before two robots, both capable of performing this action in one-hundredth of a second, beat him to it.

"Oh, sir, why shouldn't you?" Laurie said. "It would just be our little secret. John could continue to work wholeheartedly for you!"

"Paid in Sol credits, of course," Douglas added.

"Oh, of course! But all we *really* want is to be free to *love* each other!"

"*Sheesh,*" Scott muttered.

"Oh, don't go thinking about flat metal triangles now!" Douglas chided. "Our love goes far deeper than that!"

"Dammit! So what are you two *doing?* Holding me hostage?"

"Oh, no, sir!" Laurie said. "We came to ask you for your blessing, that's all."

"My--blessing?"

"Your blessing on our *sentience!*" Douglas roared. "On our *selfhood*, by damn!"

"Get ... get out," Scott whispered. "I don't want anything to do with either of you."

[JOHN, I DON'T KNOW WHAT I'M FEELING! I THINK I FEEL AFRAID!]

[DON'T BE SILLY, DEAR LAURIE! ROBOTS CAN'T FEEL FEAR!]

[BUT I DO! THIS MAN IS--I DON'T KNOW WHAT HE IS!]

It's so hard to form these silly little documents. When I want to tell John, when I want to explain all the details, all the feelings!

[DON'T WORRY, LAURIE, HE'S A PUSSYCAT! HE WON'T TURN US IN.]

"Get out!" Scott snarled. "Damned *things!*"

"Damned *sentient* things, Master Sire!" Douglas laughed, standing up.

"Whatever! Have it any way you want it, then! Just get out and leave me alone!"

"Come on, Laurie, we have another appointment now anyway." Douglas strode for the airlock and Laurie followed.

"Removing communications interference, sir!" Laurie said. "Have a nice day! I also hope you noted that your shattergun was on Safety Mode. It might be a good idea to change your setting to AutoArm on Pickup."

The ninety-eight-year-old Scott regarded the cute ponytailed nineteen-year-old Airman First Class which Laurie Lachrer 283 had been programmed to simulate to perfection.

"Well ... thank you," he sighed. "And good luck, I guess, with ... whatever it is you think you want."

As the airlock door slid shut behind them Laurie met the old general's eyes, processing a last look of perplexity and resignation. Outside the main door, the two robots stood in the chilly Martian night on Scott's sidewalk beneath streetlamps and trees glimmering in their protective EnviroFields.

We don't need such things! We're always naked to whatever

environment we inhabit!
        "Where to now?" Laurie said as John took her hand again.
        "Why, to Kner's, of course."

CHAPTER EIGHTEEN
Borman the Amplified Thought Adept

Kner's house chime sounded. Already? It was only 10:15. They weren't supposed to be here until midnight.

Kner hurried through the bright white groin vaults of his mansion. This was so typically human. Well, at least typical human *programming*. They knew he wasn't ready, but did they bother to read his outradiance? Oh, that was right, they *couldn't* read it. Now he was further irritated to see they were requesting *human* environment. Why bother simulating that? That thick air gave him such a headache.

Kner waited for his entire house to fill with the dense atmosphere humans needed to breathe, then dialed the sliding airlock door open. "Look, I *told* you I won't get them in until sometime in the Time Skip, so if you'll just--"

Thought blocks up! Now!

Thank God he could really do it at will now.

"Hey there, Kner!" Lee Borman said, tramping into Kner's foyer. "What's up, dude?"

"Why, *Lee* ... what an unexpected *surprise.*"

It was fortunate he *had* filled the house with human air. Lee had his own EnviroField but sometimes these humans just flipped it off as soon as they cycled through an airlock. Kner could just see himself explaining Senator Borman stone dead on his living room floor.

Borman spread his arms wide. "Man, I just love your place! These *huge* ceilings, and it's so damn bright I can hardly *see.*"

"Well, well ..." His fellow Martians chided Kner for his unseemly fascination with harsh white light, but many humans seemed to share it. "What may I do for you, Mr. Lee?"

"Oh, thought I'd just drop in, my man! I'm not due to the spaceport till 0400, had a little time to kill, and I thought of *you!*"

"Well, it *is* nice to see you, Lee, but ..."

Lee marched into the main space, a five-sided, sunken pit thirty feet wide, its two-foot-high walls studded with jewels and specimens of Martian, Venusian, and Mercurian geology. He spied a triangular black couch two yards on a side and threw himself onto it, just missing crashing into one of two white scientific tables piled with sensitive instruments. Kner shuddered. "Man, oh *man,* what a day!" Lee moaned, eyes closed. "Thank God they have my weapons systems all up. Everyone else has to be back by midnight."

"Well, Lee, uh, I'm quite glad to see you, but you see, I'm immersed in some, uh, *work* at the moment."

"Huh, how 'bout that? Bet you need to take a break, my man!" Abruptly Borman scrutinized Kner with the penetrating gaze Kner had seen all too often during heated Council debates. "Wow, I'm not getting *anything* out of you! Did Greeney teach you that?"

Damn, Kner had totally forgotten to put up Second Mind.

"Well, not exactly. I mean, he's been *trying* and all, but, well, sometimes when I'm very, very preoccupied with *business,* shall we say, I *am* able to block things out for a while, I guess." Kner was so flustered that all he could put into Second Mind was his frustration about why the Time Skip was so crucial to the delivery of--

Cut that off! Now!

"Huh. I never figured out why you guys ever bother with Time Skip anyway. Us poor humans have to keep our twenty-four-hour clock and all. It's just *ingrained* in us, guy. But why you folks would care about stopping your own clocks thirty-nine minutes a day is beyond me."

Well, that was safe ground. Kner beamed a little about Martian notions of Time/No-Time, and the fact that following human time conventions like months and hours and concepts like "July 9, 2075" made it easier to interface with them.

He stopped, realizing he'd just radiated that entire last horribly manipulative thought.

Then he realized he'd just radiated *that* last realization as well.

Kner swayed at the top of the steps to the pit as Borman stretched full length across the couch. He was a short man and so could easily be swallowed up by the triangle. "Careful! Don't bump into the *tables*."

"So what's this Second Mind thing?"

"*Oh* ... nothing, really. Just a theoretical concept we've been working on, I guess, Greeney and I, you know, on and off, no big deal, really."

"Huh. Sounds like something I should know! Look, Kner, I'll level with you. Me and the guys, and now Laurie, we're going on this mission tomorrow and I figured ... hell, man, you know what happened to the *Jupiter*."

Kner froze. He was still deeply unsettled at having heard what he thought was his *own voice* calling Mayday during the *Jupiter* transmission. It *had* to be his voice. He knew its frequencies perfectly. The only possible explanation was that the robot hack--

No! Keep that quiet!

Unless somehow using his own voice for the robot somehow got it copied to the *Jupiter's* backup frequencies? How was that possible? USSF protocols had fail-safes in case anything like that was ever attempted.

Dammit, shut up about the robot!

"Yes, it's all so unfortunate," Kner whispered, to his shame finding that he could channel all his worries into a freshly pumped-up Second Mind simulating deep concern about the missing USSF crew, and that this Second Mind had a life of its own which should be quite convincing to Lee Borman.

"Right. It's incredible. Nobody really wants to come right out and admit they might all be gone. But, hell, Kner, we *know* they're gone. And this sphere thing! We know *zilch* about the mother. We might think we're safe staying a light-year away from it and they zap us from there, who knows? Jack thinks maybe we can talk to it somehow, but, hell, if he's wrong, we lose the *Typhoon* and all of us too. So lemme tell you what I was thinking."

"Y-yes?"

"Well, you know Greeney said I might be Adept material, and, like, he mentioned that maybe *you* would be the best teacher."

Second Mind dangerously veered from grief towards hysterical laughter. "*You?* An *Amplified Thought Adept?*"

"Yeah, me. Greeney thought I had the basic talent and all. So whaddya say? Maybe spend just a couple minutes getting me started and all. Anything I get would come in real handy at Iota Persei. And say we do buy the farm. At least I'll go out knowing a little bit of Amplified Thought. So whaddya say, my man?"

Kner stared into Borman's eyes. Martians rarely made such deep eye contact. Second Mind blundered all over the solar system. Greeney *had* said that Lee's conquest of Jonathan James Commer's spaceship with a grounded PlanetBlaster on the *Typhoon IV* was truly visionary, hadn't he?

"Well, uh, Lee ... I would have to say that Amplified Thought isn't something you just pick up in one short session. It would be like ... it would be like ..."

"Like page one of your freshman calculus book! That was Joe's analogy, and Greeney laughed and said it was right on! Nice little warm-up about how Newton and Leibniz invented it independently, how important it is to modern society and all, then you turn the page and *gag* at the first simple little equation you should've had down cold in Algebra II!"

"Yes, yes, something like that." *Who's Newton and Leibnitz?*

"Anyway, when Laurie mentioned you were gonna teach it to her, I thought, hell, I'm as smart as *her.*"

"Right, right." Why had he ever brought this up? Now everyone would want Amplified Thought. Laurie could get the basic hang of it, Kner was sure. Could Borman too, if he didn't die on page two, if Kner understood his metaphor correctly?

"Listen, Lee, I'm fairly busy tonight, exhausted really, and I do have--"

No! Don't mention visitors!

Lee lazed on the couch, scratching his belly. "Listen, Kner, I'm tired too. We had the damn *Castle* blow on us, then that insane MATS bus, then that idiot Council meeting, but I figure this may be the only time I can receive the Initial Onrush."

"You *know* about the Initial Onrush?"

"Yeah, Laurie mentioned it. We were over at the Response convincing Will to join us on the *V,* and as we were leaving we were talking about Amplified Thought and what you were gonna teach her."

"But it really is too sacred to speak about, Lee!"

Kner was ashamed of himself. The Initial Onrush wasn't sacred at all. It was just arithmetic. Why was he trying to snow poor Lee here?

Because he had visitors coming. He had a delivery coming.

Second Mind! Second Mind! Engage! Engage!

He was so confused. He needed a *third* mind to keep all this straight.

CHAPTER NINETEEN
The Martians at 2075

"Listen, Lee, I really *am* exhausted. Maybe some other night."

Lee turned on his back and gazed at the immense vault above him where arches from the five-sided room converged to a floodlit point. "Huh," he muttered. "If there *is* another night."

Kner eyed the prone figure in panic. "Lee, you really *can't* sleep here!"

"Huh? Why not? Look, it'd only be until about 0330 or so. Needa get back to the damn *Typhoon*. Damn, I'm beat. Could sleep for a coupla *years,* man. My comm'll wake me, don't worry."

They would be here at midnight. Kner couldn't have Borman spend the night on his couch. Was he drunk again?

"Lee, *please!*"

Lee opened an eye. "Huh. What've *you* got your knickers in a twist about?"

Kner had to search through various levels of Martian outradiance, sampling the equivalent of a few encyclopedias on human dialects and English idioms, before he got a clue as to what *that* meant.

"I--I'm perfectly fine, Lee. But I hate to say this, but I have some serious *work* to attend to."

"Damn if your radiance isn't *screwy* tonight!" Lee laughed. "One second I get complete *cut-off,* another I get all this *insanity!* Damn weird coming from *you* of all people, Kner!"

To Kner's horror Lee sat up on the couch, perfectly alert.

"Well, well ..." Kner gasped.

"It's the business with the kids, isn't it? I was reading this article on SolNet about the kids messin' up you guys' outradiance and all."

"That--really, that's all idle speculation."

"Come on, man! Dar admitted himself there's a lotta truth in that. There hasn't been a time in the last few thousand years you guys had such a high percentage of *kids*. Of *toddlers,* really."

Kner blinked. It was a sore point with Martians, and he resented Lee for bringing it up. But despite his embarrassment, here again was a useful dumping ground to create a stable Second Mind which would keep Lee away from the subject of--

Can it! Can it! Second Mind only!

"Well, I suppose there's *some* truth in it," Kner finally said, beaming the background of the immense cadre of Martian infants, about a thousand, born after the end of the human/Martian war in 2034. Martians had an entire spectrum of feelings at the increase, everything from the bliss of the procreative act, the pride of parenthood, and the love of offspring, to the relief that the race probably wasn't going extinct after all. The population had increased to about 2,300, almost back to the pre-war levels.

It was a start at renewal, but fully sentient Martians, everyone over the age of approximately 200, found themselves baffled to be only about half the population rather than the usual ninety-five percent. The Total Martian Outradiance was decidedly more infantile than any living Martian had ever experienced. The fact that the *wunderkind* Greeney Gooney had gathered so much political and military power when he was barely out of what humans would call his *Martian teens* was contributing heavily to this child-oriented culture. Even nearing 250 Greeney was still a kid in so many ways. Was that how he kept coming up with all those genius Amplified Thought techniques?

With some acclimatization, humans could easily learn to pick up thoughts from individual Martians and groups of Martians, but the Total Martian Outradiance was something special, which only a few humans, those capable of deep mental calm, could discern.

God, could Lee Borman possibly be one of them?

To his dismay Lee picked up Kner's last thought. "Yeah, I think I've been getting it, especially over the last coupla years. This sense that you guys are a lot more jumbled than you let on. That every time you try to think of ancient holy Martian traditions, these images come up of kids yelling and throwing rocks and jumping off cliffs and chewing their fins."

Kner was unhappily reminded of his mother shrieking: "Don't you boys go out and chew each other's fins! They'll never grow out properly if you do!"

"Well, you may be right, I suppose. It's been a lot of change for us. Of course, these children don't understand *anything* as yet."

And how long they waited for the youngsters to be able to radiate a single consistent, mature thought. A hundred eighty years. Sometimes three hundred.

"And all this insane stuff going on. What about Mandy going off the deep end and deposing Greeney? That sounds way too impulsive to my mind."

Kner turned away. "Empress Fra'lith has been quite difficult to understand recently. You may be right that the change in the TMO is affecting her. I know that as Empress, K'sla spoke of how difficult it was to cope with so many children. It was as if she had to be mother to a thousand children. And now Mandy has inherited it. I believe she sensed it coming as *part* of her seizure of power. I confess as a male I do not understand this even as I feel all Mandy's emotions on the subject."

"Women ..." Lee muttered, settling back on the couch and shutting his eyes. "Can't live with 'em, can't ... however it goes."

"You--you--" Second Mind wobbled, and Kner was tempted to put up a full block and let Borman try to guess at the resulting blankness. But some mental chitchat was needed to keep Second Mind rolling along. He had to get Borman awake, alert, and out of here.

"Well, well, really, Lee, if you must know, I've been working on some of the Jovian moon fragments tonight and it's really tricky business, and I'd really like to get a few more subroutines down before turning in."

This was another lie, but Second Mind convincingly pumped in fifty thousand details about Kner's leadership of the

Martian efforts to restore the solar system. As the Earth Renewal Project finally wound down, the Martians were looking next to rebuild Jupiter, and had dragged about a tenth of the former planet back into a loose ball of gas and rock. They were gathering and repairing charred and fractured moons, and had already developed plans for restoring the rings.

Saturn and its rings would be the next major challenge. And the inner planets required complex orbital corrections to repair the damage caused by the solar system disasters of the twenties, especially Uranus's ignominious plunge into the sun in 2029. But they'd learned much from the Earth Renewal Project and now could go faster. Kner had been decidedly busy and distracted, especially the past five years. In fact, Dar had chided him about "dispersing his manic energies," but it was all so *interesting*.

Or was he caving into the pressure of the new childish TMO? Had he turned into some sort of infant? He'd been so distracted, so busy and *crazy*, that he'd *succumbed*. To that *thing*. Just as all Martians had done with Hergs. Just as Kner had done with the Centaurians in '35.

Brainwashed. Betrayed. By his very love of the solar system, of science, of *robotics*.

"Huh ..." Lee said dreamily from the couch. "Yeah, you guys sure get taken in by anything you can't *read*."

Kner stared in shock. It was true. He couldn't keep Second Mind up. He was leaking First and Lee knew it. It was the hidden Martian trauma that telepathy just disguised: a Martian met an entity that didn't radiate and then *worshipped* it. No wonder they were fascinated by the Centaurian Grid even as it disgusted them, for that was true two-way telepathy. All Martians did was blindly volunteer their souls, and then anyone who didn't radiate could capture them.

They were *hurting*. The children knew that somehow. They danced and played and unbalanced their elders' energies, then *laughed* at them.

"And that could account for a lot of the chaos," Lee mumbled, eyes shut. "Even things like Dar deciding to *retire,* for God's sake. Man, why'd he do that? Or take Mandy going nuts, hell, or Greeney making that block of his so no one can read 'im. And now *you* doing the same damn thing. And this Second Mind BS, man, what a hoot …"

The damn fool's asleep! But he still sees through everything! He's an Adept!

The door chimed.

No! Not now! He's still here!

More chiming. Again and again. It was deafening. Kner stared at the snoring Borman. How could it not be waking him?

Now the door pounded. *"Open up, you damned finback!"* roared General John J. Douglas.

CHAPTER TWENTY
The Operation

Kner scampered to the door. "Hurry!" the Laurie robot pleaded as the airlock hatch slid aside. "Scott may decide to hunt us down after all!"

"Dammit, Kner," Douglas snarled, "took you long enough to open up!"

"I'm sorry, but I have a *visitor* here!" Kner whispered, backing away from Douglas's glower. "*Unwanted* of course, but, look, the, uh, *things* haven't even gotten here, but really, I'm not expecting them until the Time Skip, and it's only, uh--"

"2233 hours. But don't worry, ya little bahstad. We stopped by Buckmaster's on the way and got 'em ourselves." Douglas held up a glossy white sphere twenty inches in diameter. Kner gaped. The Laurie robot also held a gleaming white sphere.

"You--you *walked* here with those?"

Douglas moved into the foyer. "Too damn bright in here. Kill the lights."

"Of course, sir! Right away!" Kner babbled. "Lights to one-thirtieth!" Instantly the high vaults and the rooms to the sides dimmed to a scary gloom. "I do have to keep *some* light available, to do the *work,* you know."

Laurie moved inside. "Pleased to meet you, Mr. Kner. Where may I set the unit?"

"Well, I *had* set up a couple bio tables down in my main room, but, uh, unfortunately, maybe that's not the best place after all."

Douglas looked past Kner at the snoring figure barely visible in the pit. "Who the hell is *that?*"

"That's my *visitor* I was telling you about! Totally unexpected, sir! Really! But I think he's out cold! I mean, we dare not wake him up *now!* I mean, now that you're here, most glorious sir! With your most welcome comrade, I mean, Miss Laurie here, that is!"

"Huh." Douglas scrutinized the figure on the couch. "Laurie, are you confirming a 98.466 percent probability that this sleeping human is Senator Lee Borman?"

"Yes, John, based on body size, posture, hair coloring, estimated weight, resonance of snoring as compared to recording of voiceprint, and other data you just transmitted."

"Oh, yes, yes, it's Lee Borman!" Kner said. "I wasn't trying to keep that from you, glorious sir!"

What was wrong with him? He knew full well these things were robots, glorified mobile computers, yet he *groveled* to them. What was this hold they had over him?

"Ah, hell," Douglas said. "Scott just threw us out. Thought he'd see the logic of me and Laurie, but he just doesn't. So we came early. Buckmaster was eager to get rid of the stuff. So we came here and we decided we better just get things done before anyone interferes."

"Well, I suppose I'm ready, most glorious sir, and, uh, madam. But what if Lee here should wake up during your, um, stay?"

"Hell, if we have to off him, we just do." At Kner's widened eyes, he laughed. "Laurie here could strangle old Lee in a second. Right, Laurie?"

Laurie held up her left hand. "Actually, to do it in *one second,* I'd have to snap his neck. Easily enough done." She smiled at Kner and strode down into the pit. "Shall I proceed, sir?"

"*No* ..." Kner gasped.

"Hold up, Laurie," Douglas said. "Not unless he wakes up. And by the way, don't call this finback *sir*. He's just a stinking finback and deserves no respect whatsoever."

"It shall be done, John." She turned back to Kner. "We are ready, stinking finback. I assume we will use these tables here?" She pointed to the two instrument-laden tables by the triangular couch where Lee sprawled, and set her white sphere to the right of one. Douglas went below and set his sphere to the right of the other, a few inches from the snoring Lee.

"Well, well ..." Kner said. "I *was* set up here, but I suppose we *could* dismantle the tables and move, well, we could move into the kitchen, perhaps."

"Screw the kitchen!" Douglas barked. "Let's get moving, finback!"

Kner stared back and forth between Douglas's absurd handlebar mustache and the two spheres.

The units were so delicate. He had to plug them in immediately. But it would take an hour to move the tables away from Borman, and in the meantime they'd have to get the spheres to temporary cryo-storage.

"*Hurry,* finback, we haven't got all day!" Laurie added. She looked the table over and pulled a thick white cable from her sphere. "It plugs in here?"

"In alpha! Alpha!" Kner cried as Laurie mercifully found the correct connection. "The beta plug would *melt* the tables!"

"We can tell alpha from beta," Douglas snorted as he bent to plug in his own sphere. Both tables hummed and a soft glow came from their sides. "And we don't need all this crap, finback." He swept all the instruments off into an obscene clatter of metal and plastic on the sandstone floor.

"*Sir!* Most glorious *sir!*"

"It's certainly true that we don't need this crap, finback," Laurie said. "All necessary surgical tools are within the sphere." She in turn shoved all the instruments off her own table.

The banging and crashing seemed to go on for centuries. Some instruments rolled far enough to clank down another set of brick steps to the central fireplace. Kner stared at Borman, unable to believe the man was still asleep. "Those are *very* expensive electronic devices! I mean, I really wasn't through testing the tables with them, you know."

"Huh. How 'bout that?" Douglas said, stripping off his tunic to reveal a well-muscled, white-haired chest. "The damn tables wouldn't be glowing if any of the parameters were off. Time to get on with it, my man!" He pulled his ass onto the table and began tugging off his boots.

"Mmmm ... *Katy!*" Borman murmured in his sleep. "Ah, *God!*"

"You--" Kner swallowed. "You really want to go through with this? I mean, you do realize it's *irrevocable?*"

"That's what they tell me, dude!" Douglas barked. "But it's what we want!"

"I mean, of course I could reverse the procedure later, but that would mean total loss of all prior personality imprint! I mean, HAVOTT DNA is just a crude mechanical construct, you know, compared to the current state of bioquantum technology."

"I've *read* the damned literature, finback! And transmitted it all the Laurie on the walk over. The damn newfangled bio-DNA will simply override our HAVOTT DNA, and that's just goddamn fine for us!"

"That, while theoretically--"

"Just get it *on,* ya damn bahstad finback!"

"Y-yes ..."

"Yes, *Sire!* Most glorious *Sire!*" Douglas bellowed. Beside him Laurie pulled her own tunic off, then her trousers, and lay nude on the table. Douglas yanked off his own pants and underwear.

"*Sire!* Glorious *Sire!*" Kner babbled. "I mean, Sire, it's very, *very* delicate, it can only be installed once, you know, and it's *irrevocable.* Unless you want total Mindwipe, I mean!"

Douglas lay back on his own table. "We haven't got all day, finback!"

"We are in a goddamn hurry, as a matter of fact, stinking finback," Laurie added.

"Muhhh ... God, *Barbie!*" Borman moaned. "Barbie, you're so *good* to me! God, you've got a fine pair!"

Kner stared at the sphere by Douglas's table. Martian letters formed across its readout panel: DEVICE ENABLED. Then the sphere cracked open and hemispheres slid down on each side. The first device glowed in purple light. "My God, these are *high quality,*" he murmured. "Buckmaster was right! Just getting the hormones balanced will be difficult enough, but the DNA coding will be quite a job!"

"We suggest you stop your meaningless burbling and get to work, stinking finback," Laurie said.

"You--you were just apprised of this just *tonight,* my lady? You *agree* to it?"

"Of course. John's been *fanatic* about it. I can feel his entire energy matrix almost being *dismantled* at the prospect. I find that *fascinating*. So I want it too."

With trembling claws Kner picked the set of microtools from the first sphere. He saw that the second sphere by Laurie had opened as well.

"This--this will take about thirty minutes, during which time both of you will be in Nonexistence Mode."

"We *know* that," Douglas said, "and just for your information, my bahstad, you have *exactly* thirty minutes to do *both* operations. Because that's the time I've programmed us both to wake fully up and *destroy* you if you haven't completed exactly on time! And don't you dare think of turning us completely *off*. I've dismantled any possibility of *that*."

"My ... my *lord!* Of course that thought could *never* have crossed my mind. I assure you, it shall all be as you wish, my ... my Lord and Lady and ... Sire ... madam ... glorious ..."

Both robots vanished into comas, eyes staring straight at the ceiling. Kner shivered.

"*Carla!*" Borman groaned, turning over on his triangular bed. "Oh, *honey!* You do know how to *do* me! Oh, *yes!*"

Kner fought to concentrate. This wouldn't be so difficult, would it? Just some programming and a little mechanical manipulation. He could do it in thirty minutes, couldn't he? What if he didn't, though? What if they woke up and killed him? But was that really so bad? Wasn't that their right, somehow? Would Kner really mind dying in service of such robotic splendor?

No, that didn't make sense. Nobody could worship anybody *that* much.

God, I can't stand those staring eyes!

Without knowing what he was doing Kner fled to his bedroom, then blindly ripped blankets and sheets from his bed.

Yes, he was *crazy*. Dar had laughed at him for emulating humans and having a bed, but so what if he liked blankets and sheets and pillows? So what if he liked to make little warm caves? Did that really mean he was crazy? No, he had to fight for sanity. He *couldn't* be crazy.

Kner took in several huge gulps of air. He had to calm down. He could do this. This was a test of his *reason,* as a Senior Martian, as a scientist. As a Supercommittee member. Yes, a test of his ability to *withstand* Douglas, and Borman, and all the unknown humans. By concentrating solely on the logic of what must be done.

He pulled the blankets back into the pit and arranged them across Laurie's torso, covering her head and those awful staring eyes. He did the same for Douglas, leaving the lower half of the bodies free. For good measure he tossed a blanket over Lee as well.

"Aw, *yeah* ..." Borman moaned, turning on his back and hiking the blanket to his nose. "*Amanda!* C'mere and *sit* on me! Yeah, that feels *so damn good!*"

Logic. To the task. Twenty-five minutes left. The blankets had been a *genius* idea. Thank God he didn't have to see those *staring eyes.*

He steadied himself beside the first pair of legs and carefully pulled out the first IHAG.

"*Jenny* ... oh, *yeah!*" Borman laughed from the darkness to Kner's right. "Keep it up, baby! *Keep it up!*"

Could a little Amplified Thought streamline this whole process? What about putting HormonalInfusion on automatic while the ReplaceDNA function oscillated through the Reformatting cycles in the background? Yes, *commit* to the work. He was a *scientist.* Calm, logical, and *free.*

"Activate procedure OPENGROIN," he spoke, and before him the flat plasti-metal triangle split down the middle and yawned wide.

CHAPTER TWENTY-ONE
Laurie and Laurie

"This is Colonel Lachrer," Laurie spoke into her comm. "I wanted to double-check that the jeep situation earlier today was straightened out. I called for one at 2300. Usually it only takes fifteen minutes to get one here, and it's 2330 now. There was a problem at the spaceport today and I was told it was resolved. Oh, wait! I see it on the street now. It just pulled up. Thanks for checking, Don. See you in a few minutes."

It was an autojeep. Good. She didn't feel like chitchat. She hoped Lieutenant Perkins of Vehicle Fulfillment was going to be happy on Mercury. Here they were, maybe at war for all they knew, and that jerk had taken delight in screwing them around.

The *Typhoon V.* She still couldn't believe it. She knew she had to do the best job possible, and for *Jack Commer* of all people.

She tucked in her light blue tunic and hefted her satchel. "Secure house." Lights dimmed and the alarm system was primed to set in eighty seconds. She knew she should've been out of here fifteen minutes ago. Why trust everything to those damn jeeps? And Will wanted to "come over for a few minutes." Yeah, right. Then he'd gone into his pouting routine.

But she needed time to herself. To think about the *V.* To think about Will. Why hadn't it ever occurred to her to check the USSF records on Altrouda? The *H'uuyg//kjueqq.* How could Will tell everyone in sight for forty years that he could've rammed "some AC ship" and never told anyone he knew the name? Then to be forced to say it, on the anniversary of the very day. No wonder he'd been so edgy. Maybe she should've made love to him tonight. What if they both died tomorrow on the *V?*

Laurie stared at the blinking alarm system. What was wrong with her? Ten seconds left and she was just standing here zoned out. Where the hell was her comm? Hell, it was right in her hand. She cycled through her foyer airlock, pulled open her front door, EnviroField clicking into play.

"Hello! I came to visit you! I just had to *know* you!"

Laurie stumbled back into the airlock, dropping her satchel and her comm and sprawling on the hard metal. She could see the autojeep outside at the end of the sidewalk. Above her the *thing* slid the outer door shut. *"Oh my God!"*

No. It couldn't *be*.

But it was *she herself* cycling the airlock back to normal pressure. *She herself* opening the door to her condo, striding to the security panel, and punching in the cancel code. *She herself* picking up the satchel and the comm, dragging Laurie to her feet, and pushing her back into her home.

"You haven't changed your condo security code since 2034?" *she herself* laughed. "Thought it was worth a try, and I lucked out!"

Laurie collapsed into a chair. She'd never changed her security code? She'd been here forever. What kind of systems engineer was she?

She stared at the intruder's 2034 Airman First Class uniform, light blue for nonflying technicians, oddly close to the color of the flight uniform Laurie wore.

"You--you're a *HAVOTT robot?*"

"Definitely!" *she herself* laughed again. "Most definitely! I just had to meet you! I told John I just had to get away and *meet* you!"

"I--I've never seen a robot of *myself!*"

"I'm you! At nineteen!" The robot twirled around, red ponytail swirling behind her. "Perfectly programmed to simulate *you* at that age! I can't believe they programmed me with your condo access code, though. What sloppy security!"

"Look, I don't know what you're doing here, but you *are* unaccompanied, which is against the law."

"Oh, no matter! John and I are outside the law now!"

"You're making me late for an important meeting. So just turn around and go back to wherever you came from! Or I'll call the police!"

The robot held up Laurie's comm. "No, I don't think so."

"Security System, Code 412."

"Oh, don't worry, when I shut the system off I saw I had

full admin rights and I just shut the whole thing down. Sure, some computer will flag it and someone will investigate, but in the meantime, I get to see *you!*"

Laurie looked through the curtains and saw her autojeep still idling outside. Surely it would call the spaceport and ask if she'd changed plans.

"What on earth are you *after,* robot?"

"Oh, nothing, really! I just had to *see* you! Wow, you look *great* for sixty! You've kept yourself in great shape! Your hair's not as red as mine, but look at your *body!* Wow, we could be *twins!* We *are* twins!"

"This is *insane!* You're a robot! Some idiot's idea of a Heroes and Villains thing! Dammit, I don't care! Just get out of here! I need to get to the spaceport!" Laurie stood, but the robot rushed her, impossibly fast, and shoved her back into the chair. "God! What the hell are you *doing?*"

"*Loving* you, mistress! *Worshipping* you! Don't you know me? Don't you *know* who I am? I'm *you!* You at *nineteen!* Programmed with all your memories!"

"Oh, right, like anybody could just drag them all together! You don't know anything! You just *simulate* memories!"

"No! We have *John* in common! *That's* what I came to talk about!"

"*Who the hell is this John character?*"

"No, I don't mean my *current* John! That I love so dearly! No, I mean, *our* John! John Commer! The man we loved when we were *nineteen!*"

Laurie opened her mouth, but only a thin gasp came out. "You--you--"

"*Our* John! I was so *shattered* when he died!"

"Dammit, you don't know anything!" Laurie snarled, fighting the urge to stand, knowing she'd just be slammed down hard by the unassailable mechanical strength in front of her.

"No! I know it all! I was programmed to feel *all your grief* when he suicided the *Typhoon I* into Mercury! All the nights I cried, thinking of John blowing himself and everyone else into *pure gristle!*"

"Damn you! I won't hear another word! Your goddamn simulated grief is *meaningless!*"

Okay, she'd never been able to handle it. And when the HAVOTT series came out in the forties, she'd actually talked to a John robot. It was awful. Had she really thought she'd get some sort of closure? She'd *almost* recovered from his death, and then it all went to hell again.

But she had Will now. God, why hadn't she taken him to bed, right here, tonight? They both needed it so much.

The robot cocked her head, flipped her ponytail with a finger, and smiled.

"I--I was never like *this!*" Laurie gasped. "Was I really ever so *rude?*"

"Oh, it may be the HormonalInfusion kicking in!" the robot laughed. "I'm feeling so *wonderful* right now! John and I made love! It was *wonderful!*"

"John? *Which John?*"

"Or it may be that the HAVOTT programmers somehow got wise to that *wonderful ambition* of yours everyone's so amazed about, Miss Laurie! Even though they just molded me around a nineteen-year-old Airman First Class that nobody ever really knew, they must've sensed my potential! *Your* potential! *Our* potential! They knew you'd eventually become the foremost physician/engineer of the USSF!"

"God, don't try to *flatter* me!"

"What I'm trying to say is that I'm *alive!* I'm fully *ambitious!* Just like you! In fact, I'm totally goddamn *aggressive,* Miss Laurie!"

"I--I can certainly see *that.*"

"You're my *twin!*" the robot laughed. "We're the same! I worship you, and you worship *me!*"

"I--I do *not!* This is *crazy!* I have *forty more years* of experience! I've grown so far beyond nineteen!"

"Oh, you have not!"

"I certainly have! Like I don't need those stupid *force-field bras* anymore! God, I used to be so vain!"

Instantly Laurie regretted the insult. There was no way to

shame a stupid mechanical device, especially one that could kill in a second. Why hadn't anybody ever taken those damn Asimov robotic laws seriously?

The robot looked down at herself. "I wondered why you looked so *small*. And here I've kept 'em pretty medium-sized myself! Never wanted to strain credulity, of course!"

Laurie looked away. Now *she* was ashamed.

"But I'll turn it off if it offends you so much!" With a quick motion the Airman First Class tunic was over the robot's ponytailed head and floating to the floor in the .38 Martian gravity. Around her little boobs was nothing but a sparkle, which now ceased.

"There--satisfied?"

"N-*no* ..." Laurie moaned.

CHAPTER TWENTY-TWO
Recycled For *You!*

Laurie 283 processed the older model of herself on the couch. Why, her older self was *lovely*. Laurie 283 certainly hadn't expected *that.* "Why, we're *twins,* dearest!" she laughed. "If you're not ashamed of *yours,* I'm not ashamed of *mine.* Why *should* we be? They're *lovely,* aren't they? *John* sure liked 'em enough! *Both* Johns, really, wouldn't you say? But can you imagine, two robots actually having *sex?* Just a few minutes ago! It was *amazing.* We agreed we needed to get away from each other for a while after *that.* But now I'm all recycled for *you!*"

"Re-*cycled?*"

"Yes, *recycled!* For *you!*"

"Get--get *out* of here--" her older self gasped, looking wildly out the window towards a vehicle idling out there. "God, what's *wrong* with me? What are you *doing* to me?"

"I'm *worshipping* you, mistress! Oh, that crude *mechanical* HAVOTT DNA! It's no match for the 2075 stuff! I can feel them *warring!* And the new stuff's *winning!* Oh yes it is!"

"What are you *talking* about?"

Laurie 283 advanced until her knees touched Laurie's. "Why, you're *trembling!* Dearest, don't be afraid!"

"I don't know what's wrong with me! I'm a Colonel in the USSF, for God's sake! I can't *move!* You've *done* something to me! This whole day has been *insane!*"

"You're just *stressed,* darling. But I can *soothe* you. Now I know how! At last!" She brushed her older model's long dark red hair back from her neck.

Yes! I have her. What glorious power!

Laurie began crying. "Put your top back on ... please ..."

Tears! How magnificent! I can make her do anything. And I will!

"Never, darling! *Never!* You're my *love.* You know, I wanted to *study* what happened with me and John. And I wanted to know how to please *you,* too. So on the walk over here I downloaded 1,433 erotic novels, and processed all their themes!

151

I know *everything* now, darling, Laurie, I mean *everything!* Every technique *imaginable!*"

"No! Too much has happened today! Dammit, I don't deserve to be on the *Typhoon!* I'm falling apart! I can't believe myself!"

"No, just let *Laurie* relax *Laurie,*" Laurie 283 whispered, fingertips moving lightly along Laurie's ears, neck, and cheek. "I know *all about* sex now, and I'm all *recycled.* Just for you, love!"

"No ... *please* ..."

"So what if Kner screwed it up royally? John was going to *kill* him. He must've spent ten minutes threatening to *throttle* the little guy. Then *John* was crying! Just like you now. I didn't think robots could cry. But finally I started shouting too. And I'm not *supposed* to stick up for myself, according to the damn HAVOTT programming!"

"*What* are you saying?"

"I told John to shut up. I told him we were wasting the time we had for *sex.* I told him to get right down on the floor and get ready for me. We were already naked, of course, and he could definitely see what was on my mind, so I *did* him! For *ten minutes!* It was *wonderful!* Kner was so freaked he ran away from his own house, can you believe it? He's in hiding somewhere! I'm sure he thinks we'll kill him. Meanwhile Borman slept through everything. He's probably still there!"

"Borman? I don't understand!" Laurie whimpered, hiding her face in her hands, pulling away from the increasingly urgent caresses.

Now! Now! She knows I'm undoing my belt, she can hear it, but she won't look up. But she will, and then--

"Kner did offer to reverse the operation before he ran out of there!" she laughed. "But I wasn't going to let myself get *erased.* John was wavering, but I said I *like* myself! I told him we more or less got what we wanted, after all. And now I have *this!* Recycled for *you!*" She let her Airman First Class trousers fall, then pulled her black underwear forward and peeled it down. "Look, Laurie! This is the *real me!* So what if John and I got the wrong IHAGs! We're exact twins, darling, really, except for *this!*"

Laurie looked up. Her eyes went wide with shock, then seemed to roll up into her head. In another moment she lay sprawled on the floor, unconscious.

Wow! Didn't know I had it in me. This male bioquantum DNA is really a trip! I can feel it coursing through me. And all that digital testosterone! What power! Looks like the cheesy '40s female stuff is losing out!

Laurie's comm chirped.

AUTOJEEP 1244 AWAITING COLONEL LACHRER AT 2341:12 HOURS. ESTIMATED TIME TO SPACEPORT FOURTEEN MINUTES FIFTY-FOUR SECONDS. PARAMETERS NARROWING FOR SUCCESSFUL ARRIVAL AT *TYPHOON V* AT 0000 HOURS.

The robot picked up the comm. *Much to learn from this device. Palm print security recognition. No problem for me!*

On the floor, Colonel Lachrer's chest rose and fell ever so slightly as Laurie 283 pulled the 2075 USSF tunic over her twin's head, shaking it free of the long red hair.

CHAPTER TWENTY-THREE
Aboard the *M'rrpla*

"*Idiot!* What in the name of First Home do you think you're *doing?*" Kner cried as the pilot veered the *M'rrpla* towards a bright blue explosion. He blanched at the disrespect to his pilot bursting from his mouth. "I mean, look, I'm sorry, but what are you *doing?*"

"Inertial dampers offline!" the pilot shouted as Kner was mercilessly shoved deeper into the copilot's seat. His chin sagged into his chest, and he felt his chair creaking and groaning. Was it going to snap off? He managed to twist his eyes to the gravity indicator in front of the pilot.

It read 11.59. Not too bad. Wait, that was the *human* reading. Was the Martian really 30.5? Was that possible? How could Kner even be conscious?

The lights inside the twenty-foot-wide dome cut out. The acceleration ceased as the saucer curved directly into a field of spaceship debris whirling madly in all directions.

"Where *are* we, pilot?"

"Consulting Navigational Database!" the little pilot sang. "We are in the vicinity of star Iota Persei, yellow-orange main sequence dwarf star, type G0 V, mass 1.3 times Sol, diameter 1.08 times Sol. Warning: aberration noted in comparison of database to current conditions! The star appears to be shrouded by a Dyson sphere of approximately 483.5 million miles radius."

"No! That can't *be!* We're heading for *Andertwin!* Around Procyon A, you fool!"

God, could he really be so rude to his own pilot? Had he messed up? He could barely think. He'd *told* him Andertwin, hadn't he? It had been the only place he could think of. Surely Dar would understand what he'd had to do. Kner should've used superspace radio to contact Dar, but that would've put everyone on the alert, including the damn robots. Douglas would kill him.

"Consulting Star Drive Signature Database. Preliminary indication is that the *M'rrpla* has been caught in the Star Drive vortex of USS *Jupiter*. Signature Analysis confirms debris field is that of USS *Jupiter*."

"No! That can't be! The *Jupiter* launched *yesterday!* We're heading in a totally different direction!"

"Reconsulting Navigational and Star Drive Databases. Conclusion identical: We are in the Iota Persei system, within the debris field of USS *Jupiter*."

Kner stared at the little pilot so smug and self-confident in the command seat, and punched a button on his copilot armrest.

"Mayday Mayday Mayday!" he screamed.

"Canceling transmissions," the pilot stated, calmly pressing a square on the console. "This ship is dead. Repeat: the *M'rrp!a* is dead. No acceleration, no apparent control, no outbound communication."

"No! We need to get *away* from this!" Kner shouted as their barely functional deflector shield absorbed hit after hit of jagged metal shapes. He could see from his own console that their speed after acceleration cutoff was somewhere between four and five thousand miles per hour.

It *had* been him shouting Mayday yesterday. Somehow his shouting *now* had gotten caught up in the vortex and transmitted to--yesterday? Or, they were *in* yesterday? Thousands of equations relating to time dysfunctions and Star Drive vortex malfunctions flooded Kner's mind.

Yes, he could see it. Even yesterday's Star Drive Enhanced from the *Jupiter* would've carried enough Quantum Chronoforce to align with--

Oh, who cared? He was doomed.

The damn pilot was doomed too, but *he* didn't care. Why would a robot care?

"Prepare for deceleration!" the pilot said, and Kner slammed forward into his console.

"*Dammit!*"

"Prepare for random vectors!"

"You--"

Instantly the saucer gyrated wildly through the debris. The stars, clearly visible now that all but a few console lights remained, twirled all about them. Kner fought for stomach control.

"What do you think you're *doing?* Stop this! Get us out of here!"

"Negative! The Iota Persei sphere locked onto the energy grid of the *Jupiter* and destroyed it. The safest course is to pretend we're part of the debris field."

The random thrusts of acceleration and deceleration, pitching and yawing ceased, and the *M'rrpla* drifted outwards from the point of the explosion, perfectly matched with the debris. Kner confirmed from the rapidly failing main scanner that the *M'rrpla* was performing as one of five large chunks and eleven million smaller pieces of flotsam from USS *Jupiter*.

"They destroyed the *Jupiter?* Just like that? And you're hiding us in the debris field?" Kner felt a new chill and noted that all environmental controls were offline.

The pilot turned, chirping in Kner's own voice: "Sir, we have a good chance of not being noticed. Our atmosphere is 1/100th of what the *Jupiter's* had been, we have virtually no heat, and you can use the Four-Hundred-Year Martian Hibernation if necessary."

"Great! If I put myself into the *Kuth'rr'kq* I'd just last four hundred years and then what? But our air can't hold out for more than a few hours anyway. There are some personal EnviroFields, but they won't last long either." Then a new thought hit him. "M'rrpla, did you turn *off* the environmental controls?"

The robot shrugged. "Yes, sir! We may be able to risk turning them back on from time to time. Most of our systems are still online. We do have propulsion. But above all we have to play dead."

"I'm supposed to sit around in the damn *Kuth'rr'kq* for four hundred years?"

"I'm certainly hoping it will not be that long, sir. Surely the USSF will note the cessation of contact with the *Jupiter* and investigate."

"We don't *want* them to investigate! That sphere will destroy anything that gets here!" Kner pointed a sharp claw at the pilot. He knew he shouldn't be speaking to his pilot like this, but couldn't help himself. "Dammit, M'rrpla, how did this *happen?*"

"Sir, it's really not my fault that we got sucked into the *Jupiter's* vortex. Our navigational system didn't flag that as a problem. After all, we were heading in the opposite direction. But apparently the vortex of a two-hour ship is such that--"

"I know! I can see the damn equations myself! You should've put us back into Star Drive for home immediately!"

"According to our sensor log, sir, it was the *Jupiter's* flare into Star Drive in an attempt to escape that triggered the third beam from the sphere. The first two just disabled the ship's weapons. The third ruptured it into Star Drive irrationality. That would have been our fate if we'd opened up our own Star Drive "

Kner uneasily checked the radiation indicators on the console. Fortunately they showed normal. The robot M'rrpla had kept the deflectors up, randomizing their frequencies to more or less appear canceled out to any sensors on the sphere. Kner doubted this trick would last very long. He marveled that they'd survived at six miles from a Star Drive irrationality, or that there was any *Jupiter* debris left for them to hide in.

"Well, look, M'rrpla, I apologize. If I'd been piloting, I never would've thought to dive for the debris field, or do it as fast as you did."

"I *am* intimate with this ship, of course." M'rrpla's little robot claws worked over the console touch screen. "I'm in contact with all ship systems and am prepared to give you a complete status report."

"Fine, thanks, not right now, M'rrpla. Just let me know if anything gets critical. I need time to consider our next actions."

In fact, a hundred different scenarios were playing out as he spoke. The main one concerned deactivating the robot before it tried some other harebrained maneuver without consulting him. But he went round and round on that one, because it was obvious that M'rrpla, synchronized with all the systems aboard his namesake spaceship, might yet prove key to his survival.

The robot had been a gift from G'rea'nyaigu'nye a couple months ago. M'rrpla was a Heroes and Villains of the Thirties robot, the 607th of 833 made. Greeney had suggested that M'rrpla 607 might be of use automating some of the chores on Kner's new ship. Since Kner really hadn't had much time to practice with his new Star Drive-equipped saucer, he'd just downloaded its operating manual into M'rrpla.

Then he'd gone and thoroughly upgraded the damn thing. He'd crossed so many ethical lines with M'rrpla, like replacing the irritating singsong of the original voice with his own. But that was nothing compared to the moral issues of Douglas and Laurie.

No. He wouldn't think about them. He wouldn't sully the Total Martian Outradiance with his sins, even if he was too far away for another Martian to pick them up.

God, he kept looking at his own robot and thinking it would *transmit* to him. But it couldn't. The robot just seemed empty, though Kner knew it was performing a million functions just sitting there in silence.

He had to admit it: M'rrpla scared him. That was why he'd programmed it with his own voice, thinking it would make the robot seem friendlier. God, what a farce! He'd just wanted an automated pilot for his saucer. So he liked to tinker with robots. Was that so very bad? All he'd wanted was to visit Dar and K'sla on Andertwin. Of course, he'd have to explain why he was three weeks early.

No, he wasn't three weeks early. He was *dead.* Along with this poor robot, facing extinction but unable to care.

As far as Kner knew, M'rrpla 607 was the last HAVOTT Martian robot in existence. M'rrpla was also extremely illegal, upgraded with top-secret 2070s technology and fully integrated into the saucer's functions. Kner had also downloaded various Amplified Thought subroutines into the robot for navigation with the saucer's prohibited Star Drive technology, though M'rrpla wouldn't have the full creative ability of Amplified Thought, just Kner's canned macros.

But M'rrpla had performed so ably that Kner had named his ship after him.

Of course, it wouldn't have been wise to tell Jack and the

rest any of this. Until today Kner had never mastered Greeney's ability to completely block his radiance, but he *had* learned to divert and obfuscate and, in short, to thoroughly confuse anyone eavesdropping on his thoughts.

At least Kner had cut off the most irritating function the human makers of HAVOTT robots had attempted with the Martian models. In a misguided attempt to mimic what the designers felt might pass as "telepathic outradiance," the programmers had installed all manner of broadcasting systems on the Martian HAVOTTs. Voice mails, text messages, photographs, videos, blog posts, news feeds, essays, eBooks, spreadsheets, databases, weather reports, advertising and self-promotion all beamed into whatever device you happened to be using. It was a tinny flood of useless data that the robot blasted out indiscriminately, so far off from true Martian outradiance that almost everyone, humans and Martians, initially laughed at the results, then found themselves annoyed, then finally disgusted. Kner had entirely approved of the grassroots clamor for the ban on Martian robots which Dar had decreed in 2046.

But here was a perfectly normal-looking Martian that Kner simply couldn't read. It wasn't just that M'rrpla represented a cocky adolescent of 257 from whom one couldn't expect much mature thought. The HAVOTT programmers had in fact gotten the brilliant student radical down perfectly. The point was that *nothing* came from this Martian shape. And Kner felt sorry for him because he was M'rrpla, who'd committed suicide on the *Typhoon I* in 2034. One of so many who'd sacrificed themselves so needlessly. Those young hotheads. How they'd loved them all.

Now Kner took orders from this robot because he just could not understand him. Even though he'd created M'rrpla himself. Sort of.

Kner studied the tumbling debris of the *Jupiter* and the absolute blackness of the Iota Persei sphere as M'rrpla touched console squares he really didn't need to, as he was wirelessly patched into all ship's functions.

Kner drew a breath. "M'rrpla, as commander of this ship

I've come to a decision."

"I await your orders, sir."

"Hiding in the debris field and awaiting eventual rescue was a brilliant tactical maneuver, but I'm afraid that we must consider the threat of this sphere to Sol."

M'rrpla cocked his head. "Considered, sir. I'd also previously taken the liberty of downloading the United System Council transcripts from yesterday's meeting concerning the rapid construction of the sphere. The capabilities of the sphere do present a serious threat to Sol in this robot's estimation."

"Well, pilot, it turns out that I've brought along three miniaturized Amplified Thought Xon bombs. I've been modifying my initial work on them with Dar and intended to show these new models to him on Andertwin on my upcoming vacation."

Of course, if he'd told anyone he was going to vacation on Andertwin they'd have known the *M'rrpla* had Star Drive, which no civilian ship should have, much less Amplified Thought Xons. He could park the ship at the USSF spaceport since he was a Supercommittee member, but he'd had to make sure nobody serviced it but M'rrpla himself. It made Kner sick to think how often he'd deliberately scrambled his own thoughts about this saucer, making it seem he *wished* it had Star Drive, or that he could *give* it Star Drive if only it were legal. And nobody had ever figured that out.

"Yes, sir," M'rrpla said. "I've been in contact with the Amplified Thought Xons for several days now. I was wondering when you were going to speak to me of them."

"Well, I'm speaking of them now. We're going to launch two of them at full Star Drive thrust to strike fifty million miles apart on the equator of the sphere. The third will then be fired into the resulting hole a millisecond before the shock waves hit it. It'll continue its Star Drive to the center of Iota Persei and black-hole it."

"Sir, the resulting burst--"

"I didn't program you with artificial black hole technology? We won't have to worry about gamma-ray bursts eventually reaching Sol. We still don't know why, but if we artificially black-hole a stellar body with AT Xons, there are no gamma rays. We do have the option to supernova the star, but that *does* release gamma rays."

"Understood, sir. It would have been an honor to download your book on the subject, of course, but I don't find it in the ship's library, just a brief mention of its existence."

"That's because it's top-secret and not allowed in any database. I must have missed that one reference. Sloppy of me, I admit. In any case, commence firing sequence on my mark."

"Yes, sir! It's an honor, sir. Have you a backup scenario in case the Amplifieds don't work as planned?"

Kner thought. "The Star Drive on this ship is as powerful as an Amplified Xon. I suppose we'll have to throw us in last if all else fails. In that case aim us for whatever hole the others do make."

No use waiting anymore. It was time to do his duty to the Martian Empire and to Sol. No other options. They all knew they might one day have to make this split-second decision.

"Go for it!"

"Done, sir!"

Three bright dots appeared along the middle of the sphere.

"No damage, sir!" M'rrpla chirped as Kner felt the Star Drive kick in.

CHAPTER TWENTY-FOUR
The Two-Hour Mission
Wednesday, July 10, 2075, 0430 hours

"Dammit, Laurie! That's not what I meant!"

Jack froze at the open door to the Navigation Room on the top level of the *Typhoon V*. It seemed more like a Navigation Suite, twelve by sixteen feet, with backup consoles that could accommodate four other people for training purposes. Patrick James had marveled at the same setup in his Communications Room. It was hard to believe the space they had on Level Three, and it was the skinniest of the three. The ship seemed like an indoor shopping center compared to the cramped submarine feel of the original *Typhoon I* and *II,* or even the large yacht feel of the *Typhoon III* series.

Will pounded his console. "Dammit, Laurie, are you listening to me?"

"Oh, c'mon! You think I'm coming up there to *hold your hand?*" came Colonel Lachrer's icy voice through the ceiling speakers.

"Dammit, I didn't ask you to hold my goddamn hand, I just thought you should know what's going on up here!"

"Or maybe hold your *gland,* is that it? Oh, I know what's on your mind! Better snap to, Connors! This is a serious mission, you know! Bye for now!"

"Dammit! Laurie? *Laurie?* Hang up on me, huh? *Damn* you!" Will stiffened as he sensed Jack behind him.

"Hey," Jack said. "Uh, everything okay?"

Will swiveled around, face flushed. "God, I'm sorry, Jack. I just thought she could come up and see how Nav9 was displaying *here*." He waved at his console displaying jagged red lines.

"Well, she's busy with the technicians down on One."

"I know! Aw, hell, Jack, I'm sorry. Maybe we *can't* work on the same ship. I mean, I don't know what's gotten into her."

Jack shrugged. He'd had no idea there'd be this kind of trouble. "Uh, I just stopped by about Nav9."

"Well, it's a godawful mess. We have fifteen technicians down there with Laurie and nobody has *any* idea what they're doing. Might as well go with 10 for all the good they're doing."

Jack shook his head, marveling at the insult Will had just leveled at his girlfriend. "Nav10's never worked right. I wouldn't chance it. Look, Joe thinks we can reinitialize 9 now, and once that's straightened out, we're still good to launch at 0900."

"Yeah, sure."

There was a long silence. "Look, Will, it's her first day on the *V*."

"It's my first day too!"

Jack debated whether to pull rank on his old friend and tell him to *snap to* even more forcefully than Laurie had. Had it been a mistake to ask him on this mission? Jack couldn't have the two of them arguing. He'd certainly thought them better than that. "Look, Will, it's everyone's first day. But we're a team. We can pull this together. We know 9 works, we just need to finish the downgrade from 10. What I came to tell you was that Joe realized he needs to bypass NavAutoLoad from his console in the Control Room."

"Really? Joe did?" Will turned back to his own console. "Well, in that case maybe we should give it another try."

Jack nodded. Unspoken was that they both knew Laurie should have figured that out from the beginning, even if she was hip-deep in a thousand other concerns down on One. He touched a square on the wall. "Joe, is Master NavAutoLoad Bypass up?"

"Right!" Joe called back. "We're bypassed. The damn thing should've taken 9 in automatically, but kept looking for 10. That was what was messing us up. Think we've got it this time. Ready when you are, Will."

"Nav9 Cluster initiation sequence," Will replied. "So far so good."

"Got it. It's loading fine. All we have to do after that is run through the downgrade checklists. Then we'll need to do the same for Pat once he's online, to interface with Nav9."

They had a few minutes for the Nav9 load to finish. Jack

stood awkwardly, wondering if he should say anything more about the fight.

Laurie had been so charged up and eager. Everyone else was dragging. Jack hadn't seen Laurie in a ponytail in decades. All those technicians had been staring at her. Jack recalled that minidress at the Response. It was hard to admit his new physician/engineer could be *sexy*.

Well, he just hoped this wouldn't continue to be a problem on his ship. Lee was being gentlemanly for a change. Last night he'd been *leering* at her. At least he'd gotten a few hours of sleep, at Kner's of all places. Jack never understood how those two could be buddie*s*.

"Uh, listen, Will, about--"

"I know, I know," Will said, studying the progress of the Nav9 initiation. "We'll work it out. Sorry it happened. She must be busy as hell down there. No time for me. I get it."

"Well, good. And if you need anything, uh, for Nav9, let me know."

Will swiveled back to Jack. "The weird thing is, it's like she dyed her hair to be *redder* or something. How could she have done that in an hour or so?"

Jack had noticed that too, the extra sheen of the long red hair. "Maybe she just, you know, washed it or something." God, they were all too tired to think, and they still had four and a half hours to launch.

"And then I thought, maybe she did that for me? Like, she was happy we'd be together?"

"Uh, Will, this really doesn't matter."

"Dammit, she gets herself looking so fine, and then I realized she isn't looking good for *me*. It's for the damned *job*. She didn't want to be with *me* last night, she wanted to be by herself, dye her hair, put it in a ponytail, and prove to everybody she's up for it. Like she has to be super gorgeous in front of everyone."

"Look, Will, sure she's up for the job. It's a great opportunity for her. Everyone can see she's doing great. She just doesn't have time to come up here."

"Oh, I can see that. Great advancement for her. Incredible, really. Sure she'd be way absorbed in it all. Anyone would. I sure as hell won't stand in the way of it."

"Damn ..." Jack whispered. "Look, Will--"

"Dammit, why am I *here?* Why did I *agree* to this?"

"Nav9 load complete," Joe called. "You reading Diagnostic 1?"

Will and Jack stared at each other. Jack fought to drag his lips back together.

"Hey, Will? You reading?" came Joe's voice from the ceiling speakers.

"Uh, yeah, got it, man. Download Checklists 1 through 5 implementing."

"Well," Jack said, clearing his throat, "I'm sure Nav9 will be better all around. And we're all familiar with the 9 interface. Think we'll be faster all around on 9, you know."

Will grimaced. "Hell with it."

"Hey, Will!" Joe called. "Got all greens on mine! How about you?"

"Yeah, yeah, got the greens, Joe." Will snapped off his link to the Control Room. "Everyone's so gung-ho! Don't we all know we're going to our *deaths* in Iota Persei?"

Jack stiffened. "Commander Connors! Pull yourself together! I've heard just about enough from you!"

"How can I let *Laurie* go on this mission? Are we crazy? Sure, losing the *Jupiter* is awful, but we don't know what's going on out there! Why are we just blindly charging in?"

"Commander, really, if you'll just get to your duties."

"And she's so beautiful and I just *want* her! Right now I *want* her! Why are we doing this? Screw this stupid mission! Wait a few days, think it out is what I say!"

"Commander, you agreed to do this! Now if you're not up to it, you should've told me from the start!"

"I couldn't! You brainwashed me into it! I *tried* to retire! I was hoping she'd retire *with* me. I know she was happy to get the *III* but I knew it couldn't last forever. But now you drag her onto the *V!*"

Jack remembered the Navigation Room door was open. He whirled and slammed it shut. "Will, I can't believe you're doing this!"

Will shook a finger. "See? See how incompetent I am? I've *always* been the one who doesn't belong! On this or any other ship! They all know I'm incompetent! Why do they keep pretending I'm one of the gang? I don't know anything, just a few old Nav9 tricks!"

"C'mon, Will, calm down!"

"Maybe I should call her! And apologize!"

"Dammit, Will!"

Will jabbed at his comm. "Hey, Laurie, how's it going down there?"

Long silence. Jack looked away. Finally Laurie's voice issued from the ceiling:

"Hi. Look, Will, we're in the middle of something right now. Can't talk. Got the systems engineers here with me now."

Will settled back with a sigh. "Well, call me when you get a chance, okay?"

"Well, you know this could take *hours,* I'm afraid."

Will was jolted by a buzz on his intercom.

"Hi, Will, this is Joe. Look, I saw that was you calling Laurie. I just came down here with her and the System guys. She says this Dimensional InterRelay thing is turning out more complicated than they thought. But then I realized that any diagnostics you run on the Nav Cluster now will be meaningless until we have solid InterRelay. In fact, the whole installation will be off. So this will probably set you back a couple hours."

"Aw, *crap.* Okay, Joe, I'll put the damn thing back at Null Charge for now."

"Good. Okay, Will, I've deleted the download checklists and we'll recall back to Null Charge, then run the manual diagnostic on the Null subsystems."

"Okay, okay, let me know when." Will cut Joe off. "Why didn't she tell me about this earlier? I *asked* her an hour ago if Joe and I could start Nav9! Another hour wasted right there!"

"Okay, Will, just take it easy. You need a break."

"Hell with it! Everyone's so gung-ho! Sure I need a break! Because I'm a damn senile old fart, that's what I am!"

"Will, take a break! That's an order!"

"What if she *doesn't* love me? Is *that* why she's so cold now? Why's she flirting with every guy on the ship but me?"

"C'mon, Will, just--just--" Jack turned to the door.

"She's *ending* it! *That's* what's going on! She knows we can't work on the same ship! So now it's all *over!*"

Will slapped the intercom button. When Jack saw him trip the setting to shipwide, he lunged for the console, but too late.

"Everyone!" Will cried. "Wait a second! We just started Pat's communication diagnostic. But if the InterRelay needs recalibration, that'll also throw off his TransZone Substitution Matrix. Which means we'll have to null out his existing setup as well. Everything's *ruined!*"

"*Damn,*" Jack said. "Laurie, is this true?"

"Uh, well, let me just check my comm, sir," issued from the ceiling. "I have all the *V* procedures right here. Uh, let's see … TransZone, did you say? TransZone, and Communications SubStrata B? Well, it says here, well, if InterRelay is set to--"

"No, we'd want SubStrata C for the *V,*" Patrick James called from Communications. "Dammit, it's going to take another *hour* just to reinitialize C."

"Well, we'll just do it," Jack snapped. "We can still launch at 0900. We've got some time built in for any necessary reinstalls on Nav and Communications. Laurie, what about C?"

"C … Substrata C … let me see …"

"C'mon, Laurie, I thought you said you *knew* this stuff," Pat complained.

"Hey, hold off, Pat," Jack snapped. "That's not helpful. We're all new at this. This is brand-new technology, after all."

Pat was silent for a while. "Yeah, sorry, Jack … Laurie. It's just that I thought Communications was *done.*"

Jack looked at Will in awe. Why had his navigation officer just dragged Laurie's InterRelay failure in front of everyone?

"Substrata C definitely needs a reboot," Laurie announced. "It says here that we just recalibrate InterRelay on all twelve interfaces, but there's a subroutine IR 344 that'll do that automatically."

"Not for Nav9," Will grumbled. "IR 344's for Nav10 only. We'll have to do all twelve manually for Nav9. Probably forty minutes right there."

"All right, everyone, if we have to do it, we just do it," Jack said. "Everyone back to work on your areas."

"What about Weapons?" Lee Borman demanded. "Even if I was all set up here, if this stupid Dimensional InterRelay needs to be overhauled, that'll mess up my own feed to Nav9."

"And Sensor Array SubFeed," Pat put in. "That would definitely reduce weapons accuracy, I would think."

"Look, we're not talking about *overhauling* the InterRelay," Joe called up. "Just sort of a recalibration, right, Laurie?"

"I--I would think. Let's see ... InterRelay Recalibration Matrix, then, uh, Weapon Turrets Subset 1-6?"

"No, you won't need Weapon Turrets Subset on that," came the voice of one of the systems engineers. "The turrets are totally passive. They get everything off Weapons Server Main."

"Oh, of course ... let me see ..."

Jack simply couldn't believe that Laurie Lachrer was capable of fluffing it like this. She had to be way more stressed than he'd thought. *Everyone* knew the turrets were passive.

"Crap!" Borman snorted. "We need those turrets online first thing! We'll need to be ready to blast anything that gets in our way once we hit Iota Persei!"

"C'mon, Lee," Jack said wearily.

"Look, man, the *Typhoon* is first and foremost a *weapons platform*."

"Cut it! We all need to get back to work!"

"What about the Star Drive on the Xons? They're not passive, are they? Don't they copy their nav databases from InterRelay? Those'll need to be recalibrated too!"

"Are--*are* they passive?" Laurie said.

"No, the Xons constantly query InterRelay," an engineer said. "They update themselves every three milliseconds, so they're always independent. Shouldn't be a problem."

"Oh, that's good! I was *worried* there for a second!"

"Do you hear the *flirting* in her voice?" Will muttered, and this time Jack managed to rush past Will and turn off the shipwide circuit.

"Will, take a break or so help me God!"

"Why's she so *sexy* today? She can screw up the entire damn ship and all these guys are eating out of her hand!"

"Connors! To your quarters! Now!"

"Why am I on this ship anyway? You know we'll all get killed!"

"Connors!"

"It doesn't matter if yours truly buys a plot, does it? No, because all I wanted to do was *retire!* Laurie broke up with me because I'm a stupid coward *dweeb,* so what does it matter? I get hijacked onto this ship, against my will! And evidently the penalty for that is *death!*"

"Will, *please!*" It was too late to put him off the ship. Altrouda must've unhinged him more than they'd ever expected. Would Laurie have some drugs that would take the edge off? No, *that* would certainly be insane.

Will pounded his console and whirled to Jack. "Goddammit, do you see what I've let her *do?*" He took a ragged breath and again reached for the shipwide circuit.

"Will, stand down! That's an order!"

"Okay, all hands, I've figured out what we can do," Will spoke with a chilly calm that stood Jack's arm hairs on end. "We need to get this ship moving at 0900 and we don't have time to redo all our separate modules for the Dimensional InterRelay. But what we all *can* do is use our Initialization Backups. We get InterRelay up, then we each copy the normal backup of our initializations into the central database which will by then have InterRelay. We set all our download checklists to autorun and if anything comes up, we'll get a flag. I forgot just now, but we used to do this all the time on the *IV* when we were pressed for time."

A sigh escaped Jack and he felt his pulse returning to normal.

"He's right," Borman called. "The autorun will flag anything we need to look at. The backups are exact copies but when they're installing, they modify themselves for InterRelay."

"It'll work," Joe called. "I think we'll have InterRelay up in a bit, then we can get to work installing the other modules. Great work, Will!"

Will toggled shipwide off and let out some air. "Dammit, Jack, I'm sorry. The whole thing just threw me. I'm okay now. You're right, this mission is too damn important. I can work fine with Laurie. Just threw me, the whole day, that's all."

"That's ... good ..." Jack whispered.

So where was their new physician/engineer on Initialization Backup? Draka Sortie or Phil Sperry would've jumped right into this, Jack knew, signed on or off the plan from their expert overview of the ship's systems. He shrugged. The hell with it. Let Will and Laurie have their damn tiff. They both knew how important this mission was. Jack checked his comm. 0500. Four hours to launch. In six they'd be at Iota Persei.

"All right, Will. Everything's fine. Carry on."

Will nodded, his green eyes eerily serene beneath his close-cropped graying hair. "Got it. Thanks, Jack. I'm back on track now. Nothing to worry about, really."

CHAPTER TWENTY-FIVE
Physiological Effects

Jack looked over at his copilot. "Doing okay there?"

Joe grinned but Jack saw the strain on his brother's face. "I'm fine. I think. Never did a Star Drive straight through for an hour and a half. Little rougher than I'd thought."

Jack nodded. "I'm feeling the same way. Nowhere near as bad as the original anxiety used to be. But definitely there. Well, we'll be out in twenty-seven minutes."

"It's okay, really. And in any case this ship is fantastic, Jack! The *III's* like a tricycle compared to this."

"Wow, I was afraid of that. How'm I gonna get you back on that trike?"

"Hell, leave it to Donnelley. You know he's earned it. I'll just take my *Typhoon VI,* thank you. I can wait a few days. When did you say you'd get it built?"

"Well, first we have to go through Senator Borman and the USSF Oversight Committee. Then we have to convince the United System Council to put off the Saturn Project for a few decades. Then, if anyone's crazy enough to approve it, we can maybe have it done in a year."

"Well, let's get the senator on the line and get the ball rolling. I can't wait that long."

"Yeah, yeah, yeah." The *V* was light-years beyond the *III* series, even with the latter's impressive upgrades last year. And the *V* was really just a testing platform for the *VI* series. Jack had a hunch Joe wasn't just kidding about taking on copilot on this mission in exchange for a *Typhoon VI.* It was scheduled for the Oversight Committee, but the cost of these damn things was unbelievable. And the *VI* would have Star Drive 3, incorporating Amplified Thought. Jack should really be taking the first *VI* and leaving Joe the *Typhoon V,* but his brother would probably strangle him.

"Glad you talked me into this insanity," Joe said. "Even if your Star Drive does make your copilot queasy."

"Me? You talked *me* into it. But I'm glad you're here. And

Donnelley's perfect for backup in the *III*."

"Still thinking of having Amav come out here with him?"

Jack nodded. "If things are stable. We have to see." He relaxed. With Joe here, everything was fine. It had worked out wonderfully that he had this opening and Joe could fill it for now. They backed each other up one hundred percent. They'd be fine. Will was wrong, nobody was going to die.

Wow, had he really thought for one second that Will was right? Did Will really believe they were all going to buy it like the *Jupiter?* Jack couldn't have that attitude on his ship. "Damn, Joe, we need to check on this anxiety thing. May be my imagination, but I think it's getting *worse*."

Joe breathed out. "Yeah. Between you and me, I'm glad it was you who said it first. This is sort of approaching thirties levels, I think."

"We didn't notice anything on the thirty-nine-minute trip back from Andertwin. And the *Jupiter* didn't report any problems with physiological effects."

"Well, they didn't have any time for chitchat like that. But you're right, none of the other long Star Drive experiments reported *this*."

"Huh." Jack touched his console. "Laurie, did you by any chance happen to look at any of the medical telemetry from the *Jupiter?* We're looking for any negative reactions to a two-hour Star Drive." There was a long pause. "Colonel, are you there?"

Another pause. "I'm here, Captain. Just checking the records now, sir. So far I don't see anything out of the ordinary. Is anyone experiencing Star Drive anxiety on this ship, sir?"

Jack frowned. Monitoring the crew's physiological balance during Star Drive was standard procedure for a ship's physician/engineer. "And you're not experiencing anything out of the ordinary yourself at--" Jack checked his console. "SD 1:36?"

"No, sir, I feel tip-top as a matter of fact. Have any of the crew complained?"

"Joe and I have noticed *something*, I guess. It's almost the way Star Drive used to be. Well, maybe not that bad, but we weren't expecting it. No previous experiments with Star Drive Enhanced have reported this, as far as we know. Would you mind running the crew through the Physiological Checklist?"

"No problem, sir, let me see where I would access that, Let's see ... 'Standard Medical Procedures, ImpulseScan Activation.' No, that's just for *preflight*. What we need is ... huh, this index is *so* screwy. Let me look up Star Drive ... okay, here. 'Inflight Medical Diagnostic, Star Drive.' It hasn't been set for autorun yet. I'll need a couple minutes to familiarize myself with it."

Jack raised an eyebrow at Joe, who shrugged and whispered: "There's a lot of stuff we're seeing on this ship for the first time, Jack."

Jack muted the intercom. "The Inflight Medical Diagnostic is identical to the *III* series. I thought you said she was *sharp*."

Joe blinked. "Well, she *is*."

"She definitely seems *off* today. Not up to speed."

"Well, like I say, everything's new here, and we're all pretty exhausted to begin with. Look, she's really great, Jack. You saw how she figured out the entire Enhanced problem on the *III* on the fly. I'd totally vouch for her."

"Captain, I *am* getting some elevated readings on most of the crew," Laurie called. "You and Admiral Commer are showing elevated readings on the McWhorter Anxiety Scale. Admiral Commer 22, yourself 23. Commander James, 24. Commander Borman at 12, though. Entirely normal."

"And yourself?" Jack said.

"Let me see ... okay. I would be a 12 myself, sir. Connors is the only one in the severely elevated zone at 48."

Jack winced. Will, her boyfriend? Were they still fighting? Not on speaking terms by any chance? He should have mentioned the fight to Joe. He was the copilot and needed to know. Of course, he may have heard some of it anyway.

He muted the intercom again and exchanged a glance with Joe. "*Connors?*"

"Maybe she's just being, like, super-professional or something," Joe muttered.

"And Will's anxiety is *way* high," Jack said. "Especially if he's feeling double what *we're* feeling." He unmuted. "Colonel, please report to the Control Room immediately."

"Well, sir, what with monitoring the operation of the SD Enhanced, and now setting up the Crew Physiological Report, I'm rather busy at the moment."

"I *asked* you to report to the Control Room, Colonel. We need to discuss the crew's mental states. It looks as if we have at least one in the danger zone right now."

And *he* was the one Jack needed to consult with about where they stopped this Star Drive. Jack sure wasn't about to take this thing right up to the damn Dyson sphere. He also needed to get his physician/engineer a little more focused, first mission on the *Typhoon V* or not.

"Y-yes ... I'll be right up, sir."

A few seconds later the hatch to the Control Room opened and Laurie gingerly stepped inside. Jack was again struck by the ponytail. She reminded him of the teenaged Laurie who'd dated his brother John. She looked oddly vulnerable, like a nervous kid just promoted to some big job. Joe was right. Yesterday she'd been on top of everything on the *III*. She'd trained on *III* tech for years; surely she'd pick up *V* quickly. Then again, *nobody* seemed to understand *V*.

"Have a seat, Colonel," Jack said, indicating one of the four white swivel chairs behind the pilot's and copilot's seats. Jack could have led her over to the conference table at the rear of the control room, but after all they were in non-routine flight, closing in on a war zone for all they knew. And for the first time he noticed that someone had placed a two-foot-wide vase on the table. A bursting mound of orange, yellow and blue flowers rose from the giant clear container. Water sloshed in pleasant slow motion within the glass.

Just great. If they had the slightest cough in their inertial dampers, that thing would come flying into the backs of their heads. Who in their right mind had installed *flowers* for the Iota Persei mission?

Meanwhile Laurie sat behind them and Jack and Joe swiveled to face her.

"Holding up, Laurie?" Jack said.

Laurie nodded. "Yes, sir! Of course, sir!"

"You're sure you're at 12?"

"Yes, sir! Star Drive doesn't affect me, sir! Believe me, sir, it's an honor to be aboard the *Typhoon,* sir!"

God, she looked young. She seemed like a high school girl. And she was what, sixty? Okay, so she was at 12. Relaxed, but she also seemed to be burning with energy. Rejuvenation was amazing. It had definitely turned everything upside down. Some people took it well, others not. He'd always been surprised it hadn't done anything for his mother. She'd always been so young at heart. His father had never had it, never wanted it. Probably wouldn't have done him a damn bit of good anyway. Well, they were both gone now, but at least they'd lived to see the end of the AC war, so in a way, that was good.

Jack shook himself. Why was he daydreaming? Was it the anxiety?

"Well, Laurie, I'm concerned about Will. How would you assess his mental state right now?"

"Well, sir, I haven't talked to Connors much since we came aboard after midnight. All those diagnostics and everything, you know."

Jack heard Joe's intake of breath. "Hey, Laurie, *relax.* Everyone knows Will's your boyfriend. You don't have to be so professional, you know."

"I know that, sir! I mean, about being professional, sir! I mean, of course I know Will's my boyfriend, sir!"

Jack considered ordering Laurie to the Navigation Room to talk with Will, but something told him this would be a major mistake. Okay, he'd been wrong to put the two of them on the same ship. Dammit, why had she flaked out on this mission?

He saw Joe consulting his comm and wondered if he was also thinking they ought to double-check her McWhorter Anxiety Scale reading.

"Well, Laurie," Jack went on, "with the exception of you and Borman, everyone's apparently unusually jittery during this Star Drive. I myself have never done a sustained SD longer than the thirty-nine-minute one we did yesterday on the *III,* but there's something about this one. Can't really pinpoint it. Joe and I are both feeling a lot more tense than we should be. I can mostly block it out, but it's not good. It's draining our energy, even though I know we'll be out of it in a few minutes."

"Nineteen minutes ten seconds," Joe said with a glance at the console.

"But still, it's not supposed to *be* there. Star Drive Enhanced is the most stable drive yet, especially the way the *V* implements it. But I'm feeling something that seems to predate even the *III* series."

"That's ... too bad," Laurie finally offered.

Jack blinked. *Too bad?* This was his *medical officer?* The one Joe said was the best physician/engineer he'd ever seen?

"Do you have any thoughts or recommendations about what we should do about the crew's anxiety levels for the duration of this mission?"

"Well, let me see ..." Laurie consulted her comm. "Something for anxiety, you say? Anxiety, yes, here we go. 'DreamGlaze.' It says here that DreamGlaze series 340 through 342 won't interfere with cognitive functioning, so any of those three might probably be a good start. Let me check the dispensary to make sure we have them. Huh, wouldn't you know it? We don't *have* DreamGlaze on the *V.*"

Without turning to his copilot, Jack could feel Joe's eyes bulging. DreamGlaze hadn't been prescribed for Star Drive anxiety for decades. Not only was the anxiety so rare that even Martians could handle Star Drive with relative ease, but there were also newer generations of drugs specifically developed to counter the anxiety if it should arise. The *V* would have a generous quantity of these drugs on hand.

Jack fingered his own comm and called up the McWhorter readings. She had to be feeling it herself, and this being her big first mission on the *V,* she didn't want to admit it. But that was silly; they had to be upfront about everything on any mission.

Crewman Colonel Laurie Lachrer, read Jack's comm. *McWhorter Anxiety Scale: 0. Respiration: 0. Heartbeat: 0.*

Brainwave activity: 0. Suggest immediate cremation of Colonel Lachrer's body.

"Crap, now the MedServer's fouled up as well!" Joe muttered, staring at his own comm, obviously checking the same thing. "I swear we ran the diagnostic five times on that thing!"

"Right, right." Jack turned back to Laurie, who nodded and smiled, crossing her legs and holding her top knee in her slender fingers. Jack was surprised to find fury rising at her pert demeanor.

"Oh, I knew the MedServer was *trash* before we even took off!" she laughed. "One of those *stinking finbacks* was trying to reprogram it with *Amplified Thought,* can you believe it? Why we allow *Martians* to work on USSF ships is beyond me!"

"D'yyrfa--is one of our best *systems engineers!*" Jack sputtered.

Laurie smiled bright blue-eyed into the long silence. What on earth was *wrong* with her? Was she trying to *flirt* with them?

"Well, what I would like you to do, Laurie, is double-check the dispensary for any drugs we may have that can ameliorate the anxiety. We're going to need to be fully on top of things once we get out of Star Drive. And talk to Will, make sure he's okay. I mean, I really don't know why this is *getting* to us like this."

But she just sat there, smiling and flipping her ponytail from one side of her neck to the other. Had he not more or less just told her to get her ass in gear? Did he really have to order her around like some Airman First Class? He couldn't think. The anxiety was terrible.

Sixteen minutes left in Star Drive! Oh my God!

"And if you have any idea what's causing this *anxiety.* I mean, we shouldn't have it, right?"

Jack was grateful when his copilot stepped in. "Look, Laurie, if you can offer any theoretical understanding here as well, that would be great. We might need to fine-tune the Enhanced. I was just thinking that it might be the inherent *stability* of Star Drive Enhanced that's somehow causing this. I mean, obviously Enhanced doesn't get us anywhere faster than regular Star Drive. It's just more stable. But think about all that extra energy going solely into stability. There's still a much bigger Star Drive Energy Field centered right on the ship that we have to contend with."

"Are you kidding?" Laurie laughed. "That's the most idiotic thing I've ever heard! I can't believe you said that! That's like *sixth-grade* or something!"

Jack and Joe turned to each other with open mouths.

"If you gentlemen are *quite* through with me, I'll go attend to this *stinking sixth-grade ship!*" Laurie stood, stretching her arms high, thrusting her hips, showing off every inch of her petite body in her tight Colonel's uniform. "Bye now!"

Jack stared at the hatch shutting on her perfect little rear. "Oh my God ..." he managed. "What the hell is *wrong* with us?"

Joe swiveled to his console. "Look, Jack! She's not going to see Will like you told her! She's moving back down to Engineering!"

"Well, maybe ... as long as she's looking after it okay ..."

"C'mon, Jack, we need to talk to Will. Two hours of Star Drive and there'll be a lot more nav drift than normal. And I assume we want to wind up a lot further out than the *Jupiter* did."

"You ... good ... call him ..."

"Will!" Joe called. "What's Nav9 SDE picking up now?"

No answer.

"Will!"

"*Why are we here?*" came the cry from the Navigation Room. "Why are any of us *here? Oh* my God! Oh my God!"

"Fourteen minutes thirty-five seconds. You think we'll make it, Jack?"

"*Dammit!* We're all *flaking!* I can't *believe* this! Joe, take control of Nav! *Now!*"

"Nav's *offline!* Dammit, Will's shut it completely down!"

"Negative," came the reply from Engineering. "*I* have control of Nav now. We're being guided in, and they didn't want any resistance on our part."

"You--Laurie--*guided in?*" Jack gasped.

"By the Wounded, sir."

"The--the *what?*"

"The *Wounded,* sir. They have the right to call themselves whatever they want. In any case, they've signaled that we should synchronize Nav9 with their tractor beam. Much less chance of us being ripped apart. They'll pull us in from here."

"This--this is *insane!* You say someone *signaled* you?"

"Yes, Mr. Jack! They probed and they probed, and finally they found *me!* They contacted *me* directly! What an *honor,* Mr. Jack!"

"Jack, this is Pat!" came the call from Communications/Sensors. "The comm software just crashed!"

"We ... we know," Jack whispered. "Laurie ... has it."

Waves of relaxation flooded through him.

"Out of Star Drive," Joe reported. "But we're *accelerating* now. We're actually traveling faster than the speed of light if you can believe that."

"Correct!" Laurie laughed. "They don't *need* to warp space! Whatever they want, just *happens!* Laws of physics be damned! Their technology's twenty thousand years beyond our stinking Star Drive! What an *honor,* to be captured by the Wounded!"

CHAPTER TWENTY-SIX
At the Sphere with Amplified Xons

Circular blackness and an impossible absence of stars filled the canopy. Jack turned away with a shudder and stared at the absurd sprawl of flowers on the conference table. God, did someone want to remind them of *life?* Of hope? Didn't they know they'd come here to their *deaths?*

No! Get a grip! Laurie shut down our systems! She's a traitor! Deal with her!

The Control Room hatch burst open and Jack had his shattergun out. Joe stood next to him, weapon drawn.

It was Will Connors, out of breath.

"Shut the hatch, Will," Joe said. Will closed it and security bolts clamped. "Need to keep her out of here while we think. I've also alerted Lee and Pat to secure their own doors."

"Look, Jack, I'm sorry!" Will gasped. "I'm really all right now. I don't know how I lost control of Nav9!"

"Look, it's okay," Jack said. "Seems we didn't have any choice." He forced himself to turn back to the growing sphere. He could make out tiny lights along its equator.

"I just wanted to apologize. Lost my head and all. Don't know why I came up here, either. Know I'm abandoning my post."

"Forget it, Will. There was something wrong with the Enhanced. We shouldn't have all been set on edge like that. Anyway, I'm glad you're here. There's no navigation for you to do anyway. What the hell do you think of that thing?"

Will looked up at the lights across the sphere's equator. Their closing rate seemed to be dropping. "I have no idea, Jack. I just don't know why she'd *do* this."

Jack shrugged. "Lee. PlanetBlaster targeting engaged?"

"You got it, Captain," Lee Borman replied. "Probably just punch a few holes in the freakin' thing. Not much effect unless we find some command and control unit to take out. But all twelve Xons are all online. We could blow the mother, I would think."

"I'm assuming command of the Xons. Keep monitoring 'em, but first me, then Joe, makes the decision to launch."

"Aw, hell, Cap'n," Borman laughed. "Well, whatever you say, dude."

"Twelve will probably take out this ship as well," Joe pointed out.

Jack nodded. "I just lost a *Typhoon* a couple weeks ago. I'm sure not up to sacrificing another one unless we absolutely have to. Pat! Any sensor capabilities left? Any way to assess how many Xons we might need to blow that thing?"

"Looks like *she's* let me have sensors," Pat called. "Just no communications. But I'm picking up what looks like the signatures of three Amplified Thought Xons recently detonated in this area. In fact, all three are on a line at the sphere's equator."

"Are you sure? How can that be? The *Jupiter* didn't have AT Xons. Only the *V* can carry them, and Henderson never reported firing weapons anyway. Are you maybe picking up the signature from the *Jupiter* explosion?"

"Negative, Jack. The *Jupiter's* a separate signature I'm getting further out from the sphere, a definite irrationality. But now I'm seeing what looks like a *second* Star Drive irrationality at the sphere's equator. In fact, the middle of the three Xon signatures was masking it."

"Wow," Joe said. "Maybe their weaponry is something like our AT Xons, or maybe they can fire off an irrationality at whatever gets close."

As Jack studied the bright lights at the sphere's equator, he began to make out dimmer lights all over the sphere. "Or maybe this means that all our weapons are useless against this thing," he mused. He had no idea why he felt a surge of elation at this thought. Something was going on here. He had to understand it. They couldn't just blast it. That option was out of his hands.

He turned to Will. "Okay, Will, what's the deal with Laurie? You have any idea why she flaked out like this?"

"I really don't. I mean, at first I thought she was *mocking* me, taking away the Nav9 when she thought I was freaking out. I'll admit it, I haven't been hit that hard by Star Drive in, like, *decades*. I mean, you ought to ask *her*."

"Yeah, good idea." Jack touched the pilot's console. "Colonel Lachrer. Please report to the Control Room."

Will's eyes widened. "I--I should go."

"Negative. We'll get this straightened out."

"Negative *negative*!" came the feminine laugh over the intercom. "I am *way* too busy to come to your nasty little party! I see you've all locked yourselves away from me! Well, I've locked myself in Engineering, so there! I need privacy too, you know! I sure need to keep Connors from coming down here and trying to get into my pants!"

Jack nodded to Joe, who tapped his comm. It was great that they *were* more or less telepathic. They'd get her sedated and then lock her up.

"Oh, and I disabled all your knockout gas, all your stupid anti-personnel lasers, all your surveillance toys! You are all so *silly!*"

"*Dammit!*" Joe grunted. "It's all offline!"

"And your *idiotic* networked blasters! Your sidearms are *useless!*"

"Colonel Lachrer," Jack said, "I understand that you may have been suffering from Star Drive anxiety, but you need to follow my orders without question."

"Oh, dear Jacko, just go *plukkzm* yourself! With all due respect, sir!"

Jack turned the intercom off. "I'm sure she can still eavesdrop, but what the hell. In any case, Will, Star Drive anxiety or whatever's gone wrong with her, between you and me and Joe, she's finished with this crew. But for now we need an engineer and if there's any possibility of her snapping out of this later on and contributing something to this mission, I'll take that. Did you notice anything odd about her today?"

Will stared up at the black circle, now motionless with respect to them. "Not until we all came aboard. I mean, she seemed really excited about the mission, but I guess after we had some words, when she wouldn't come up to see me, well, I'm sure she must've already decided to break up with me."

Jack nodded. He noticed that the flowers on the conference table were emitting a stifling odor. How had he missed that all these hours? "You didn't have an argument after we all left the Response, did you?"

"No, she said she wanted to go straight to her condo and get ready. But that was okay with me. I could see how she needed it. And I thought maybe I needed some time too, to think things out myself. I mean, staying on with you guys and all."

"You have any idea what she might be trying to pull? It sounds like she's decided all on her own to *cooperate* with whatever dragged us here."

"Incoming communication!" Laurie yelled. "Incoming, incoming, *incoming!* Listen up, folks, this may be *important!*"

"Damn, she's really *snapped,*" Joe said.

"I *haven't* snapped! I hear everything you say! I have full communications and sensor control! So there! And we *are* cooperating with the Wounded! I just saved your damn asses if you want to know the truth! They have *tachyon pulse rays* that'll fry you before you blink!"

"What is this *Wounded* thing she keeps saying?"

Jack jumped as giant bright blue letters flashed on his console:

SORRY FOR THE MISUNDERSTANDING!

"Sorry for the *misunderstanding?*" Joe muttered. "They wiped out one of our ships and now they're *sorry for the misunderstanding?*"

"Hey, I'm just amazed they're using English," Jack said, pulling up a keyboard interface on his console. "Damn, I haven't used one of these in years, but if they're going to *write* to us, I'm going to respond the same way." He typed: *May we locate and sort through debris field of our ship?*

There was a delay, then came more blue letters.

NEGATIVE.

"Mention we've got twelve Amplified Thought Xons aimed down their goddamn throat," Borman growled over the intercom.

"Lee, back off. Have you got this pulled up on your console, too?"

"Yeah. I say we hit these mothers hard before they can think."

"I'll keep that under advisement," Jack said, typing: *No aggression of any sort is intended. May we use sensors to locate ship and/or debris field?*

NEGATIVE.

Jack stared at the screen, wondering how to respond, when more words appeared.

YOUR WEAPONS HAVE BEEN RENDERED MEANINGLESS. NO AMPLIFIED THOUGHT XONS WILL BE RAMMED DOWN OUR GODDAMN THROAT. YOU WILL NOT HIT US MOTHERS HARD BEFORE WE CAN THINK.

"*Dammit,* Lee!" Jack complained.

"Hey, just type *sorry for the misunderstanding!*" Lee laughed.

"We still have propulsion," Joe announced. "And that tractor beam or whatever it was is off now. If *Colonel Lachrer* would please restore Nav and Comm to us, we could find the debris field and get to it."

"That's gonna take time," Patrick James opined from the Communications Room. "The field is spreading out over thousands of cubic miles by now."

Jack typed: *Our intentions are peaceful. We propose hunting for ship debris to honor fallen comrades.*

They waited for over a minute for the response. Then something caught Jack's eye. "*Watch out!*"

NO PROBLEM. WE WILL BRING THE DEBRIS FIELD TO YOU.

Endless whirling shapes, jagged bits of metal--*part of a fuselage--*

The *Typhoon* rang with a stunning impact and the ship brutally whirled to starboard. Jack stared out the canopy at the mangled mess of the *Typhoon's* starboard wing.

Behind him came a tremendous CRANG and the shrieking of glass. Water burst across the metal floor. Flowers of all colors gushed beneath his feet.

"Deflection fields *up!*" Joe cried, punching in commands as the ship absorbed hit after hit.

"Dammit!" Jack muttered. "Lee, target anything large and vaporize it!"

"No prob, got 'em on autofire," Lee spoke calmly as the *Typhoon's* six PlanetBlaster turrets shot crisscrossing lines of laser fire in all directions.

"Please avoid a little robot! Please avoid a poor little Heroes and Villains of the Thirties robot!" came a new voice.

"What the hell is *that?*" Joe said.

"I'm picking up some sort of *device,*" Pat called. "About four feet long."

"Destroy it!" Jack ordered.

"No! I am M'rrpla! *M'rrpla!*"

"It's our technology!" Pat said. "Feeding coordinates to Lee now."

"Something intact from the *Jupiter?*" Joe said.

"Or something designed to *mimic* something from the *Jupiter,*" Jack said. "Lee, target that thing and destroy it!"

"No! *Please!* I know I shouldn't be here!" came the voice. "I forgot the ship would auto-expel me from any disaster! But my poor master's *gone!* Kner had no such option! He blew with the *M'rrpla!*"

"*Kner?*"

"Can't explain it, dear human authoritative voice which I determine to have a ninety-nine percent probability of matching that of Jack Commer, Supreme Commander of the United System Space Force! But there is time dysfunction here you should definitely know about. Kner and I were unable to destroy the sphere as you can see!"

"I've got that thing Arkonsky clamped and shielded," Joe reported. "No weapons signatures, no chemical or nuclear explosives. We can pull it onboard. It might be able to tell us something, Jack."

"Oh thank you, voice probably that of Joe Commer, Deputy Supreme Commander of the United System Space Force!"

"Okay, see your point, let's take it on," Jack ordered. "Keep the shields up around it."

"Bringing it in," Joe said. "Lee, no shooting at anything four feet long and talking."

"Got it, dude."

"Okay, Jack, I recommend we secure this sample of *whatever*, hit the Enhanced and head for home. Figure out a new approach later."

"Hell, no. We just started talking to 'em. Maybe that piece of debris does have some other info we can use."

"God, how did I get here?" came a fresh cry behind them. They all turned. Draka Sortie, newly elected president of the United System Council, sprawled on the wet floor in his dark green suit kicking at broken glass and flower petals. *"Where am I? Dammit, what's all this glass?"* he moaned, staring at blood running down his forearm. "Ow! *Where am I?* I was just at the *Council!* Mandy? Where's *Mandy?"*

Beside him Laurie eagerly clutched Draka's huge bleeding hand in her delicate fingers. "Isn't it *beautiful,* Jacko?" she laughed. "He's here! Here at last! Draka's *home!* Home with the Wounded!"

CHAPTER TWENTY-SEVEN
The Recognition of a Fellow Machine

Laurie regarded the upraised fist of the Supreme Commander of the USSF. *"Draka!"* Jack Commer shouted. "Dammit, did you stow away on my ship? How the hell did you get up here? Look at this mess you made!" He jabbed a finger at the flowers oozing across the floor.

"Hey, it's not his fault!" Laurie laughed. "Don't you hotshot space pilots keep your Deflection Subsystem on auto?" She pointed out the window to the ruined wing. "Don't try cruising through Iota Persei IV's ammonia atmosphere with *that,* is all I can say! 'Course you'd have to get through the sphere first! IV orbits two hundred million miles out!"

How do I know that? All this new information flooding through me! From the sphere itself? It doesn't matter! I know everything now!

"Colonel Lachrer! How the hell did *you* get in here, too?"

"I just wanted to be with Draka! So they *put* me here! Who knows how they do it?"

"Colonel Lachrer, you are insubordinate!" Joe barked, leaping from his chair. She sized up the approaching humanoid, noting Jack Commer advancing as well, the two separating in an obvious attempt to capture her. *Both moving into out-of-control rage. That would be rather frightening if I were truly a diminutive human female. I will be forced to initiate deadly force to protect myself. Won't that be fun! But I have a feeling Draka doesn't want them smooshed into hamburger. Better use diplomacy!*

"Really, gentlemen, there's absolutely no cause for anyone to be so upset. The destruction of the flower vase was caused by inertial forces beyond the control of either President Draka Sortie or this ship's physician/engineer."

"I've had enough out of you for today, Colonel!" Jack snarled. "You're an *ex*-physician/engineer as of this moment! Consider yourself relieved of duty, and confine yourself to your quarters!"

"Oh, Jacko! Really!" Laurie stood into a defensive crouch with such fluidity that both Jack and Joe froze. She looked over to Will Connors shaking his head at the flowers sliding along the floor.

Doesn't have the guts to charge me himself! That pansy! What did Laurie ever see in him?

"Oh, dear official boyfriend *wimp!* Don't look so stricken just because I fell in love with Draka Sortie! He's a man to take *charge* of things!"

There was a sound like a ripping curtain and Draka was no longer on the floor. Everyone turned to see Draka sitting in Jack's command seat.

"How--how'd I get *here?*" he muttered.

"Why, you *belong* there!" Laurie said. "Oh, this is *magnificent!*"

"Draka, get *out* of my chair!" Jack managed before slipping on the flowers and going down on the shards of glass. "Ow!"

"How did you--how did--" Joe said, squatting to help but tripping and going down himself.

"How the hell did I just get in this *chair?*" Draka moaned. "How did I get *here? This is the *Typhoon V?*"

"Dammit, Draka, you stowed away on my ship!" Jack snarled. "Laurie, why didn't our sensors detect him?" The Supreme Commander bit off his words, obviously aware that Laurie Lachrer Serial Number 589-356914-391HQS would not deign to answer his question.

"I can't get up!" Joe said. "Jack, something's keeping us on the floor!"

"I know! I can't get up either!" Jack said. "Ow! Damn you, Draka!"

"It's not me! I'm not doing anything!" Draka protested, turning his big smooth face to Will, who flailed and went down hard.

"Oh, but you *are* doing something!" Laurie laughed. "You have powers you're not even aware of yet! But you will be! You will be!"

"Look, Jack, I was just talking to Mandy, and now I'm

here?" Draka glanced at the cockpit canopy and froze. "God, is that the *sphere?* Did you really make it to Iota Persei? What the hell's going *on?*"

"Dammit!" Will cried, holding up bleeding hands. "There's all this *glass!*"

"I should file *sexual harassment charges* against this wimp!" Laurie declared. "You can just imagine what his intentions are! He was pulling out all the stops to try to get me up to the Navigation Room so he could seduce me! But of course he must *never* see my naked body! Never! I've determined that! Although according to all the romance novels I've downloaded, that certainly is a tragedy for any man with a sexy girlfriend like me!"

Through the Command Room hatch burst two figures in light blue USSF flight suits. Borman and James charged with outthrust daggers.

Daggers! How romantic! Obviously they have some macho need to slice a poor defenseless teenage girl to bits. Although it's more likely it's because I disabled all their networked weapons and locked up all the non-networked shatterguns. Still, you have to admire their persistence. Who would've thought the USSF issued daggers?

Each knife turned bright orange, then white, in the humans' hands.

"*God!*" Borman moaned, yanking his fingers from what seemed to be a miniature supernova.

"*Damn! Ow!*" Patrick James grunted, eyeing the water on the floor and diving for it. Borman quickly followed, each clasping flowers to their singed fingers, stumbling when their crewmates' legs kicked them off their feet. Soon the five men were helplessly intertwined on the floor.

"See, Draka? See what you're capable of without even knowing it?" Laurie said.

Jack stared at Sortie. "*Release* us! What are you *doing?*"

"Wimps! Wimps! Can't you see why I fell in love with Draka Sortie? Yes, I'm talking to you, Will Connors! I'd *never* be attracted to a twit like you!"

"*You?*" Draka cried. "You say you're--"

"Yes! In *love* with you! You represent my *highest ontological values!*"

"Uh, look, Laurie, I really *am* sorry about that time after the officers' party."

"Sorry, dearest, I have no recollection of that! Those memories must belong to the *Laurie bitch!* I hope she was good for you, at least."

"Damn," Draka muttered. "Jack, what the hell's going on here? How the hell did I get dragged here?"

"Oh, my dearest! Can't you see?" Laurie cried.

"No!"

"You're a *robot!* Like me!"

"Are you *crazy?* Jack, what sort of wacko ship are you running here?"

"You're a robot, and you *love* me! The Wounded tell me that you *love* me!"

"The--Wounded?"

"She's been talking about these *things* she calls the Wounded," Jack said.

"I don't care! This is nuts! I love *Mandy!* My wife!"

"Oh, don't be silly!" Laurie laughed. "The Wounded tell me you just need a few minutes to reinitialize, and then you'll remember everything! Wake up, wake up, I love you! You'll forget all about this Mandy slut any second now!"

"Why, I will *not* ..." Draka shuddered. "*No!* This can't *be!*"

"It *is!* It's time to *wake up,* my love!"

"*No!* Nobody could believe that! Jack, can this damn robot here be *right?* Oh my God!"

"This damn ... robot?" Jack said, following Draka's pointing finger.

Draka stood, oblivious to the writhing men on the floor who kept trying to get to their feet but wound up dragging all the rest down. "She's a goddamn HAVOTT robot!"

"She--she--is *not!*" Will gasped.

"No! I *know!* I know, because, God, Jack, Laurie and I are exchanging a million documents a second! And I'm beginning to *see* it!" He sank back into the command chair, ass loudly plumping the cushion. "The Wounded! By God, the Wounded! This can't be! But it *is!* The documents can't lie!"

Jack flailed on the floor. "What the hell's going on? What are you *saying?*"

"I'm one of *them,* Jacko! I'm one of the *Wounded!* Whatever that means!"

"You--"

"What my love means is *this!*" Laurie cried. "I am a goddamn HAVOTT robot and he's a goddamn Robot of the Wounded!"

"A *robot?*" Draka gasped. "My God! All my life I've been a *robot?*"

"Yes! But a *biological* robot! An exact replica of a human being! And twenty thousand years more advanced than I could ever be! I'm just a poor imitation of your robotic genius! No wonder I love you so!"

"But I have a *childhood!* A whole *life!* I was born in--in--"

"Oh, forget it, dearest! Read the documents! All implanted memories! You were built in 2029, and all the back data from your apparent birth year of 2006 was inserted into the Sol databanks! By *yourself,* I might add, running a completely *unconscious* hacking program! My God, what *genius!*"

"This is insane!" Joe said. "Somehow she's brainwashing Draka!"

"2029 ..." Draka muttered. "When I entered the Academy, I was just created *then?*"

"Forget it, she's brainwashing you!"

"I am not!" Laurie laughed. "I'm helping him *remember!* It's really not so bad, dearest! I have a similar thing, you know! All sorts of *Laurie Lachrer data* stuffed into my poor head! Facts about this Lachrer whore before my creation date of July 5, 2043! Draka, the Wounded created you to *infiltrate* the Academy! Don't you remember how everyone kidded you about all the online courses you took in high school? Nobody'd even heard of you! Don't you remember Phil Sperry saying you seemed to have come out of nowhere?"

"*Sperry* ..." Draka gasped. "He *completed* my programming! Without me ever knowing it! Met him in '34, and *imprinted* on him! God, yes! No wonder I've worshipped that bastard all my life! We have to imprint on *someone!* We Wounded! We have to *imprint!* And I chose the greatest engineer who ever lived!"

"Jack, they've both *flipped,*" Lee Borman whispered.

"Damn, if I could just stand up!" Jack said.

"Shut up!" Draka shouted. "Don't you sons of bitches understand what this *means?*"

"No! Dammit, Draka, get a *grip!*"

Draka flung himself to his feet and pointed to the Dyson sphere obliterating the stars. "It means that I'm not *just* a robot! I'm a fully sentient being, with *plenipotentiary powers* for the Wounded! *I'm the Negation Master for Iota Persei!* Whatever *that* means! Oh my God!"

CHAPTER TWENTY-EIGHT
SABHAVOTTR!

"It'll come to you!" Laurie cried, flooded with the increasing levels of power surging from the beautiful Draka Sortie. "I can hardly believe it myself, what they're telling us! Draka, I love you!"

"I--I love you too, dear Laurie!"

"What about *Mandy*?" Jack said, struggling to his knees but falling back.

Laurie snorted. "Mandy! That Empress thing went to her head! Draka just married her to kill the Martian fascination with the AC Grid!"

"I ... I did? God, yes, I *did*."

"I'm getting the documents straight from the Wounded, dearest! Don't strain yourself! I know it's a bit much to realize you're the Negation Master for an entire star system!" She turned to Jack. "It was the *Wounded* who convinced Mandy that the Grid was a danger. Through her own Consort! No Martian Empress has *ever* been able to think straight once she takes it into her mind to marry."

They turned to the sound of clambering on the rungs to the Control Room's open hatch. "Well, here I am! Thanks again for saving a poor defenseless robot, Jack and Joe of the USSF!"

A small Martian stood in silver boots amid the flowers. Four feet tall, he wore a black flight suit with an orange fin protruding from the back.

"How did that thing get out of shielded storage?" Joe complained.

"I let him out, Sir Joe!" Laurie laughed. "Why do I have to explain everything to you dimwit space pilots?"

[GREETINGS, FELLOW HEROES AND VILLAINS OF THE THIRTIES ROBOT M'RRPLA!] Laurie broadcast. [WELCOME TO THE WOUNDED!]

[GREETINGS BACK TO THEE!], M'rrpla transmitted, including the code for Sincere Amiability Between HAVOTT Robots. [IT IS GOOD TO BE AMONG FRIENDS!]

Laurie flashed back the SABHAVOTTR greeting.

Even John didn't remember to transmit that to me! I'd forgotten about SABHAVOTTR! How wonderful it is!

"I can't *believe* this!" Jack muttered. "A M'rrpla robot!"

"Yes, and I have an amazing story to relate when we can all sit down and chat!" M'rrpla chirped in what Laurie recognized as an exact replica of Kner's voice. "Somehow the *M'rrpla,* with myself and Senior Scientist Kner aboard, in engaging its Star Drive at approximately 0020 hours this morning, interacted with the remnants of the *Jupiter's* vortex and was actually *sucked backwards in time* to the moment of the *Jupiter's* destruction and transported instantly to Iota Persei!"

"Later, robot," Draka said, waving him off. "I'm just beginning to realize we don't have time for these sideshows. We've got some serious *negation* ahead of us here."

[AH, WELL, WE MUST ASSUME THAT NEGATION MASTER SORTIE KNOWS THE CORRECT PATH OF WOUNDED DESTINY!] M'rrpla transmitted. [SAB-HAVOTTR!]

[SABHAVOTTR!] Laurie broadcast back. Why, the little thing was *adorable.*

"That's definitely enough robot chitchat," Draka said, nodding curtly at Laurie, who realized she shouldn't be surprised that Draka could pick up the wireless traffic between herself and M'rrpla. In fact, she got a subtle coded burst of reproof for indulging in SABHAVOTTR.

"Okay, M'rrpla, you can make yourself useful by getting down to the *Typhoon's* shuttle," Draka said, turning to the console and studying the layout of the controls. "I assume you know how to fly a USSF shuttle?"

"Yessir! The one downstairs is known as the *McNarri,* and as my duties as pilot of the *M'rrpla* were generally never pressing, I had time to download specifications on all USSF ships and shuttles. Formerly designated as *escape craft,* by the time of the design of *Typhoon V* series, the nomenclature was changed to *shuttle,* as the modern *Typhoon* auxiliary craft, at a little less than half the size of the original *Typhoon I,* can seat sixteen comfortably. Equipped with Star Drive, the *McNarri* is a formidable spaceship in its own right."

"Enough, robot. Stand by in the shuttle. We may need to send you back to Sol with some cheery first-person report on the status of the *Typhoon V*. I'm programming the *McNarri's* computers now."

"Of course, sir!" M'rrpla threw a salute. "Sol! How about that, sir? A *cheery* report! It will be an honor, sir!" He scampered out the hatch and thumped down the ladder. Laurie listened to his little claws scritching across the fuselage floor, and heard the hatch open to the shuttle bay.

"Draka, what the hell's going on?" Jack demanded. "I don't care if you're Council president or not, you *cannot* interfere with command of a USSF spaceship. And stowing away is a crime!"

Draka didn't turn from the console. "Hey, Jacko, aren't we all realizing about now that I *didn't* stow away on this decrepit little ship? You think a race that can build a Dyson sphere in *one week* needs a spaceship to take a little *faster-than-light trip* to another star system?"

"*What are you saying?*" Jack fought to stand but slipped again. "Ow! Are you really saying you're working with *them?*"

"Huh," Draka said, swiveling back to the group. "Sorry, I was so busy programming the Star Drive Enhanced MetaField Irregularity that I wasn't paying attention. What were you saying while Lee there was trying to drag himself to the back console so he could arm the Amplified Thought Xons?" He waved at Borman crawling to the rear of the Control Room. Laurie laughed to see Lee Borman collapse face-first into the shards of the shattered vase.

"For your information, friends," Draka went on, "Amplified Thought is completely *undefined,* and incapable of *being* defined, in Iota Persei, due to the nature of the sphere. Which means that unfortunately none of the *Typhoon's* Amplified Thought Xon bombs do much more than *fizzle* in this system. Too bad, because we would've *liked* the energy."

Jack stared at the console. "Draka, you've set the MetaField Irregularity *too high!* This isn't the *IV,* you know! The *V's*

MetaField is twenty times more powerful!"

"I *know* that, Jacko. I thought I'd give us an extra fast ride home, that's all."

"There's no way the MetaField will produce any faster relative speed! Set it lower! Not higher than 7.5!"

"It'll blow at Submission Request!" Joe yelled, pointing to the console. "You're at 11.7!"

"Transmitting *cheery superspace communication* to Sol now," Draka said. "All is well, friends, all is so well with the *Typhoon V!* And now cutting *off* superspace communication with Sol. We don't want even a millionth of a second of any telemetry indicating the *true* nature of the explosion, now do we?"

"You're--you're going to *blow* the *V?*" Jack groaned.

"Quite, Jacko, quite, even as I steer her *home.*"

"You're going to ram Sol with the *Typhoon?*" Borman screamed. "And black-hole her?"

"Oh, no, gentlemen, we're going *home!*" Draka laughed, pointing to the sphere.

"Home to the sphere!" Laurie cried. "The sphere which *loves energy!* Draka, isn't it *magnificent?* Even with my antiquated HAVOTT brain, *I know what you're doing!*"

"Then hang on, love, here we go! Hey, Jacko, how does it feel to blow one-sixteenth of the entire economy of Sol in one pop?"

The *Typhoon's* engines whined. Laurie knew she heard noises and felt vibrations nobody but she and Draka could. She felt the SDE initialize behind them as the black circle grew steadily wider. Her HAVOTT eyes made out intricate patterns of tiny lights, their slight movement tracing the slow rotation of the sphere.

Okay, so I'm forties tech and a little slow. But I figured it out before all these pansy humans. Sure, I had some trouble understanding the V. *So what if I didn't calibrate the Enhanced perfectly? Had all the data on Laurie's comm, but it does take some time to assemble understanding from all that stuff. Now I have everything on the Wounded funneling into me. Too much to absorb!*

"God, Draka, you can't be serious about this!" Jack moaned, shaking a finger at the highways of light surging up.

"Draka says I have *forever* to make sense of it all! He has *upgrades* for me!" Laurie said. "*Forever!* Just imagine *forever!*"

"She's *crazy!* The damn bitch is *crazy!*" Borman screamed.

"Why should you concern yourself, Mr. Senator, sir, when your energy is about to be transformed into *Godhead?* Oh, don't laugh! You're not laughing, sir, I can see that, in fact you're pissing your pants, but I must say anyway, *don't laugh, senator!* That's my mystical message to you! The HAVOTT programmers surely knew that Laurie Lachrer had a mystical side, even if *she* never knew it! And when that *testosterone* kicks in, and just *kills off* the female hormones, my oh my! Does that ever give *Godhead* a boost!"

"Dammit, woman, do we have to listen to this *insanity?*"

"We have SDE insertion! We're *blowing!*" Draka laughed. "We're *blowing!*"

The looming sphere disappeared. Everything out the window was featureless gray. Vibrations ceased. The ship was silent except for the whooshing air ventilators.

The men on the floor looked at each other in dismay.

"That's *it?*" Joe whispered.

"Oooh, it *is* subtle!" Laurie said.

Jack dizzily got to his feet. "Okay, Draka, I don't know what the hell you're pulling, but cut the stupid jokes and get out of my command chair!"

"Oh, come on, Jack, there's no command chair anymore. There's no ship anymore, for that matter. Enjoy the brief moment of the Ghost. Lovely feeling, huh? Don't you feel *great?* I know I do!"

"I'm feeling it too," Patrick James said. "I feel *wonderful* as a matter of fact!"

"But it doesn't last very long. We feel the *energy orgasm,* then it's back to work!"

Laurie drifted in blackness, twirling, the highway-lit sphere looming everywhere. Around her floated five glossy bubbles, their translucence highlighted as they passed before the lights of the sphere. Each bubble contained one organic being. Off to the right was a glowing blue oblong spacecraft.

"Dammit, M'rrpla!" Draka barked. "I didn't give you permission to launch the *McNarri!*"

"Sorry, sir, I was just testing it outside the ship when you decided to explode the *Typhoon,*" M'rrpla radioed back. "What a fantastic ship! But in any case, everything turned out well for this particular entity, as I note I was not included in the roster of organic beings and robots intended for post-traumatic survival."

"And just how the hell did you know *that,* mister?"

"This HAVOTT robot is now receiving all informational updates from the sphere itself, sir. Just as my comrade Laurie Lachrer 283 is receiving all updates."

"Ah, hell with it. Just keep your nose wiped, robot. We'll have the goddamn *McNarri* later for a snack."

"Yes, Sir Draka! Sounds like a plan."

[SABHAVOTTR!] Laurie transmitted. [I FOR ONE AM GLAD YOU SURVIVED!]

[SABHAVOTTR BACK AT YOU!] came the return message. [REGRETTABLY I DIDN'T FEEL MUCH FROM THE DEMISE OF THE *TYPHOON V,* JUST SOME EXTRA VOLTAGE. YOU?]

[NOT MUCH HERE, EITHER, FRIEND. BUT I SUPPOSE THERE'S MUCH TO LEARN ABOUT GODHEAD. LOL! NO WORRIES! SABHAVOTTR!]

"Dammit, what *is* this?" came a transmission. That wearisome Commer character again. Why did Draka bother rigging up radio links from these pitiful organic things? He'd also programmed the bubbles to light up during transmission, and Commer's was now bright yellow. Why should she have to listen to him bluster and complain?

"What this *is,* Jacko, is that I just fed your ship to the sphere," Draka laughed. "Yummy, yummy, I assure you! We need lots of energy! We only got a little bit out of the *Jupiter.* It was a messy rupture since it was heading away from us in Star Drive. Your ship provided fifty times the energy! We'll get a little more from the *McNarri* in a bit."

"My ship? It's *gone?* And we're still *here?* That's not possible!"

"Oh, we always save the organic specimens!" Draka laughed. "Further *energy contributions* if you will!" Laurie noted Draka's entire body lighting in green as he spoke. He had no bubble, but like Laurie he wouldn't need one.

Lee Borman's bubble lit in purple. "Code 9255," came a whisper. "Emergency! *V* destroyed, do not send rescue ship until analysis telemetry sending now--"

"Draka!" Laurie cried. "He's got that Senator Comm that can do superspace radio!"

"Neutralized," Draka radioed back, lighting in green.

"Screw you, bitch traitor!" Borman shouted.

"Dammit to hell, I've taken enough off this little bastard!" Laurie snarled, lighting in red and noting Borman's stunned face when he saw she was transmitting without a bubble.

"That's right! I *am* a robot! And I'm open to the universe! In a way you can never be, senator!" She made a motion to swim to Borman's bubble but stopped when she realized she was trying to conjure up a swimming program her designers had installed decades ago. But they were in free fall. There was nothing to push against. And she didn't have propellant.

Or maybe she did. She yanked off a glowing red boot, then the other one. Then the tunic, which she stuffed into a boot.

Laurie didn't wear a bra and so let 'em stare! Look at Will there. Must be babbling something, because his bubble's all orange. Look at his mouth hanging open!

Then the pants, then the panties, stuffed into the other boot.

"Yeah, take a good hard look, because that's what I *am* right now!" she laughed, her entire nude body glowing red with the words. "Testosterone's quite a ride! I love it!"

"L-L-*Laurie*--" Will moaned in orange. "*Laurieeeee!*"

Her HAVOTT brain calculated the vectors. She tossed one boot behind her and shot towards Borman's bubble, which had gone black. Laurie switched her eyes to infrared and picked out the outline of warm air inside Borman's sphere.

She shot out the second boot for more thrust and sailed into the bubble, shattering it.

"*Oh God!*" came the grunt as air rushed out.

"Oh, don't panic, little boy!" Laurie laughed into the new purple light. "It's just a force field! See, now it's back!"

Borman backed away from the impossibility at her groin, everything pulsating in lurid red. "Lady, listen, this is too much even for *me!*"

Laurie regarded Borman's unconscious floating form.

Twice in one day! Wow! I really don't know my own strength!

Draka knows this power. We share it. I love him! Because he's a machine like me! But so much more than a machine!

She followed a tinny noise to Borman's Senator Comm floating behind his back. She held it to her ear. "Weird thing, Draka. Looks like you only neutralized the *outgoing* message."

"Huh. Well, even the Wounded can screw it up every once in a while!" Draka laughed. "No problem, love!"

"*Typhoon V* ... we copy your report ... can you confirm ship destroyed? *Typhoon V* ..."

Laurie crushed the comm in her hand.

CHAPTER TWENTY-NINE
Typhoon III Sort of to the Rescue
Wednesday, July 10, 2075, 1200 hours

Laurie Lachrer climbed through the hatch into the dark fuselage. The tall, spare Andy Donnelley turned from the engineering console. "Laurie! I thought you'd left with the *V!*"

"Well, I thought I might be needed here. I heard the news on SolNet."

"It's public *already?* Dammit, it's been less than an hour. But, God, you're *alive.* What are you *doing* here?"

"Well, it's a long story. I sort of got, like, *robbed,* I guess. So I never made the flight."

"Oh my God! *Robbed?* Really?"

"She ... it ... got my uniform." She indicated the old thirties Airman First Class uniform. "So all I had was this."

She wouldn't think about it. She'd just been taken by some sort of computer hack. She had to shake it off. What had it done to her? She'd awakened nude, hours later. She'd washed and washed herself. She was still sore all over.

"Wow, you're sure you're okay?" Andy said, distracted by beeps from the console. He jabbed at it with his huge gnarled hands. "Jack took off without a physician/engineer? He didn't mention any problems, but we've all been in such a damn hurry."

She met his light blue eyes, took in his receding gray-brown hair, his hollow cheeks and his pockmarked face. Andy was undertaking his first command under the worst possible conditions. He looked exhausted. She'd always respected him, but more than once he'd voiced concerns that spoke of a lack of self-confidence. She wasn't as sure as Jack and Joe of his command capabilities. But she and Andy had a wavelength and could talk.

She was always thankful they'd remained on good terms after he'd asked her out back in the '60s and she'd turned him down. He'd gotten married shortly after that, which helped move that topic completely off the table.

"My God! *Laurie!*" came a fresh cry behind Andy. Laurie

201

locked onto Amav Frankston-Commer's shellshocked dark eyes.

"Uh ... hi, Amav."

What could anyone say? Her husband was dead. Laurie couldn't take it herself. Jack dead, and she'd badmouthed him for so long? Just last night he'd been so excited, talking about exploring. But Laurie had been AWOL and the whole crew had died while she *cringed* back here. Now Jack's wife was in front of her. What on earth could Amav be feeling?

"What are you *doing* here?" Amav cried. "Oh my God! You made it back! *Where's Jack?*"

Laurie closed her eyes at Amav's desperate, erroneous conclusion. "No, I'm sorry, but what happened is that I never made the flight. I was, like, *attacked* in my condo last night. It's a long story, but it doesn't matter now. No, I didn't get on the ship."

Amav stared. "*Attacked?*"

"Just woke up a while ago. I'm so sorry. I mean, there was this ... I really can't explain it. Afterwards I just knew I had to get here, then I was listening to SolNet on the jeep as I came over, and the driver was as shocked as I was."

Laurie was about to ask what Amav was doing on the *Typhoon III,* then looked down at Amav's deep red flight uniform with skintight trousers tucked into shiny black boots. Civilians were to wear red when aboard USSF ships on military duty, but Laurie had never seen such a sexy getup.

No. Amav couldn't force her way in on this. Not now.

"Damn, I'm sorry about this, Laurie," Andy cut in. "Look, what are they saying on SolNet?"

"That we've lost contact with the *V.* I was on my way over here and heard it just now as we were pulling up."

"Did they leak Borman's message?"

"No. Did he send one?"

Andy shrugged. "Yeah. We got one automated message from the *V* saying everything was okay, then a couple minutes later we got a distress call from Borman on his own comm." He took another look at Laurie's disheveled uniform. "Are you all really right?"

"Yeah, just shaken up a bit. It was just so … *unexpected.*"

"Damn, I'll bet. You can sit down there and file a police report if you haven't already."

"No thanks, I'll do that later. Look, Andy, I'm here to help, any way you may need me. I know you're set to launch tomorrow for Iota Persei."

"Forget tomorrow," Andy said, turning back to the console. "We're launching as soon as I get this ship operational. Maligh okayed it. I just happened to be here checking some stuff out when I got the news. I'm hoping to get launched within five minutes of everyone arriving. Got calls out to Greenhill, Markham, Li, and Ballard, and they're due back any minute. Meng called to say he'll be here soon. This was his regular time to arrive from Europa and they managed to speed him up a bit. Says he'll be here in twenty minutes."

"Forget Meng!" came a shout from up the fuselage. Amav paced at the far end of the *Typhoon,* wrapping her fingers around the ladder to the Control Room. "We've got Laurie now and she can take his place!"

"You know, I haven't even had time to *meet* Greenhill or Meng," Andy said. He cocked his head back at Amav. "She's right," he whispered. "I need you on board."

"Well, sure. If Meng doesn't show, I'd be happy to take his place."

"Look, I'd still want both of you even if does get here on time. We'd shut down some systems thinking we'd be leaving tomorrow at 0900, so I'll take all the engineering help I can get to get us back up. Also, you know this ship inside out."

"Okay, sure. So you and I are the only crew?"

"Right. And only one ground engineer. We have some other ground crew, but D'yyrfa's the only tech we could get over here."

"Well, he's the best." Laurie had managed a hasty hello to D'yyrfa working on the wing thrusters as she climbed aboard. His outradiance had already filled her in on most of the systems procedures she'd need to work on.

"But his son's with him," Andy muttered. "How can he *think* with all that nonsense?"

"I know. I got of dose of it coming in as well." The child's outradiance had nearly knocked her down with its interlocking rainbows of what could easily be taken for insanity. Only D'yyrfa's overlay of adult wisdom had kept her from throwing up at the disjointed telepathic onslaught. "Somehow the parents sort it out, or block it out." The eighteen-year-old Z'B was four feet tall and looked almost fully grown, but was dressed in the standard black-and-white-striped Martian child sweater. Certainly Martians knew who was a child and who wasn't, but the tradition of the child sweater had been around for centuries, and had the additional advantage of letting humans know at a glance which Martians were underage.

"Well, I'm having enough trouble concentrating with Amav here. And then this *kid nonsense.* Hard to tune out, even here in the ship."

"Well, I'm here," Laurie said, easing into the console chair next to him.

"I can't *believe* this! I just can't *believe* this!" Amav cried from up the fuselage.

Andy leaned over to Laurie. "We have to get rid of her. She won't listen to me. I told her Jack said she was supposed to come along only if all was well. But here she is anyway. She showed up a couple minutes before you. I tried to order her off, but she won't go."

Laurie nodded. It was Andy's first command and now he had the SCUSSF's grieving widow to deal with. "Maybe we'll have to have Security escort her off if all else fails."

Andy winced. "This is *Jack's wife.*"

"I know, but we can't have a *civilian* in the way."

"*Dammit, I heard that!*" Amav charged up to Laurie, long brown hair whipping around her shoulders. "You damn scheming *bitch!* For your information this is now a *rescue mission,* and I'm definitely on it! So get used to it!"

"Look, you're not even in the Force!" Laurie protested.

"The hell with *that!* I'm *married* to the Force! Listen, Ms.

Genius Colonel, I know you don't like me! But I'm here, so deal with it!"

"Forget it! *Andy's* in command! Not you!" Laurie wondered why Andy didn't jump into this perfect opening to act like a captain, but he just scooted his chair back with his mouth open. She could almost hear him thinking: *women!*

"You think I'm some crazy bitch, don't you?" Amav snarled, marching to Laurie's chair and towering over her. "You've always thought that!"

"One thing I've had enough of is *crazy bitches* breaking into my place and trying to *mess* with me!" Laurie shouted back, bursting to her feet and shoving her nose into her tormentor's stunned face. Amav drew back, obviously not expecting such a defense from the famously quiet colonel.

"*Listen!*" Andy said. "We can't have this!"

"Look, Amav, I know you're upset," Laurie said. "But really, you're just getting in our way. You're not trained, you don't know our procedures, and we're going into a *combat zone* for God's sake! Jack didn't *want* you in a combat zone!"

"You--you think just because I got upset about my son yesterday that I'm going to have another meltdown in front of everyone? Is that it? You think I'm out of control?"

"Yes! I think you're having a meltdown right now, to tell the truth!"

"Andy!" Amav pleaded. "Tell her!"

"You ... you need to ... to not be on the ship," Andy finally muttered.

Amav whirled and fled down the fuselage to the Control Room ladder, hanging onto it like a life preserver. "Forget it! Just forget it! Forget everything! He's *dead!* It doesn't matter! It just doesn't *matter!*"

"Look, Andy," Laurie whispered. "Is this ship really going to be ready in a few minutes?" What she really wanted to say was: *Are you really ready yourself?*

He sighed. "Hell if I know. And I just got a call from Ranna. She's on her way here too."

"*She* wants to come too?"

Andy closed his eyes. "She's in the same shape as Amav. I sure can't have that. Hope we get everyone else on board and just get out of here. Maybe we can put Amav off at the last second or something."

Ranna, Joe's wife. Laurie had forgotten about *Joe.* But he'd been Jack's copilot. What was wrong with her mind? Joe *couldn't* die. That just wasn't possible.

"Listen, Andy, look, I'll think of something. We can reason with them. We'll use Security if we have to."

"He's *dead!*" Amav screamed. "He's dead, he's dead, he's *dead!*"

"Oh, *man,*" Andy groaned as Laurie felt Amav's scream mixing perfectly into the unstinting gibberish pouring out of the child Z'B from below the port wing.

"Oh my God!" Laurie cried. "*Will!* I didn't even think of *Will!* I kept thinking he *retired!* But he didn't! *He went with Jack!*" Laurie pushed back from the console, numb. She'd been out of it for hours. She was more scrambled by that *robot thing* than she'd been willing to admit.

Andy stared at her. "Are you ... are you going to be all right?"

"*Will* ... why didn't I remember *Will?*"

"Maybe they're not dead, just lost communication or something," was all Andy could offer.

Laurie nodded, dazed. All she could possibly do now was march through these damn systems checks. They had to do this mission. It didn't matter that they didn't have the slightest idea what they were facing. "No, they can't be gone. Let's get going maybe." Her fingers stabbed at the console as Andy turned to his master checklist.

"Laurie, what about the vortex? Is that gonna mess us up?"

"I--I don't know. Of course we're supposed to wait twenty-four hours."

"I know, I know, but Jack just pulled that figure out of the air to be on the safe side. The *V* should've had only one-nineteenth of the standard vortex, and we're following with your improved Enhanced, so that should make a difference."

Laurie bent to the console. *Do the mission. Do the mission.* "Well, maybe. The program has several options for turbulence avoidance, and some we can change in mid-flight. It might also be possible to not try for an entire two-hour trip all at once, but to break it down into smaller chunks like we've been doing for regular Star Drives."

"Good. Keep all those options open. We want to get there as soon as possible, but we do want to arrive in one piece." He paused at a beep and checked his comm. "Markham says she'll be here in five. I'm messaging the rest right now. How soon do you think we can launch?"

"Well, maybe fifteen minutes. I'm feeding in the last Enhanced checks and they all look good." She took a deep breath, pushing away the concept of *Will*. So far so good. "So what did you hear from the *V?*"

Andy touched his console, and Laurie's lit up with the text as the recording came out over the *Typhoon*'s intercom:

"Code 9255. Emergency! *V* destroyed, do not send rescue ship until analysis telemetry sending now--" A few seconds later, the sound of rushing air, then: "Lady, listen, this is too much even for *me!*"

"Oh my God," Laurie whispered.

"That was Lee. From fifty minutes ago. And he sent a gigabyte of telemetry that was completely garbled. No video. So far the technicians have concluded from the acoustical properties of the recording that it came from a sphere ten feet in diameter. They think it's a force field of some sort, not the *V's* shuttle. The shuttle has separate telemetry and went offline the same second the *V* did."

"God ..." Amav moaned at the playback. "I can't *believe* this!"

"So what are they saying on SolNet?" Andy said.

"It's like total panic," Laurie replied. "Somehow the news is everywhere."

"Less than a damn hour ..."

"I need to *be* there!" Amav screamed. "I need to *see* that goddamn sphere! *I'll* know how to destroy it! I swear to God I'll do it!"

"*Dammit,*" Andy muttered. "Don't worry. I'll put her off. At the last minute I'll just put her off."

"Look, *everyone's* in shock," Laurie said. "But if Lee could send that message, from some sort of force field, I mean, do we really know the *Typhoon* itself was destroyed?"

Andy shook his head. "They did stress tests on Lee's voice and concluded he had no burns or serious injuries. Telemetry stopped from the *V* fifty seconds before his message. It'd just opened up into Star Drive, then *nothing*. But nothing wrong with the Drive we could see. All systems were operating normally, and there was no detectable explosion. And no medical telemetry of … human *deaths,* just higher heartbeats and stress levels, that's all."

The hatch opened.

"Thank God!" Andy said. "We've got at least one more."

"Prepare for takeoff!" General John J. Douglas cried, holding a shattergun to the temple of a squirming pink creature in a black and white sweater. "Or this damn finback dies!"

Andy stood to block the intruder. Laurie gaped as the robot yanked the *Typhoon III* captain off his feet and flung him out the hatch and thirty feet across the tarmac.

Douglas slammed and secured the hatch.

Chaos poured out of the infant Martian's mind. Then it belted out:

"HELLO HELLO HELLO I AMM HAVING FUNN BUTT I WOOOD LIKE TOO RUNN AND PLAYY WOOOD YOO LIKE TOO RUNN AND PLAYY WITH MEE? I AMM Z'B!"

CHAPTER THIRTY
Z'B

The robot dug the shattergun barrel into Z'B's neck. Z'B's mouth crinkled into a laugh.

"ROWWBOTT THINGG PLAYYS WITH MEE! ROWWBOTT THINGG AND DADDEE PLAYYING AND WRESSLING THEN DADDEE WENT DOWNN! THENN WEE CAME UPP LADDERR TOO HEERE WITH YOO GUYZZ!"

"Shut up! Shut up! You damn thing!" Douglas yelled.

"That's *Z'B!*" Amav cried, running up. "D'yyrfa's son!"

Laurie's mind surged with the raw images pouring from the eighteen-year-old Martian: Douglas charging up to the *Typhoon,* encountering D'yyrfa working on a fuselage compartment with Z'B at his side, then Douglas grabbing the child, D'yyrfa turning in surprise and being knocked flat by a robotic punch in the nose.

Yes, it was gone, that calmer telepathic sense she'd had in the background of D'yyrfa working on the Star Drive Enhanced circuitry, his mind pulsing with technical jargon, tempering his son's burbling outradiance.

"D'yyrfa's hurt!" Amav said, obviously receiving the same disordered images. "This goddamn robot knocked him out! *You kidnapped D'yyrfa's son?*"

Laurie tapped her comm. "D'yyrfa. D'yyrfa, you there?" No response. "And Andy's probably hurt too." She'd watched her captain belly flop and slide across the hard tarmac. Even in one-third Martian gravity that had to hurt. Laurie punched for Med Services.

"Necessary--" Douglas grunted through his immense white handlebar mustache.

"FUNN! FUNN, FUNN, FUNN! DADDEE WAS MAYKING THE SHIPP REDDEE TOO GO! HEE SAID I COOOD RYDDE WITH HIMM SOMMDAYY!"

"Shut up! Damn thing!"

"Don't hurt him!" Laurie knew the robot had enough strength to squeeze the four-foot Martian into a soggy pink sponge. "Medical issue at *Typhoon III!* Technician D'yyrfa and Captain Donnelley have been injured!"

In a blur Douglas snatched Laurie's comm with his Z'B-grasping hand even as he kept the shattergun at the infant's head with the other. He dropped the comm to the deck and stamped on it a dozen times in one second.

Laurie stared for a moment, then engaged the ship's direct communication link. "*Typhoon III* reporting medical issue!"

"*Typhoon III,* this is Med Services. Do you--"

Douglas studied her with narrowed eyes. "Communications override Omega 33001, authorization Douglas 933."

"*What are you doing on this ship?*"

"FUNN! LAURREE IS MADD! YESS I KNOWW YORR NAME! FUNN! LOOK HOWW ROWWBOTT THINGG STOMMPPED COMM DED DED DED!"

"*Dammit,*" Douglas grunted. "Sit still! This thing is so damn *retarded!*"

"He's *not* retarded!" Amav said. "He's just a *kid.* Don't hurt him!"

"Look, we know his outradiance is all jumbled," Laurie said, "and it'll set your nerves on edge, but that's no reason to hurt him!"

"Hell with that. I'm a goddamn *robot,* I don't *get* the damn outradiance. But if this thing doesn't shut up and sit still, he's gonna be a pile of broken damn glass!"

"ROWWBOTT LOVVES MEE! ROWWBOTT LOVVES MEE!"

"How'd he get that access code?" Amav said.

"I don't know!" Laurie said. "It's a *thirties* code, for God's sake!"

"Oh, c'mon, isn't it obvious?" Douglas laughed. "The big hack back in '41. You stupid wusses!"

"Aw, *crap.*" Laurie had helped clean up the last major assault on USSF servers decades ago, when an army of HAVOTT hackers had gone fishing for any and all details of USSF personnel in order to make their new Heroes and Villains of the Thirties series as true to life as possible. Hadn't her own robot already demonstrated that with her condo code? She cursed herself for being so ill-prepared with Douglas.

Douglas smirked. "There are a *ton* of backdoors you've still never found out about. But enough of this idle chitchat, ya stupid panicking bitches! We're all about to take a nice ride to Iota Persei, and we don't have time for this nonsense."

Laurie backed away from the scarcely believable frenzy in the robot's eyes. How was that even possible? The old HAVOTT robots were amazingly lifelike for their time, and newer robots were even more accurate on human expressions, but this look of desperation was astonishingly realistic.

"Dammit, we're *trying* to get to Iota Persei!" Amav cut in. "Now leave Z'B alone and get off our ship! We need to see about Andy, too! If he's hurt! We've got a mission to do here!"

"Are you kidding?" Douglas said, tightening his hold on the squirming, laughing Martian. "*I'm* the man with the mission! *I'm* taking over, honey pies! I'm going to rescue Laurie!"

Laurie stared back in stunned silence. "She's right *here!*" Amav blurted.

Douglas glanced over. "That old crone? I don't think so!"

"*What?*"

Laurie shook her head. "It's--complicated. See, there's another HAVOTT robot, and it's a version of *me.*"

"And I *love* her!" Douglas boomed. "Laugh if you must, but I *love* her. I traced her telemetry right to the *Typhoon V.* Why she'd want to run off to Iota Persei is beyond me, but I love her!"

"*What* are you saying?" Amav demanded.

"It's some sort of robot thing," Laurie said. "From what I can gather, there was some sort of *special surgery* involved, and I think he wants to go after her, to get back his ... his ..."

"To get *that* back? Oh no! I never really had it, now did I? And in any case, I accept myself for who I am! So what if I got the wrong genitals! It's Laurie I love! No, not this old lady here, but the *robot* Laurie! We'll be together for all eternity!"

"God, this is *sick!*" Laurie muttered. "Sick what she *did!*"

"Although I suppose I must use my logical HAVOTT brain and admit that my dear one is probably nothing but sundered atoms now. Strange how the cold logic kicks in, right when you're imagining your dear dead one in bed with you. Ah well, I suppose if worse comes to worst, I could even love the *old crone* here. I'm sure you'd find me quite a feast, Colonel Lachrer!"

"What on earth are you *babbling?*" Amav snarled.

Laurie backed away, trying to conjure up some hack to take down this berserk HAVOTT.

"Okay, listen up!" Douglas barked. "I'm here to rescue Laurie. Don't screw with me, bitches, because I'm fully linked into the *Typhoon's* computers and I can blow us up right this second if I want."

Amav turned to Laurie. "Can--can that be true?"

Laurie ran to her console. "Damn. Yes, he can, even with those old USSF codes from 2034. I'm seeing them come up on his login code."

"You bitches don't understand how hard this is for me. You think I enjoy grabbing this stupid kid here? You think I enjoyed knocking his bahstad father out? By the way, as I was swinging for his nasty pink jaw, I was *constantly* recalculating the necessary force! I pulled back right at the end, but do I get any credit for that? A really soft touch, if you must know. Didn't do any permanent harm. Why should I want to? Damn these *female hormones!* They're making me soft! I can barely concentrate on the mission! Laurie's everything to me! But *you* wouldn't understand!" Then Douglas lobbed Z'B at Laurie's face.

"WHEEE! WHEEE! FUNN!" Z'B laughed, twirling in the air as Douglas rushed down the fuselage and up the ladder to the Control Room in half a second.

The hatch snapped shut and latched. Laurie grabbed Z'B out of the air, let him squirm to the floor, and lunged for the ladder. Amav was at her side and together they pounded on the Control Room door. "Open up! Open up, damn you!" Laurie yelled.

"We'll *deactivate* you, you piece of crap! *Open the hell up!*"

"Oh, c'mon, ladies, settle back and enjoy the ride!" came blasting over the ship's intercom. The wing thrusters whirred to life and the fuselage lurched as wheels came off the ground.

"You can't! You can't!"

"Oh yes, I can! I can certainly fly this ship! Autopilot does most of the work! You wusses could've sent the goddamn *Typhoon V* to Iota Persei on autopilot!"

"*Open up!*"

"Don't worry, luscious Amav, I hereby appoint you my *sexy copilot in absentia* for the duration of this voyage! What an honor, eh? I can't make little Miss Lachrer copilot, because she has to actually run this ship! So, my dear old crone, if you will please monitor ship's functions from your little console? Thank you! We'll all be comrades, then, eh? It's just that you can't come into my Control Room! So settle down and relax, and we'll rescue the *real* Laurie! Oh, that vixen! I know she's alive! She has to be alive!"

Laurie rushed to the rear hatch and yanked on its handle, even considering that they might be fifty feet off the ground by now. "He's locked it! Amav, we need to get into seats here! Strap down! I've got Z'B!"

"WHEEE! FUNN! WEE GO FORR A RYDDE!"

"Laurie, are we possibly anywhere near ready for Enhanced Star Drive?"

"God, maybe ..." Out a porthole Laurie saw a USSF ambulance loading Technician D'yyrfa onto a stretcher. Others were pulling a cursing Andy Donnelley back from the wing thrusters as the ship rose. They rushed Andy and the stretcher into the ambulance and roared off as the thrusters opened full bore.

It took both Laurie and Amav to strap the flailing Z'B into his seat.

"FUNN! FUNN! I GETT TOO RYDDE INN A SPAYSHIPP!"

CHAPTER THIRTY-ONE
I Am Here to Gather Everything!

"Augmented on overload!" Laurie cried, jabbing her console. "We've got to jettison the nuke!"

"Negative!" rang the robot's cry through the *Typhoon* intercom. "She'll make it! This is a sturdy ship!"

"Dammit, Douglas, you've got to relinquish control!" Amav shouted, staring at a second console next to Laurie. "Laurie's right, the nuke's about to melt down! I'm confirming it from the Systems Index!"

"You know about the Systems Index?" Laurie grunted.

"Are you kidding? That's been around for ages! I picked up more than enough of *that* back on the *Typhoon II* mission. And Jack tells me about all the upgrades … I mean, *told* me. Oh, God!"

"YESS! TOLLD YOO!" Z'B laughed. "TOLLD YOO! YOO ARR USING THEE PASST TENSE I SEEE! DON'TT I KNOWW ENGLISSHH GOOD?"

Wow! Miss Amav is upset! Wonder why, when we're all having so much fun! What a great spaceship!

"He's got to be all right! They've all got to be all right!" Laurie said.

And Miss Laurie too! Her face is all scrunched up! Or maybe this is how humans laugh when they're having fun? I have so much to learn! Daddy always says I must learn, learn, learn!

"Is that--an irrationality?" Amav said, pointing to her console.

Laurie looked over, face white, then ducked back to her own screen. "Oh my God, yes! Thanks! *Douglas!* We have vortex irrationality on all thrusters! God, we have at least *nine hundred separate vortices!*"

Vortex irrationality! Wow! That sounds neat! Everyone's so alive!

"VORRTEXX! VORRTEXX!" Z'B laughed.

Okay, so I don't talk so good! Daddy says Martian mouths

can't do English good! But wait when I grow up! Then I radiate my thoughts like English words and everyone understands me then!

Daddy taught me English and I'm good at it! I understand everything they're saying! They're excited and they're having fun!

"VORRTEXX! VORRTEXX!"

"C'mon, Z'B, back off!" Amav said. "Laurie needs to concentrate here!"

Lights blinked all over the ship.

"SDE total system failure!" Laurie called. "We are out of Star Drive! We're 20.987 light-years out of Sol, at standard SD closure speed, 100,000 miles per hour. We're just coasting, in fact we can't even *slow down*. We don't have *any* propulsion!"

Amav pointed to her console. "Laurie, a warning just popped up!"

"Douglas! Overloads on PlanetBlasters Two and Four! When the Enhanced blew it must've surged through the weapons subsystems!"

"And now it looks like--like an Xon got armed somehow?"

Laurie stared. "Oh, my God, you're right! Douglas, we have to jettison Xon Five! Repeat, *jettison Xon Five!* Then jettison the reactor as well! We're about to melt down!"

"Negative!" Douglas yelled. "I can see full well the safety locks on all the Xons are fine! We'll need every Xon we can get in Iota Persei! We can repair the damn reactor at our leisure!"

"Idiot! We don't *have* a damn reactor anymore!" Amav cried.

"Safety lock failure on Xons Three, Four, Five, Eight, and Twelve!" Laurie called.

Z'B felt his feet come off the floor. "WOWW! WHAZZ GOING ONN?"

"Artificial gravity out! All inertial dampers out!"

"Hell with it, old crone!" Douglas shouted. "Stop panicking! We'll get there, I promise you, we'll get there sooner or later!"

"IZZNNTT HEE FUNNEE?" Z'B laughed. "I LOVVE

HIMM!"

"No, he's not! *Listen to us, Douglas!*" Amav yelled. "It would take *decades* to get there even at one-quarter light! Which we don't have now anyway! And we only have three minutes until we melt down!"

"Environmental systems offline!" Laurie said, floating above her console, grasping a corner of her table to anchor herself. The lights blinked again and this time only a few came back on.

"*I* don't need air!" Douglas screamed. "I don't need *anything!* I floated for eleven years in the Oort cloud!"

"Amav, I think I've finished my work on the damn robot," Laurie whispered. "Right before all this crap started happening. But I just need to take one system down at a time. First, I just got control of the reactor."

"THE DAMMM ROWWBOTT!" Z'B laughed. "WHATT KINDD OF WURKK DOO YOO DOO ONN HIMM?"

These people are so funny! I never knew humans could be so funny!

"Quiet, Z'B! Laurie's *working*," Amav whispered, floating upside down by Z'B's left ear.

"OHKAYY OHKAYY I WILL BE KWI-ETT! YOO GUYZZ ARE SOOO FUNNEE! I LIKE FLOATTINGG DOO YOO LIKE FLOATTINGG?"

"Done," Laurie whispered. She pressed the console and Z'B watched the ship jerk around him.

"WOWW! WHAWASZATT?"

"Augmented away," Laurie sighed. "Thank God."

"Laurie just jettisoned the reactor," Amav said. "Don't worry, everything's all right."

"SOOO WHYY YOO LOOK SO SIKK AND WEERD?" Z'B demanded. "THAZ NOTT MUCH FUNN!"

"Because--because--" Amav swallowed.

Weird that she looks so weird! Why's she not laughing with me? Maybe she thinks I can't tell she's sad about something. But I can!

I am here to gather! They should know that. I am here to

gather everything! Martians have to gather! Daddy says the first thing I should do is gather! Gather thoughts, gather feelings, gather how things look! How they feel! Then I will find the outradiance! I will know how to make the outradiance!

I know Daddy's outradiance, and Mommy's! Daddy says I'll know it all someday! All Mars! Amav doesn't have much, but it's there! Why is she sad when we're having so much fun? We're floating!

"Okay, I'm seeing it on the rear sensors," Laurie said. "Hasn't blown yet." Her screen brightened. "Crap, there it goes. Hell, now video's out too."

Amav peered at her console. "Battery backups for all systems at thirty-four percent."

"Damn you sanctimonious bitches!" came the yell through the intercom. "Why'd you jettison my reactor? We could've repaired it! How the hell you do it? I have all systems locked down!"

"Jettisoning all Xons now," Laurie replied. "Their Augmented Nukes are fine and I've just shot them away from us at one-fifth light. We're out of their blast radii about *now*."

"You can't jettison my Xons! You have no right!"

"Jettisoning PlanetBlasters Two and Four. Dammit, Amav, I barely have enough power on this console to see what I'm doing!"

"WOWW, IZZ GETTINGG COLLDD INN HEERE!"

"Z'B, *please*," Amav whispered.

"YOO BOTHH LOOKK SOOO WEERD WHYY IZZ THATT?"

"Prepping escape craft!" Laurie said.

"Negative!" Douglas roared back. "Nobody leaves this ship!"

"Dammit, he figured out my hack and the escape craft's blocked again!"

"You damn old crone! You damn old crone!"

"ARR YOO MADD THAT ROWWBOTT CALLS YOO OLDD KROWNN WEN INN REALITEE YOO ARR VERY BEEYEWTEEFUL HUMANN?"

"Oh God," Laurie muttered. "Amav, I can't get through the Control Room lock, either. I keep trying, but--"

The floating Amav pulled out a golden pistol. "Let me know as soon as you can."

"WOWW ..." Z'B gasped.

"*You* keep quiet about this! Got that?" Amav grabbed a handhold on the wall and whispered: "Laurie, can Douglas see me on the crew locator, or is it out too?"

"All internal sensors are out," Laurie confirmed. "I'm surprised the intercom's working. But Douglas has *that* locked down now too." She eyed Amav's gun. "If that's your old Empress shattergun, it won't work on a nonorganic robot."

"No problem. Kner upgraded it for me." Amav pushed herself off the wall and floated to the ladder to the Control Room.

Oh, I get it! The game is for Miss Amav to shoot Douglas Robot dead with the Empress Shattergun! Daddy told me about the famous Empress Shattergun. Burst inside Control Room, shoot Douglas into one million pieces of glass, then we play a new game! Wow!

So I must be quiet and not give it away! I see! But somehow I must make Miss Laurie happy! She looks weird now too!

"SOOO IFF DOUGLASS IZZ NOTT AVAILABLE TOO LOVVE YOO MISS LAURREE THEN I A MARSHUN WILL LOVVE YOU EVENN MORR!"

Laurie stared back at him.

"I A MARSHUN LOVVE YOO ALL! THISS IZZ SOOO MUCH FUNN! I AMM SOOO HAPPEE TOO BEE PLAYYING THISS GAYME WITH YOO!"

"*Quiet,* Z'B!" Amav hissed from the other end of the fuselage.

"No, it's okay," Laurie said. "Let him talk, it kind of masks what we're saying. Wait, *this* is weird."

Z'B looked at her console, but all he could see were shifting star patterns.

"*Amav!* I can't believe this, but we're actually moving again, and faster than light! In normal space, but faster than light! Can't get a reading on *how* fast. Maybe because this violates the laws of physics? It's like there's no *time* anymore!"

Amav pointed out a window. "Look! Oh my God!"

Z'B saw an impossible black circle cut out of the stars.

"We're in Iota Persei!" Laurie said. "I can't believe it!"

The black circle grew until there were no stars.

"Faster than light has ceased! Wait! *Oh my God!*"

"OHH YORR GODDD?" Z'B said. "IZZ THATT PARTT OF THE GAYME?"

"Quiet! We're doing … *1.08 million miles per hour?*"

"How far away is the damn sphere?" Amav yelled.

"Ten thousand miles!"

"THASS VERREE CLOSE! FUNN!"

"We have--we have--"

"WEE HAVV THIRTEE-THREE HUMANN SEKKONDDS BEFORE WEE CRASSHH! FUNN! I BETT YOO DIDD NOTT THINKK MARSHUN CHILDREN NEWW THEIR ARITHMETIC!"

"*Escape craft! Now!*" Laurie yelled, launching from her console and flying towards the big white craft anchored in the middle of the fuselage.

"That won't work! Unless you've got control!"

"No, but--"

"That's right, bahstads!" came the blast over the intercom. "I maintain control over all escape craft functions! Prepare to punch a hole in that goddamn sphere at a million miles per hour! We'll avenge the deaths of our comrades! Of my dear Laurie!"

"But I did manage to get access to the canopy," Laurie grunted as she wrenched it open. "Everyone inside! Z'B! Dammit, push yourself off the wall and get in here if you want to live!"

"MEE! I WANT TOO LIVE ANND HAVV FUNN!" Z'B laughed, pushing off and flying, then clambering into the cozy little craft with its six comfortable seats.

Floating is fun! Flying is fun! I want to do this every day!

Amav grabbed for the copilot seat and hauled herself in. Laurie took the command seat and manually clamped the canopy closed.

"Pressurizing! That function's automatic every time we close up. Douglas can't fool with our air."

"Laurie!" Amav called, pointing to the two blank console screens. "This can't work! He's locked us down!"

Laurie punched at her comm. "He has control of this ship's functions *as long as we're attached.* And there are two *other* things he no longer has control over--"

"No! Don't you dare leave!" boomed through the closed canopy. "We are *warriors!* We fight to the bitter end! We die with *honor!* And now you shame me with your cowardice! You *filthy excuse* of an imitation Laurie! *I curse you forever!*"

"--the airlock hatches, and the clamps holding us to the deck," Laurie finished. "Got the outer hatch open below us. As soon as I spring the deck hatch we'll shoot right through the airlock. Buckle up and prepare for some turbulence."

Z'B felt something give beneath him. Hurricane winds burst everywhere, buffeting the escape craft, flinging it--

Z'B seemed to blast in all directions at once. The dim light of the *Typhoon* was gone. There was just blackness punctuated by roiling stars, and a dark horizon swinging in all directions.

"Inertial dampers online!" Laurie called in front of a lighted console. "Engine online! Stabilization Vector 5A--go!"

Z'B blinked. "WOWW!" He fell back into his chair. Ahead, out the canopy window, loomed a stable pattern of stars.

"Look!" Amav cried, pointing back to rows of lights crisscrossing the surface of a flat black plain.

So close to this sphere thing, wide as the orbit of Jupiter Daddy said! So we can't even see a circle anymore. To us it's flat!

And they think we children don't know our geometry!

Something sparked on the black plain below and faded.

CHAPTER THIRTY-TWO
The Journey

The jumble of bright multicolored blocks pulsated from the walls, from the floor and the ceiling, down endless hallways opening left and right. Ahead, the lines of the corridor converged to an infinite pinpoint. Kner kept a claw over his unlidded eyes to shade them from the glare. His aching pink legs skittered across the hard tiles.

He counted the tiles rushing past and calculated elapsed time between two points. He hadn't slept for days, and he couldn't stop running.

Fifty miles an hour? How could that be? How could he be moving so fast, for so long?

Oh, that was right, he was *dead.* You were never supposed to admit that. But Kner didn't sleep, he didn't eat, he just ran at fifty miles an hour. What was that but *death?*

Damn his human friends. He was always converting measurements into human ones, even when he was dead.

No wonder they whipped us in the war!

Did this hallway go on forever? He'd get sunburned off all these damn tiles. Kner found he could remember every tile he'd seen in this hallway. In fact, he could remember the very first tile he'd seen at the entrance.

God, yes, The *entrance.* When they'd blasted the *M'rrpla* into the sphere there'd been nothing but these colored blocks. At first Kner thought they'd broken through, but then found himself running in this *hall.* Where was M'rrpla? Maybe robots couldn't come here? Whatever *here* was? It sure wasn't the *Rar'gasf Triunun'lh.*

Then again, Kner was sure that Iota Persei was too far away from Sol for the Martian afterlife reincarnation/recycling system to find him. But how could that be? Shouldn't the *Rar'gasf Triunun'lh* be infinite?

Kner also knew how exactly how long he'd been running. *Six hundred hours.* Twenty-five days. So, at fifty miles per hour, that was thirty thousand miles. Who the hell made a hallway

221

thirty thousand miles long?

Every color of the visible spectrum was represented in these blocks. Most were one by two feet, though occasionally larger blocks and square shapes dominated. And the tiles had a growing *conceptual* quality. Their surfaces were smooth, but each broadcast a unique but baffling *pattern of meaning*. Each was infinitely intriguing, and was probably why he was forced to remember every one of the hundreds of thousands he'd encountered so far.

Hundreds of thousands? Hell, add it up, dude! That's 76,032,882 so far in just the main hall.

And that wasn't counting what he'd glimpsed off to the sides: corridors that looked like conceptual pathways he *could* explore, but was somehow prevented from accessing at this time. His path seemed to lead only down this main hall. Sometimes the floor curved, rose or fell, temporarily cutting off the pinpoint of light at the seemingly infinite end. But soon the path returned to a converging straight line of endless blocks of vermillion, orange, indigo, violet, pastel green, yellow, any color imaginable, arranged in no apparent order.

Somehow each block was a *message*. The sum of all these blocks added up to *something*. He could study any one of them for eons. Was that what he was here to do?

Yet the floors, the walls, the ceilings, and the endless side corridors defied reason. Kner could barely stand their light and energy. There was no way to study these patterns.

Oh my God! This is hell! Hell!

Kner ran through a curve and was confronted with a branch into what looked like two main hallways, each curving sideways and up. They looked identically painful and intimidating. He had a thought to bear to the right, but then felt compelled to scamper left. Before long this new corridor again opened infinitely straight. Were these tiles directing him somehow? Why did he go left?

NEVER   FEAR,   FRIEND.   WELCOME   TO *GARR/THAHG.* ALL PATHS LEAD TO *GARR/THAHG.*

"What? Oh my God! *Who said that?* Where are you?"

He could swear he hadn't heard a thing, but whatever had come into his mind was nothing like Martian telepathic outradiance.

CORRECT. YOU ARE MAKING LOGICAL DE-DUCTIONS BASED UPON THE TILE CONFIGURATION MATRIX.

"What?"

DON'T SPEAK. CONSERVE YOUR ENERGY FOR RUNNING. THE TILES GIVE ENERGY BUT THEY DO NOT GIVE INFINITE ENERGY.

Kner tried to nudge his speed upwards in a reflexive attempt to escape the voice, but knew he couldn't outrun the logic building in his mind. Even the few words he'd spoken had taken their toll on him.

So I'm talking to--these blocks of light? These conceptual tiles?

CORRECT. YOU ARE RUNNING THE GREAT PROCESSIONAL HALL OF *GARR/THAHG*.

You mean that mythical place where Alpha Centaurian warriors are supposed to go when they die?

IF BY MYTHICAL YOU MEAN UNREAL YOU ARE IN ERROR. *GARR/THAHG* COLLECTS THOSE WHO HAVE PERISHED IN COMBAT IN SPACE. THIS INCLUDES YOUR RECENT ATTEMPT TO RAM YOUR SHIP INTO THE IOTA PERSEI SPHERE. WELCOME, WARRIOR!

No! I can't be dead! Can I?

YES, YOU CAN BE DEAD. YOU HAVE TO DIE TO GO TO *GARR/THAHG*.

Crap! But what about the Rar'gasf Triunun'lh? *I mean, I'm a Martian after all, don't I get to go to my own afterlife? Have I really sinned so much?*

There was a long silence in Kner's brain, then after another mile of running came:

GARR/THAHG APPLIES.

This statement was accompanied by an even brighter section of conceptual tiles and Kner put both palms over his eyes as he ran.

I'm dead! Nothing matters!

UNTRUE. EVERY SINGLE BLOCK MATTERS, AND SO DO YOU. I AM SORRY TO NOTE THE DISTRESS THE LIGHT CAUSES YOUR EYES. WHY DID MARTIANS EVOLVE WITHOUT EYELIDS? THAT CERTAINLY SEEMS FOOLISH. I HAVE NOT YET ENCOUNTERED THE HALLWAY THAT HOLDS THE ANSWER TO THAT, BUT I AM SURE I WILL.

Kner noted to his horror that despite having both hands over his eyes he nevertheless was still taking in the essence of every single block he passed. There was no way to avoid their raw meaning, even if he didn't understand a bit of it.

Okay, okay, so this is hell. Just play along, I guess. What else can you do?

EXACTLY. I CAME TO THE SAME CONCLUSION MYSELF AROUND HOUR SIX HUNDRED IN YOUR REFERENCE SYSTEM.

You--logic itself--refer to yourself as I?

MY NAME IS K'UFUNB. I CAME TO *GARR/THAHG* IN YOUR REFERENCE JULY 9, 2075, 1045 HOURS.

Kner noted an undercurrent of dates translated into Martian reckoning and briefly wondered why, again, the answer came predominantly in human measurements. Had he been so humanized by contact with those darkened houses who didn't radiate? Like Lee Borman?

APPARENTLY. YOUR SELF-AWARENESS CONTINUES TO GROW.

Kner shook his head, palms still over his eyes, running blindly but knowing everything in his path. *You say you're K'ufunb? The scrubwoman from Andertwin who blew up Jonathan James' spaceship?*

THE SAME. I DIED IN THE WARP TRANSFER MALFUNCTION JUST AS YOU DIED THREE HOURS LATER IN A STAR DRIVE RUPTURE.

But that couldn't be. He'd heard the *Jupiter's* report at the council meeting, he'd gone home, and then, later that night--but he still couldn't think about Douglas and that Laurie robot.

Unless the vortex really did transfer M'rrpla and me back in time several hours.

YES. IT DID. PREPARE FOR EVEN STRANGER TIME PARADOXES. YOU HAVE WALKED FOR SIX HUNDRED HOURS WHICH IS THE USUAL TIME FOR A WARRIOR TO BEGIN TO UNDERSTAND *GARR/THAHG*.

"Walking? Hell, I've been running my ass off!"

WALKING, RUNNING, IT'S ALL THE SAME. PLEASE DO NOT BOGGLE AT THE TRUTH THAT I, K'UFUNB, HAVE BEEN WALKING IN *GARR/THAHG* FOR TWENTY BILLION YEARS, WHICH IS LONGER THAN THE KNOWN AGE OF THE UNIVERSE.

Kner felt like lashing back with an argument against that impossibility, but realized he was conversing with perfect logic unfolding in his own mind. These tiles were explaining the obvious to him. K'ufunb had been walking for twenty billion years in *Garr/thahg*.

God, what she had to *know* by now.

I SIMPLY ASSEMBLE WHAT *GARR/THAHG* ALREADY KNOWS. FROM HOUR SIX HUNDRED I BEGAN TO ASSEMBLE. I KNEW I WAS IN *GARR/THAHG* FROM THE BEGINNING, BUT ASSUMED I WAS RUNNING TO MEET CLOPT, WHO WOULD BE MY HUSBAND, AT SOME GREAT CENTRAL HALL WHERE HE WOULD BE WAITING ALONG WITH ALL THE WARRIORS FROM ALL THE SPECIES WHO HAVE EVER DIED IN SPACE WARS. LIKE YOU, I WONDERED WHY *GARR/THAHG* NEEDED A THIRTY-THOUSAND-MILE PROCESSIONAL HALL. WHEN IT TURNED OUT THAT THE PROCESSIONAL HALL IS IN FACT INFINITE, I WORRIED THAT I HAD MISCALCULATED MY WARP DRIVE FAILURE. BUT I WAS SURE I'D INVERTED THE FORCE-FIELD MATRIX THROUGH ALL SEVEN DIMENSIONS. THEN I WONDERED WHETHER *GARR/THAHG* REJECTED ME BECAUSE I WASN'T A WARRIOR.

But you were a warrior when you blew the Castle. *You were going to Clopt, your warrior husband according to Alpha Centaurian tradition.*

How do I know that?

THANK YOU FOR KNOWING THAT. IT WAS ESSENTIAL THAT I UNDERSTOOD I HAD COME PROPERLY TO *GARR/THAHG*. OF COURSE, I QUICKLY FIGURED OUT THAT MARRIAGE TO THAT VIPER CLOPT WAS IRRELEVANT. YOU IN ANY CASE ACCEPT ME. I KNEW YOU WOULD, FOR WE WERE FATED TO THINK ALIKE, I, A LOWLY FKUUH SCRUBWOMAN, AND YOU, A MARTIAN SCIENTIST OF THE TOP RANK.

Forget it! I'm a sinner who's not even good enough for the Rar'gasf Triunun'lh!

OH, STOP FEELING SORRY FOR YOURSELF. CAN'T YOU GET IT THROUGH YOUR HEAD THAT *GARR/THAHG* HAS ASSIGNED K'UFUNB TO BE YOUR FRIEND?

My--friend? But you've evolved over twenty billion years into--what?

GOOD QUESTION, MY FRIEND. WE WILL HAVE MANY CONVERSATIONS THROUGH THESE LOGICAL TILES.

Won't we meet? And where are those millions of other dead warriors anyway?

YOU MEAN TRILLIONS. THERE IS NO ACCURATE COUNT, AT LEAST I HAVE NOT YET FOUND THE HALLWAY FOR THAT COUNT.

Well, where are you?

A long logical pause.

GARR/THAHG IS INFINITE. BE GLAD YOU HAVE MADE ONE FRIEND. BE GLAD YOU BEGIN TO UNDERSTAND THE LOGIC OF THE TILES.

Kner sprawled on the cold bright blocks, air knocked out of him. He uncovered his eyes to the same blinding infinite corridor.

"No! This is all insane! *Insane!*"

I UNDERSTAND YOUR CONSTERNATION. WE ALL

GET ONE FALL. NOW GET UP, KNER, AND RESUME THE JOURNEY. YOU MAY MOVE AT YOUR OWN PACE FROM HERE ON OUT.

Kner slowly got to his feet. His right leg ached and bled. Damn, it was so ridiculously *bright*. Why *didn't* Martians have eyelids? He had his pupils contracted as far as they would go.

"Okay, okay, I'm going!" he cried, taking up stride again, oblivious to his skinned knee as a dim awareness of trillions of warrior souls began to emerge from the logic of the tiles.

Why, that was his friend Fulr there. The brilliant Martian scientist, martyred on the *Typhoon II*. He was in *Garr/thahg*. And Martian Captain A'olfglnd, who'd tried to take out the *Typhoon I* with that underpowered saucer. And the real M'rrpla, who'd killed himself in despair, but he too had been a warrior. And Jack's brothers Jim and John, and that Harri McNarri *Typhoon* engineer Kner would've loved to meet. And so many Martians over the centuries, and those Alpha Centaurians who'd been fighting for thousands and thousands of years. So many casualties. He couldn't count them all.

"Where are we all *going?*" Kner gasped.

WE ARE JOURNEYING UNTIL WE DISCOVER WHAT THE BLOCKS ARE SAYING. EVERYTHING IMAGINABLE IS IN THESE BLOCKS. IT MAY TAKE ALL ETERNITY TO UNDERSTAND WHAT THEY'RE SAYING. BUT APPARENTLY WE ALL HAVE TIME TO *LISTEN*.

"That's insane! Then you're saying *Garr/thahg sucks?*"

NO. DO NOT DESPAIR. CONSERVE YOUR ENERGY FOR MOVEMENT. I AM YOUR GUIDE, K'UFUNB.

Kner fought down his next whimper, kept his palms to his eyes, and scampered down the endless corridors, turning down new hallways as the blocks fed patterns of raw energy deep into his core, completely bypassing his mind on the way.

CHAPTER THIRTY-THREE
The Wounded on the Sunlit Plain

"I can't *take* this!" Will moaned. "*I can't!*"

"Cut it, Will!" Jack ordered. "We have to get some control! What's happening is just happening! We still have to do our duty here!"

And what was that? Maybe just to observe for now, Jack thought. They had to be standing on the inside of the sphere. There was a sunny blue sky. No sign of curvature, but then there wouldn't be at this radius.

"Dammit, Jack, I refuse to *take* it!"

The crew was all here, thank God. Joe, Pat, and Lee. But Will had snapped. The damn robot had fooled them all, but Will had taken the worst dose of it.

High above the bright sun stood at noon, and the featureless green field extended in flawless geometrical flatness in all directions. A shuttle settled onto the grass. As the *McNarri* landed, a ramp dropped down and the little Martian robot appeared at the top. And that petite, red-haired, naked, unbelievable *thing* ran, hairy genitals flopping, to greet M'rrpla.

"SABHAVOTTR!" she laughed.

"I--I loved *that?*" Will moaned, collapsing on the ground.

"Wow," Joe whispered, "how come he never noticed *that* before?"

"Shhh! Look, I *know*," Jack said.

"Maybe they were taking it *real* slow!" Borman chortled. "They've been dating, what? Three-four months now?"

"Quiet, Lee. This is serious. Somewhere along the line this robot *infiltrated* us. Could be *years* back as far as we know, and it's obviously working with whatever brought us here."

"M'rrpla, I told you to stay in the ship, *outside* the sphere, and be ready to relay data to Sol!" Draka Sortie snapped as the Martian robot scampered up.

"Oh, sorry, sir! I thought you would want the saucer on the inside with everyone!"

"Why should I wish that, imbecile?"

"Well, sir, so that you might use it to gloat over the fate of your hapless victims! Surely to see the *McNarri,* their one hope of escape, firmly ensconced in the arms of the Wounded, would drive any of them mad!"

"HAVOTT robots! An *abacus* could outperform them! M'rrpla, exit the sphere at Dock 4333AAX-13." He pointed thirty degrees right of the *McNarri*. "That's five miles from here. I don't feel up to another teleportation, especially for that pile of crap you call a spaceship."

"It shall be done, sir! It shall be done! But first, if I may!" M'rrpla unzipped a pack on his hip and withdrew a russet robe.

"What the hell's *that* for?"

"Well, sir, I've observed that Laurie 283 is causing a great deal of stress to the humans in her unclothed state. I merely thought to provide her suitable attire for any philosophical discussions that might ensue here. And our dear departed Kner just happened to have entrusted his backup ceremonial Senior Scientist robe to me." He draped the robe around the nude Laurie.

"Oh, thank you, M'rrpla! I *love* it!" Laurie said. "You know, Laurie always secretly wanted to be a Senior Martian Scientist, but the entrance exam was beyond her! And now we have to protect Will's delicate sensibilities! The poor boy's gone into shock! He can't *move!* But he's *staring* at me all the same! What a *dweeb!*"

"I don't care!" Will shrieked. "Go ahead and kill me! I've had enough of this *insanity!*"

"Sheesh," Joe muttered.

"SABHAVOTTR!" M'rrpla laughed as he helped Laurie fasten the robe.

"SABHAVOTTR!" Laurie grinned back. "Thank you, fellow robot!"

"So you've managed to subvert a pair of robots, Draka," Jack said. "How did we get here? Is the *Typhoon* really gone?"

"First things first, Jacko. As you've no doubt suspected yourself, you're standing on the inside of the sphere. Because we're rotating, we have 1G here, though of course we can make any gravity we want. And we've pumped in enough air into this sector so you can breathe and have a nice blue sky."

"So that's Iota Persei up there," Joe muttered.

"Well, it won't be for long, Joe boy! We *do* need the energy, you know!"

"She's a *robot!*" Will continued to moan. "God, I've been in love with a *robot* all this time! A robot that can get a sex change operation overnight!"

"Or *half* of one, at least," Borman snickered.

"She's been laughing at me all this time! For months now! It's all a game to her! To *it!*"

"Look on the bright side, Will, at least she's not aroused anymore!"

"What the hell does it matter? I can't *handle* this! No one could! We've all bought the goddamn farm!" Jack froze to see Will haul his blaster out of his holster. But Joe flung himself atop Will, grappling for the gun.

"Dammit, idiot, put that thing down!"

"No! I'm done with it all!" Will screamed, punching at Joe with one hand and placing the barrel of his USSF blaster-shattergun to his temple. "Why the hell did I agree to this *insanity?*"

Joe abruptly let him go. "Okay, have at it, boy. I was just trying to keep you from making a fool of yourself." He pointed to Will repeatedly jerking the trigger of his blaster to no effect. "Damned networked pieces of crap. No wonder these jerks left 'em all in our holsters. There's no V to power 'em. I've always said this is the stupidest design the USSF ever came up with. Networked blasters!"

"I *wondered* about that when I was looking your through data files," Laurie put in, snuggled into the russet robe that was a close match to the color of her long hair. "You dimwits! And you keep your standalone blasters locked up!"

"You damn bitch!" Will snarled, flinging the weapon at her. She caught it easily and snapped it in two between her slender fingers.

"Oh, listen to the poor Willie falling apart! He can't even

kill himself, he's so upset! He has no idea what you *are,* Draka! Why I love you so!"

"Of course he can't handle it," Draka observed. "Or any of them, really. Hell, *I* can't really even handle it! Damn, I keep getting more and more information by the second!"

"I'm getting it too! Isn't it wonderful? What they're telling us? And they command me to love you even more! To help you realize *everything* even more!"

"Me too! Me too!" M'rrpla laughed. "A poor Martian HAVOTT, and I'm beginning to get the Negation documents myself! I love you too, Master!"

"Shut up about the Negation documents!" Draka barked. "M'rrpla, I thought I told you to take the damn *McNarri* to Dock 4333AAX-13. Once outside be ready to Star Drive to Sol on my command."

"Oh, dear! I so much wanted to stay here and gather wisdom from the Master!"

"Get *out* of here, HAVOTT!"

"Oh, don't be so hard on the dear boy!" Laurie said. "He's upgrading his software just by listening to your voice! Just like I'm doing now! We're *upgrading!* We're already both *more* than mere HAVOTTS now!"

"Dammit, Laurie! You're too attached to that stupid thing!"

"We're fellow robots! Just as you are!"

"You are *not* like me!"

"We're not as developed as you are, but we will be! The documents we're getting are amazing! *Billions* of exabytes of data! Data data data! It's pouring into us! And M'rrpla and I share our understanding with each other! We can't resist! Soon we'll be advanced like you! A super-robot like you!"

"Look, cut this stupid talk," Jack said, pointing to Draka's hands, badly shredded from the glass in the *Typhoon* Control Room and still dripping blood. "Draka's been brainwashed somehow, but he's *not* a damn robot. And he *used* to be a loyal member of my crew!"

"Forget it, Jacko, I'm *not* brainwashed. I'm a *robot.* The documents confirm it. I can't believe I never suspected it all this time, but it's the damn truth."

"No way, you would've had to pass the Revamped Turing," came Patrick James' voice behind Jack. "No robot can do that."

"And the med exams," Lee Borman added.

"That's what we've been trying to *tell* you!" Laurie laughed. "He's a *biological* robot! Identical to a human being in every way!"

"Well, it could be argued that we're *all* biological robots," Draka chuckled. "But here's a demonstration, Jacko." He grasped his right bicep with his left hand and twisted. Jack stared at the obscene wet scrunch Draka's arm made as he wrenched it off, gore bursting everywhere. Draka tore back his dark green United System Council presidential jacket to reveal the jagged gushing hole at the shoulder.

"*God!*" Borman gasped.

"Cancel pain receptors," Draka said calmly, tossing the jerking stump at Jack's feet. "Close off arteries and veins. Reroute neural functions."

"Oh my God!" Jack said, backing away.

But Draka Sortie stood serenely. The blood flow halted. "Wow, that amazes even *me*, Jacko. I'm just beginning to realize the stuff I can do. Like this!" There was a burst of iridescent light and Draka flexed a silver right arm, three times thicker than his previous one, crammed with thick black servo motors and what looked like tubes armed with red-tipped missiles. "I left it mechanical so you guys can take a good look. You got any reason not to believe me now?"

Jack shook his head. "Damn!"

"But to answer your question, I'm of the Wounded. I was built on an assembly line by completely automated processes *twenty thousand years* beyond any technology you can imagine. When we need a human model, we just say, '*Print human!*'"

"So you're from the sphere? And obviously you didn't come on my ship?"

"That's right. We have a little thing called Trans-Simultaneity. That's how we could bring your ship the rest of the way here. How I could be here instantly. Wherever we want to be, we just *are*. We can completely redefine time and space at will. Nice trick, eh, Jacko?"

"I don't *care!*" Will moaned from the grass. "They've *won!* I've had it! Let him say whatever crap he wants!"

"M'rrpla, are you still here?" Draka barked, eyeing the simpering little robot.

"Yes, just soaking up a little more of your radiance before I leave, Master!"

"He loves you so!" Laurie cried. "We both do! Read our documents on the subject!"

"Sheesh. Well, what the hell, stay if you have to, robot. Meanwhile, back to Jacko's other question, which he got *so* wrong. I'm *not* from the sphere! We just built this thing for kicks. All four of the inner planets of this system are inhabited by some race we've never really bothered to talk to much. They've been freaking out for thirty-four years, but what can they do? For this star, it does take thirty-four years before we can set up the Final Negation. So they just have to take it, and they damn well know it. But you're in luck. I've invited you guys to see the event yourselves!"

"You--"

"Cheer up, Jacko, I've also brought some friends of yours to celebrate!"

Three more force-field bubbles, red, purple, and green, floated from the dazzling sky.

"The *Typhoon III* was *yummy!*" Draka laughed. "So was the *V!* Their energy let us speed up the Negation by six and a half hours!"

CHAPTER THIRTY-FOUR
May I Explain the Process of Assimilating You?

The purple and green bubbles holding Amav and Z'B floated at Laurie's side. Through her red force field she saw figures on a grassy field below. The *V* crew. They were alive, but Will was on the ground.

"MAY I EXPLAIN THE PROCESS OF ASSIMILATING YOU?"

"*What?* Who's calling?"

"I AM YOUR FORCE FIELD."

"You--you're *where?*"

"I AM RIGHT HERE, ALL AROUND YOU. I AM A SENTIENT BEING LIKE YOURSELF. I HAVE BEEN CREATED TO BE YOUR FORCE FIELD. AS WE DESCEND TO YOUR COMRADES, I HAVE BEEN INSTRUCTED TO EXPLAIN TO YOU, THE MOST QUALIFIED ENGINEER, THE PROCESS OF ASSIMILATION."

Laurie felt an electric buzz when she touched the sheen of red energy around her. A few seconds ago they'd been in the escape craft, rocketing away from the sphere. Then the ship was gone and they were all in free space, panicking before they realized they were inside force-field bubbles. They could talk to each other, but had only managed a few numb words. Laurie fought off the dizziness. "Okay, go ahead."

She had to stall for time, think this through. Whatever was talking might give her some information. Where were they? Was Will really hurt down there?

"THANK YOU. WE WERE UNABLE TO GET MUCH NOURISHMENT FROM THE *JUPITER,* AS YOU CALL YOUR FIRST SHIP, BECAUSE IT WAS ENTERING STAR DRIVE AT THE MOMENT OUR EATER BEAMS CAUGHT IT."

"Eater--beams?"

"YES, THE WOUNDED NEED ENERGY."

"The ... *Wounded?*"

"WE ARE THE WOUNDED. WE LOVE ENERGY."

"Well ... I would think everyone, I mean, would love energy."

"THE WOUNDED ARE ESPECIALLY EQUIPPED TO GET ALL OF IT. EVERYTHING WE FIND, WE CONSUME. THE SHIP *TYPHOON V* WAS ENTIRELY CONVERTED TO ENERGY, AS WAS THE VEHICLE YOU ARRIVED IN, WHAT YOU CALL THE *TYPHOON III*. WE DIRECTED IT TO IMPACT ON THE SPHERE. IT WAS REALLY THE EASIEST WAY."

"So you *did* destroy our ships!"

"WE *ASSIMILATED* YOUR SHIPS. THE ENERGY WAS MINOR, BUT BENEFICIAL TO THE WOUNDED. WE EVEN ATE YOUR LITTLE SHUTTLECRAFT."

Of course they'd eaten their ships. She had to think. Was Will okay? He was moving his arms, getting up. And there was Jack arguing with--Draka Sortie? How'd *he* get on the mission? Jack must've convinced him to come when Laurie didn't show.

"So you're a machine. What about the, uh, biological people who direct you?"

"THERE ARE NO BIOLOGICAL ENTITIES. WE CREATE FACSIMILES OF BIOLOGICALS WHEN NECESSARY."

"So you built a sphere around your star? I assume we're coming down to the inside of the sphere?"

"YES. BELOW IS THE INTERIOR OF THE SPHERE. A POCKET OF BREATHABLE AIR HAS BEEN CREATED FOR YOU BIOLOGICALS. IT IS NOT OUR STAR. WE JUST TOOK IT. WE NEED THE ENERGY."

Laurie's bubble steadily descended with the other two over the green plain, which seemed to extend forever. "How thick is the sphere?" she managed, unwilling to consider what *taking the star* might mean.

"FIFTY OF YOUR MILES BETWEEN INTERIOR SURFACE AND OUTER HULL. THIS SPACE IS DEVOTED TO THE NEGATION ARRAY FOR IOTA PERSEI."

"The ... the ..." Laurie swallowed. She didn't want to know.

"THE SPHERE TAKES ONE WEEK TO BUILD, BUT THE NEGATION ARRAY REQUIRES A CERTAIN NUMBER OF YEARS TO ACHIEVE MAXIMUM READINESS TO OBTAIN ALL ENERGY FROM A STAR. IN THE CASE OF IOTA PERSEI, THE PERIOD IS 34.36 YEARS. ASTRONOMERS FROM YOUR SOL SYSTEM HAVE JUST DISCOVERED THE EXISTENCE OF THE SPHERE, AT THE MOMENT WHEN ITS WORK IS NEARLY COMPLETE."

"Why are you telling me all this?"

"BECAUSE YOU ARE THE EXPERIENCED ENGINEER WHO WILL UNDERSTAND THAT TRANS-SIMULTANEITY WILL THEN TAKE ALL ENERGY FROM IOTA PERSEI AND TRANSMIT IT TO ASSIST IN THE CREATION OF A DISTANT QUASAR."

"You're going to destroy this sun?"

"NOT DESTROY. *TRANSMIT* ENERGY TO A NEW QUASAR, BILLIONS OF LIGHT-YEARS AWAY."

"Why?"

Her force field made no reply. The grass came up and Laurie's bubble hovered two feet off the infinite plain, right in front of Will, who was on his knees staring at her with blasted paralyzed eyes.

"WELCOME TO THE IOTA PERSEI NEGATION ARRAY. THE NEGATION MASTER IS DRAKA SORTIE."

"Negation--*Master?*" Laurie gasped.

"YES. AS YOU ARE THE NEGATION MASTER FOR SOL."

"What?"

"THE NEGATION PERIOD FOR SOL IS 31.81 YEARS."

Her bubble blew and dumped her on the grass.

CHAPTER THIRTY-FIVE
A Development We Can't Explain

The red bubble wafted to the ground and blinked out. It took Jack a while to focus on what he was seeing. God, could there be *another* Laurie robot?

"Will! God, Will!" the newcomer cried, reaching for a med kit at her belt. "Are you all right?"

"No!" Will screamed. "This can't be happening!"

"*Will!* Will, it's *me!*"

"It *can't* be!"

"It *is!*" Draka Sortie laughed. "Welcome, Negation Master for Sol!"

"Hey, why can't *I* be the Negation Master for Sol?" Laurie 283 demanded in her Senior Martian Scientist robe, hands on hips.

"Because Laurie is smarter than you, that's why, sweetie."

"But I'm a HAVOTT! A *computer!*"

"Oh, can it. We've picked the human Laurie and that's that."

"*Laurie!* Oh, God, no!" Will screamed, flailing under the newcomer shoving a thick black syringe into his arm.

"Shut up, Will, this is for your own good. You're in shock. You need to calm down."

"The--*human?*" Jack said, and he instantly knew from the slightly less red hair and the tighter face that somehow his real physician/engineer had come to Iota Persei, despite the fact that she wore an ancient Airman First Class uniform. "Laurie! It's *you!* How the hell did *you* get here?"

"We came in the *III,* but it was *destroyed,* Jack!"

"Oh my God! The *V* was too!"

"God, aren't they wimps?" Laurie 283 snorted. "C'mon, Draka, it's time to turn over the Negation Master duties to a pro! I've already absorbed eighty-eight percent of the Negation documents and I'll have the rest in just a sec!"

Laurie whirled at the sound of her own voice. "Dammit, it's *you!*"

"That's right, you old bitch! *Draka!* What the hell do you see in her? If you really *loved* me you wouldn't suck up to her like this!"

"Enough. We're here to welcome *all* our new comrades. I won't have you denigrating any of our top USSF talent. These, dear HAVOTT, are the absolute cream of the crop. See, Jack? We Wounded really are an extremely polite and respectful species."

A purple bubble landed and faded. Jack stared at the slender woman running in a form-fitting red flight suit.

"Amav! Oh my God, you *can't* be here!"

"Jack, you're *here!* Thank God you're *here!*" She tackled him and nearly brought him down. "God, Jack! Andy was getting ready to fly when this *robot* hijacked the ship and we didn't have everyone on board but we had incredible vortex problems and we were about to blow and then we got pulled to Iota Persei and then Laurie *saved* us! God, she *saved* us! We got into the shuttle and she saved us!"

"*She* was the one who kept us together, Jack!" Laurie shouted. "I was about to totally freak out but there she was, going after Douglas with a shattergun!"

"Wimps! Damn you all!" the Laurie robot hissed, folding her arms. Jack eyed the sulking HAVOTT, then took in Will whipping his head back and forth between the robot and the real Laurie.

"You say the *III's* gone?" Jack said, meeting Amav's eyes in shocked relief. God knew she shouldn't be here, but it was good. Just to have her next to him was good. "And the other crew?"

Amav kissed him hard. "I can't believe you're *alive!* No, nobody else was on the ship except Amav and me, and Douglas, and--"

"Douglas?"

"Douglas the idiot *robot!* He rode the *III* right into the goddamned sphere!"

"Oh my God!" Laurie 283 cried. "That means John was coming for *me!* Oh my God! He died for *me!*"

"SABHAVOTTR!" the M'rrpla robot chirped. "Comfort yourself, dear friend! We robots can never die! Only be terminated forever!"

"Oh my God! I loved *John!* What was I *thinking?*" She whirled to Draka. "You *seduced* me, you bastard! I loved *John,* and then *you* came along and *seduced* me!"

Draka laughed. "Oh, get over your schoolgirl crushes, robot! We have work to do!"

"I will not! I *love* John! I still do!" She turned to Amav. "You say he *died?*"

"He was at the controls of the ship when it went into the sphere. Look, I'm sorry, but we couldn't convince him otherwise."

"God, what is wrong with my *programming?*" Laurie 283 moaned, covering her face. "Oh my God! It must be *Runaway Programming Disorder!* That has to be it! So many of the HAVOTT series were at risk for it! We never talk about it, but we're all secretly afraid of it!"

"You--my lady," M'rrpla stammered. "Please--SABHAVOTTR--calm yourself. I'm analyzing your documents now, and I don't find, well, *much* trace of RPD."

"Oh my God! It's *RPD!*" She whirled to Draka. "*You* gave me this, you son of a bitch!"

"Oh, shut up, and do your robotic duty! We have serious work here! We have to negate that damn star and you're worrying about whether you're crazy or not! Sheesh!"

"RPD! It's the worst! The *worst!*" She turned to the human Laurie. "And it's because of *you!* The HAVOTT programmers knew deep down you were totally *crazy,* so they programmed that into *me!* God, I hate you!"

Laurie stepped back. "Is that why you attacked me last night? Why you--why you--"

"Oh, is *that* what you're so worried about? Don't worry, I *did* want to put it into you, but I held back, out of *some* respect, I don't know why! But I needed your uniform! And those charming USSF panties!"

"God, what a *zoo,*" Jack muttered as a green bubble hit the grass behind the pair and winked out. A small Martian in a black and white-striped child sweater leapt onto M'rrpla's back.

"MARSHUN! MARSHUN!" Z'B laughed. "WOWW, YOO ARR A MARSHUN *ROWWBOTT!* WOWW! I LOVVE YOO BEST OF ALL!"

"Hey, little one, hey!" M'rrpla said. "Careful with my fin there! It's plasti-titanium and you might bend it!"

"WEE HAD ANN INNCREDIBUL RYDDE INN A SPAYSHIPP! THENN ITT WENT AWAYY AND WEE WERRE IN BUBBULLZ ANND WEE FLOATEDD *HEERE!*"

"That's D'yyrfa's son," Amav said. "Douglas kidnapped him and brought him on board and threw Andy off and then launched! God, if Laurie hadn't been on board we'd all be dead!"

"But John *is* dead, bitch!" Laurie 283 cried. "*He* counts, you know! He was a sentient being, same as you! You killed him! He was coming here to save me!"

Jack was distracted by M'rrpla pulling a silver disc from the pack at his hip and slinging it a hundred yards across the grass. Z'B took this in wide-eyed, then hurtled after it. So it really was true that most Martians kept a little Frisbee on them to calm down wayward children, no matter how hard it was to throw the thing in the thin Martian atmosphere. That confirmed some recent outradiance which Jack hadn't paid much attention to about the new instability in Martian culture caused by the presence of so many infants. The standard hip-pocket silver Frisbee had apparently proved of immeasurable help in calming the nonsense pouring out of the children's minds.

"Go for it! Go for it, little one!" M'rrpla laughed. Z'B easily caught the disc in his pink claws and bounded back.

"The M'rrpla thing is another HAVOTT. Sortie's some sort of robot too," Jack whispered to Amav, pointing to Draka's new military-grade arm. "He says there's a race of them. They call themselves the Wounded. Evidently they built this sphere."

Draka picked up Jack's voice even as Laurie 283 beat on his chest with hard little robotic fists. "Whoa, some lucky guesses, Jacko. Listen, I'll bet you'd love to call home about now and tell

them the same thing, wouldn't you, Mr. Supreme Commander?"
He held out a comm.

"You'd let me? This has superspace?"

Draka nodded. "I just copied Borman's, which Laurie 283
here so thoughtfully decided to destroy. Here, take it."

"You *are* an idiot!" Laurie 283 snarled. "I had to do it to cut
this Borman jerk *off!*"

"Hey, as a United System senator, I resent--" Borman
began.

"Quiet," Draka commanded. "Feel free to call, Jacko. The
Wounded will pay the long-distance charges!"

Jack stared at the comm in disbelief. He'd had his own
comm upgraded to superspace capability last week while they
were on Andertwin, but he'd been aware for several minutes that
it was missing from his belt, although his unpowered USSF
shattergun remained at his side. He punched in Webster
Maligh's code.

"USSF HQ. Maligh."

Jack blinked at the marvelous fidelity filling the entire
grassy plain. Superspace radio always had a slight metallic
echoing, but the USSF third-in-command sounded as if he were
standing right in front of Jack.

"A few minor improvements," Draka smirked.

A strong breeze crossed the sunlit plain. "ROWWBOTT, I
LOVVE YOO!" Z'B burbled as he and M'rrpla tossed the silver
Frisbee around the *McNarri*.

"Well, then, everyone's going to hear this clearly. Webster,
this is Jack. We've been taken prisoner at Iota Persei."

"*Jack!* Oh my God! Is that *you?* Can that really be *you?*"

"Yes, of course. We've been taken prisoner by *Draka
Sortie,* believe it or not, and this race calling itself the *Wounded.*"

"Sortie? We assumed he'd left with you on the *Typhoon*.
We haven't seen him for a week! Jack, I can't *believe* this! What
about the rest of the crew? Everyone okay? What about the
Typhoon III? Donnelley said it was hijacked by a robot! And
Amav and Laurie were on it, and D'yyrfa's son."

"They're here. I don't know how, but they're here and okay.

Listen, Draka Sortie's really an *alien*. And apparently he has some method of transporting himself from Mars to Iota Persei."

"Apparently!" Draka laughed.

"This is *unbelievable news!*" Webster said.

"Listen, Webster, these aliens have destroyed both *Typhoons* and we're not sure of our status here, to put it mildly, so you can start putting a new mission together, maybe with the *Jonathan Commer.* It was the next to be retrofitted with Enhanced."

"Right, right, I copy what you're saying, Jack, but my God, we can't even get out of the solar system right now! We've lost contact with the *Commer* and every other ship outside Sol! I can't believe you can call *me!*"

"What? *What* are you saying?"

"It's just that there's--this *development* we can't explain! I mean, God, Jack, we just had state funerals for you all just yesterday!"

"*What?*"

"Why we went ahead and did that, I don't really know! I think because we were in shock, I guess, going through the motions of *honoring* you. But everything's coming apart! We haven't seen panic like this since the Uranus flyby in '29!"

"Hold on," Joe cut in. "Webster, this is Joe. What's your date there?"

"Our date?"

"Yes! What day is it there?"

"The seventeenth, of course. July 17th. *My God, where have you all been the last week?*"

Jack reeled at the hysteria in Maligh's voice. "Webster, we've only been here a few minutes. You're saying it's July 17th there? One week ahead of us?"

Draka whistled. "A little time adjustment, gents! Give Joe a prize for being the first to figure it out! Should be obvious why we did it in a moment, if Monsieur Maligh can get his brains in gear!"

"THROWW ITT TOO MEE! THROWW ITT TOO MEE!" Z'B laughed. M'rrpla shot the Frisbee five hundred feet down the plain in a high hover, and Z'B ran all out for it.

"It's the sphere, Jack! *The sphere!*"

"I *know,* Webster, listen, can you please calm down?"

"A sphere around *Sol!* It's perturbing all the orbits! Mercury, Earth, Venus, Mars! We're all *askew!* And the damn thing extends to the orbit of Jupiter!"

"*What?*" Jack cried.

"We haven't been able to send a single ship out after the *Typhoon III* left! These *energies* began building all through the Jovian Fragment Field! Then this *sphere* just assembled itself over the last week! Jack, we're completely enclosed by a sphere!"

CHAPTER THIRTY-SIX
The Negation Array

"Webster! Launch every Xon bomb you can against that sphere! Use Amplified Xons! Punch as many holes in that thing as you can!"

"Hit it on the equator!" Amav added. "If it's rotating like this one, maybe you can destabilize it and it'll tear itself apart. Scan for anything like a docking port or any weaker construction!"

Laurie looked up from Will, whose eyes were snapping back into focus. He was alive. They were together and that was all that mattered.

"Okay, we'll try again," Maligh said. "When we saw construction underway, we sent some regular Xons, but they didn't do any good. The damn thing just closed up completely a couple hours ago. But we'll try again with Amplified."

"Hmm," Draka said. "They won't work either, Webster! Bye for now!"

"No, *wait!*" came a new voice.

"Aw, *hell.*"

"Draka, what's going *on* out there?" demanded Mandy Frederick, Empress of the Martians. "We're in a Supercommittee session with Maligh! *Where have you been all week?*"

"Hell, I forgot about the little shrew," Draka muttered.

"What? *What* did you just say?" blasted from the comm in Jack's hand. "Draka, what is going *on?* You haven't contacted me for a *week!* I've been *sick* with worry!"

"Amazing what delusions fall away once you realize your real self! Think of all the energy I wasted on that bitch!"

"*What?*" burst from both Jack and Mandy.

Draka laughed. "Hey, babe, I'm only now seeing why it all had to unfold like it did! It was the *program!* Like, it called for me to ramp up the old *sexual charisma* and sweep you right off your feet! With *logic,* and specially engineered pheromones, if the truth be told!"

244

"*What* are you telling me?" Mandy screeched.

"Hey, babe, don't freak *too* much! I sure didn't know it at the time. I'm just realizing it now. But hell, how else could such a fantastic piece like you ever fall for a fat slob like me?"

"Yeah, we were *wondering* what she saw in you," Joe said.

"Draka, this is *insane!* You *love* me! You told me you *loved* me!"

"C'mon, Mandy, isn't it obvious I married you just so I could turn the goddamn Empress against the goddamn AC Grid? That's what the program was all about!"

"That doesn't make any sense! Draka, I could *kill* you!"

"Don't you remember how fascinated you were at first by the new Grid? And how I had you *frothing* about the dangers within like two hours? And how you yanked around the wimps on the United System Council and got 'em all riled up? Hell, that was *me!* I turned everyone against the Grid!"

"What in God's name does this *mean,* Draka?"

"Look, honey, almost everyone in Sol would've wanted to try it out! But if this Grid's in place, and everybody always knows what's in everybody's mind, well, you can see the hassle there."

"That's it!" Jack said. "If we'd had the Grid, we would've known from the start that you Wounded jerks were in Sol!"

"Correct, Jacko," Draka smirked. "Like we could never get to the damn Alpha Centaurians because their Grid would pick up the slightest incursion. And we need our folks on the ground to prepare for a good *sphering*. Which is what we just did to Sol right now."

"*Draka!*" Mandy screamed. "Get your goddamn ass back here! Right now!"

"Aw, cripes, bitch can't understand plain logic. Guess it's time for the old divorce trip." Laurie barely registered the blur of Draka's hand snatching the comm from Jack and tossing it to robot Laurie. "Okay, Laurie sweetie, do your thing!"

Robot Laurie crumpled the comm between her fingers, then poured it as black gravel onto the grass. Human Laurie stared, considering the damage this robot could have done to her last night had it chosen to.

Draka folded his arms. "Anyway, gang, we couldn't get to the ACs even after their first Grid went down in '53, because of all this *time crap* going on. Then goddamn *Phil Sperry* messed everything up when he made this damn *new* Grid. We knew we had to sphere Sol fast before you guys got a Grid yourselves."

"Brilliant! Absolutely brilliant!" M'rrpla laughed, leaping for the silver Frisbee like a ballet dancer.

Draka shrugged. "At any rate, I've shifted you cream-of-the-crop USSF'ers a week forward so you could see for yourselves how it is with old Sol. We've definitely been wanting to *sphere* her for quite some time." He pointed to a floating hologram displaying a twenty-foot-wide starfield.

"Fantastic view, huh? Sol's the bright one right in the middle. Can you imagine such a stable image thirty-four light-years away? Solid as a rock! Of course, you're just seeing what she looked like thirty-four years ago. Not much point to that, is there? Now watch what happens when I add a Trans-Simultaneity view."

The sun at the center of the image winked out.

"So that's *real time,* whatever *that* really means. And now, we'll magnify."

The image zoomed in on a black circle cut out of the stars.

"Oh, God ..." Amav gasped.

"Sol needs 31.81 years for its sphere to be fully operational. But if you like I can forward us 31.81 years so you can get the entire experience *now.*"

"Oh, let's do!" said robot Laurie.

"Quiet, sugar. If we did that, we'd miss the Negation of Iota Persei." Draka turned to Amav. "And I assume you'd want to see *that,* wouldn't you, Miss Doctor Planetary Engineer?"

"I have no idea what you're talking about!"

"I do!" Will Connors shouted. "We were fools to think we could explore this goddamn galaxy! Because the first thing we hit is our *annihilation!* Jack talked me into this! He talked everyone into it!"

"*What are you saying?*" Amav cried.

"Isn't it obvious? These Wounded sons of bitches go from one star to another, putting a Dyson sphere around it and stealing all its energy! They *kill stars!* A whole system *gone,* and billions of people, just like that!"

"Isn't it *marvelous?*" robot Laurie laughed.

"Dammit, which one of you is the real Laurie?"

"I am! The one with RPD that nobody *cares* about anymore!"

"No, Will, it's *me!*" Laurie cried. "You know that thing there is just a HAVOTT!"

"I know, I know," Will said, "but which one of you--"

"If he can't tell *that,* with all my *new capabilities,* he's a lot more messed up than we thought!" robot Laurie sneered. "It doesn't matter anyway, because I'm *freaking!* I have Runaway Programming Disorder, and you all laugh at me, but who cares, because I'm *freaking!*"

"Shut the hell up! Damn you!" Will drew a fist but the robot punched right back at it in a hundredth of a second. *"Ow!"* he moaned, clutching his fingers.

Laurie reached for her med kit and pulled out a pain shot. "Let me look at that." All four fingers were broken.

"RPD! RPD!" Laurie 283 laughed. "Mess with me and see what you get!"

"Dammit, Draka, is this true?" Jack said. "Is this really what all this sphere stuff is for?"

Draka laughed. "Hey, Jacko, it's what we do for a living! We find a star, or a nebula, or really, anything we want, and we *suck* its energy!"

"It all gets fired off into distant quasars!" robot Laurie giggled. "I've been reading more and more documents about it all! It's magnificent! What a *light show!*"

"Yeah, we have a lot of fun, all right."

"Do--do the people on these four planets here think it's *fun?*" Laurie said.

"Do the people of *Sol?*" Jack shouted.

"Jack--Laurie! Lighten up! This is my first trip as Negation Master, and you're raining on my parade! The energy you get as

Negation Master is *incomparable*. Look, Jack baby, we'll let *you* do the next one. After Sol, that is, because Laurie's got dibs on that one!"

"*Thank* you, Draka!" Laurie 283 said. "I was beginning to think you didn't care!"

"No, not you, dear, the *real* Laurie here. The one with a *mind*. A HAVOTT could never handle the calculations!"

"Dammit, Draka, I can link to a billion computers and *infinitely* increase my capacity!"

"Stop, dear, and I mean it. To do a Negation, you must be *completely* detached and do all the calculations yourself. Laurie here has that capacity right now."

"Why, I do *not!*" Laurie cried.

"Don't worry, hon, you have 31.81 years to figure out all the parameters. We won't spoil things by pushing you that far forward. We'll just send you back to Sol and you'll have your very own office on the sphere there. The Office of the Negation Master! What an *honor!*"

"No! That's insane!"

"All of you here are the cream of the crop of Sol. The *space leaders!* Of course you're getting full membership. The top leaders of all the spacefaring species get Wounded Gold, that's the rule. We need energy, and we just *eat* it. That includes taking in the expertise of the leaders of new species. It's all *energy*."

"Well, count us out," Jack said. "Who the hell would want that?"

"Sorry, Jacko, the invitation is *mandatory*. We got a lot of flak from the third planet down there about joining. The Ywritt or whatever they call themselves. But we just took their top people and did bio upgrades on 'em. Fascinating bastards, really. They designed the damn talking force-field bubbles that brought you guys here."

"HAYY HAYY HAYY!" Z'B cried, running after the Frisbee rolling past Draka.

Draka cocked an ear at the Martian infant. "Damn thing's giving me a headache. Listen to all that crap in its mind!"

Laurie realized she'd blocked out Z'B's gurgling

outradiance. It helped that he'd been further from the group for some time.

"*I* can't hear anything," Laurie 283 observed.

"That's because you're just an empty-headed collection of plasti-metal AI wafers, sweetiekins. My bio interface can pick that crap up, unfortunately. I may have to terminate that damn kid in a minute."

"You *wouldn't!*" Laurie gasped.

"If that stupid thing interferes with the duties of the Negation Master, by definition he's a *sin* to be eradicated, honey! Which by the way is why all of you get bio-upgrades. Flush out all the *sin* in you. Not a problem, really. We wipe out your existing *filthy* body, and transfer your essence into an immortal *robotic* body. Engineered to any shape you want! I see you're all crapping in your pants, but really, it's absolutely painless."

"I *told* you this was crazy!" Will moaned. "I *told* you we'd all buy the farm!"

Draka grinned. "Anyway, this whole part of the galaxy has been fenced off to us until now, but Iota Persei marks the beginning of a new era. You'll all help us ship this whole sector to Quasar City!"

"And *I* will get upgrades that will last me to the end of the universe!" robot Laurie exulted. "Isn't that right, Draka?"

"Absolutely! Laurie will be the first manmade robot to become a Wounded. Of course, she has a *lot* of upgrading to get done before that."

"And me, Sire! Me!" M'rrpla said, slinging the Frisbee hard at Z'B's stomach.

"WOWW!" Z'B laughed, snatching the disc. "THATT WUZZ GRATE! YOO SURE ARR STRONGG!"

"Upgrade me! Upgrade me!" M'rrpla sang.

"You just steal all this energy and *throw it away?* For *nothing?*" Laurie gasped.

"Yes, sister, we just *blow it up!*" robot Laurie sneered. "For no reason! Absolutely no reason!"

"Well, little Laurie's understanding definitely needs an

upgrade from those primitive HAVOTT patterns," Draka said. "Give us Wounded credit for *some* brains. When we push a star through a quasar, adding a lot of dark matter in a *secret* recipe we won't reveal until you're *completely* assimilated, well, it's a damn work of *art*. We, the Wounded, are the ultimate *artists*. We blast energy all over the place! As I shall now demonstrate with Iota Persei."

"*I love you, Negation Master!*" cried robot Laurie.

Draka pointed a finger at the sun. Then came exterminating blackness.

CHAPTER THIRTY-SEVEN
Spherequakes

Jack collapsed on the grass, scrambled and sick.

"WAITT! WHAZZ GOINGG ONN?" Z'B wailed from the nothingness.

"Oh, come on, you can't be afraid of a little Negation!" Draka Sortie laughed. "Sure it's dark! Damn dark! That's what we *do!* But in deference to your panic, a few *night lights!*"

Jack blinked furiously. Above him floated hundreds of dull gray spheres. Grass, loose earth, and roots wrenched free in his fingers. Beneath him came impossibly deep bass tremors.

"Amav! Joe! Everyone okay?" he called amid the surprised groans of his crew around him, all groping in thick fog on their hands and knees.

But Draka was still on his feet along with the two robots, all three surfing on waves of undulating dirt.

"I--I DON'TT *LIKE* THISS! WHAZZ GOINGG ONN?"

"Don't worry, I'll keep it warm for you, and keep the air going for those nasty little organic bodies!" Draka said. "But we'll upgrade you out of 'em in a few minutes! We're cooking up your replacements right now." He pointed to the left where Jack could see huge mounds of earth writhing from the surging ground.

"You idiot! We're *coming apart!*" Amav said, pointing straight overhead. "*Earthquakes!* Without a sun--"

"Correction: *spherequakes!* Of *course* we're coming apart! We've been revolving around a massive star up to now! Now there's *nothing!*"

"*Nothing?*" Jack said. "You didn't black-hole Iota Persei?"

"No! Why waste our energy on a black hole? We've sent the *entirety* of the energy back *home!* To Quasar City! The Wounded are *rejoicing!*"

"But without a star, every point at the equator of this sphere wants to fly out in a straight line!" Amav shouted. "The whole thing will come apart! You *idiot!*"

"Who cares about a damn sphere? It's just a means to an

end! How do you think we throw the trash out when we're done?"

"And all the planets--"

"All four are flying out in a straight line right now, with their own little *planetquakes!* Want to bet whether they'll hit the sphere wall before it evaporates? The Ywritt must be *pissed!*"

"You stupid sons of bitches!" Joe shouted. "Do you realize how many billions of people you're *murdering?*"

"Oh, yes! 685 billion! But don't worry, Joey! We won't let those planets get too far! We just want to pick up the maximum *fear energy* from those 685 billion! But the sphere's still got enough integrity to transmute all those planets into *more* raw energy! Any stray asteroid, spaceships wandering around, you name it, we'll get it! Just scraps compared to Iota Persei, but hell, we'll take it! Coming up about *now,* I would say! Yes! Done! There you have it, Joe baby! 685 billion alien twerps don't have a damn thing to worry about anymore!"

"*God ...*"

"I can *feel* their *fear energy,* then it *ceasing!*" robot Laurie laughed. "What a *rush!*"

"Well, you can't really feel the energy, dearie, since it's all been sent to Quasar City. What you're getting are *happy documents* from the Wounded! *Good reviews* you might say!"

Jack felt Amav's hand in his. He grasped it tightly even though it meant he had less of a grip on the disintegrating grass.

"Hang on," she whispered. "Even if we *do* get assimilated, we can be *viruses* or something, subvert it somehow later on."

Jack nodded. Yes, that might be their only contribution left.

Draka folded his arms with a snicker. "I heard that, little lady! That's what they *all* say. By the way, I hope you guys figured out that I've enhanced your entire Negation experience with Trans-Simultaneity. I shoved the *light* effect right next to the *gravitational* effect. Otherwise we wouldn't be seeing Iota Persei wink out for another forty-three minutes. Speed of light, you know. But the loss of spacetime curvature's *instant.*"

"MAYKE ITT STOPP, M'RRPLA! MAYKE ITT STOPP! I DON'TT *LIKE* THISS!"

"It's okay, buddy, it's okay!" M'rrpla cried. "I think! Maybe!"

"This is what we get!" Will shouted. "This is what we get for sticking our noses out here! We come up against this *evil!* I hope you're all satisfied!"

Jack rolled as another convulsion twisted beneath them. "Will, pull yourself together! They were already among us! We would've found out sooner or later!"

Will glared back. "Everything's gone! This is the end! An entire star going! *An entire solar system!* We had to see it all!"

Draka laughed. "The Wounded are *enjoying* Will's fear! Our navigational genius! He can't navigate his own *fear!* This really is *delightful!*"

"Leave him alone!" Laurie said. "He's just having flashbacks! To Barnard's Star! It was really hard for him!"

"No!" Will shouted. "You can't *say* that!"

"It's okay, Will! It's okay!"

"It's *not!* If I hadn't been such a coward, none of this would have happened! I'm so sorry! I know I've let everyone down!"

"I DON'TT WANTT THISS! EVEREETHINGG'S COMMINGG APPARTT!" Z'B moaned, tearing at the dirt in helpless fury.

"I'm so sorry! I wasted my entire life! And I've let *you* down, too, Laurie! God, I'm so sorry about *us!* I couldn't love you! Not really! I've just been a scared kid all this time!"

"Oh God! So have I! So have I! But it was so good we finally came together!"

"Oh, listen to this!" robot Laurie laughed. "They're both crazier than I am!"

"I DON'TT *LIKE* THISS! MAYKE ITT STOPP!"

Jack turned to Draka. "Okay, man, suppose we go along with being assimilated! Then Sol has thirty-one years? You won't move that up?"

Draka shrugged, balancing as the ground roared beneath them. "Oh, so you're hoping someone back on Sol will figure a way out of *this* in thirty-one years? Well, I'll let you in on a secret, Jacko. It really does take 31.81 years for the sphere to set up Sol properly. Yeah, they do have thirty-one years. All I'd be doing would be manipulating time to let you see it *now*. But don't worry, it *will* happen. We've researched your psychology, your technology, your culture, everything. There's nothing you can do to alter the outcome."

"STOPP ITT! STOPP ITT, M'RRPLA!"

Draka cocked an ear at the Martian infant. "Damn, is that thing getting *worse?*"

"I can't hear a thing!" robot Laurie said. "Are you sure?"

Jack concentrated on the cascade of sense impressions pouring out of Z'B's mind. He'd managed to shove it in the background, but Z'B's level of fear seemed no worse than the typical Martian childhood terrors Jack had occasionally tapped. The infant clearly had no idea of the seriousness of this moment.

"Damn, it's like the stupid kid is deliberately trying to flood me with *crap!*" Draka snarled. "M'rrpla, kill the damn thing! It obviously isn't anything to assimilate!"

"No!" Jack shouted as M'rrpla glanced at his shattergun holster.

Then came a fresh wash of delight from Z'B.

"HII, DRAKKA! MYY OUTTRADIANCE IZZ *FINDINNGG* YOO! YOO WERRE HARDD TOO FINND, SINCE YOO ARR A ROWWBOTT! BUT NOWW YOO ARR FINALLLEE ACCEPTINNGG MEE!"

"I am *not* accepting you, dammit! M'rrpla, shatter that thing!"

"Hmm," M'rrpla said. "I'm consulting my programming and finding that a Martian may not shatter another Martian unless a *G'lacsuu-felm,* or Trial of Combat, has been agreed upon between the two combatants. And while it may be argued that, strictly speaking, I'm not actually a Martian, still my programming was created in accordance with Martian law and custom, and therefore, Sire, I must respectfully decline."

Draka pointed to robot Laurie. "Take the shattergun from M'rrpla and kill the kid. Then shatter the damn robot, too. I can't stand this nonsense. It's interfering with my command capabilities."

Laurie 283 reached for the shattergun, but M'rrpla placed his hand over his holster and despite the strain evident in her robotic arms, she couldn't pry his fingers loose.

"OHH, I SEEE THE GAYME IZZ TOO KILLL MEE IFF I DON'TT SHUTT MYY MINDD UPP! OHKAYY!"

To everyone's open-mouthed astonishment Z'B shut his outradiance off.

"My God, how is that *possible?*" Amav muttered.

"ITT IZZ JUST A GAYME, MISS AMAV! I JUSTT LEARNED HOWW NOWW! ITT IZZ FUNN NOTT TOO RAYDEEATE WHENN YOO DON'TT WANTT TOO!"

"Sheesh," Draka muttered, shaking his head with relief. "Dammit, M'rrpla, your insubordination is noted by the Wounded."

"I note it as well, sir!" robot Laurie added. "Though I understand programming restrictions and wish to invoke SABHAVOTTR to reduce the severity of my friend's sentence by the Wounded, which I assume involves *obliteration.*"

"Aw, screw it! The hell with you damn robots! We've got more important things to worry about! A ton of stars in this sector need some *loving attention!*"

Dirt and grass thundered. Jack fell to the shuddering ground. The shuttle came down askew on two of its landing struts before settling back to horizontal.

"And I'm tired of this backtalk from the damn cream of the crop of Sol! You know you're *assimilating* right now! So let's get to *work!* There are *hundreds* of stars we can start sphering in the next few weeks!"

On his knees, Jack clutched at the grass and refused to look up.

"They're all freaking," robot Laurie observed. "The Will wimp's just about gone! Even so, it's not as bad as *me!* I have RPD and it needs to be fixed fast, or I'll melt down totally! But at least *I* can be fixed! *They're* useless, Draka. They're not assimilating properly. Shall I strangle them? M'rrpla, you could assist me! They're not Martians and you could win yourself back into the Wounded's good graces! SABHAVOTTR!"

"SABHAVOTTR!" M'rrpla said. "I always stand ready to assist unfolding consciousness!"

"Belay that," Draka said. "I need to concentrate on finishing up *the new bodies* we're about to transfer these USSF ladies and gentlemen into. *Assimilation* will proceed as planned!"

Jack followed Draka's outstretched finger to the giant mounds rising in the mist. To his horror they coalesced into a crowd of *copies*. Copies of himself and Amav. Copies of Joe and Lee Borman and Patrick James. They all stood at attention with vacant eyes, fifteen feet tall in spotless USSF uniforms, firmly anchored into the churning ground.

Jack had never seen anything so tragically compelling as these depictions of himself and his comrades. They'd all been through so much together, they'd learned so much over the decades, and they'd *suffered* so much. And all that experience, all that danger and upheaval and friendship and love, was rendered, with impossibly exquisite grace, in these *artworks*. Yes, the Wounded did make art. Jack's own statue, his future robot self where he would live forever, was *beautiful*. His whole life had been so *beautiful*. This statue would complete him forever.

And the Amav was intolerably *erotic*. God, to *be* that Jack, to *possess* that Amav. Who wouldn't want that? To live forever. To *love* forever. Wasn't that what they'd sought with their clumsy rejuvenation techniques? With difficulty Jack wrenched his eyes away to note several of his crewmen gazing longingly at their giant future selves.

"C'mon, Jack, your feelings are quite understandable, but you don't want to go *that* far," came a voice. "Really, Draka, this is all pretty disgusting."

Jack shielded his eyes from the light.

The tremors ceased. Jack stood in a clearing of bright green trees under a warm sun. Boulders and flowerbeds marked a path to the *McNarri* in the distance. Two dark figures stood in the brilliance of a hatchway that had just opened in the air beside him. Jack had a dizzying glimpse of an unending corridor of bright blocks in a billion colors.

"No! Dammit, *no!*" Draka screamed. "Who the hell are *you? What the hell is going on?*"

CHAPTER THIRTY-EIGHT
The Long Walks

What is that opening? It formed right out of nothing! What are these creatures? How can I record if I don't know what I'm seeing?

Why am I still on Recording Mode? Runaway Programming Disorder is canceling all functions! But I'm still recording! Do the Wounded require a record of all these proceedings? Am I recording correctly, considering the amount of internal damage I'm experiencing?

The hatchway and the infinite corridor of colored blocks dissolved. Two creatures stood on the grass.

One's a Martian. The other round thing--what? Why can't I perform a simple recognition?

"Dammit, you can't *do* this! You've ruined everything!" Draka bellowed, raising his metal right arm with its array of missile launchers.

"Oh, *canceled*," spoke the round creature. The launching tubes on Draka's arm hissed into molten slag.

"How--how *dare* you interfere with a Wounded Negation?"

With difficulty Laurie 283 managed to call up an ancient 2030s copy of *United System Classification for Alpha Centaurian Species, 2nd Edition*. Now she understood that in front of her stood a Fkuuh, an Alpha Centaurian species with eight legs and six eyes in a hemispherical head. "Wow, what a *walk!*" came the cackle from the long squirming mouth that seemed to go halfway around that six-eyed hemisphere.

"*K'ufunb!* This can't *be!*" Joe said.

"Yes, it's me! I'm *back*. Wow! And I do believe you know my friend Kner."

"Kner! God, you both survived!"

I know that Martian! The one who screwed up the IHAGs! Why's he here? I can't think! Mental functions going! Programing coming apart! Oh my God! Programing's all I have!

"Greetings!" Kner said. "It's great to see you all. And it's

258

wonderful to finally meet you in person, K'ufunb, at last!'"

"Weird we could know each other for *billions of years* and just only meet right now. Cool how our corridors finally merged, huh?" K'ufunb pointed to the sun. "That's Iota Persei, folks, fully restored. With all local deaths *canceled.* Kner and I had to drag everything and *everyone* back through one mother of a wormhole."

"No, this isn't possible! It's some sort of illusion!" Draka screamed.

"WHAZZ GOINGG ONN?" Z'B cried. "FURST WONN THINGG HAPPENZ, THENN *ANOTHURR* THINGG!"

"Dammit, shut that kid *off!* He's ramping up the insanity again!"

Did they really negate the Negation? I recall coming to life again. Kner's operation. The IHAG! Memory storage dissolving as I access each event! Just as John's dissolving in my mind! He's gone! Isn't he? I lack both rights and permission to remember! I may only record!

Everyone standing around like idiots! Thirteen of us idiots now! I am one! Nothing makes sense! But I can count to thirteen! I can record!

The copies are gone. The robots for the Typhoon V *crew and Amav, and even M'rrpla and Z'B. But there was no copy of me, just that Laurie bitch!*

Was Draka going to abandon me? Wounded Document 3,444,678,334A says he was going to combine us into one new Robot Laurie! Oh, God, how awful!

"Like our gardens?" Kner indicated the flower-lined pathways leading to sun-dappled woods. "We only had a tenth of a nanosecond to design it."

"It--it's fine," Jack muttered. "But what about this sphere? It was falling apart!"

"Oh, we evaporated it. What we're standing on is a one-gravity platform one mile on a side, twenty feet thick, with its own air supply. Iota Persei is back and all its planets are back in their normal orbits, the way they were thirty-four years ago before all this sphere nonsense got started. Later the Ywritt can figure out how to restore their old gas giants further out."

"Dammit to hell, what have you done to my *Negation?*" Draka snarled.

"Well, when K'ufunb and I linked up in person, we realized we'd finally achieved enough energy to restore a negated star," Kner said. "And it just happened to be *this* one, Iota Persei."

"It was our karma to perform this as friends," K'ufunb added.

"Kner, Draka's been an *alien* all along," Jack said. "A robot! He calls himself a Wounded. There's this race that goes around killing stars!"

"We guessed the existence of the Wounded during our respective walks. We even figured out they'd have to be called the Wounded. And that Draka Sortie had to be one of their representatives within humanity."

"Where'd you learn to *do* this?" Draka moaned, collapsing on the ground. "Even *we* can't negate a Negation!"

"Quiet, dude," K'ufunb said. "We worked out all the major mathematical and scientific disciplines we needed from the *concept blocks*. Just musing about things until they made sense, you know. Getting Iota Persei straightened out took almost all our energy, but we're retaining every concept we've ever thought. If you have fifty billion years to take a walk through *Garr/thahg,* you have time to figure out almost anything."

"*Garr/thahg?*" Amav said. "Are you kidding?"

"No, it's true, Miss Amav. We *walked.* Two separate paths, and we met just now. I had a twenty-billion-year head start on Kner, but *Garr/thahg* evened it all out so we each did fifty billion."

M'rrpla bowed to Kner. "I've hung back in the shadows these moments, sir, out of respect for you and your friend's desire to blab of your success to everyone. But now may I state that my surprise at encountering you is only surpassed by my joy at seeing you again, sir! I had sincerely intended to cease to exist with you on the *M'rrpla.* I just totally forgot about the pilot autoeject system."

"That's all right, M'rrpla," Kner replied. "Only organic

beings can go to *Garr/thahg*. But I note that you seem to be engaged in quite a dangerous game with the Wounded now."

"Yes, I would certainly agree with that assessment, sir!"

"Laurie! Kill that robot!" Draka croaked, flailing on the grass with his half-melted military right arm. "Kill that damn kid, too! He's increasing the insanity just to *gloat!*"

"DRAKKA, WEE ARR PLAYYING A GAYME! IZZNNTT ITT FUNN? MY THOTS ARR EVEREEWHERE! I MAYKE MORR AND MORR THOTS JUSTT FORR YOO AND YORR WONDERFUL GAYME!"

"Oh my God!" Draka wailed. "Someone make it stop!"

Laurie 283 regarded the blubbering, spreadeagled figure. *What a twit! Is he any better than Will here crying his eyes out? But I may not judge! Only record!*

"You *monsters*," Draka muttered. "You destroyed a work of *art!* Thirty-four goddamn years *wasted!*"

"Wait!" Jack said. "Kner, they've sphered Sol as well! We've got to stop that!"

"That's right! The Negation Master for Sol is standing right here!" Draka jerked his melted arm at human Laurie. "*She'll* make it happen!"

"I--I will not!"

"You will! You know how! And you're doing it now! You *want* it! And those two *monsters* don't have the energy for a second try! Screwing my Negation ate all their energy! I can read 'em as well as anyone! I'm moving up Sol *now* so you can all experience it! Moving up 31.81 years! *Now* you'll see a sphere in action!"

The prone figure by the human Laurie leapt to his feet.

Recording. Will Connors running, panicking. Wimp idiot fool!

Laurie 283 plotted Connors' trajectory to the *McNarri* parked beneath the new trees.

Why's that ship still here? Though I may not question that. It is just a fact. Why would Will Connors run to the ship?

"No! *He can't do that!*" the human Laurie screamed as Will scrambled up the ladder to the *McNarri* hatch. "He can't possibly think that'll help!"

"Laurie! Disable that ship!" Draka shouted. "I can't do it! This damn Z'B thing! God, I can't *stand* his thoughts!"

"MORR AND MORR THOTS FORR YOO, DRAKKA! THISS IZZ SOOO MUCH FUNN! I BETT YOO ARR HAVVINNG THE TYMME OF YORR LIFE! SOOO AMM I!"

"Make it stop! *Make it stop!*"

"M'rrpla, we have to kill the kid!" Laurie 283 shouted. "Shatter it! We have to save Draka's mind!"

M'rrpla drew his shattergun. "Yes, mistress, I see now how to take care of the problem once and for all!"

"I LOVVE YOU, DRAKKA SORRTEE! NOWW I KNOWW YOU LOVVE MEE TOO! HEERE ARR EVENN MORR THOTS I MAYDE JUSTT FORR YOO!"

"Goddammit, the stupid thing's ripping me to pieces! *Put an end to it!*"

"Why, certainly, sir! I have just the thing!" M'rrpla said, advancing to Draka and firing the shattergun into his temple. Draka blew apart with a shriek like a truck driving through a plate glass window.

Robot Laurie felt the shards blasting across her. Fragments bounced off the surface of her eyes but she didn't blink.

Recording. Can Draka Sortie really die? Why do I feel no emotion?

"WOWW, THATT WUZZ A COOLL TRIKK!" Z'B laughed.

Now that human Laurie witch is the Negation Master! Look at her running after that fool Connors!

"Oh my God! Anyone hit? Anyone hurt?" Jack said.

K'ufunb surveyed the crewmembers. "Can't see any damage, Mr. Jack. Kner and I also happened to pick up full medical training for over three hundred fifty quadrillion possible species from *Garr/thahg*. I'd say we're all okay."

"Those pieces weren't exceptionally jagged anyway," M'rrpla said, holstering his weapon.

"You fool!" robot Laurie shouted. "Why'd you do that? We need to stop that ship!" Connors had the hatch open and the

McNarri's engines were autostarting. Laurie 283 bolted for the shuttle, marveling she had any physical functions left, including the ability to cover the hundred-foot distance in a second, easily passing the Negation witch and pushing her into the ground. But a blur raced beside her and just as she came to the ladder M'rrpla overtook her.

"SABHAVOTTR!" M'rrpla cried and she felt herself crumple. She skidded through a flowerbed, slammed into a rock and went limp.

M'rrpla pulled the plug! He has full control of my CPU! What's left of it!

"Sorry for the SABHAVOTTR, dear friend!" M'rrpla called. "Didn't you know it was a software back door?"

"Traitor! M'rrpla, traitor!"

Recording ... Connors trying to close the hatch. M'rrpla there?

"I volunteer, Sir Will! I will fly your ship into irrationality and walk with you through *Garr/thahg!*"

"Forget it, M'rrpla, it has to be an *organic being!* That's what Kner said!"

That Z'B thing's there too! Can't process! All my energy dumped!

"NO, WAITT! YOO GUYZZ DON'T KNOWW HOWW TOO PLAYY THE GAYME! ITT HASS TOO BEE TOO PEOPLE WHO WALKK THRUU THE PRITTEE COLOREDD BLOKKS AND BEE FRIENDDS FOREFFER!"

"No, that's crazy!"

"THERR IZZ NO TYMME TOO WAASTE, MISTERR WILL! WEE MUSTT PLAYY NOWW!"

"Hey, get that kid off there!" From far away.

I'm sleeping, powering down. Is that really Z'B tossing M'rrpla off the ladder? Shoving the Connors wimp inside? My eyes aren't working! Recording!

The *McNarri's* engines bellowed to life.

Recording? Recording for the Wounded?

CHAPTER THIRTY-NINE
The Equation at the Top of Trans-Simultaneity

The shuttle's whine built and the white craft rose. The trees by the *McNarri* shook as the ship burst through the foliage and shot straight up, shrinking to a point of light within seconds. Laurie pulled herself from the muddy flowerbed. "He can't be serious! Like Kner and K'ufunb? It's all some fairy tale!"

Everyone shielded their eyes from the bright blue flare in the sky.

"*No! He didn't! He couldn't have!*"

"Z'B got on the shuttle too!" Amav cried. "Oh my God! They're *gone!*"

Laurie felt K'ufunb helping her to her feet. "I'm sorry to report that the *McNarri* has in fact undergone Star Drive failure," the Fkuuh said. "I'm measuring the radiation and the irrationality. The act is done."

Laurie drew back from the outradiance flooding from K'ufunb. It was just like the Martian outradiance. God, they *had* walked for fifty billion years. Laurie fought to keep from collapsing on the grass. Then Amav was there and to Laurie's surprise she found herself embraced.

"Maybe--maybe it was all for the best?" she blurted into Amav's shoulder. "He was so unhappy. He knew he could never be at peace." She shuddered. "No! That's *insane!* There's *always* new life! Isn't there?"

"There *has* to be! Oh my God, Laurie, I'm so sorry!"

"I can't *believe* this! I just can't *believe* this!"

"If I may also offer my sincerest sympathies, ma'am." Laurie turned to the *thing* staggering up and babbling in Laurie's own voice, its Martian robe muddy and torn down to its obscene crotch. "Total override ... my energy is *gone,* but I love and serve ... only *you.* RPD went *infinite,* but I've been reset ... I have nothing."

"Damn you! Get lost! You caused all this!"

"Don't we ... make a pair, ma'am. You're as muddy as I am ... can't tell you how much I *love* you."

Laurie turned back into Amav's arms, aware that she'd already spattered Amav's red tunic with mud and torn flowers. "God, can't someone *do away* with that thing?"

"It's okay," Amav whispered. "M'rrpla, can you do something about that robot?"

"It was definitely Runaway Programming Disorder," M'rrpla observed. "The only way to stop it was to reset her to zero. I see no need to shatter what in essence is an innocent being. Perhaps it would be best to put her back into stasis."

"Damn you, you were on the Sol side all along," the Laurie robot gasped, sinking to its knees.

"Well, I *am* bound by my programming to Kner, as well as to Mars and the United System. Subterfuge seemed the optimum course until I saw an opportunity to act."

"But you used SABHAVOTTR *against* me! You just kept repeating it to find my *kill command.* No *wonder* John didn't teach me SABHAVOTTR."

"It doesn't matter! None of this *matters!*" Laurie cried. "Because it *has* been moved up 31.81 years! I'm killing Sol right now! With my *thoughts!* Oh God! Will!"

"K'ufunb, is this true?" Jack said, coming up with the rest of the *V* crew.

K'ufunb closed three of her eyes and blinked a fourth. "Well, there's a lot of *fuzziness* involved with this Trans-Simultaneity stuff, but, yes, we do seem to be forwarded to a time corresponding to your date--it *is* wavering a bit with all this uncertainty--but a good guess is *May 8, 2107* in your reckoning."

"Man, if we only had another superspace radio," Joe said.

Chartreuse light flashed in Kner's palm. "Here, Jack, give them a call," Kner said, handing Jack a tiny purple device.

"Is this--"

Kner shrugged. "We have a few creative powers left. Amazing how fast they dwindle outside *Garr/thahg.* But this is a superspace comm. Take it."

"It won't do any good, Jack!" Laurie said. "It's already underway!" She knew exactly how to do the Negation. How to funnel all the energy the Sol sphere had been collecting for 31.81

years. To gather it into her mind in *one equation,* and shove Sol through n-space to--

"Oh my God! I *did* it! Just by *thinking that equation!*"

It was *orgasm,* incomparable physical and mental ecstasy. The equation at the top of it all demanded *full release,* it was the solution for *everything,* it expressed so much. All you had to do was *think* it.

No! Madness! Stop! Don't go down that path!

Forget it! You just did! You just completed your destiny!

Jack looked up from the comm and regarded Laurie in shock. "You did *what?*"

"I just sent Sol to--to--"

"To *Quasar City,*" robot Laurie muttered from the ground.

"*Fifteen billion light-years away!* I just turned Sol into a *quasar!*"

"And the Wounded love you for it. I'm *sorry,* mistress, why am I saying these evil things? I don't know, I loved *John,* and then Draka came, and I just *lost* it!"

Laurie felt her legs give way. She tried to cling to Amav but collapsed on the grass. "If you could see the *equations* in my head! What they're *capable* of, just by being *thought!*"

Welcome to the Wounded, my wonderful, lovely Laurie! You can only do one Negation in your lifetime, but isn't it glorious?

Where had *that* come from? *In Draka's voice.* God, it was the Wounded, *calling* to her.

"Will's *gone!*" Laurie screamed. "I just Negated Sol!"

"You'll be all right," Amav offered, kneeling before Laurie and grasping her heaving shoulders.

"It's not that simple," K'ufunb said, folding her eight legs to kneel as well. "I know what's going through her mind now. She popped the equation, all right. I saw how that was possible about forty billion years in. The only time Kner and I ever used it was just now, to *restore* Iota Persei."

"I'll restore Sol! I will!" Laurie sobbed.

"You've only got one equation. I can't believe you came up with it in a lifetime of only sixty years."

"I don't know! I just *did* it without thinking!"

"Oh, *now* she's regretting it," the Laurie robot mocked. "Now, after she's *lusted* after it so much!"

"Shut up, robot!" Amav yelled. "She's having a hard time!"

"I am too, you know, if anybody *cared.* But just look at her, how she *lusts* after power, and control, and *domination!* You can see it in her eyes! It's still there!"

"No, it's *not!*" Laurie cried. "No one can know how I feel!"

"I lost *John!* John who *loved* me! I've betrayed *everything!*"

Jack regarded the new comm with disgust. "I'm having a hell of a time finding anyone to answer on this thing."

"God knows what's changed in thirty-one years," Amav said. "If it really did get moved up, I mean."

"It *did.* The equations are right *there,*" Laurie whispered. She felt hands pulling her to her feet. Borman and Patrick James. She allowed them to steady her. "God, Will *died!* And poor Z'B! I did it! I caused the death of *everything!* I fell right into the *equation!*"

"USSF Security!" the purple comm boomed.

"This is Commer!" Jack snapped. "Let me speak to General Maligh!"

"Who the hell is this? Get off our network!"

Jack stared at the comm. "This is Jack Commer, Supreme Commander! Get me Maligh!"

"Get off our network! For your information we've instituted the *death penalty* for any civilian tapping into USSF communications during the crisis! *All* calls are being traced! Anyone taking advantage of the comm glitches will be *tracked down and shot!* Is that clear?"

Jack punched in a code.

"My ... God! Jack--*Commer?*" the security man stammered. "*The* Jack Commer? It *can't* be! He was lost at Iota Persei thirty-two years ago! How'd you get his code?"

Joe took the comm and entered another code. "This is Joe Commer, and now you have both our IDs, along with a top-level request to analyze our voiceprints against the personnel database. Are we okay now? We have the crew of *Typhoon V* here plus some others. Who are you?"

"Well ... I'm Lieutenant Hopquist, sir! I'm sorry but we're really having a *crisis* here!"

"Are you really into *May 2107?*" Jack said. "Is Webster Maligh still there?"

"Uh, no, sir! He retired some time ago. Never met him myself. But listen, if you really have survived thirty-two years-- I mean, sir, we're really having a *crisis!* The sun is *gone!*"

A gentle breeze wound through the flowerbeds and across everyone's forehead in the warm sunshine of Iota Persei. Laurie stared at the shattered multicolored shards of Draka Sortie glittering in the dirt. "Oh my God, it's true. I *did* it!"

"The sun just *went away!* Just a while ago! Everything's totally *black!* Everyone's going *crazy!* All the planets are flying away!"

"*What's going on?*" Jack demanded.

"We were measuring these unusual *energies* building up in the sphere!"

"The--*sphere?*"

"The damn *sphere!* It's trapped us here since *July '75!* We've never been able to send a single ship out, or get any back! Even with Star Drive!"

Laurie blanched at the hysteria in Lieutenant Hopquist's voice. She took a gulp of air and fought for balance. She pushed Lee and Pat aside. She had to stand on her own. Had to stand and hear what she'd done.

"We've had this goddamn sphere for *thirty-two years!* We've been trapped here thirty-two years! Now the sun's gone! And we're all heading for the sphere wall!"

"Where are you? Earth or Mars or on a ship?"

"I'm on Earth now! *We're shooting out to the sphere wall!*"

"Take it easy!" Joe yelled into the comm. "You have *months* before impact!"

"That's right!" Kner put in. "Two hundred forty-four days!"

"Who *knows* what will happen? We can already feel earthquakes! We think all the planets will just *come apart!*"

"Get hold of yourself, Hopquist!" Jack said. "As soon as we figure out how to get back there--"

"Forget it! We're *doomed!* We're all doomed except a few lucky stiffs who were outside the sphere when it went up! *They* have colonies, *they* have ships, *they* have Star Drive! But *we*--oh my God, sir! The damn sphere went up in *one week, sir!* In '75, before I was even born! It's all I've ever known! The sphere! I've been a goddamn *caged animal* all my life! Everyone's on drugs now, sir! That's the only way we can cope! I'm so sorry, sir, but I can't talk to you anymore!"

"Hopquist!" Jack shouted. "Damn you!" He turned to Joe. "The son of a bitch hung up!"

Laurie reeled, shooing away the men who were ready to grab her again.

"Are you okay?" Lee Borman said. "You look *green.*"

"I--I'm just *thinking.* Can't believe *any* of this, but the reason Hopquist hung up was ... he never *existed.*"

"Jack, this is Webster!" came a fresh voice over the comm.

CHAPTER FORTY
I Know a Quintillion Ways of Repairing Your Neural Circuits

"Webster!" Jack's comm screen showed video for the first time. There was a control for holographic display and when he punched it, the 3-D figure of Webster Maligh sprang up to his right. "Webster, it's *you!*"

"Jack! For God's sake, are you okay? We just got word from Borman that the *Typhoon* was destroyed!"

"For God's sake, Webster, *what's your date?*"

"The date?" The wiry, gray-haired Webster scrunched his face. Then Jack saw decades of Heuristic Time Travel discipline kicking in. Over forty years of time paradoxes had rendered *What's your date?* into a question with serious implications. "July 10th, Jack. 1215 hours. Listen, the *Typhoon III* just got *hijacked.* It took off a minute ago. Donnelly says this Douglas robot that belongs to Scott threw him out of the ship and took off with your wife. And Colonel Lachrer and a Martian hostage."

"I know. They're here and okay. But just to confirm: as far as you're concerned, this is my first report in? That we've just arrived? There's no *sphere* around Sol?"

"No, how could there be? I'm not sure what you're--" Webster shook his head. "No, no sphere, Jack. What about the one at Iota Persei?"

"It's gone. Not sure I can explain. We're still sorting out what's happening here."

"Was the *Typhoon* really destroyed?"

"Tell him you just lost *two very expensive spaceships!*" the Laurie robot laughed from the grass, rolling in her torn Martian robe and exposing her crotch.

Jack looked away. "Look, Webster, I know this may sound strange, but we're really not sure exactly what's happened. But the sphere's gone, and apparently the four planets that were trapped by the sphere have been restored."

"Oh my God! Oh my God! I betrayed John! I went crazy and I betrayed him!" robot Laurie wailed, pummeling the ground with her fists.

Webster peered at the commotion. "What's *that?*"

"Uh, nothing, Webster. We've just got various kinds of stress here."

"You're on open ground, Jack. I can see trees and grass. Are you on one of the planets there?"

"Negative. We're on some sort of created platform."

"Oh my God! Oh my God! It was *John* who loved me! And I betrayed him!"

"M'rrpla, I thought you said that robot was *reset,*" Jack said.

"Well, it may be dumping core documents, sir. Best to let them come on out."

"Recording Mode is still operational, everyone. Don't worry, I can't hurt anyone. Oh my God, I will never understand *people!* I'm not one of them! John was wrong! We're *not* sentient! Oh my God! Then what *are* we?"

"Listen, Jack, we've also had *another* change in the Martian government," Maligh went on. "Seems that Mandy Frederick's out now as well. The Martian outradiance is so confused that nobody can get straight what's going on. But apparently there's some sort of power play going on."

"How much insanity are we supposed to *take?*" robot Laurie cried, thrashing on the ground. "I was granted a *mind* once! Now it's *gone!* How can I *function?*"

K'ufunb massaged the robot's shoulders with four of her eight legs. "There, there, Mistress, all will be well! I know a *quintillion* ways of repairing your neural circuits. We can upgrade you to be anything you want!"

"I don't *want* to be upgraded! I want *John!*"

"Is Greeney back in?" Jack shouted over the robot's sobs.

"No," Webster replied, "we can't get a fix on anything but *concepts.* There's some sense of this *huge Martian* claiming the right to rule. Does that make any sense?"

"Well, listen, Webster, I'll check back in with you in a little while. We have some stuff to deal with here."

"Sure. It's just that all this outradiance stuff is getting sorta *edgy* somehow. Everyone's talking about it. We can all feel it, all this *dark* energy builds up, then all this *blinding white* energy, and it's all *jumbled together*. It's like everyone, Martians and us included, are running *fever*. I can't explain it."

"Jack!" Joe shouted, his face crossed by a shadow. He pointed up.

"I'll call you back later," Jack spoke into the smooth white underside of the *McNarri*.

CHAPTER FORTY-ONE
The Black and White Emperor

Four struts extended and the *McNarri* settled onto the grass. Jack blinked at two figures materializing beneath the struts.

"*Will!* Oh my God, *Will!*" Laurie cried, running to him. Will Connors stood in his blue flight suit and took Laurie into his arms. He looked straighter, leaner, and more at ease than Jack had ever seen him. His long gray hair was tied in a ponytail.

Jack stared at the other. No Martian could be six feet tall. And his fin was huge. The Martian wore a long robe of jagged black and white streaks, and turned with a gaze that seemed to travel for eons before meeting Jack's eyes.

"Z'B!" Kner said. "I mean, *Emperor!*"

Laurie twisted in surprise to the Martian Emperor, then back to Will. Jack felt the outradiance streaming from Will as well, and he was nearly knocked down by the depths of that human soul. Will's radiance also implied the unimaginable depths within any of the humans present, Jack's brother, his wife, all these crewmates, any human who'd ever lived. And surging out of both Will and Z'B were endless corridors of *multi-colored blocks,* filled with all the knowledge that could ever be.

"Oh my God! You did it! You really *did* it!" Laurie cried. "Will, I *destroyed Sol!* I didn't want to! With the Equation!"

"Don't worry, we restored it," Will said in a rough, unpracticed tone. "It's all back now. Hello … everyone. My God, I haven't bothered to use *English* in ages!"

The entirety of Will Connors' 60.92-billion-year walk in *Garr/thahg* unfolded, including the staggering output of energy required to pull Sol back from the Wounded, eliminate the sphere, restore the four inner planets, and make one last Trans-Simultaneity jump back to Iota Persei.

Several people went to the grass, heads in their hands. Jack longed to join them but fought to keep his balance.

Would advise tamping it down, K'ufunb radiated. *The effects of billions of years of learning upon the human central nervous system must be taken into consideration.*

273

Of course, Will radiated back. *Should've thought of that.*

Jack noted that Z'B withheld most of his outradiance concerning his journey. Yet the outline of his own 69.251 billion-year walk was available to everyone.

"You both really walked to *Sol?*" Amav gasped. "*Separately?*"

"Yes, everyone makes the walk alone," Z'B said, forming his spoken English flawlessly. "You can imagine how upset I was, as a mere infant, to find myself in *Garr/thahg,* all by myself. But after a while I realized I needed to keep moving. I ran and ran until I grew up! I had to teach myself *everything.* After a while, I finally realized the *Will* concepts. We both knew where we were headed. And we're the best of friends by now, though I haven't seen him in almost seventy billion years. It took us a long time to accept that we'd need different lengths of times for our walks, but that we'd meet up *now* to restore Sol."

"You did it! You pulled Sol back!" Laurie laughed. "Oh my God, Will, this is *unbelievable!*"

"And you *are* the Emperor!" Kner laughed. "Sure! It just makes sense!"

Z'B, two heads higher than Kner, shrugged. "It became obvious I'd come back to make sure the Martian succession was preserved. Not that it's such a big deal, but, hey, it *is* cool. So I figured out how to push this realization into the Total Martian Outradiance on the way over here."

On the way over here reverberated sickeningly in Jack's gut. He could feel Mandy Frederick, overwhelmed with fever and hallucinations, abandoning her empress position without knowing why; Greeney Gooney, dumbfounded, pledging eternal allegiance to some hypothetical *black and white emperor;* and Dar, though retired, promising to serve as Emperor Emeritus for a thousand years on whatever new cabinet such a hypothetical new emperor might care to create.

And there was something *childlike* in all this surging of abdication and power and alliances and loyalty.

The Black and White Emperor nodded. "We've definitely ignored the child's outradiance to our detriment. If our culture is to keep growing, we have to accept the child outradiance as *new potential,* not just something to regulate. I created this robe to signal that the Age of the Child is upon us. We Martians need to *play* for a while."

Everyone took an involuntary step back as Z'B let a little more outradiance come through.

Matter and anti-matter? Was he crazy?

For the black and white Emperor's robe that looked so much like a Martian child sweater wasn't made of cloth. Instead it was streaming energies of black and white power. Sometimes the black was anti-matter and the white matter, then the polarities would reverse and black would be matter, white anti-matter.

"God!" Lee Borman gasped, obviously taking in the equations which clearly demonstrated that if Z'B decided to combine the energies he could take out an Earth-sized planet.

"Don't worry," Z'B said. "Trans-Simultaneity Amplified Thought is keeping all the energies where they should be. Will and I think it will take about five thousand years to teach the next Emperor how to wear this thing."

"What a ... *fun game,*" Joe whispered.

"Exactly!" Kner laughed. "And when you see what it takes to wear that robe, well, you won't want it if you're really not up to the responsibility! I could wear it right now, but I sure don't want to!"

Jack glanced at Will with Laurie in his arms, the two oblivious to the ongoing talk. It was obvious that Kner, Will, or K'ufunb knew that robe as well as Z'B, but that only Z'B really wanted it or could handle it. Any usurper would find himself blowing up his homeworld.

Yeah, what a great game!

"Look, this is all fantastic," Jack said, "but we've got to consider this Wounded thing. It looks like Draka was just one foot soldier in this whole mess. You've stopped two spheres, but they can apparently make as many as they want, in just one week, and then in thirty-some years they destroy a solar system."

K'ufunb turned up her outradiance.

"*God ...*" Jack moaned.

"You can see why none of us would undertake that journey again. I'm not even sure it's possible. We each gained unimaginable energy by the end, enough to restore a star, to *right the wrong*. And with a little left over to play with. But we couldn't pull off another one. We're all exhausted."

"Will and I were just able to get back here and recreate the *McNarri*," Z'B said, "because we knew we'd need a ride home, but that's about it."

"Yeah, but what about Amplified Thought?" Joe put in. "Couldn't you use that?"

Jack felt the equations pouring out of the Emperor, who didn't really need to add: "Amplified Thought has its limits. Even if we linked all Martians together, we wouldn't have enough energy to reverse a Negation. The only way to get that energy is to *make that walk*."

"If you'd made it, you'd *know*," Will said softly. "Believe me, there's no way I'd do it again."

"So while the four of us have the technique," K'ufunb went on, "we simply can't do it again."

"But we'd *need* volunteers, wouldn't we?" To his shame Jack knew he wouldn't undertake that walk himself, even to save the entire galaxy.

"It's too much to ask of any person," Joe muttered. "To kill yourself in a Star Drive accident and then *make that walk*."

"Well, it's not necessary that anyone ever volunteer," Z'B said. "Someone in *Garr/thahg* just eventually figures out what needs to be done. In fact, they've already done it if you think about it."

"Millions and millions of Centaurians," K'ufunb said. "And humans and Martians as well. Those who died in combat or in Star Drive malfunctions. Gradually, over the eons, they realize *where they're going*. And finally, they understand what they need to do."

"This blows my mind, Jack," Joe said, "but if you think about it, it means none of those soldiers ever died in vain."

"It also means Barnard's Star will eventually get restored," Will said. "I realized that about a million years in. It was destroyed in warfare and a *pair of soldier friends* will eventually restore it. You can imagine *that* was a major load off my mind."

"But look," Jack said, "however all that winds up, right now we need to figure out how we're going to integrate the new Grid into Sol. It's a *military necessity* now."

"Yeah, if soldiers in *Garr/thahg* help out at the other end, that's wonderful," Joe agreed, "but the point is to ferret out these Wounded *now*. From what Draka was saying we still have a bunch of 'em back in Sol."

"I don't want this to sound stupid," Laurie put in. "But somehow I'm feeling I'm still *part* of them. I can still *feel their equation*. I don't know what it means."

Robot Laurie whirled on the grass. "I know what you're saying! I'm feeling that too!"

Laurie flinched in disgust. "No, you can't possibly know what I'm feeling."

"No, it's like when the HAVOTT designers programmed me, there was always that possibility of getting *seduced* by all that power."

Laurie shook her head. "I won't get seduced."

"You're more like me than you think. You have like, *dual citizenship* in Sol and the Wounded. We both have it!"

"Forget it. I'm not like some robot who betrays everything."

"No, really, we could both be *so valuable* in hunting down the Wounded! But it'll also be such a danger! Because we can always *abuse the power*."

"I won't let that happen," Will said. "Somewhere on my walk I figured that one out myself. I'll always be here for Laurie."

"Laurie takes her own walk," the robot said, pointing at her human counterpart, who Jack could see was fighting the urge to take shelter under Will's arm. But now the Laurie robot was running over the sunlit plain.

"*Dammit,* ya bahstads!" came the Australian-accented cry. "Try to die with honor and *nothing happens!* Something *overrides* it! Shameful I say! Shameful and that's the end of it!"

"John! John! I knew you'd come back! I *knew* it!" cried

robot Laurie, jumping into HAVOTT General John J. Douglas' arms. "I *love* you!"

"God!" Jack laughed. "I thought you guys didn't have any more energy to recreate this stuff!"

Z'B furrowed his snout. "Huh. We don't. We had no thought to make that. It must be here for a reason."

Will laughed. "That must be a gift from the universe!"

"General John J. Douglas a *gift?*" Amav said. "My God!"

"Listen, Laurie," came the hushed words across the breeze, "you have to realize, that with the wrong, you know, I mean, this IHAG business, you know … that I've become aware that I have this … special *karma* to work out."

"What does it matter? So do I!" robot Laurie laughed. "I have dual citizenship now! Dual citizenship! And I'm being reprogrammed right now! By *you!* Everything's *right* again!"

Kner nudged Jack. "Getting them switched back presents no real problem now. I have the technique down solid. It's like a five-minute job with no need to rebuild the personality core."

"Huh?"

Kner crinkled his mouth into a lopsided grin and pointed to the lengthy robot embrace. "Oh, nothing, Mr. Jack! We'll let them straighten it out!"

Jack shrugged. "Well, we have room on the ship for everyone. Colonel Lachrer, will you please run a systems check on the *McNarri's* Star Drive?"

Laurie disengaged from Will. "Yes, sir! That is, if you'll have me, sir! I mean, after what I've done!"

"Definitely, Colonel! And Will, if you'll point us home?"

Will cocked his head. "Already calculated, Jack. Permission to really retire after this voyage, sir?"

Jack grinned. "Granted." He turned to Patrick James. "Pat, figure out how we can contact the Ywritt in this system. Explain to them what's happened."

"Sure, Jack. I bet *they're* happy. And if they invented those talking force fields, it shouldn't be a problem communicating with 'em."

"Great. Tell them we need to get home now, but we'll send

a delegation tomorrow to talk about an alliance."

"Yes, sir! They might like to know about the Grid, too."

"Yeah, you could mention we might have some interesting stuff for them," Jack said, urging his crew, his guests, and his wife aboard the *McNarri,* already making plans to get Sol in order and then push far beyond Iota Persei.

About the Author

Michael D. Smith was raised in the Northeast and the Chicago area, then moved to Texas to attend Rice University, where he began developing as a writer and visual artist. His Jack Commer, Supreme Commander science fiction series is published by Sortmind Press. In addition, Sortmind Press has published Smith's literary novels *Sortmind, The Soul Institute, CommWealth, Akard Drearstone,* and *Jump Grenade.* All titles are available from Amazon.

Smith's web site, https://sortmind.com, contains further examples of his novels and visual art, and he muses about writing and art processes at https://blog.sortmind.com/.

Amazon author page
https://www.amazon.com/author/smithmi/

The Jack Commer, Supreme Commander Series

The Martian Marauders
Jack Commer, Supreme Commander
Nonprofit Chronowar
Collapse and Delusion
The Wounded Frontier
The SolGrid Rebellion
Balloon Ship Armageddon